MORE THAN A WOMAN

"I am Mrs. Merriwether to you, Major Sheridan."

"You will never be Mrs. Merriwether to me."

Her son's gaze landed on Tony, although the little boy continued to pat Phys. Tony leaned over, took his hand and showed him how to stroke the dog's head. Phys grinned a silly dog grin in appreciation.

Felicity looked at her carriage and back at him. "Where will you be going?"

"I'm taking an assignment in India."

"When?"

"A few months, if all goes well."

The boy studied him curiously a moment before starting to speak. "Are you—?"

Felicity's gloved hand clamped over the boy's mouth. Her movement brought the foursome—his dog, her son, and the two of them—in a tight circle. He reached out and touched the back of her gray silk gown, and she froze.

The material felt particularly fine, rich, with just the faintest drag as his fingers slid down to the small of her back. She felt the same to him: wonderful, magical, almost more than a woman. Dear God, how he had missed touching her. . . .

<u>BOOK YOUR PLACE ON OUR WEBSITE</u> <u>AND MAKE THE</u> <u>READING CONNECTION!</u>

We've created a customized website just for our very special readers, where you can get the inside scoop on everything that's going on with Zebra, Pinnacle and Kensington books.

When you come online, you'll have the exciting opportunity to:

- View covers of upcoming books
- Read sample chapters
- Learn about our future publishing schedule (listed by publication month *and author*)
- Find out when your favorite authors will be visiting a city near you
- Search for and order backlist books from our online catalog
- Check out author bios and background information
- Send e-mail to your favorite authors
- Meet the Kensington staff online
- Join us in weekly chats with authors, readers and other guests
- Get writing guidelines
- AND MUCH MORE!

Visit our website at
http://www.kensingtonbooks.com

THE WEDDING AFFAIR

Karen L. King

ZEBRA BOOKS
Kensington Publishing Corp.
http://www.kensingtonbooks.com

ZEBRA BOOKS are published by

Kensington Publishing Corp.
850 Third Avenue
New York, NY 10022

All Kensington titles, imprints and distributed lines are available at special quantity discounts for bulk purchases for sales promotion, premiums, fund-raising, educational or institutional use.

Special book excerpts or customized printings can also be created to fit specific needs. For details, write or phone the office of the Kensington Special Sales Manager: Kensington Publishing Corp., 850 Third Avenue, New York, NY 10022. Attn. Special Sales Department. Phone: 1-800-221-2647.

Zebra and the Z logo Reg. U.S. Pat. & TM Off.

First Printing: June 2003
10 9 8 7 6 5 4 3 2 1

Printed in the United States of America

ONE

"Don't you think that young man there should make a wonderful suitor?"

Felicity Merriwether tried to ignore her mother's unsubtle hint and gave only a cursory glance at the man descending from the carriage in front of them.

Felicity answered by rote. "I can't marry yet. It would be utterly improper."

Her plain outside, plush inside carriage inched forward, then stopped in front of the wide stone staircase. A liveried footman opened the door.

"To marry now, yes." Esmirelda Greyston raised her Chinese fan in front of her face as if that should keep the servants from knowing she was scolding her grown daughter. "But one doesn't bring a gentlemen up to scratch in just a few weeks. If you wait out the full year to cast your lures, the end of the season will be upon us."

"Charles will need a father to guide him," added her father.

A twinge of guilt made Felicity wince. Would Charles suffer if she remained unmarried? That was the one area where she suffered any qualms about her decision. However, Layton, during his life, had done little more than provide her son with a name.

"Actually, as I remember," Felicity said as she was handed out of the carriage, "if one is quite determined, a few weeks is more than enough time to convince a gentleman to hang up the ladle."

Felicity was determined to be quite irresolute this time around. She didn't want a new husband. One had been more than enough, but her parents were of the opinion that a woman without a man's guidance and protection was like a ship without a rudder. It was just a matter of time before she crashed into a rocky shore.

"Felicity, if you are not going to let me assist you, you really do need to find someone to look after Layton's business interests. You can't postpone that forever," said her father in an attempt at reasonableness.

She bit her tongue rather than try to make her parents understand. If she kept from responding, the discussion would die a natural death once they entered the assembly rooms—well, were it not for her mother's insistence on pointing every eligible man out to her, as if being a widow made her blind to their preening.

Men, most specifically one man, had caused her no end of trouble. The last thing she ever wanted to do was invite one back into her life. So that was why, when she entered the ballroom and realized *he,* the father of her only child, was there, she averted her head.

Major Anthony Sheridan felt her gaze the minute she arrived. For just an instant her liquid brown eyes met his and erased six years. Then she turned her back on him and reminded him of the chasm of betrayal that separated them.

"I say, are you all right?" asked Lieutenant Randleton. "Look like you've seen a ghost."

No, Tony had just been given the cut direct by the woman who'd once promised to be his wife. She was supposed to be his reward for surviving the war. And he had survived. His memories of her warm brown eyes, the softness of her skin, and the supple curves of her untutored body had intruded on his thoughts at the oddest of moments over the years. She'd made him the gift of her innocence, and the gift haunted him, at times made him reckless or made him cunning, and made him want both to die and to live in the mud on the Peninsula.

He should have come home and taken back his place in society with her by his side. But she must have known much sooner then he did that he couldn't fit in here.

But he'd be damned before he let her force him out until he was ready to go. His voice cut across the idle chatter of the ballroom. "Felicity."

She swung around. Her gray dress swirled around her slender form and shimmered into place, causing a shudder to course down his spine as he remembered the beauty of her body without any adornment at all.

Jewel-toned skirts swept back, the crowd parted before him like the Red Sea as he lurched across the floor toward her. His limp made him impatient with his painstaking progress.

Her smooth white brow furrowed as he advanced. Her sable hair was wound in a simple topknot at odds with the elaborate curls and crimping of the women around her. Her gaze dropped to his wounded leg. He said her name again to draw her attention away from his infirmity.

Flanked by both her parents, he considered how best to separate her from her regiments. He didn't have to when she stepped forward and held out her hand.

"Major Sheridan, it is a pleasure to see you again. Have you been home long?"

He stopped, his gaze jerking to her face. She had circumvented his confrontation.

"It has been forever," she continued blithely in a singsong voice. The frown lines etched deeper into her forehead with every word. "I'm Mrs. Merriwether now."

She had changed. No longer the impulsive, reckless bride-to-be he had left behind, she was a married woman with her own strategies. Her clothes and demeanor were simply elegant, and gave him the impression of an understated determination to deny the passionate part of her

nature. An aura of maturity and restraint enfolded her, right
down to the fingertips of her gray gloves.

Obviously, a discussion of the past wouldn't be tolerated
in the middle of a ballroom with the half the ton looking on.
Years ago, she'd begged to join him in her last letter, and
then he learned she'd married another man. He wanted to
know why. He wished he'd kept the letter, but it had been
bloodstained and torn. He hadn't known it would be the last.

He smiled slowly.

He had always admired a worthy adversary and gave due
respect to one who had outmaneuvered him. If he made the
attempt tonight, he would fail to get to the bottom of why
she had betrayed him. The reckoning would come, though.
No one ever got the better of him.

"Not quite forever, Felicity."

Felicity swallowed hard. Tony was back. He was back
and at the same ball she'd been persuaded to attend.

He had changed in so many ways. His brown hair was
shorter than it had been, and laced with gold where the sun
had kissed it. She'd noticed that in spite of that noticeable
limp, he walked with command and authority in every step.
But it wasn't until he stood directly in front of her and finished his slow perusal of her that she noticed his
winter-cold, dead eyes.

The lack of small talk made her jittery. But Tony had
never been one for idle chatter. A man of action, he was
more likely to do something forceful and unexpected, like
sweeping her into an embrace.

Though he wouldn't sweep her into his arms. She knew
that. The thought—wish, really—was bizarrely out of place.
He'd made it clear in his last letter that he didn't want her
with him.

Yet, why had he called out her name? Twice?

She couldn't help but look at him, his bearing at once
military-straight and noble, squint lines etched in white
against his tanned skin.

She stared straight into the pale blue eyes that had once

held hers with such warmth. Now they appeared so light and menacing, they seemed almost inhuman. He stood towering over her, too close yet not close enough. Her heart pounded in a mad battle rhythm.

She glanced down at the leg he favored. "You were wounded."

"Twice in the same leg."

His delivery was so flat, she marveled that he had even acknowledged her statement.

She heard her mother's gasp behind her. Tony was breaking all the rules. Calling out her given name in a crowded ballroom, referring to his limb with an accurate word like "leg." Next thing, he would be asking about his son—did he even know that her pregnancy had resulted in a son?

Felicity couldn't let that happen. She shook her head and stepped back, ready to end this charged encounter.

"Captain Lungren always says I lead with my right . . . foot, therefore this limb"—he patted his thigh with a slight wince—"always bears the brunt of the attack."

His lifted eyebrow spoke volumes. One shouldn't have to be so circumspect with vocabulary with a woman he'd known intimately. Or perhaps he hated to admit to a weakness, any weakness. She stared at him, trying to discern a betraying emotion in his icy-cold eyes.

The corner of his mouth lifted in a wry way. "Did you think I wouldn't return home?"

Suddenly she wanted to blurt out that Charles was well and a lively child in spite of Layton's constant rebukes. She wanted to shout out that she was now a widow. She wanted to cuff Tony and demand to know why he had treated her so shabbily.

During her indecision, his gaze had dropped to her mouth, and suddenly she knew why he had called out her name.

"There was always that possibility," she answered coolly.

His eyes flickered with a coldness that made Felicity want to escape.

He didn't care about his son, didn't care if she was married, didn't give a fig about her well-being. He just wanted what she had so foolishly given him years ago and paid for every day of her life since.

That night had been one of the most special in her life, and he cheapened it by revealing that it was nothing more than a sensual encounter to him. She hated him for that. If he thought she would fall back into his arms, he was sadly mistaken.

She would not make that blunder again. She searched desperately for an expression to mark her vehemence. Not unless pigs flew—that was it; she would sleep with him again when pigs flew. Tony was a nasty piece of work, and she had been too naive to realize it years ago. "Well, it has been lovely seeing you again, Major. I—"

"I arrived home yesterday. I was delayed in Brussels." He had finally deigned to answer her first question.

He wasn't going to let her walk away. Fine. A jolt of fresh anger stabbed her. She'd just chat him into madness. He'd always detested idle prattle.

"I hear Brussels is packed with tourists. My niece was to visit there and see the battlefield at Waterloo before she returned home. But she took ill and had to book passage on a ship directly bound for England." She opened her fan and began waving it. Why did they keep these assembly rooms so warm?

"She wouldn't have enjoyed it. It is a gruesome place." He looked away.

Felicity waited, made uncomfortable by the odd matter-of-fact tone of the conversation. She was thinking of pigs, and he was talking of war, however indirectly. "Well, then—"

"I thought only of home."

There was something so stark in his words that Felicity wondered if that battle—the whole ghastly war—had robbed Tony of compassion. She fought the urge to lay her hand on his arm. He may be a hard, ruthless man now, but there had been moments of tenderness before. She couldn't have been so wrong about him then. "Well, you are home now."

"Not for long." His eyes held hers steadily. "What niece?"

"My niece by marriage, Diana Fielding." What did he mean, *not for long?* "She attended finishing school in Switzerland and is finally coming home after a dozen years there. She should have come home sooner but for the war and both her parents passing away. Now I shall give her a season. I'm quite looking forward to her arrival."

"When?"

Tony couldn't be interested in this. Felicity glanced over her shoulder, looking for her parents, who had discreetly moved across the polished wood floor. Could they think Tony was an acceptable suitor now? "Her ship is due to arrive two days hence. I'm sure she is a lovely girl. She writes me the sweetest letters."

Tony's gaze dropped, and Felicity realized that her agitation was making her breathing rapid and her chest was rising and falling in a distracting cadence. Underneath it all was this spreading heat that her fan was doing little to combat.

Tony latched on to her elbow, and Felicity nearly squealed in alarm. Her heart pounded harder, if that was possible. With a firm and sure grip, he tugged her across the floor.

Memories of the last time she'd seen him, his naked body bathed pale gold by the moonlight, rose unbidden in her mind. His touch, then so firm and purposeful yet tender and caring. By the time she realized he was forcing her to go with him to some unknown destination, it was too late to refuse.

"Tony, where are you taking me?" she hissed.

"It must be cooler by the windows, or there might be a balcony. You are overheated."

She yanked her arm free of his grip and nearly smacked herself in the face. Quite likely she hadn't needed to pull so hard, as his grasp wasn't tight enough to be bruising—just controlling. However, she might need the smack to bring her to her senses. What was she doing, letting him lead her off to a garden path? "No."

"No?" He seemed taken aback, as if no one ever told him no.

"That's right, no."

"No, it isn't cooler by the windows?" He faced her with a deceptively placid expression. "Or no, you are not over-heated?"

"I don't wish to be dragged across the room like a half-wit."

"I wouldn't have bothered with a half-wit."

"If I am overly warm, I should prefer something to drink." She wagged her fan faster.

He leaned close to her and whispered, "Are you over-warm?"

Felicity realized that she'd made a poor choice in words. "Overwarm" could mean too daring, which was not her meaning at all and not quite what she had said. She snapped her black-edged fan shut with an attempt at nonchalance. "Not in the least."

She wished he would take his low voice and his tall, lean form elsewhere. The challenging lift of his eyebrow invited her to remember that night long ago in far too much detail. She needed to find a balcony or a cool drink.

Alone.

Before she melted into a complete idiot and forgot the damage that one wonderful night had done to her life.

"Shall I fetch you a glass of lemonade?"

"That would be lovely, Major." Did he remember that as her preference? Or was it just a lucky guess?

He bowed and then limped away.

A half hour later she still didn't have her glass of lemonade, and Tony was nowhere to be seen. And where was the surprise in that?

* * *

Suicide. It couldn't have been suicide. Tony stared across the dimly lit drawing room at the body stretched out on the trestle table, brought in by the undertaker. Yet there was no doubt that his captain, who had survived six bloody years in the war to defeat Napoleon, was dead. Over thirty thousand men had fallen at Waterloo; Captain Lungren hadn't suffered a scratch. Had he returned home only to blow his brains out?

It didn't make sense.

Tony hadn't believed Lieutenant Randleton until they had arrived at Lungren's estate. Randy had waylaid him after he walked away from Felicity at the ball. His reddish-brown hair was mussed as if he dragged a hand through it, and his freckled face creased with concern when he gave Tony the awful news.

"If I had been here, I could have prevented this," Tony said to Randleton.

"What could you have done?"

Tony rubbed his face. "Talked to him, put his mind at ease. I am sure I could have done something."

Across the room Lungren's three dark-haired sisters huddled together like a row of black crows on a hedgerow, fluttering and swarming around the emaciated undertaker and a barrel-shaped Lord Carlton, the local justice of the peace.

A wave of pity washed through Tony. The women hadn't even had time to leave off their mourning for their father and two older brothers, and now they would continue without a head of the family.

"Was it too much for him? The responsibility?" Why had Lungren done himself in? "It doesn't make sense."

"He didn't seem the type, did he?" Randy shook his head and seemed to take great interest in rubbing the toe of his shoe across a bare spot in the faded rug.

What had happened? What had prompted a vital young man, full of life and with a bright future, to this end? "Had you seen him? Did he seem of sound mind?"

"I met him last week. He seemed fine, as carefree as ever. He was off to stake his fortune with Bedford. Joked about how he actually had more than captain's wages with which to wager."

"Who is Bedford?"

"William Bedford, of the Devonshire Bedfords. Bit of a Captain Sharp, I've heard. He and Lungren got along famously."

"Birds of a feather?"

"I should think so. They seemed rather fast friends." Randy scanned the gaggle of women. "Should we do something for them?"

"We ought to marry them," muttered Tony, mulling over what could be done to assist the family of his captain.

"Good God, no!"

"Then marry them off. Find suitable candidates." Tony turned to his lieutenant.

"Not me." Randy backed away, shaking his head.

"Come, now. I'm sure they're not so bad when they're not dressed in black and all Friday-faced." Really, Lungren's sisters, while not diamonds of the first water, weren't hideous either.

"Your command doesn't extend so far as to include telling me to marry anyone."

"Oh, give over, Randy. I'm just roasting you. But we should make sure that they are settled properly since Lungren isn't here to do it."

"I don't think that Lungren would have put much effort into seeing them settled."

"The matter wouldn't have been so urgent if he were here to head up the household, now, would it? Besides, Lungren was most resourceful. If his sisters wanted for husbands he would have scrounged up a willing sacrifice or two."

"He needed three. He couldn't have persuaded that many men to agree to marriage."

"Now there is just you and me."

Randy cocked his head, regarding Tony skeptically. "You have first choice, sir, but count me out."

"I can't marry. I'm bound for India once this leg mends. Wouldn't be much of a life for a wife."

Across the room one of the sisters raised her hand in front of her mouth and choked on a sob. Another spun away from the group; and only the glassy-eyed eldest stood her ground, but she swayed back and forth on a nonexistent breeze. They were still in shock, reasoned Tony.

He and Randleton had grown far too inured to death. They were here to help, not make light of the situation.

The undertaker pursed his lipless mouth.

Tony strode forward. "What is it?"

"It is customary for the family to wash and dress the body. I am not in the habit of—"

"Now, now," Lord Carlton, with the assurance of long-held authority, cut him off. "Just because the lad did himself in doesn't mean these young ladies should suffer for it."

"We'll take care of him." Tony turned to the glassy-eyed sister. It was something they could do.

Tony turned to his lieutenant and issued a one-word command. With the ease of many years of working together, Randleton began arranging the furniture so that they would be able to wash and dress the body in something other than the stained breeches and blood-soaked linen shirt Lungren wore.

Addressing the eldest sister, Tony removed his jacket and rolled up his sleeves. "Miss Lungren, I'm sure he has his uniform. Bring it to me."

The undertaker looked as if he might object to a suicide being buried wearing a uniform of His Majesty's army, but Tony quelled his objection with a single glance.

Lord Carlton reached out to steady Miss Lungren, and she jerked away, giving Tony an abrupt, tight-lipped nod. "I'll get it."

In a far gentler manner than Tony managed, Randy sent

the other two sisters off to fetch basins, washrags, soap, and towels.

"You will be back with the casket in the morning, sir." Tony made sure his tone to the undertaker implied an "or else." "Captain Lungren was a worthy soldier and served me and his country well."

The undertaker touched his forehead in a gesture of abdication and slouched off to take his leave.

"He's a bit squeamish about suicides." Lord Carlton had a don't-cross-me tone to his voice. "But I'll see to it—he'll do what needs to be done."

Tony glanced at the bullet wound in the forehead of his former captain. "Will there be an inquest?"

"I see no need. I'll have the doctor fill out the death certificate. No need to drag these poor gels through any more hell, what with their unfortunate mother and everything else." Lord Carlton shook his head. "Two brothers and a father taken by wasting diseases, and now a third brother dead by his own hand. Perhaps the losses were more than the captain could bear."

"An inquest would settle any doubt," said Tony.

"There is nothing to settle. He was alone in the library. The servants were all in their hall having supper. No one else in the house but his sisters, and they were in their rooms."

Tony rubbed his forehead. He had no real reason to object to the baron's conclusion. Tony had just thought his men were safe, their futures secure, once they returned to England.

Lord Carlton had drawn himself up but slowly relaxed when Tony made no further objection. "I'll just take my leave of the family. It's getting quite late."

Lord Carlton was no doubt anxious to return to his fire. He'd had the situation well in hand when they arrived. He seemed a capable man, perhaps a bit used to having his way, and not willing to expend a great deal of effort to confirm what on the surface seemed obvious.

Damnation, if Tony hadn't lived and fought by his light-hearted captain, he wouldn't have questioned the foregone conclusion either. But he still wondered how Lungren could have sunk so quickly and totally into despair.

He walked the middle-aged gentleman to the door, assuring him that he and Randy would see to the deceased and put themselves at the service of Lungren's sisters.

When Tony returned to the drawing room, his lieutenant was alone with the body. Randy had begun the task of washing away the dried blood from Captain Lungren's wound. "Major Sheridan . . ."

The formality of Randy's addressing him by his rank made Tony brace.

". . . would you take a look at this?"

Tony stepped forward and clearly saw the oblong, not round, not star-shaped wound. The world tilted under his feet. Reaching out, he braced himself against a chair back. He drew himself up. A superior officer never showed weakness, never admitted to pain.

He heard himself asking the question and watched Randy raise the head so they could both confirm what the shape of the wound already told him. The bullet had not followed the course it should have taken if Lungren had pulled the trigger.

Randy looked closer. "There aren't the powder burns I should expect. Didn't Casey . . ."

"Yes."

". . . have flash burns?"

"Yes." One of his officers had taken his own life during one of the protracted campaigns. There was absolutely no doubt that the supposed path of the bullet was all wrong, but also, the pistol had not been pressed against the captain's skin, which made the presumed method of death impossible. "Lungren didn't kill himself."

TWO

"My, my, our Captain Sheridan is now a major," Lady Greyston murmured behind her lazily fluttering fan.

"He isn't 'our' anything." Felicity glanced around at the thinning company in the ballroom.

"Well, wouldn't it be a fine match if he married you now, after all these years?"

"He doesn't want to marry me, and I don't want to marry him." *Or anyone else.* Felicity barely restrained herself from rolling her eyes. The real danger was that she could succumb to the same sensual madness that had taken her before. Pigs had to fly first, she reminded herself.

Lady Greyston's fan stopped. "You aren't considering him for your niece."

"No." Wouldn't that be lovely: the father of her child, married to her niece. The thought was too bizarre to contemplate. "It's time we went home."

"Other than Major Sheridan, I don't think you spent time with any gentlemen."

"No, I spent time with the hostesses, whom I hope will issue other invitations. One gets excluded by forgetting the niceties."

"Well, you should let me worry about that."

"I would, if you would remember that Diana is to be included in the invitations."

Lady Greyston pursed her lips.

Felicity's parents were going to drive her berserk in a fortnight. They were absolutely convinced she should be seeking out a future husband for herself. "I know you don't know my niece or even care if she should have a season, but it shan't be as easy for her to secure entrée into the ton as it was for me."

Diana's father, like Layton, had been in trade, and in spite of being raised as a lady, Diana would find some doors eternally shut.

"Well, I don't understand a bit of it. We have dropped everything in our lives to see you through this season so that *you* might find a husband."

Felicity closed her eyes. If she had known that was what her parents thought, she would have refused their company, or better yet, never told them she was going up to town. "There was no need. I did not want or expect you to leave home. Nor do I intend to find another husband."

Her mother's response was an impatient hiss. "We couldn't very well let you attend the season alone. It would be utterly improper. You are far too young and . . ." Her mother let the sentence dangle, her meaning made clear by her lifted eyebrows.

What her mother left unsaid was that a girl who was foolish enough to get pregnant during her first season was not to be left to her own devices at any age.

That Felicity had triumphed over her stupidity by finding a decent man to marry her, albeit one who had a little less than desired in the matter of breeding, was conveniently forgotten. That she had learned from her mistake and had no intention of repeating it didn't count at all.

"You should consider Major Sheridan."

"Why? Six years ago you thought my acceptance of his suit ludicrous."

Her mother replied with great patience as if Felicity were still as foolish. "He was a careless young man with no way to support you as a wife."

"Yes, I understand a captain's wages are inconsequential in comparison to a major's. What do you suppose the difference is? A farthing a week? I suppose I could actually afford tea on that."

"No, Felicity, you could support him now with your dower portion of the estate."

Felicity laughed. The idea of Tony allowing himself to be dependent on her tickled her. As if that would ever happen. "He and all the other fortune hunters. I swear, I could do better. Don't you suppose there is a penniless earl or two? Maybe a duke. Why, perhaps one of the foreign princes. I hear the Coburgs have pockets to let."

"You are not *that* deep in plump current, Felicity."

"Mmm," agreed Felicity. What her parents didn't know couldn't hurt her. "Quite unseemly of us to speak of something so vulgar as the blunt. I must have been married to Layton for far too long."

"Which is why you should consider Major Sheridan. He has excellent breeding to recommend him above all else," replied her mother, quite missing the point that Layton, for all his immersion in trade, had never talked about money.

Felicity feared that if she mentioned the irony of her mother's using the very argument Felicity had used nearly seven years ago, her mother wouldn't appreciate it. Having a great-grandfather who was an earl didn't make Tony anything other than a younger son of a younger son. "And far too much pride, I fear."

"Is that a bad thing?"

Not as long as it kept him from marrying her. She smiled. Now if she could just figure out how to avoid the pushy, protective presence of her parents, all would be well.

"Should we alert Lord Carlton?" asked Randy.

"No," answered Tony.

Randy lifted his reddish-brown eyebrows. He wouldn't go so far as to question his superior officer out loud. Then again, there were times when it was far better for Tony to explain to his subordinates why he chose a particular course of action.

Tony lowered his voice. "Whoever did this thinks they got away with it."

"You don't believe Lord Carlton would put much effort into finding the culprit."

There was that, too. Tony wouldn't have said it, but he nodded.

"Probably wouldn't put much stock in our experience with bullet wounds." Both of them had seen more men shot, stabbed, wounded, and killed, in every conceivable method of warfare, than anyone should ever see. Randy calmly finished cleaning Lungren's too-still face. "What do you think? Someone he fleeced?"

Tony rubbed his temple, trying to understand why someone would kill Lungren. "Possibly."

"A jilted lover?"

Tony rolled his eyes. "Pistols aren't the usual method employed by women. Poison is. So a jilted lover is doubtful."

"Servant?"

"All in the hall at supper. Where is the library?"

"First door on the left."

Tony turned on his heel and moved to the doorway of the drawing room. The eldest sister stood there—what was her name? Rosalyn? Or was this one Jocelyn? The youngest he remembered as Carolyn. "Miss Lungren, will you show me to the library?"

Her glassy-eyed look sharpened for a moment. "Oh, you wish to see where . . ." Miss Lungren stood rooted to the spot.

"If you would just point, I'm sure I can manage to find the room on my own."

"Why?"

How much had she heard? Randleton moved behind Tony. "There might be a note."

Anger flashed across the woman's face. "No. There wasn't a note."

"Have you looked thoroughly?" asked Tony. He knew there wasn't a note. Murder victims didn't leave notes, but it gave him and Randy an excuse to search the room. "Do you know of any reason your brother might have . . . ?"

Her head moved side to side in a more distraught manner than an ordinary "no" would have taken. She stepped back and bumped against the door frame. Her voice shaking as she spoke, she said, "Perhaps you should look; perhaps I did not look well enough. Perhaps . . . perhaps I was distracted."

Worried she was on the edge of collapse, Tony reached out and grabbed her elbow. She jerked back. It reminded him of the way Felicity had moved so quickly away from him earlier in the evening. "Miss Lungren, you should sit down."

"No, I'm fine." She stepped forward as if she regretted recoiling. "I don't want to sit down."

"Please, you are very distressed." He should comfort her, but the thought that Felicity was waiting for him to return with a glass of lemonade kept his arms by his side.

Rosalyn spun on her heels and marched down the passageway, as if she had barely gotten up the nerve to return to the place of her brother's death and was afraid to go slowly lest the courage desert her. Tony was hard-pressed to keep up with her, given his limp.

She threw back the door and then hovered near the doorway. Tony had to shoulder by her to get into the library. Across the room, two low-slung wing chairs flanked the fireplace. One had a large, dark stain flowing down from just below where a head would rest. A maid was on her hands and knees behind the chair, scrubbing the wooden floor with a flat brush, a reddish-brown stain covering a towel near her knees.

"Molly, you may stop."

The maid flattened her mouth.

"No, let her continue." Tony's eyes flashed along the pristine row of bookshelves not four feet behind the chair, and then back to the grim-faced maid. He wanted to question her after Rosalyn left the room. "She won't disturb us."

"The estate papers are kept in that desk." Rosalyn pointed.

Then, as if she had marked the escritoire as a buoy to swim to and cling to for safety, she darted across the room to it.

Her face was so pale, Tony wondered what strength she was drawing on to offer assistance to them. She had to be near collapse.

She pulled out a drawer.

Randy caught his eye. The concern and the question *Should we tell her?* was as plain as the freckles on his face.

Tony shook his head. She didn't need any more shocks tonight, and they needed proof before making accusations.

"They're gone!" Rosalyn shrieked.

Suddenly there was a flurry of paper in the air as she tossed aside the contents of the drawer and leaned over to yank open another.

Tony headed toward her, but Randleton beat him there. The lieutenant wrapped his arms around her flailing arms. It was amazing she had taken this long to turn hysterical.

"Let's get her out of here," hissed Tony in a low command.

"No! The papers. The deed to the estate. I have to find them!"

She tried to wrench away from Randy's restraining arms, but with Tony in front of her adding his sure grip to her shoulders, she broke into sobs.

"What has he done?" She covered her face with her hands.

"Most likely moved the important papers to another place. They'll turn up."

"No, oh, no." Rosalyn resumed her swaying, dragging Randy back and forth. "He said . . . he said . . . Oh, God, I'll kill that man."

Randy recoiled from the distraught woman.

Tony continued to grip her shoulders, although he, too, had been shocked by the vehement declaration right after learning Captain Lungren had been murdered. But she couldn't be referring to her brother; he was already dead. "Who said what?"

"He said he had to repay a gambling debt. That's why he had that man come here. Oh, what has he done?"

"What has *who* done? Who had to repay a gambling debt?"

Rosalyn snapped at him. "My brother had to repay Bedford. Dear God, how I hate that man." She jerked away from Tony's grasp but was trapped by Randy, behind her. Randy belatedly stepped back. She hastily sidestepped, then paced back and forth in the small amount of open floor space in the library.

"He has been nothing but an evil influence. Gambling all the time, all hours. The drinking, the whor—" Rosalyn clapped a hand over her mouth.

Randy needed to work on how telling his face was. Yes, they both knew that Lungren had not needed any influence to commit those debaucheries, but obviously his eldest sister hadn't known.

"Bedford was here? Tonight?"

"Yes!" Rosalyn stamped her foot.

Tony and Randy exchanged looks. What did this Bedford fellow have to do with Lungren's death?

Meg Brown wiped the damp brow of the girl lying in the bunk. The ominous creaking and the sway of the lantern overhead marked the rough seas. They hadn't even reached the English Channel.

"Are we within sight of the white cliffs of Dover?" asked the girl, Diana Fielding, lately of a Swiss finishing school.

"We're close." That was a lie. Meg felt no remorse. She was good at lying, and besides, she meant it for comfort.

"Good, I've missed England."

Meg curled her nose. Meg had not missed England. Yet here she was, returning to everything she'd never had.

"I'm anxious to meet my aunt," whispered Diana.

Your very generous aunt, thought Meg. The one who had unknowingly financed Meg Brown's return. Although, as much nursing as the young miss required, Meg had earned every ha'penny.

Diana, who epitomized the wealth and gentle manners of a lady—although she did not have the blue blood Meg could claim—was sicker than a poisoned dog. Meg felt an odd mix of pity and envy. The girl had everything to look forward to: a position in society, an aunt determined to give her a proper season, and no doubt, enough blunt to induce a respectable man into the parson's trap.

Meg, on the other hand, had endured every kind of hell known to women. She was stuck in this cramped cabin, tending a sick girl she barely knew. All because that was what the wife of an officer in His Majesty's army would do. Meg wasn't a wife. A camp follower, more like. But there was no future in that. With the Corsican monster defeated, soon there wouldn't even be any armies left to follow.

"My cousin is the only real family I have left."

"What about your aunt?"

"Aunt Felicity is only my aunt by marriage." Diana breathed hard for a few seconds. "Not a blood relative."

Meg was tempted to warn her to conserve her strength, but it hardly mattered now. If it comforted the girl to talk, well, then, Meg could listen. She had always had too soft a heart. Besides she couldn't go anywhere on the ship, because the captain had been keeping a close eye on her. A very close eye.

"Her young son, Charles, is my first cousin. But everyone else is dead."

Then Diana would be surrounded by family soon. Meg bit back the uncalled-for response and dipped the rag in the basin to wipe Diana's forehead and wrists again.

"My parents are dead. Uncle Layton is dead." Diana closed her eyes. "I often wondered if my destiny was to perish so far from home in Switzerland."

"Of course not," Meg reassured her.

Meg was no longer sure that she herself was destined for anything better than her mother's fate, being a wharfside doxie once her looks faded and the only ones that would want her were the smelly old drunks who didn't care beyond that she had the right parts.

Each opportunity she grabbed to take her closer to the life she knew she was entitled to live and had begun to fight for ended up having an unforeseen drawback. Every respectable soldier she had done laundry and cooking for in the hopes of a decent proposal ended up facedown in the dirt, and she'd have to start all over again. She'd come out further ahead when she just lay on her back.

"I thought they might have forgotten about me, but then Aunt Felicity started writing me. I have every letter still." Diana lethargically pointed toward the trunk in the corner. Her arm flopped down as if she could no longer support its weight.

Meg gently placed Diana's arm on the bunk. "Yes, you should try to sleep now."

This service, which Meg performed for Diana in hope of some small return of a respectable connection, would be worthless. The girl was deathly ill and would not last long enough to offer any assistance. Meg could only hope this aunt would appreciate her chaperoning and nursing care—and compensate her. Still, Meg continued her efforts.

It was a crying shame: Diana had everything in life that Meg coveted, and she wouldn't live to enjoy it.

His purpose clear, Major Anthony Sheridan lurched across the dark, smoky room. Armed with knowledge of the man's clothing description provided by the maid Molly, and a physical description from Randleton of wavy blond hair, turquoise eyes, and a slight build, Tony scanned the room with precision born of command. He spied his target and drew to a halt beside the man's chair. "Are you Bedford?"

The man looked up from the baize-covered table heaped with markers and vowels, leaned back in his chair, and held his none-too-clean cards against his chest. "Who wan's ta know?"

Tony had no time for games or banter. Already he had crashed through the protected portals of the exclusive Watier's gambling club when Randy's negotiations hadn't progressed far enough to gain them civilized entry. He raised his voice several decibels. "Are you Bedford?"

Tony glared at the man. Bedford stared back at him. The unfocused but brilliant blue-green eyes gave him away. Other gamblers, those sober enough to notice the confrontation, turned in their direction.

"It's him," whispered Randy, pulling up at Tony's elbow.

"Did Captain Lungren give you the deed to his estate?"

"I won it, sir."

How could he have won it? Lungren was too good at cards, too shrewd about what to risk. How many times had he warned them never to wager what they couldn't afford to lose? Though, of course, Lungren almost always won.

"I should like to speak to you."

Bedford stared at him. He shut his eyes and opened them as if that would make Tony go away.

Tony wasn't going anywhere until he got some answers. He put command in his voice. "Now!"

It was as he leaned close that he saw the red markings of a court card in Bedford's lap.

Was the man even now cheating? Did he know the pattern of stains on each card? The flickering light of too few candles would make it far too easy for sleight of hand. Rage sliced through Tony. Had Bedford cheated Lungren out of his estate? Or was Lungren able to outsmart the swindler and preserve his holdings only to have Bedford shoot him?

"You, sir, are a cheat."

Bedford dropped his cards to the table. He slowly stood. His face contorted with a smug anger that made Tony's blood boil. "Sirrah!"

Bedford had to be the man who killed Lungren. Tony

could take care of him right now, administer swift, military-style justice. "You killed him."

"What? I merely won at cards." Bedford turned to look at the other gamblers at the table, as if to sway them into thinking Tony was not in his right mind.

Tony slowly unbuttoned his glove and drew it off.

Bedford's unsteady gaze returned to Tony, and with too much cunning he said, "I did not force his hand—"

That was enough for Tony. He slapped the smirk right off William Bedford's face.

The despicable man knew he had staged the scene to look like a suicide.

William Bedford leaned heavily against the table and said the only words that were acceptable: "I demand satisfaction."

"My pleasure, sir," the tall major said with a bow.

The pleasant alcohol glow that had surrounded William just a few minutes ago was changing into a confusing black haze. Had he just challenged a military man, no doubt proficient with lethal weapons, to a duel?

The naming of time and place and seconds was going on around him, and William stared at the floor, where the knave of hearts stared back at him. Where in blazes had that card come from? William vaguely remembered holding that card a couple of hands earlier, but where had it come from now?

The major pivoted and left the room, ignoring the porter who had come to escort him out. His red-haired companion and second trailed behind him and looked back at William as if he were insane. Likely, he was.

William Bedford leaned over and checked his pocket watch. He waited at Chalk Farm for his opponent. Would he show?

William paced back and forth. The low, rolling hills of the countryside protected them from view of the main road. He understood now why this matter had resulted in the public slap that left no recourse but a challenge or humiliation. Not only the slap, but the accusation of cheating.

Lungren was dead, by his own hand, just after he'd signed the deed to the estate over to William. No wonder Major Sheridan had thought him involved and had pulled off his glove to slap William.

By the code of honor no apology for the blow was acceptable, but William wasn't above bending rules when necessary, though he usually stopped short of outright cheating. The last thing he would have done was cheat his friend out of his estate. He hadn't dreamed that Lungren would kill himself. If he'd had the merest inkling, he would never have let his friend sign over the deed. He would have remained there for the night, the week, the month just to stay Lungren's hand.

He heard the jingle of harnesses and the roll of carriage wheels and realized he was sweating. His opponent, Major Sheridan, lately of the Peninsular campaign, was war seasoned. No doubt he thought nothing of shooting a man. Doubtless he had done it many a time before. With that limp, he would choose pistols. Not a chance he would bring swords and they might satisfy themselves with first blood.

This was not the outcome he had intended when he faced Captain Lungren and allowed the stakes to rise impossibly high. Lungren had been remarkably cool as he exchanged the deed to his property for his vowels. William wanted to shout that it was all a mistake.

He bent over and rested his hands on his knees. He felt dizzy and sick. It would be just his luck if he cast up his accounts just as Sheridan arrived.

The major descended the steps with perfect military posture that marked his control. He wasn't suffering a humiliating battle with his nerves. Sheridan's icy blue gaze shot through William and chilled him to the core.

William straightened, as if Sheridan's disdain brought what little honor he had to the fore.

Sheridan stripped off his coat, a blue morning coat rather than his red uniform. He unbuttoned his buff waistcoat.

"I would have allowed him to grant me an annuity in lieu of the deed."

Sheridan paused only the space of a half second before continuing to remove the waistcoat. "He's dead. Shall we get on with it?"

William shivered and wondered at Sheridan's cold statement. How many times had Sheridan spoken those words? How many men had fallen under his command, under his watch? How could the man be anything but cold?

"Is it to be pistols, then?"

"Show him the barkers, Randy."

William unfastened his jacket with trembling fingers. Although the air was frigid, his shaking was not due to the February weather.

Lieutenant Randleton brought out a carved walnut box and flipped back the lid. Inside, red velvet cradled two elegantly tooled dueling pistols, their handles inlaid with mother-of-pearl.

William's second moved to inspect the weapons. "Capitol set of poppers."

"Spanish, you know. The major got rather fond of things Spanish."

"He bring 'em back with him?"

"Didn't bring any of his Spanish things back with him. Found them here in London."

"By Jove, not at that place off Bond Street, near Clifford Street?" exclaimed the man who had volunteered his services to William after the unexpected slap.

Dread crawled up William's spine as he listened to the two seconds discuss the pistols, as if he and Sheridan weren't about to kill each other with them.

"I believe so," answered Randleton. "Dusty little shop with all sorts of odd weapons."

"I say. I believe those pistols are cursed."

Randleton gave a tight-lipped shake of his head.

"Burn my breeches if those aren't the very pistols used for grass before breakfast just over a year ago by . . . well, by two men I know. They were pearl-inlaid and Spanish-tooled," said Bedford's second.

William didn't want to hear about curses. He could hardly keep the contents of his stomach down just thinking of their deadly purpose. He stared across the field, where the major had limped out into position. The sight of the two men dropping ball and powder into the barrels and packing them down wasn't doing his puling stomach any favors.

"Had it from the shopkeeper that there was a curse. Now, what was it? Something about marriage." William's second tapped a finger against his lips. "Ah, yes. The winner shall gain a jolly good wife; the loser shall be leg-shackled to a horrid bride."

"Are we ready, gentlemen?" Sheridan's deep voice boomed across the field with a commanding authority impossible to ignore.

William suffered a turn for the worse. His stomach roiled. Probably a good thing he hadn't eaten breakfast.

"I say, are you quite all right, sir?" asked the jackanapes William had pressed into being his second. "You look as if you might flash your hash."

"Let's get on with it, do," William managed to grind out.

The two assistants measured the field and pointed out where to stand. There would be no pacing with Sheridan's bad leg.

One of the pistols was pressed into William's hand. The heavy weight punished the wrist not used to holding anything heavier than a deck of cards. The Spanish tooling marks cut into his palm, while the mother-of-pearl felt smooth. He prayed that the target practice he'd done yesterday behind Manton's would assist his aim.

He lifted his gaze to his opponent. Sheridan's eyes darted around as if surveying the lay of the land. Was he expecting the authorities to stop them? William shook his head at the fleeting hope of salvation. Sheridan's icy blue gaze snapped to him, no doubt provoked by the small movement of William's head.

Chills ran down William's spine. He couldn't look away from that penetrating stare. How many Frenchmen had looked their last into those winter-cold eyes?

"Are you ready, gentlemen?" asked Lieutenant Randleton.

William squeaked out an answer that vaguely resembled a yes.

Major Sheridan gave an imperturbably calm "I'm ready."

"Aim . . ."

William brought the pistol up and sighted down the barrel. He strove valiantly to keep his knees from knocking and his aching wrist steady.

"Fire."

His finger slid off the trigger and he fought to reposition it without dropping his sights. He heard the click of Sheridan's pistol, and time stretched as he waited for the spark to ignite the powder. One heartbeat, two heartbeats . . .

His heart had grown so large, it pounded in his gut and his throat at the same time. He managed to pull his trigger, heard the click and the chattering of birds, the sway of the breeze in the leaves of the trees. Sheridan's narrowed eyes stared through him. If William lived, those pale eyes would haunt his nightmares.

The detonation of the pistols in quick succession blasted his ears. Pain ricocheted through his eardrums, and the world tilted madly. The sky tumbled toward the ground, and then the faded yellow grass rushed up to meet his face.

THREE

Felicity smoothed her gray gloves over the back of her hand and adjusted her hat. Seeing the man, first his head, then his shoulders as he ascended the steps, she said, "Stand up straight, Charles."

She leaned over and picked up the worn valise that had belonged to her husband, and transferred it into her left hand. As the balding middle-aged man approached the locked door where she stood, she extended her hand. "Mr. Blume, I presume."

The man eyed her skeptically, but Felicity kept her hand extended and her voice calm and purposeful. "I'm Mrs. Merriwether, Layton's widow, and this is my son, Charles."

Mr. Blume looked as if he'd swallowed sour milk. Finally, when it became clear that Felicity wasn't about to move from in front of his office, he gave one halfhearted shake of her hand.

"Since you are such a busy man, I thought it best to take care of matters first thing in the morning." Felicity smiled without baring her teeth. She had never felt less like smiling.

Mr. Blume, her husband's London banker, had been avoiding her. He mumbled something that sounded suspiciously like "meddling woman" but was spoken too low for her to be sure. She had sent several notes requesting a convenient time for her to call, without receiving an answer, and arrived at his office only to be repeatedly told by the young man who was his secretary that he was otherwise engaged and could not see her.

"I'm a bit preoccupied, Mrs. Merriwether."

Felicity nodded. "I see, but we shall have to take the time to sever our business relationship, and I have the time now, Mr. Blume. However, it will take quite a space for me to be sure all of Layton's holdings are intact and the necessary audits of his accounts are complete."

"You can't do that!"

Felicity stepped to the side of the door. She was glad her gray kid gloves concealed her damp palms. "I'm sure this discussion should take place in your office."

Her eyes on the door, she waited until he slowly withdrew a ring of keys.

Mr. Blume fumbled to insert his key in the lock of his office. Felicity swept through in front of him and, without waiting, opened the door to the inner office and took a seat. Charles followed her and climbed into the morocco leather chair beside his mother. Felicity perched on the edge of her chair. She removed a copy of Layton's will. After the banker seated himself, she placed it on top of the papers scattered over Mr. Blume's desk.

"As you can see, Charles is too young to manage his father's businesses and Layton named me as the sole trustee until such a time as Charles reaches his majority."

Mr. Blume's disgust grew apparent on his face. He picked up the will and read it. "This can't be right."

"Mr. Blume, whether you like it or not, I am the one you have been dealing with for the past two years. Layton's long illness precluded him from making business decisions and I—initially with his guidance and approval—have completely taken over the management of his holdings."

"He wouldn't have let a woman run his business."

"Businesses, Mr. Blume. There is the coal mine in Cornwall, the textile mill in Cumberland, his ownership of the sugar plantation in Haiti, the thirty-three percent share in the Moore, Merriwether, and Turner shipping company . . . Shall I continue?"

Mr. Blume shook his head.

"Are you sure you wouldn't like me to list his various investments, also?" She did want to make sure that the banker understood that she knew Layton's holdings down to the last farthing.

Charles watched her with a wary eye. He could probably hear the tightness in her tone.

"I could list the income of each, quarterly or annually."

"That won't be necessary."

Felicity didn't really want to switch banks. Many businessmen would not even deal with a female, but she was bound and determined to be given her due for the work she had been doing for years as Layton's illness progressed to the point where he was incapable of making any decisions. She'd be damned before she'd apologize for being an intelligent woman.

"I'm sure the most satisfactory arrangement for all of us would have been if Layton had continued to manage his own affairs, but his death precludes that."

"Surely there is some other relative—your father—who could shoulder this burden for you, Mrs. Merriwether."

Her involuntary snort should have been clue enough to what she thought of her father's financial ability. Felicity couldn't possibly trust her father to understand the intricacies of her husband's investments.

"A future husband, perhaps," suggested Mr. Blume weakly.

"Why, I'm surprised you would suggest that, Mr. Blume, knowing as you do how ill-equipped and inept Layton's brother-in-law, Thomas Fielding, was with finances."

Mr. Blume had to admit to himself, at least, if not to her, that Layton's brother-in-law was a disaster in the financial arena. He'd run through his wife's fortune before his death, while Layton had steadily increased his wealth from an almost unheard-of equal split of their father's holdings between Layton and his sister.

"Have there been any troublesome issues that have surfaced for you in the last two years, since I have been in charge?"

His response was reluctant. "No, madam." Mr. Blume leaned back in his chair and cupped his chin in his hand. "You have made your point."

"Are we going to have problems, Mr. Blume? I know it is not to your liking to do business with a woman, but I am afraid that is the way it will be for several years." He'd had no problem when he hadn't realized he was dealing with her. "If it is not convenient for you to arrange a meeting when I request one, then I am afraid I will have look into other banks."

"That is not necessary, Mrs. Merriwether."

Felicity nodded. "Good, then. Just so there won't be any confusion, I will continue to manage my son's inheritance on the off chance that I should remarry. I will not turn over my son's finances to a future husband or anyone else. Also, I will be bringing Charles along on all business meetings, so he can learn as he grows up."

"Yes, ma'am."

Felicity heaved a sigh of relief. "Now, I should like to talk about arranging a suitable dowry for my niece." Her penniless niece, but Felicity didn't think she needed to make the point again about how inept her father—a male—had been.

The door to the inner office opened, and the secretary started to usher in a man in a scarlet uniform. "Mr. Blume, you have a visitor, Captain . . ." the secretary paused in the middle of his introduction as he recognized Felicity from her attempts to gain entry to Mr. Blume's private office. His jaw fell slack. "I'm sorry, I didn't realize you had visitors."

Charles took that moment to pipe up. Looking straight at the captain Felicity had never met before in her life, he asked, "Are you my papa?"

"Do roll him over." Tony stared dispassionately at the still form of William Bedford, lying face down on the ground. The two seconds had run over to him but stopped as if afraid to touch the man.

"Perhaps you should be off, sir," said Randy.

"I doubt it." Tony lurched across the field. He rather suspected Bedford was just as sound as he was.

Bedford's second rolled the pale man to his back. A trickle of blood dripped from his lip. "You've killed him."

"What happened to him, sir?" Randy exchanged a puzzled glance with Tony. "I didn't see. I was watching you."

Tony knelt down on his good leg and pulled out a handkerchief to wipe the blood from the corner of Bedford's mouth. He waved with the dueling pistol, lightly held in his other hand. "I rather suspect I should not be so enamored of all things Spanish."

Bedford's eyes flicked open. His gaze drifted to the spot of blood on the handkerchief, and he blanched. He grabbed Tony's shirtfront. "I must ask a favor, sir."

Tony held his tongue.

"In my carriage is a packet with the title to Lungren's estate. There's also a quitclaim deed, duly witnessed by my solicitor. Do take it to Captain Lungren's sisters."

"You might take it yourself."

Bedford's eyes flicked to the handkerchief and back up.

"I suspect you bit your lip when you fainted," said Tony.

"But you shot him," said Bedford's second.

"I don't believe so. He didn't have the look of a man who took a bullet. I have seen more than a few men brought down by one."

Bedford sat up gingerly, as if he expected the task to be difficult.

Randleton raised his eyebrows. A crack shot like Tony had far too much experience to be thrown by a fit of nerves at twenty paces.

"I regret to say that I missed. We should have gone for Mantons after all." He collected Bedford's dropped pistol and handed the pair to Randleton. "I felt it kick sideways when I fired. I suspect all the pretty work was decorative only."

Bedford dabbed at his lip with his fingertips, probing the

slight wound. Would he withdraw his generosity now that he knew he wasn't dying?

His second seemed to recall the rules of engagement at this point. "Are you satisfied, sir?"

Since Bedford had issued the challenge, it fell to him to answer. His expression held disgust and wonder. "I am satisfied."

Tony began to struggle painfully to his feet. Randleton knew better than to offer assistance.

Bedford leaned forward and brushed off his breeches. "Will you discharge this errand for me?"

Tony paused.

Bedford's face had grown red. "As you are Lungren's— *were* Lungren's—senior officer, perhaps it should come better from you. I should think I am persona non grata in that household." He looked down at the ground. "I had no idea he would kill himself. I did not mean for this to come to pass."

For the first time, Tony stopped to consider how little he knew about his opponent. Had he misjudged Bedford? Convicted him with circumstance and coincidence? "What did you mean when you took his home?"

Bedford's voice shook, but he emphasized, "I *won* his home."

Tony cocked an eyebrow. By honor he was expected to accept the outcome of this duel as the final word in the matter. He could no longer accuse Bedford of cheating, but murder was a different story. If he could find proof or induce a confession, he could bring the matter to Lord Carlton's attention.

"I should have been happy to allow him to grant me an annuity, if he had mentioned his difficulties to me. I did not prompt him to wager his home." Tears began to drip down Bedford's cheeks, and he swiped at them, looking away.

Tony crossed his arms and stared at his opponent. Perhaps he had leaped to the conclusion that Bedford was out to relieve young men of their superfluous wealth. But Lungren, while young, was a seasoned veteran who should have known better than to stake his ancestral home on the turn of a card. "Perhaps I was hasty in assuming your methods were foul."

"By my word, I was uncommonly lucky that night." Bedford frowned and fingered the lip that had started to fatten ever so slightly. "Or devilishly unlucky."

Tony cast his eyes to the horizon. Wispy clouds danced across the pale sky. The day was placid. The birds, momentarily silenced by the blast of the pistols, once again chirped in the trees. The breeze rustled leaves, and the faint babble of running water of a nearby brook reminded him that life runs on.

So different from a battlefield, where the hiss and crack of gunshot, the boom of cannon and heavy gun, the screams of the dying and wounded, and the shouted commands pounded him from every side. Facing Bedford, Tony had almost been confused by the lack of distraction. In battle he'd shot men and turned to the next danger before they hit the ground.

After the hostilities, the silence would turn ominous. The birds didn't sing or return to the place of carnage. The air grew putrid and heavy with the stench of blood and death.

Yet it wasn't so different in that you could assess a man quickly, intuitively watching him behave under the pressures of gunfire. Suddenly, Tony was sure Bedford was not the type of man who could shoot a man in cold blood just to take his property. Would such a man arrange for the property to pass back to the rightful owners in the event of his death?

"Upon my word, he was my friend, too," whispered Bedford.

Tony suddenly felt weary. Had he become so callous, so inured to death that he jumped to it as a solution before considering anything else? Perhaps it was as well that the pistol had wavered and he missed his target. As for Bedford's shot, hard to say. It might have gone astray for nerves or by poor design of the fancy pistol.

Bedford lowered his head and rested his hands on his knees and gave into the tears that he had tried to stem.

Tony had seen too many soldiers succumb to fright in battle and had witnessed their deep humiliation afterward. He put a hand on Bedford's shoulder. "It's over now. It shall be breakfast for two after all."

Bedford winced and shook his head. "I can't believe I am such a coward."

Tony squeezed and removed his hand. "We've seen bluff and bluster men acquit themselves worse, haven't we, Randy?"

"Many a time," agreed Lieutenant Randleton.

Bedford waved them away.

Tony knelt down and put his arm around Bedford's shoulder. Tony spoke in the low, soothing tone he used with his men. He had given a thousand variations of this speech. The first time he'd barely been twenty-one, hardly more than a boy himself. "You know courage is not being without fear. Courage is containing and controlling that fear until the crisis is past. You held steady until you got that shot off."

"I missed. I'm no good with guns. I don't even hunt," whispered Bedford.

"I missed, too, and I assure you I don't as a rule."

A new sob shuddered through Bedford. "Why would he kill himself? Why?"

Tony exchanged a look with Randy. "That's what we should like to know. I fear I jumped to the conclusion that you were responsible."

"I can't believe I fainted."

"Come, we'll find an inn to serve us, and we'll regale you with tales of what really happens to men facing bloodshed for the first time." Tony watched Bedford. "Unless, of course, I have made a lifelong enemy of you. I should understand."

"You must have been terribly upset to learn Lungren had taken his life."

"He served me well." The words were inadequate to explain the debt of responsibility Tony felt toward his men.

And he was back at square one. If Bedford hadn't killed Lungren, who had?

Bedford straightened. "Very well, sir. Breakfast for two it is, or four." He turned to his second with an inquiring look.

"Ah, yes, and I shall look forward to seeing how quickly each of you falls into the parson's mousetrap."

Bedford's appalled expression mirrored Tony's feelings to a tee.

"No time soon, I'll wager," said Tony.

"Within a twelvemonth, I'd hazard," disagreed the ninny Bedford had brought to the fray.

No, Tony didn't intend to marry. Ever. He had meant to once, but never again would he succumb to that cork-brained notion. Felicity had perhaps done him a great favor in discarding his suit the minute he left England.

Home again and alone with her son in the little-used green drawing room, Felicity pulled Charles up to her knees. He squirmed against her, impatient with the change in plans. She had promised a trip to the toy store for reward if he behaved well in Mr. Blume's office, and he had, except for that one question she needed to discuss with him. "Darling, do you remember what you said to that captain at the bank?"

Charles blinked his pale blue eyes at her.

"You must not go around asking every man we meet if he is your papa."

"I do not ask every man," answered Charles with the imperturbable logic of a five-year-old. "I did not ask mean Mr. Blume or that other man. I only ask army men."

Fortunately her son's question had been laughed off. Felicity had mildly suggested that now she was out of her widow's weeds, her son was hoping she would marry, if only to get himself a new father. Only Charles wasn't looking for a new father. He was looking for his *real* father.

How did Charles know that Layton wasn't his natural father?

Felicity rubbed her forehead. "Why would you ask such a thing? You know Layton Merriwether was your papa."

"No, he told me he was not my real papa. He told me my *real* papa was an officer in the army."

Oh, Layton, thought Felicity.

Charles's lower lip thrust out and trembled. He was so brave and vulnerable at the same time, she hated to chastise him. Yet he tottered precariously on the verge of destroying Felicity's reputation.

"He should not have done so. It was not kind of him." But then, Layton Merriwether had never been kind to Charles. When he wasn't chastising him, he had ignored him. "You cannot go around asking men if they are your father. It makes your mama look very bad."

Charles's face scrunched up in confusion. He really could make her look wicked without realizing what he was about.

Felicity tapped her lip. She really couldn't have Charles endangering the respectability she'd bought so dear. "You should have asked me."

Charles leaned his elbows on her knees and asked with perfect seriousness. "Do you know who my papa is?"

Ah, the innocence of youth. Felicity bit the inside of her cheek to keep from smiling. "Of course I do, darling."

Charles scowled at her. "You didn't ever mean to tell me."

She swallowed her regret that, unbeknownst to her, Layton had informed Charles of his paternity. "I did not feel you were old enough to understand."

"I am not a baby."

"No, but you're not grown, either." He wasn't out of short coats yet. "If you were older, you would understand that you can't go around asking strangers who your father is."

"I'm glad *my* real papa fought The Monster in the war." Charles looked altogether too earnest.

Was her son building his natural father into heroic proportions in his mind? Did he think his sire was a noble creature who deserved his worship? And should Felicity shatter his dreams or let him have them?

She noticed the belligerent set to Charles's chin and thought of Tony. If Charles had inherited determination from him, he wouldn't let the subject drop. Ever.

"All right, if you promise not to tell anyone, I'll point him out to you before we leave London."

"He's here? He's in London? When can we see him?" Charles pushed back and ran to the door as if he would run right out to find his father.

Felicity moved to him and knelt down in front of her son. "Promise you'll never tell anyone that Layton Merriwether wasn't your father."

Silence hung in the air while Charles pondered the situation. His face took on a sulky look, his lower lip thrusting out.

"Very well, then. I shall not point out your real father." She rose with a rustle of gray silk.

"Mama, wait!"

She knelt back down and brushed the golden-brown curls off her son's forehead. "I need you to promise, else I shall not point him out to you."

"Why?"

There were a thousand whys. The main reason was that Tony knew of his existence and had never expressed one iota of interest in him. She didn't want her son hurt with the painful truth. She searched for an explanation her five-year-old son could understand. "Well, if you tell everyone you are not a Merriwether, your cousin Diana will be all alone in the world. She won't have a single relative left."

"You." Charles looked at her narrowly.

"I'm only her aunt by marriage. But she believes you are the son of her mother's brother and the only true family left to her." Gads, that was weak, thought Felicity.

He frowned as if seriously considering the hasty excuse she'd given.

"Please, Charles, there are other reasons, which you will understand when you get older."

His face took on a determined look. "I'll promise not to tell anyone if you promise to tell me everything about him."

"Charles, you cannot add conditions. You must promise not to tell."

"Upon my honor."

She hated that he looked so hopeful. He hardly asked for anything. She didn't want to deny him this. Where was the harm in sharing a few details? His real father, after all, was a war hero.

At his age, Charles wouldn't understand that his father had left his mother in a terrible coil and discarded her like so much rubbish when she grew inconvenient. "All right, I shall tell you a little about him."

"And I can meet him?"

"No, not meet him. I'll point him out, but you must promise not to speak of it to anyone." Felicity swallowed her reservations. What harm could come of pointing out his father from a distance?

Charles pierced her with an icy blue gaze. "Can we go to the toy store now?"

The question startled a response from her. "Of course we shall."

With a sweet, cherubic smile Charles tugged her toward the door.

Felicity pulled on her gray gloves and buttoned the cuffs. She'd called for her carriage, and a footman opened the front door for her and Charles. His little hand tucked in hers, she made it down the first two steps before she realized she was being watched. The sensation spread through her like butter melting on a scone. She unerringly looked across the street to meet Tony's eyes.

He leaned against a wrought-iron railing around the small square. He straightened, breaking the liquid relaxation of his pose and dropping a barrier between the unbidden memory of the untried young man he had been and the tightly controlled officer he had become.

In one of his hands was the end of a lead to one of the biggest dogs Felicity had ever seen. In the other hand he held . . . a glass?

He raised the glass and held it out. His mouth curled in a dangerous half smile, while Charles jerked at her hand.

Felicity felt as if she were wading through water as she was half tugged across the street toward Tony. His pale eyes flicked over her, perhaps marking the changes and the difference after six years. The dog he held began to thump his tail against the ground and lunged forward, half-sitting.

"I brought you your lemonade."

"Look at that dog, Mama. Look!" her son's voice squeaked with excitement.

Tony's gaze lit on her son, and she could see the animosity, the coldness, the almost unadulterated hatred, and she pulled Charles closer to her.

What kind of man hated his own son?

FOUR

William Bedford stared at the letter on the salver as if it might sprout fangs and bite him. What did one do when the dead were communicating to him? Although Lungren had obviously been alive when he had written it. If the letter was a suicide note, William had no desire to be the recipient of such a missive.

Reluctantly he reached for the single sheet and popped the seal. Of course, if he was to know more, he supposed he had no choice but to get on with it.

My dearest Bedford,

By the bye, now that you have the title to my estate—my former estate—I should warn you that it is not the prize it seems. The farms and rents that are left after the sell-off my predecessors have managed to effect are not enough to support the daily expenses of running the household. Of course, if you should manage to oust my sisters, expenses might be trimmed considerably. However, things have fallen into such a state of disrepair that I am afraid only a good bit of blunt shall make it worthy. Blunt I do not have.

I, however, by the time you read this, shall be on a long journey to a new land. Do keep this to yourself, old chum. . . .

William set the letter down, his hand shaking. Fury

spurted through him. He grabbed the offensive single sheet and wadded it into a ball to throw in the fire.

He couldn't quite bring himself to consign Lungren's last words to the flames. He smoothed out the paper and began again.

. . . I shall have to level you if you speak of my whereabouts to anyone. America is a new and exciting land that I wish to see. Perhaps I shall make a new home there where a man is not encumbered by the shadows of his family. I didn't think it fair to leave you with such a burden without warning you it may be best to stay away. I should think it much better if you didn't tell my family that you own the property. Then they just might content themselves with blaming me for their misfortunes. Perhaps my sisters will see to getting themselves settled in marriages as they ought, rather than looking to this brother to provide for their future.

I know this letter must seem quite strange. But I have reservations about my father's and brothers' deaths. I cannot with any certainty make accusations and cannot quite think if I should. Anyway, I have decided my health will thrive in the climate of Colonies, not that of my home—which does not feel like home any longer.

I am of course brother to those still there and ask you to not be utterly cruel, but do as you think best. Perhaps if I make my fortune in the New World, I shall return willing to extricate you from the hungry hand of the estate I have burdened you with.

I must conclude now as I am off to dinner at a local establishment. As you know, I never dine at home, other than at first, the food is much to be preferred at the Boar's Head Inn.

And you thought you had won such a prize!

Yours,
Lungren

What in the blue blazes?

William reread the letter. Did this mean that Lungren hadn't meant to kill himself? Of course it did, but had guilt over abandoning the women of his family got the better of his conscience anyway?

The more times he read the words, the more sinister they sounded. Had Lungren killed himself at all?

Tony stared at the woman he had once thought to marry, once thought he wanted more than life itself, and realized he still wanted her. The powerful desire dismayed him and shocked him with its intensity.

She stood before him holding the hand of a boy, cruel reminder of her married state. A reminder that cut him to the quick.

Why had she turned her back on him? Did she marry this Merriwether chap just for the money?

She stood away from him. Her expression was cool, remote, although her eyes flashed angrily. There was no way she could totally subjugate her passionate nature.

She could have been *his* wife. If fate had played its hand differently, she would have been his. That child—what was he? Three or four? His eyes were still the pale blue of infancy—that child could have been his. Instead she warmed another man's sheets.

"Last night I was called away on an urgent matter. I didn't want you to think I forgot my promise." He held the glass of lemonade out to her.

Felicity's lips tightened. That mouth, that had once so freely opened under his and welcomed his kisses, locked against him.

She steadfastly ignored the glass he held out. She looked up the street, where a carriage rounded the corner. "I'm afraid we're about to leave."

She stepped backward.

Her son had other ideas. "Mama, the dog! I want to see the big dog."

Phys gave a little whimper and scooted toward the child.

"Stay, Phys." Tony put his hand in front of the dog. The Irish wolfhound was of a size to worry any mother. However, Phys was indiscriminate about attention. Anyone who would pet him was all the crack with him.

The boy yanked his hand free from Felicity's and galloped toward Phys.

"Go slowly; you don't want to startle him." Tony tightened his hold on Phys's lead just the same. "Take this," he shoved the glass into Felicity's hand. "He's big, but he's gentle," he said to reassure her.

"Come, Charles, the toy store."

Charles paused, caught between the two warring attractions.

"You had best go to the toy store. That is an opportunity not to be missed," Tony said to the little boy.

"Why do you call him Fizz?" Charles's milk teeth looked tiny in his little mouth.

"Phys—it's short for Physician." Tony shifted his gaze away from the tyke and looked at his mother. "Felicity, I want to talk. Would tomorrow be a good time to call?"

"I am *Mrs. Merriwether.*"

He wouldn't use that name. "You still call me Tony."

She curled her nose at the lemonade and held out the glass to a footman from the carriage, who relieved her of it instantly. She smoothed an unwrinkled gray glove over the back of her hand and tugged on the cuff. "I'm sure it was a slip."

Tony had the feeling he was missing something. Her son had knelt by Phys, and Tony felt obligated to make sure his big, clumsy dog didn't do any damage. He watched the small boy with one wary eye.

"You don't like lemonade any longer?"

Her brown eyes focused on him with a look layered with pity and exasperation.

What prompted that expression?

He wanted to rail at her, to learn the reason why she had turned her back on their engagement, but this was England, and he had to learn to be a civilized gentleman all over again. Not that he'd learned all that well the first time.

"I won't continue to hound you. I won't be here that long." As he said the words, Tony realized they may not be true. He would be here in England until he saw justice served for Captain Lungren. "I just want to know that you are happy, Felicity. That the man you married . . ."

What? He tried to finish the sentence with "makes you happy," but the words wouldn't leave his mouth.

Her response, for all its bluster, was slow to arrive. "I am Mrs. Merriwether to you, Major Sheridan."

"You will never be Mrs. Merriwether to me."

Her boy's gaze landed on Tony, although he continued to pat Phys's head. Tony leaned over, took his hand and showed him how to stroke the dog's head. Phys grinned a silly dog grin in appreciation.

Felicity looked at her carriage and back at him. "Where will you be going?"

"I'm taking an assignment in India." He rubbed his leg.

"When?"

"A few months, if all goes well." When his dratted leg returned to normal.

The boy studied him curiously a moment before starting to speak. "Are you—?"

Felicity's gloved hand clamped over the boy's mouth. Her movement brought the foursome—his dog, her son, and the two of them—in a tight circle. He reached out and touched the back of her gray silk gown. She froze like a man suddenly brought face to face with the business end of a bayonet.

The material felt particularly fine, rich, with just the faintest drag as his fingers slid down to the small of her back. She felt the same to him: wonderful, magical, almost more than a woman. Dear God, how he had missed touching her.

The boy glared at him over the edge of her hand. There

was something endearing about his expression, even though Tony would have wished him and the dog miles away at the moment. Something in the boy's disgust almost reminded Tony of himself. He couldn't imagine how he would have reacted if his mother had clamped a gloved hand over his mouth at any given moment.

An observation broke free in Tony's mind. The little boy's small clothes were all black, quite Quakerish. Felicity wore gray. Yet, her parents had dressed much as usual. Some detail from last night knocked at his brain. A detail he once wouldn't have observed, but war had made him pay attention to the smallest of things, because he had found a trivial observation often proved important. Last night Felicity's fan had been edged in black. "By God, you're a widow."

She straightened and eased away from Tony's hand, and without removing her palm from Charles's mouth, she firmly led her son to the waiting carriage.

Tony grabbed the glass of lemonade from the impassive footman. Tony quirked an eyebrow at the man.

"Yes, sir, she is a widow," he said under his breath.

He gave the man a brief nod and turned and gave Phys a sloppy drink of lemonade. His dog stared at him as if he had played a cruel joke on him.

"Sorry, Phys. I guess lemonade isn't quite the thing anymore."

"Pigs, pigs, pigs," muttered Felicity as she half hoisted Charles into the carriage. "When pigs fly."

Fortunately, Charles grew more concerned about pigs than he was about the affront to his dignity. He didn't like being picked up anymore.

"I have to buy pigs at the toy store? I want soldiers."

"How about both, some animals and soldiers? It is a good idea for you to know what animals are on your farms."

"Do I grow pigs?" Charles appeared thoughtful.

"You raise pigs."

"Flying pigs?" asked Charles with a squeaky uncertainty.

"No, wallowing pigs." Felicity smiled. "And cattle, and chickens—lots of chickens."

"I didn't think pigs could fly," he said with his confidence restored. "Was that man in the army?"

Felicity sucked in a deep breath. That man, that man was a hazard. One touch and she was all a-quiver. Yet she had no intention of throwing her hard-won freedom away. She didn't intend to marry again. "Yes, he is a major."

The real danger was that the thought of an affair tempted her far too much, but she didn't want to be trapped into marrying again.

Then there was Charles.

"Is that man as rude as Mr. Blume?"

"What?" Felicity quickly shook her head. "No, why did you think he was rude?"

"You looked at him like you look at me when I say something wrong." Charles shrugged. "You looked at Mr. Blume that way."

"Charles, love, I was mad at Mr. Blume because he didn't want to talk to me about business."

"Why does that matter?"

"Some men, lots of men, think ladies aren't intelligent enough to run businesses."

Charles tapped his finger against his lower lip. "Perhaps they are afraid women will run them better than they can."

Felicity's grin broke across her face. "Why, that may be it. That is quite astute of you, Charles." However, she couldn't let Charles ruin necessary relationships out of loyalty to his mama. "But then, it may be difficult for a woman to concentrate on running a business when she is raising children. So you mustn't hold it against Mr. Blume. We shall have to work with him a long time, and you will be working with him when you are older."

"Are you going to have more children?"

"I should have to get married again, and I don't plan to do that."

"Grandpapa says that is why we are here in town."

"No, we are here to get Diana married, not me."

"So why were you mad at that man?"

Felicity closed her eyes and considered her options. She could tell Charles the truth about his paternity and be done with it. Except how shocking would it be for her son to learn that his father was someone who angered his mother, someone he called "that man"?

"His dog liked me, but I don't think *he* did."

No, and that was the unfair part of it. "Major Sheridan doesn't know you well enough to know if he should like you."

"Is that the man Grandmama says you should marry so they can go home?"

Felicity rolled her eyes. "I shall have to have a talk with Grandmama."

Charles ducked his head down and looked guilty. "I suspect I shouldn't have listened."

"I suspect not. You know it is not proper to eavesdrop."

"I know. May I still get toy soldiers and toy animals?"

Felicity gave a rueful shake of her head. "Yes, you may."

"May I get a dog?"

"No, we have dogs at home. We don't need one in London."

"I want a dog."

"I don't."

"Grandpapa says I can afford anything I want."

"That is neither here nor there." He looked eager to protest her decision. She cut him off before he had the chance. "No dog, Charles, and that's the end of it."

Her bright cherub settled against the squabs, in a snit. He wouldn't stay that way long. Raising him with a proper appreciation for his wealth and what he might do with it was not easy. Really, they could afford to have a dozen dogs with a footman assigned to the care of each, even rent a fully staffed town house just for dogs, but she worried that Charles's character would be ruined by his wealth before he had a chance to learn responsibility.

Her indulgent parents were not helping. Perhaps the only thing she could do to get them to leave her alone was agree to marry someone.

Meg Brown leaned her elbows on the rail of the ship and stared at the inky water at the mouth of the Thames. She was coming back to where she started. The thought made her desperate. She would not—could not—return to what she had been.

The twinkling stars seemed to laugh at the notion that she could become something, someone better.

She rubbed her hand over her forehead and looked underneath her arms to either side. Not seeing anyone, she turned around and surveyed the darkened deck. She had to be sure no one was about. The creak of a mast made her start, although the sound had become familiar to her.

The slapping of sails, which she had also grown used to hearing while on deck, was curiously absent. Instead, the cloth was lashed to the spars and the ship drifted only as far as its anchor allowed it to move. On the morrow they would navigate upriver when the sun illuminated the shore and the tide was right. It was now or never.

She couldn't decide if the death of the young woman below was a godsend or just the culmination of a disastrous trip in which she had resorted to tactics she'd hoped never to use again. But that was what one was left with when one was born to a ha'penny whore. No matter that her father was an earl. She was nothing and certainly not respectable. No matter how many times she tried to rise above the circumstances of her birth, she got knocked back down again.

She'd done her best to act the part of an officer's wife, albeit one who couldn't seem to locate her husband. Now the young woman who had the good fortune to be born into the right class had up and died. Meg shook her head. It was a sad thing.

Was it any wonder a certain thought, as dangerous as it was, had popped into her head in the lonely hours of the night?

She walked across the deck to the open hatch. Gripping the rope railings, she descended the stairs. She moved as quietly as a church mouse through the narrow passageway to Miss Fielding's cabin.

Who would know if Meg became Diana Fielding? Who could possibly be the wiser? Who would be hurt?

Certainly not Diana—she was dead. Not the dead girl's relatives—they hadn't seen her in years.

From now on Meg would be Diana, but what she was to do with the real Diana's body made her squeamish. Yet she couldn't leave the body to be found after she left the ship, or her charade would be over before it started.

Inside the cabin, Meg lifted Miss Fielding's body as she had done a dozen times before. This time it wasn't to help her to the bulkheads or to the galley; this time Miss Fielding didn't cooperate. In fact, for a moment she seemed to resist, but it was just that the corpse had begun to stiffen.

Meg had to hold the body like a dancing partner as she made her way through the narrow hall. Meg was sure every passenger could hear the thumps along the walls, the awkward, macabre dance the two of them performed.

Meg reached the stairs, and what had been a wisp of a girl became a lead weight. Climbing up as she held the body wouldn't work. Their similar heights made it impossible for Meg to get her burden high enough to reach the next step. She struggled, lifting and straining. For ten year-long seconds, she didn't think she would get Diana's body up the steep, narrow stairs.

Desperation made her curse silently—and rudely enough to make a sailor blush. She succeeded in getting the body balanced on the second step, only to tangle her feet in her skirts and Diana's lawn nightgown, sending them toppling forward. Trying to break the fall and muffle the sound, Meg clutched at the rope and pulled the body close as they landed. She stifled a scream as she came to rest face to face with the dead girl's mottled face.

How loud? Oh, God, how loud had that been?

Ignoring the shooting pain in her shoulder and knee, Meg scrambled over the body. She grasped under Diana's arms and yanked her up the stairs. The corpse's head thumped on a riser, and Meg froze.

Was that louder than the fall?

When no one came out to investigate the noise, she resumed her grim task. She bit back the hysterical apologies that rose to her lips as Diana's head bounced on each stair.

Sweat streamed from under her arms and trickled down her sides. She tugged and strained, sure that she would be discovered any second.

Blowing like a hard-ridden horse, Meg finally wrestled her charge to the deck. Even though she hadn't spotted a night watchman, there could be one. Wrapping her arm around the dead girl's waist, she tugged her toward the stern.

She hardly looked as she pushed the torso over the railing and heaved the legs up. The body balanced on the rail, like a street-performing acrobat. Meg shoved with all her might.

Diana's body tumbled down the stern of the ship, thumping and rolling until the sickening splash at the end. Meg tried to think a prayer, but she could only will away her panic and attempt to breathe normally. Sweat clung to her skin and made her feel sticky, while the sea breeze chilled her damp face.

"Mrs. Brown?"

Meg whirled around to see the captain, buttoning his breeches and with his shirt hanging open over an ale-swollen belly. His momentary confusion at finding her wouldn't last long.

Her heart thundered in her chest. She spun around, trying to see down in the water, sure that Diana's body would float near the ship until daylight. Visions of the corpse, tangling in the anchor's chain and being pulled up while Meg stood by shackled and bound, crowded her thoughts.

She'd made too much noise. She should have figured out a way to lower the body. There were ropes all around. Ropes she could have tied around the corpse to guide its descent into the water. Ropes they could use to hang her from the creaking mast.

Thoughts spun around in Meg's mind in a horrible whirlpool of self-recrimination and half-invented lies. At the same time Meg knew nothing would get her out of this. Slowly she spoke. "Hello, Captain."

FIVE

Tony scratched Phys's ears while the dog thumped his tail on the parquet floor. "One good thing: we shall have carpets in India, so you won't disturb any neighbors below us with all your thumping."

Carpets were hardly a reason to value an assignment in India. But there were fortunes to be made there.

Even that failed to strike an appropriate enthusiasm for his requested assignment. Tony rubbed his injured leg. It would be months before the wound was fully healed. Besides, he was probably a bit blue-deviled by Lungren's murder. Phys whimpered and put his head in Tony's lap.

Felicity's being a widow did not matter. All he wanted from her, at most, was an affair. He wouldn't give her another opportunity to jilt him. He certainly couldn't take her with him to India. She may have wanted to see Spain at one time, but India was hot and dirty. She was obviously too elegant, too fastidious for a country like that.

While an affair was not the most gentlemanly of intentions, a discreet relationship with a widow was not unheard of. They would just have to be circumspect.

Only when Phys stopped thumping his tail did Tony realize there was knocking on his door.

"Good grief, Phys. What kind of a dog are you if you don't let me know when there is a guest?

Phys gave a halfhearted *woof.*

"I know, you thought your only duty was to make me get out and walk you." Tony rose from his chair with difficulty and limped to the door. "That is what I get for naming you Physician."

Tony swung back the door and found Lieutenant Randleton. Just the man he needed to cheer him up. Much better to talk to a man instead of an uncomprehending dog. Although perhaps Randy had probably come around so early because he had news pertaining to Lungren's gambling exploits.

"Did you discover anything?" Tony stepped to the side.

"No, I didn't learn anything of significance, but Bedford has something he wishes us to see." Randy stepped inside.

Bedford stood behind him, his pleasant features twisted up tight. What was worrying him? Tony gestured him inside.

Bedford about jumped out of his skin as Phys nudged him, as dogs were wont to do. "What in blazes is that monstrosity?"

It was unfortunate that Phys stood as tall as a small pony and was able to nudge anywhere he wished.

"Phys, sit." Tony pointed to a corner. "My dog, Physician."

Phys chose to sit where he stood, in front of the entrance, so Tony waved toward the chairs as he closed the door. Bedford edged gingerly around the dog. Phys started to follow him.

"Stay."

Phys gave Tony an objecting look and then made a sound not quite a growl, more of a good-natured protest, when Tony stared him down. Phys lay down and assumed a posture reminiscent of the Sphinx, looking eagerly at the men.

"Don't even think it, Phys. Or I shall have to lock you in the bedroom."

Phys put his head down sadly on his paws. Tony limped across the floor. Bedford held out a crumpled paper. When Tony took it, Bedford gnawed on a fingernail.

"What's this?" asked Tony.

Randy moved to stand beside him and looked at the writing.

Bedford lowered his hand and stared at it half a second, as if wondering how his finger had gotten in his mouth. "A letter Lungren wrote me, apparently just before his death. Please just read it."

Tony started to read, but Bedford shifted impatiently from one foot to another. "I don't think he killed himself," he blurted out.

Tony lowered the letter. His dog seemed to be ready to shower Bedford with canine affection, so the man couldn't be a complete bastard. They might as well include him in their inquiries. He would know more about Lungren's last days than either of them. "We don't believe so, either."

"You've already read it?"

Randy and Tony exchanged a look.

"We saw the body," answered Randy.

Bedford blanched. "My God, you knew before this?"

"Suspected." Randleton was ever one to go gently.

"Strongly suspected," modified Tony.

"What—what was it about the body?"

"We've seen a few men shot," said Randy.

"No powder burns, so the pistol was not against his skin."

"Probably at least six inches to a foot away," added Randy.

"The gun had to have been pointed down." Tony put his finger against his head at the bullet's angle and pulled it away a few inches. "Hard for a man to manage that kind of shot."

Bedford looked mighty pale. He backed toward a chair. "Oh, my God!" Bedford clapped a hand over his mouth and sat, unfortunately a foot shy of the chair. From his ignoble position on the floor he whispered, "You thought I killed him."

"Obviously, I was wrong."

"You intended to kill me."

"Lady Justice thought otherwise." Tony bowed.

Phys made a mistake that any good-natured dog would make. Sure that Bedford had dropped to the floor just to play with him, the hound bounded over with a gleeful exuberance.

Bedford gave a squeak of alarm and shielded himself with his arms.

"Phys, heel!" shouted Tony. His leadership abilities were slipping if he couldn't control his own dog. "Get over here, you corkbrain."

Tony shut his slinking dog into the bedroom while Randy helped Bedford into a chair.

"What now?" asked Randy when Tony returned to the room.

"I didn't find anyone grossly wronged by Lungren on my inquiries last night," said Tony. He read the entire letter, then passed it to Randy.

"I say, have you returned the title to Lungren's estate?" asked Bedford tentatively.

"Not yet. Want it back?"

"Good God, no! Not if that is why he was killed."

"He says right here it is near worthless," pointed out Randy.

"Yes, but if someone *thinks* it is worth something, I don't wish to hold on to it."

"While we didn't find anyone in London who gambled away a fortune thanks to Lungren, he did fleece half of the raw recruits. His murder could have resulted from a long-standing grudge," speculated Randy.

"Perhaps we should not simply hand over the title to the estate," said Tony. It wasn't wise to abandon any advantage until the motive became clear, and the letter muddied the waters a bit.

Bedford shook his head. "I don't want any part of it."

"You don't want to find his murderer?" asked Tony.

"Not by being the next victim, I don't."

"He obviously trusted you enough to send you a warning." Randy held up the letter. "He must have suspected all might not go as he planned. He thought it mattered who owned his estate, and warned you to keep quiet about it."

"Appears to me he was counting on your assistance," Tony added. "We three do have the advantage of knowing that Lungren was murdered, while the killer believes he's gotten off scot-free."

Bedford swallowed hard. "All right."

"Well, then, we shall just have to stick together, won't we, gentlemen? We do not want any more suspicious deaths." Tony looked at Bedford. "It should be quite interesting to see who is most concerned about the whereabouts of the title."

"What is our next step?" asked Randy.

"Why, I think we should make a condolence call on Lungren's sisters tomorrow afternoon and dine together at the Boar's Head Inn afterward."

"Not today?"

"No, I have another call I need to make this afternoon."

Felicity took one look at Charles in long pants and spun on her heels. Once out of the room she clenched her fists and slammed through the rooms until she located her parents in the breakfast parlor.

"What is the meaning of this?" she demanded.

"What is the meaning of what, dear?" Felicity's mother split open a scone and buttered it.

Felicity practically sputtered. "Charles is wearing a skeleton suit. Why is he out of short coats?"

Her father lowered the newspaper he held. "I told you I was taking him to my tailor. He doesn't need to be in mourning anymore."

"I said for you to have some short coats made up. He was not to wear long pants until the age of six."

"He's nearly six years old now," said her mother.

"Not until April. This is not good."

"Felicity, no one will remember that he was a little early. No one pays much attention to children."

"I'll never get him out of them now." What boy would willingly go back to short coats? What were her parents thinking?

Her father raised the newspaper.

"It would have been a waste to have new short coats made up when he will only wear them two months," argued her mother.

She could afford to have clothes made for each wearing and dispose of them afterward without making a dent in her wealth, let alone touching Charles's.

Felicity wanted to rail at them, but she clapped her mouth shut. She didn't want to have a childish pet in front of her parents. That would only make them think she needed chaperoning even more. She forced herself to breathe slowly. "I cannot fathom why you thought I would condone the slight to Layton's memory."

"We weren't trying to dishonor Layton's memory," said her mother with a wavering voice.

"Trying or not, you did."

"You may not have cared for Layton's social status, but he was a good enough man to save me from certain disgrace. And his money is now saving you from ruin."

Her father threw down the paper and left the room.

"He doesn't like to be reminded, and we just thought it would save you a little to have Charles move directly from mourning clothes to long trousers."

"It would be best if you and Papa made arrangements to return home."

Her mother put her fingers in front of her mouth and went teary-eyed. "Oh, no. We *can't* do that."

"Why not?"

"A young woman cannot live alone. Your father and I would never forgive ourselves if there was a whisper of scandal. And how could you avoid it if you insist on being part of polite society?"

"I'll hire a companion."

"Felicity, you know that is not enough."

"What is enough?"

"If you had a husband to look after—"

Felicity almost stamped her foot. "I can't marry. I'm in

mourning. To marry would be far more scandalous than living on my own, with my son and my niece in residence."

"I know that you can't marry, but if you were to enter into
an agreement with a gentleman . . ."

Felicity wanted to yank out her parents' twiddle-brains
and feed them to the birds. Didn't they understand that it
was being engaged that had got her into trouble in the first
place?

". . . a gentleman we could trust to watch out for you
and, well . . ."

"Marry me by special license and damn the scandal if it
should prove necessary?"

"If you are going to be so forthright about it, well, yes,
Felicity. You could certainly afford to take a wedding trip to
the Continent should there need to be some ambiguity
about certain dates."

Felicity threw up her hands. "Very well."

Meg squeezed her eyes shut, opened them, and looked at
the man lying beside her. He was finally sleeping. Moving
slowly as a sun-drunk cat, she slid back the covers and
reached for her sweat-stained dress. Tears stung at the backs
of her eyelids. She swore: *Never again.* Once she set foot on
England's shores, *never, ever again.*

She would be Diana. It had cost too much to turn back
now.

The captain caught her wrist.

She nearly screamed.

"We never talked about that noise."

"I thought you were asleep. I was trying not to make any
noise."

"Last night. The splash."

"What splash?" Meg begged all the saints in heaven to
help her keep her voice steady.

The captain held his silence, his hand a steel manacle
clamped over her wrist.

"If you must know," Meg began as if quite put out. "It's really quite disgusting, but Miss Fielding . . . her illness . . . well, there were some of her soiled linens and . . . and waste . . . and well, several of her books that she was sick on, and I wrapped them up and threw them overboard. She wanted to save them, but I couldn't stomach packing them in her trunks, so when she fell asleep, I got rid of them."

She held her breath, waiting on his response.

His grip loosened. "What are you going to do when she discovers they're not there?"

"I do intend to see her safely delivered into the bosom of her family, and I think she means to ask them to retain me as her nurse, but as dear as Miss Fielding has grown to me, I shall have to take a coach straightaway for Kent. My husband's people are there and are expecting me."

"I thought your husband's family lived in Derby."

Had she said that? She was going to have to be more careful of her lies. "Oh, no, that's *my* family. Well, and some cousins of his, which was how we came to meet."

"You have been quite helpful with her."

"You should be grateful."

The captain gave her a measuring look. Christ, she'd slept with him. What more did he want?

"I should go help Miss Fielding dress. She doesn't seem to be able to do much for herself," said Meg, pulling her clothes on now that he'd let her loose. "She has been unwell, you know. I'll be relieved to turn her over to her relatives."

"I should see her safely into the arms of her family."

Meg hoped that the captain would content himself with letting her take over his responsibilities to his passenger. If he insisted on taking Diana off the boat himself, there would be hell to pay.

"You must have a thousand things to do, and I have kept you from your sleep. Let me discharge this errand for you."

He smiled. "I suppose you'd like to help me out."

Meg wanted to punch him in his yellow teeth. How like

a man to think she would be grateful for enduring his ham-fisted caresses. She gritted her teeth. "It is no trouble."

Meg forced herself to chatter as she drew on her under-garments. "I do so hope that I carry no contagion, for I should not like to bring so poor a gift home with me, but then surely, if Miss Fielding's illness is catching, I should be under the weather by now. Although my husband always said I had the constitution of a horse. The whole regiment would be tormented by aches and fevers, and I barely suffered so much as a sniffle. I suppose I must count myself fortunate in that regard."

Meg smiled. Maybe he'd worry the next time he sneezed.

"Very well, Meg. I do have many duties to see to this morning. I shall leave Miss Fielding in your capable hands."

He grabbed her wrist again. "By the bye, there is no Mr. Brown, is there?"

Meg couldn't stop the tears that pooled in her eyes. "Yes, there is. He was hurt; they took off his arm. We haven't . . ." She pointed toward the bed. ". . . haven't in a long time, not since the surgeon . . ."

The captain patted her hand and looked as if he couldn't wait to be rid of her.

She thought the amputated arm was a nice touch. She chomped the inside of her cheek to control her expression and held her eyes open wide.

She only had to get off the ship, keep Diana's aunt from getting on the ship or coming into contact with anyone who knew her as Meg Brown, and convince everyone that Miss Fielding would slip off the ship with no one seeing her.

Meg was doomed.

Tony stared at the note that had arrived just as he was showing Bedford and Randy the door. It was short and to the point: *If you still wish to call on me today, I shall be at home until noon.*

Not much time, and no signature. But that was common

when ladies made assignations. However, assignations didn't normally take place in the morning, and he needed to walk Phys first. Well, there was no point in appearing too eager to play fiddle to her bow. And he was none too sure of her mood.

He ought to have his head examined for wanting to bother with such a mercurial woman. The only thing he knew was that Felicity was passionate when it counted. He'd never met a woman before or since who made his blood rise to such a fever pitch.

Tony rubbed his thigh as he stood in front of her town house and raised the brass lion's-head knocker. He had perhaps overtaxed his leg the night before, going about town trying to discover if Lungren had made any mortal enemies with his unfortunate talent for swindling the unwary.

The butler took his card and nodded. "I'm to put you in the green drawing room. If you would follow me, sir."

Tony entered the house. Like most London houses it had a simple design, although with a grander simplicity than most. The colonnaded entry hall led to a wide staircase with gleaming mahogany risers. Tony's boots clicked unevenly on the finely veined rose marble as he followed the butler. The carpet on the stairs absorbed all noise and made Tony feel as if he walked on clouds, especially since the midday sun gleamed down on the wide staircase and glinted off the gold-plate-and-Venetian-glass gas girandoles in the entry hall.

Tony had the sinking realization that if he had married Felicity, she would have lived in tents or cramped billets that would have fit in her London entry hall with room to spare, much like the austere quarters he lived in now.

A footman and two maids scurried by as Tony was shown into a spacious room. The butler drew back the heavy green velvet drapes and tied them with thick gold-braid cords. In spite of the coal fire burning in the malachite fireplace, the room had the feel of little use.

The plush mint-and-emerald carpet felt comfortably

thick under his feet. Marble sphinxes and lions seemed ready to leap at him from every corner. An ornately decorated chaise longue invited a body to recline and become bait for the snapping crocodiles that curled up the carved legs.

The door clicked open, and Tony turned from the window.

"Have the carriage brought round, if you please. We shall be leaving shortly."

Felicity entered the room wearing a lavender wool pelisse with gray corded trim, and a matching gray bonnet already on her head. He should have realized the first time he saw her that she was in half-mourning. He ticked off almost forgotten society rules in his head. That meant she'd been a widow more than six months but less than a year.

What dismayed him more was that she had gone so far as to purchase outerwear in half-mourning colors. Most people didn't bother.

"We don't have much time, so I'll be brief." Felicity moved across the room and perched on the edge of the chaise longue.

She turned and met his eyes, and a flood of tenderness rushed through him. Her look was uncertain, much the same as it had been all the years ago when she met him at the basement door and smuggled him up the servants' stairs to her bedroom. Was he about to be met with a similar offer?

He stepped forward and was stopped short by his limp. "Please accept my condolences for your loss. I hadn't realized before yesterday."

She batted away his words with an impatient hand. "It was a blessing, really."

"Your husband was ill a long time, then?"

She blinked, then looked down at her gloved hands. "Yes, several years." Her voice firmer, she said, "Do sit down, Tony. I have a request. I can't make it if you are hanging over me."

He moved to the end of the chaise longue and risked the crocodiles and sat down. He reached for Felicity's hands.

He didn't like it a bit that she'd married this Merriwether fellow, but he liked seeing Felicity in distress even less.

She allowed him to take her hands in his. His heart stepped up a notch as he rubbed his thumb over the fine kid leather of her glove.

"I have to leave soon to fetch my niece." She hesitated and then began again in a rush of tumbling words, "This is a horrid room, is it not? But we shan't be disturbed. We hardly ever use the room, because the carvings used to scare Charles, and we got out of the habit. The rose drawing room is much more cozy."

He didn't want to hear about her son with this Merriwether fellow. Although he empathized with his sentiments about the carvings. "Mmmmm."

"I shall redecorate it one of these days, but I have had no time to spare. It was like this when Layton bought the house for me."

His blood curdled. He really didn't want to hear anything about her dead husband's gifts to her, either. "What is your request?"

She bit her lip and then spit out, "I should like you to tell my parents you are affianced to me." She hesitated a moment while he grappled with what she said. "Again."

"No!" Tony jerked to his feet. His leg nearly faltered, and he ground his teeth, fighting for control, standing still instead of stalking to the door. "I have no desire to marry you."

"I know that. And I do not want to marry you. I want you to tell my parents that you *intend* to marry me, so they will go home."

The scorn in her voice scorched him. He wasn't sure if her not wanting to marry him hurt worse than her vehemence about knowing he didn't want to marry her. He checked his emotions; the only thing he wanted from her was an affair. Engagements, pretend or otherwise, weren't worth thinking on. The silk of her gown rustled behind him.

"I'm making a hash of this," she said. "I thought I'd have

more time to explain. I don't want a public announcement. I couldn't possibly announce that I'm engaged; I'm still in mourning for another four months. I just want—"

"An affair?" He swiveled around and stared at her. His leg was killing him, so he lurched forward to lean his weight against the back of the chaise longue, inches from where she sat primly on the edge.

"No, absolutely not." Her eyes flashed, but she had the guilty look of someone telling a falsehood.

That passionate nature of hers would win out in the end. There was only one way to know for certain. He reached out and touched her cheek.

Her breath spilled out, and he caught the last of her gasp against his mouth. A half-dozen years dropped away as his lips pressed against hers and her lips parted. She tasted sweet and tart—lemons? Her bonnet knocked him in the forehead, and he wanted to swing around from the back of the chaise and deepen the kiss. Yet he was afraid he might fall on her, and his leg was giving him every indication that it would buckle the minute he tried to put weight on it.

He pulled back. With her eyes closed she leaned toward him. He feathered a gentle kiss on the corner of her mouth.

Her eyes popped open, and she pushed him back. "Stop it."

"Certainly," he said, dragging his thumb across her fuller lower lip. He drank in the deep, soulful look in her brown eyes. He almost wanted to say yes to any request she made.

"Listen. I've thought this out. If you pretend to be my fiancé, my parents will go home, and then, when you leave for India I shall just tell them you jilted me"—she frowned—"or I jilted you."

"I think you've forgotten who jilted whom."

Her eyes flashed. "I haven't forgotten." She pushed his hand away from her cheek.

He folded his arms and leaned against the back of the chaise longue. He would get his answer before he left the house. Why had she jilted him all those years ago?

"You see, when my parents wanted to come with me to London, I thought it would be a beneficial change of scene for them. Society provides so many pleasant diversions for young and old, don't you agree?"

She talked faster and faster, without waiting for his reply.

"But now they think that the only reason I am here is to get a husband for myself. They are practically ignoring that I intend to present my niece. You know, they are ashamed of her lineage. I can't get them to leave by fair means or foul."

"And how does that concern me, Felicity?"

"I'm asking you to pretend a private engagement to me. They will trust that I am in capable hands and go home."

Perhaps she hadn't understood him the first time. "No. I have no intention of marrying. I will not enter into a sham engagement, either."

She clenched the lapel of her pelisse in one hand. "You owe me at least that, Tony."

"No, madam, I believe you owe *me*. Did you ever intend for us to marry, or was I just bait so you could land a bigger fish?" He gestured around the opulent room.

She stared at him and finally shook her head in a bewildered way. "How could you doubt that I intended to marry you? After what happened, how could you doubt that?"

"Lying in hospital for six months, battling with surgeons daily to let me keep my leg, wondering if I would die from the gangrene, leaves a lot of time for doubts when you had already married another man."

"What was I to do?" Her anger was back. She stood and paced across the room. "You told me to stay in England, that you didn't want me there with you."

"Spain was no place for you. I couldn't have taken care of you, protected you. It was a bloody war, damn it. You wouldn't have been safe there." His voice had risen to a shout.

She snapped back sarcastically, "I'm sorry, I wasn't that strong."

He continued leaning against the chaise and watched her

stalk across the room. She was angry, fuming. Was she hurt when he told her not to come to Spain?

"If your answer is no, then good day, Major Sheridan. Please do not return."

"I'll consider it on one condition."

She stopped and waited, her back to him.

"That we pick up our 'pretend engagement,' exactly where we left our real one." He pushed away from the back of the chaise and willed his leg to behave. He wanted to see her face.

"You mean an affair."

"Just a few months and I'll be out of your life." And God help him, she'd be out of his system forever.

Her arms hung at her side, and her shoulders slumped.

"It is fair, Felicity. You want something from me; I want something from you."

Her reply was the merest whisper. "No. I cannot go through that again."

He had almost reached her. The room was far too large. Her response confused him. She had given herself to him long ago, enjoyed their one night of passion. He'd seen it in her eyes, in the delicate flush of her skin, tasted it in her kisses. What had happened to make her reject the hope of experiencing that bliss once more?

He put his hands on her shoulders and felt her shudder. Had her husband been cruel? Leaning close, he spoke in a low, soothing voice. "It's me—Tony—and you know I would never hurt you, misuse you, or force you to do anything you don't want to do." He rubbed his thumbs in soothing circles. "Your promise would be enough for now."

She spun away from him and swiped her gloved hand under her eye. "You already did all that."

What had he ever done that made her think that?

The door to the room cracked open and out of the corner of his eye Tony watched Felicity struggle to compose herself.

"Mama?" The word was plaintive. "Are we going? The carriage is waiting."

"In a minute, Charles. We are almost done."

Charles saw Tony and scooted in the doorway. "Oh, did you bring your dog?"

The little boy stood, a touch of blue in the green room. His short jacket was blue; his long pants down to his buckled shoes were blue. His eyes were a pale, pale blue—not of infancy but of the kind that stared back at Tony from his shaving glass every morning.

For a second Tony forgot how to do simple arithmetic. But his brain quickly added it all up and there was no avoiding the obvious answer.

His leg faltered, and he sat down hard on a couch with reclining-lion arms. "You're not yet six, are you?"

SIX

"Almost," said Charles as he skipped into the room. "I have a loose tooth." He opened his mouth and waggled one of his lower teeth. "Mama says it is impolite for a gentleman to sit when there is a lady standing."

Tony nodded solemnly at Charles. "I expect your mother shall have to forgive me."

Felicity rubbed her forehead. What madness had prompted her to think she could convince Tony to do anything he didn't want to do? He hadn't done the honorable thing when she'd written him about her pregnancy. Why did she expect him to do the right thing now? Or at least do something to help her?

"We need to leave. Diana will be waiting."

"I shall come with you."

"Absolutely not necessary." She just wanted him to leave.

"Not bloody likely to be helpful, either," he muttered.

Felicity put her hands on her hips, ready to tear into him. What was he thinking? It wasn't like Tony to be rude. Forceful, arrogant, but not rude. "I agree."

He massaged his thigh with both hands. "I shall go with you. It is the least I can do."

She didn't need him to go along. What's more, she didn't want him along. And if she could just get the appropriate members of her family to come along, she would leave him behind.

"Come along, Charles. We cannot keep Diana waiting." Felicity adjusted her bonnet—when had it become askew?

Oh, her step had faltered. When he kissed her, when her world tilted upside-down.

Thank heaven Charles had come in shortly after that. She blessed the stars that Charles had gotten past his fear of the carvings. Lord knows it wouldn't have taken much for Tony to have convinced her to sprawl on the chaise longue with him.

"Pigs, pigs, pigs," muttered Felicity. She would not succumb to the idiocy, this insanity, this enchantment, ever again. But his touch, like before, had been so gentle and persuasive, and he made the thought of an affair far too easy to imagine. His kiss made her lips tingle, made everything tingle.

"What did you say?" He looked at her, and for the first time she marked some humanness in his pale blue eyes. He looked as if he was in agony.

Her burst of concern for his welfare irritated her, but she was helpless to avoid voicing her worry. "Are you all right? Shall I have my carriage set you down somewhere?"

Tony stood. The pain blanked from his eyes, which once again grew stony, cold, and distant. "At the dock to retrieve your niece." He held out an arm toward the door. "Shall we?"

"How badly were you hurt?"

"Not so badly this time." His reply was maddeningly uninformative.

"How bad was it the first time?"

"Bad."

"Tony," she said with exasperation. Had his injury interfered with his intention to return home in enough time to marry her? Had he thought he would die?

She shook her head. Without some indication from him, just the curt letter telling her to stay home, she'd had to find someone to marry her before her predicament became obvious.

He placed his palm against the small of her back and guided her through the door. She shouldn't have asked. She desperately wanted to give him a chance to explain, to tell her that if she had traveled to Spain he would have fulfilled his promise. She wanted to believe in his honor.

But she had to face facts. The man had no nobility of character when it came to her. He had just insisted on an affair in response to a very minor request to pretend an engagement in front of her parents. Just when she'd given up on his reply, he answered her.

"Shot the first time. Stabbed with a bayonet the second time, but I'll spare you the details."

"You were shot?" asked Charles, his eyes big.

"I'm asking for details," Felicity pointed out.

Tony nodded, and in a low aside that made her shiver, he said, "Later."

The tone was full of pillow-talk promises. She rolled her eyes. There would not be any later. In fact, if she walked a little faster, she wouldn't have to put up with his guiding hand at the small of her back. Her feet seemed reluctant to speed up the pace.

When they reached the entry hall, Felicity inquired of her butler if her father was ready to leave. The butler sent an underfootman to inquire.

The longcase clock showed a quarter past noon. She'd told her father they were leaving at noon. After another minute ticked by and Felicity fretted that Tony shouldn't be standing on his leg, Lady Greyston clattered into the room.

"Your father just sat down to eat nuncheon." Her mother turned her attention to Tony. "How pleasant to see you again, Major Sheridan."

Felicity sighed. It was very like her father to use this kind of technique to avoid accompanying Felicity to retrieve her niece. "I told him we needed to leave at noon. We cannot just leave Diana waiting on the docks."

She didn't know why she bothered protesting. It wouldn't make a bit of difference.

Tony's hand pressed against her back.

"Well, then, send the coach," said her mother.

"Let us go, Felicity," said Tony. "The docks are no place to leave a young lady alone. Charles, to the carriage."

Felicity bit her lip as her son followed Tony's command without question. The little traitor.

At first they followed Charles to the door, but Tony's hand slid around her waist and pulled her back. After Charles skipped down the stairs, Tony pivoted, swinging Felicity around him to face her mother.

His gaze fastened on Felicity as he spoke, "Lady Greyston, you should be the first to know that Felicity has done me the honor of agreeing to be my wife."

Felicity's squeak of outrage was cut off by Tony's minute shake of his head. Then her mother was hugging Tony.

"That is simply wonderful news," said Lady Greyston.

His pale blue eyes met hers, and Felicity was suddenly chilled by the determination she saw there.

"Of course, we cannot announce our plans publicly or risk word getting out until Felicity is out of mourning." Tony managed to inject the pleasant words with a hint of steel. "That is why we have decided not to tell Charles until later."

Her mother nodded, let loose of Tony, and reached out to hug Felicity.

Felicity tolerated the hug. Her mother's emotions were heartfelt as she rubbed Felicity's shoulders. "See there, I knew things would work out for the best," she whispered.

Tony continued his thinly veiled warning. "I shall be around often to be sure that everything is all right and to allow Charles to get to know me. So you and Sir Edmund need not have any worries on that score. I understand you must get back to the country."

Felicity stared at him, both amazed and resentful. How was it he could sound so firm and not be thought of as a great blaggard, while she came across as shrewish and spiteful saying the same thing?

On the other hand, admiration aside, they had not agreed to this. What was he about? Did he think he had made a bargain with her?

"I never agreed to anything," she hissed as they descended the stairs to her waiting carriage.

"I know," he answered simply.

"If you think—"

"We'll discuss this later."

If not for Diana waiting on the docks, Felicity should have insisted, but Tony jerked his head in Charles's direction. She had to bite her tongue. They really could not sort this out in front of Charles.

Tony turned his head and stared out the window as they drove through town. Did he think he could force her hand by presenting her with a fait accompli? Could he tell how very tempted she was by that single kiss?

As they exited the carriage at the wharves, Felicity was far too aware of his palm resting against the small of her back. His touch and stance were protection from the jostling of the crowd. With the merest pressure of his fingertips, he guided her through the throngs of people and cargo. And she followed as though they were dancing.

She wanted to hold his arm and steady his hobble as he walked, but she sensed he would resent that and held back. All the time she thought it strange that her onetime fiancé, who had abandoned her so recklessly in her moment of need, was asking the dock men for information, learning where Diana's ship was berthed, playing the role of protector. Did he think she was incapable of finding her way?

"Why the frown, Felicity? We are almost there."

She stopped and swiveled away from his light touch. "What are you doing here? Why are you helping me now?" Her voice was low, and she tried to smooth the frown from her face.

"Because now I can." He faced her squarely, his eyes heavy-lidded. Slowly his gaze dropped from her face and moved down her body and back up again. There were pauses as his inspection stopped at her hips, her chest, her lips.

Heat rose to her face and flowed down her body. It was

the look of a man used to getting his way with women. His meaning was too clear. Because he thought he could expect an affair in return.

She shook her head, not quite certain if she wanted to step forward into his arms or back away. As it was, she only stared at him, almost but not quite shocked. She'd opened that particular door a long time ago. "I will never repeat that night, Tony. Never. It was a mistake."

His grip tightened on her elbows, and the searching in his expression faded, replaced by a look she couldn't fathom.

She wanted to yank away, to tell him to stop troubling her hard-won peace. Finally, she had control of her destiny, and he threatened it with the reminder of that perfect night. That there could be more perfect nights, more passion, more heat, more . . . babies.

His voice was low, with that edgy burr that made her melt, "What happened afterwards might have been a mistake, but that night was not."

She hadn't been brave enough to tolerate the disappointment of her parents, or being shunned by society. She couldn't risk a future child being born illegitimate and ostracized forever.

She turned sharply and rushed toward the ship where Diana was waiting. With Tony limping along behind her, Felicity skirted through the throngs of dockmen, shifting crates, and piles of supplies and goods.

She dodged the toiling men and wharf-rat boys and ducked as a mast creaked and groaned overhead. Feeling a little silly, she shaded her eyes and looked toward the small ship that had brought her niece to England. She needed to set aside her tangled feelings about Tony and concentrate on Diana's needs.

A dark-haired young woman stood clutching a reticule and chewing her lower lip. Felicity could see, even from the distance of several yards, that the girl looked apprehensive. Was that her niece?

Felicity stopped.

Hadn't Layton told her that Diana resembled the portrait of his sister, with nut brown hair and. . . ? That was twelve years ago when the girl was eight. Layton wasn't necessarily an accurate reporter of details, either.

Felicity glanced back to see Tony steadily making his way toward them, but his progress was hindered by the traffic of the workers. She winced, thinking how easy it had been for her to weave around the obstacles. He ought to use a cane, she thought.

She moved toward the girl who kept taking tentative steps away from the gangplank and the somewhat steady flow of sailors on and off the ship. "Diana?"

"Aunt Felicity?"

The girl's voice shook, and Felicity moved forward to embrace her niece. Diana seemed startled by the affectionate embrace and belatedly responded. Obviously the poor girl had been too long away from her family.

"Did you bring Charles?"

"He is in the carriage, waiting eagerly to greet you."

Tony gained their side. Felicity put her hand on his elbow. "This is my niece, Diana Fielding. Diana, this is Major Anthony Sheridan."

"Pleased to meet you." Diana bobbed an awkward, almost subservient curtsy. "It feels so strange to be on land and back in England." She cast a glance over her shoulder at the ship and shuddered.

"Takes a little while to get your balance back, doesn't it?" said Tony.

Diana stared up at him, wide-eyed, nodded, and then proceeded to stare at Tony. Not that Tony wasn't handsome, in a roguish way, but her niece was staring as if she wanted to devour him.

"How was the trip?" asked Felicity.

"The trip was fine. Could we go?"

Felicity was taken aback by the abruptness of her niece's request.

"Where is your baggage, Miss Fielding?" asked Tony.

Diana suddenly looked at her aunt, and Felicity could see her throat work as her niece swallowed. Tears sprang up in the girl's eyes.

Felicity was torn between sympathy and an odd animosity that seemed to spring from nowhere.

"Mrs. Brown! Mrs. Brown, have you found your party?" Diana flinched.

Felicity might not have separated the voice from the surrounding shouts and the screech of gulls around them if not for Diana's reaction.

Her niece spun around to stare up the gangplank, where a middle-aged man had started down. "That is the captain," she whispered, and her whisper wavered.

She closed her eyes and seemed to steel herself. She opened them and tossed a halfhearted wave in the captain's direction as if to say, "All is well." Then she turned a pleading gaze to Tony. "I believe the trunks are over there."

She strode across the dock to the growing pile of baggage and bandboxes being carried from the ship by the sailors.

Tony took off after her. Felicity started to follow when she heard the gruff voice behind her.

"You must be Mrs. Merriwether."

"Yes," Felicity answered while watching Tony lean close to Diana and hold out his elbow to her. Diana wrapped her arm around his and clung much too tightly to his arm.

Felicity nodded to the captain, aware that she hadn't heard above half of what he said. The ship's masts creaked, and Felicity looked up, wondering if the ominous sound portended the fall of the mighty timbers holding the furled sails, or if the noise was just an expected sound of the ship.

"Mrs. Brown has been a great help during the voyage. She often took Miss Fielding her meals and the like."

"Very good," said Felicity.

"Miss Fielding was ill most of the voyage."

She had probably missed the explanation of who Mrs. Brown was, while she watched Tony lean over and offer Diana his arm. She didn't like the way Diana leaned against him. She didn't like Tony's overly attentive manner toward her niece. The girl was pretty in a dark-eyed and dark-haired way Felicity hadn't expected.

She wanted to run over and interpose herself between them. Once upon a time she would have followed the impulse.

"If you need any more help with Miss Fielding, let me know."

Felicity jerked her head back toward the captain. "I'm sure we won't need any further assistance. Thank you so much for everything."

"If you would like me to show you to her cabin . . ." The captain gestured toward the gangplank. Felicity took one look at it and decided she really didn't like the idea of climbing up the narrow, sloped board with only cross slats for traction. She liked the idea of Tony navigating it even less.

No reason to board the ship. At least none more than the mild curiosity that tempted Felicity. "That will not be necessary."

Tony advanced toward her, alone, lurching around coiled ropes and cartons littering the dock.

"But . . ." said the captain.

"Felicity, your niece says she feels unwell. If you would like to take her home, I can see to her trunks."

The captain crinkled his forehead. Felicity thanked him again and hurried toward her carriage. She didn't have time to puzzle out that expression. She was too busy trying to ignore the relief she felt. Tony's solicitous care of her niece was probably due to Diana's state of health and not any amorous motives on his part.

Or Diana's.

Truth to tell, Meg suspected she was simply having hysterics or a fit of the vapors. She sat in the carriage, alternately wishing her newly acquired aunt would hurry or never arrive. Silently reproaching herself, Meg clenched her fists.

What had she done?

The memory of Diana's body toppling down the stern rose unbidden in her mind.

Meg giggled, then quickly clapped a hand over her mouth. Horrified that such an inappropriate response had erupted from her lips, the enormity of what she'd done struck her. She reached for the door handle, wondering what would happen when she was caught. Would they think she had murdered the girl? Christ, she wouldn't be able to talk or sleep her way out of that.

"Are you getting out?" asked the small boy who studied her balefully. Charles, her cousin Charles. Diana had been so eager to meet him.

Meg wanted to run, to forget that she'd ever thought of impersonating Diana. She removed her hand from the latch. She couldn't now. Her few belongings were stashed in Diana's trunks. She would have absolutely nothing. If she fled now, she'd be working flat on her back before nightfall.

She had no choice but to go forward, pretending she was the sickly Diana.

She shook her head.

Was the captain even now alerting Felicity to her masquerade? Meg had the terrible suspicion she was doing everything wrong. The major had looked at her quite strangely when she offered to solicit help from the dockmen to move Diana's trunks.

"Are you scared?" asked the boy.

"Terrified," muttered Meg.

"My mother is very nice. She only yells at her mama and papa. Mr. Merriwether used to yell all the time, but he is dead now."

She was being reassured that the family life Diana would have was not so terrible. Meg was afraid she would be forced back into prostitution or worse before night fell. She put her fists to her head. *No more, no more, no more.* No more sleeping with strange men who cared nothing for her. *I'm Diana. I'm Diana. I'm Diana,* she chanted to herself.

"Diana?" Felicity opened the door. "Are you all right?"

"Oh, I'm so sorry." She was sorry, sorrier than she could ever express. Tears dripped down Meg's cheeks.

Felicity patted her hand and handed her a handkerchief. "There, there. If you are not feeling well, it is understandable."

Which only served to make Meg feel worse. "I'll be fine momentarily. I'm sure I will." If she could just stop shaking. Stop the sure suspicion that it was just a matter of time before she was put to death for murder.

"We will get you home and see what can be done to make you feel better."

Meg reminded herself that Diana had been sick—sick unto death, actually. "I should like to take a rest before dinner, but in truth I am much better than I was before leaving France. The trip has been quite restful, and that helps. If I tax my strength too much, I shall end up in bed."

Felicity studied her as if surprised at her answer.

As she spoke the words, almost an exact quote of Diana's rather quixotic explanation of her illness, Meg wondered what strength-sapping things a girl in finishing school could have got up to. "The battlefields were horrific . . ." she said vaguely. "There was no avoiding—" She broke off, uncertain of what to say next.

Felicity squeezed Meg's hands.

The gentleman, Major Sheridan, tossed a wry look in Felicity's direction. "We must get her home. I'll see to her luggage."

Felicity swirled around and gave a hard look at the major.

He stepped back and held up his hands. "No recompense necessary. Take care of your niece."

Perhaps things were not going as badly as Meg thought.

Meg relaxed her fists. "I am so very sorry to be such a nuisance."

Felicity—Aunt Felicity—gave a slow shake of her head and said to the gentleman, "Very well." She turned brown eyes that were full of concern on Meg. "You are not a nuisance."

His expression still wry, Tony handed Felicity into the carriage. She tapped on the panel between the closed coach and the coachman's box. The carriage lurched forward.

Meg swiveled to look out the window, wondering about the tall major with the unusual eyes.

"Is he . . . ?" Meg's voice trailed off. She could not ask if he was Felicity's lover. The unworldly Diana would have no understanding of that kind of relationship, nor would she ever ask such an impertinent question.

Felicity's face flamed, and the question was understood even though Meg had stopped herself from speaking it out loud.

"He is just an old friend." Her expression said clearly to stay away.

"I understand," murmured Meg. Of course she would stay away from him. She planned to keep her distance from any man she couldn't bring up to scratch.

Shouts outside the carriage had both women looking out the window, and Charles jostling them, trying to see, too.

"What is it?" whispered Meg.

The shouts and the running men, one with a grappling hook and another with a length of netting, made the cause of the commotion all too clear.

"Oh, my God, they have found a body in the Thames," said Felicity.

Meg clamped a hand over her mouth, tasting bile as the skin of her face went cold and clammy under her palm.

"Mama, I think Cousin Diana is going to lose her breakfast," said Charles.

SEVEN

Bedford stared at the closed door. Nervous sweat trickled down his back. He wanted nothing to do with visiting the remaining Lungrens. He was the last person on earth who should have been charged with this responsibility—who should be charged with any responsibility, for that matter. Yet he couldn't ignore it.

He'd tried, but Lungren's shade was disturbing his peace. Not that he actually believed he was being haunted by his former friend and gambling companion, but too many times last night he'd woken up in a cold sweat for no reason at all. "Hell, man, if you were looking for someone to avenge you, you should have gone directly to your major."

As he was speaking out loud to a ghost that wasn't there, the door swung open and a maid looked at him as if he might be dicked in the nob. To tell the truth, she might be right. "I am here to see the Misses Lungren."

"Yer name, sir?"

"William Bedford." William fumbled for his card case and finally retrieved a calling card. He didn't recognize the maid. He'd only been here a couple of times, and usually late in the evening.

"I shall see if they're at home," she said and closed the door in his face.

William looked down at his blue coat. Was it so threadbare that it looked secondhand? Should he have his landlady turn the cuffs and give a newer look to the sleeves? Maybe he'd do better to commence a flirtation with a seamstress working in one of the Bond Street shops. Perhaps he could get the work done for free.

Maybe it was the sorry horse he'd ridden that prompted the maid to leave him standing outside. A man was in dire straits when he couldn't even hire decent horseflesh. He turned to retrieve the tethered nag and go back to town when the door swung open.

"They will see you in the drawing room. They are having tea with the other callers." The maid stepped back inside, closing the door and scurrying away.

William stepped into the darkened interior and felt disoriented as he waited for his eyes to adjust. Should he guess his way to the drawing room? In previous visits he'd almost always been shown directly to the library. Perhaps he should smell his way. He sniffed. His nose wasn't good enough.

"This way, sir." Impatience colored the maid's voice. She stood halfway down a passageway, next to the sagging stairs that dominated the entryway.

He gave her a long look and a slow smile. Obviously he needed to practice charming women. Especially since it looked more and more like he would need to marry a woman of means, most likely a horse-faced heiress since his breeding wasn't good enough to recommend him to a pretty one.

But the maid only rolled her eyes as she opened the door for him.

Inside the room, Major Sheridan and Lieutenant Randleton sat stiffly with mismatched teacups in their hands. The three Lungren sisters stared at him with varying degrees of animosity.

William managed to stammer out his condolences, which had the younger sister nodding; the middle sister turned toward a window, and the oldest kept up her glare.

"Not sure you were going to make it," said Lieutenant Randleton.

"How do you take your tea?" asked the youngest sister.

"With a fair bit of cream," William answered politely.

The eldest sister—what was she, about thirty?—poured tea in a chipped cup and added the tiniest drop of cream.

He took it with a mannerly thank-you and found a seat in a chair that had seen better days. He didn't see a tray of scones or sandwiches and sighed. He could have used a bit of nourishment since he hadn't broken his fast yet. In fact, he'd overslept dreadfully.

He had been out quite late, gambling to win enough to buy himself dinner at an inn and hire a horse to get him here. Unfortunately, Lady Luck had only grudgingly smiled upon him last night, and then well into the morning hours.

He'd had to send a note telling the two officers that he would meet them at Lungren's house rather than ride out together as they'd planned.

He raised his cup of tea and leaned back in the chair.

The eldest sister intensified her glare until William wished someone would say something—anything. Unfortunately, his wish was answered in the worst possible way as he took a sip of his nearly clear tea.

"Do you have the title to our estate?" asked the eldest Miss Lungren.

William swallowed too fast and scalded his throat, which was another reason he liked a generous amount of cream in his tea. He managed to croak out a solitary "No."

Miss Lungren flounced back in her seat with a roll of her steely eyes.

William cast a glance in Major Sheridan's direction. How long did he mean to keep the secret of the paperwork?

"You still have not located it?" asked Randleton.

"No doubt he just put it somewhere else for safekeeping," said the middle sister, Jocelyn. "It should hardly matter if we find the papers or not. Who would concern themselves with them? I am sure you are wrong about his gambling the estate away, Rosalyn. He was such a good boy."

He was hardly a boy, and he was rarely good. The look passing between the major and his lieutenant mirrored William's thoughts.

"The war was so terrible," said Carolyn, the youngest sister. Although by William's calculations she must be twenty-four or more. Why weren't any of the sisters wearing mobcaps? They were all old enough to be past their last prayers.

"The war did not kill him, madam," said Major Sheridan.

The eldest met his comment with a piercing look. William was starting to wonder if she knew how to do anything beyond glower. It was no wonder she was unmarried. A man would be lucky to survive supper with her, let alone a marriage.

"He never was a gambler before," said Miss Jocelyn, with a belligerent set to her chin.

"Why else would he have done what he did?" asked Miss Carolyn. She leaned forward and plucked at an unraveling thread in her lace mittens.

Undoubtedly concerned that she was on the verge of tears, Randleton leaned toward Carolyn and spoke to her in a low tone.

They weren't learning anything from the sisters except that they had a distorted view of their brother. William had heard innumerable tales of how Lungren had fleeced dozens of men after warning them he was about to take their money. William was as fond of him as the next fellow, but he didn't cherish any illusions about Lungren's character. The man had not been exactly a candidate for sainthood. He'd been too clever by half, and extremely capable, which was what made his murder such a queer thing.

Major Sheridan rubbed his thigh and stared out a window.

"Perhaps he felt he could not adequately meet his responsibilities," offered Randleton after a glance at his superior officer.

"Of course he could. We told him what he needed to do. We went through all the books with him," protested Rosalyn.

"He was the baby of the family, but we were fully prepared to help him," said Jocelyn.

"He had some odd ideas. Certainly we could not manage

with less than three upstairs maids." Rosalyn handed a cup of tea to her sister.

"Oh, no, we could not let Molly go. She has been with us for sixteen years." Jocelyn set her teacup on a side table.

"We had no assurance she would get another position." Rosalyn shook her head.

Jocelyn mimicked her older sister, shaking her head, too. Good God, had all Lungren's efforts to reduce spending met with this insidious resistance?

Major Sheridan's attention snapped back to the sisters. "He may have been young, but he was more than capable of running a small estate like this one. Devil take it, he was my best procurement officer ever."

Bedford winced for Major Sheridan's cursing in front of the sisters. The youngest blinked as if surprised. The eldest turned her glare toward Sheridan, who had resumed looking out the window.

William leaned over to see if there was something outside that had caught Sheridan's attention. Only an overgrown garden lay beyond the glass.

"We never would have got the library clean if not for Molly," said Jocelyn.

William stood, the thought of what the maid had needed to clean jarring him to his feet. Molly might have preferred to be let go.

"He really didn't need to do anything. Ros and I have been managing the estate for quite some time."

William paced over to the empty fireplace. The room was chilly. All three of the girls wore heavy wool shawls. The tea was weak and bitter, obviously made from used leaves, so they were not completely unaware of the need for economy.

"It occurs to me that since you no longer have any brothers to escort you about town, Randleton, Bedford, and I could perform that service for you. I am sure Lungren would have wanted us to help you get settled," Major Sheridan said.

William felt suddenly queasy and hastily took a noisy sip

of his tea. The youngest sister, Carolyn, leaned forward, her expression taking on a hopeful gleam.

The two elder sisters looked, well, rather disgusted—however, probably not nearly as disgusted as William felt.

"Not that you would want to go about town right away," added Randleton. "But after Easter, when the season picks up."

"Your brother did express a wish to see you all find husbands," added William, doing the pretty in spite of his reluctance. Surely escorting the sisters must be part of a master plan of Sheridan's. He must think there was some information to be had from them, although William couldn't see it. They had just blindly accepted that their brother died by his own hand, without questioning it once.

Suddenly that struck him as strange. The family should be the last to accept the truth of the matter in a death by suicide.

Rosalyn's glare made William fidget like a rabbit.

"I am sure we can continue on, much as we have. There is no need for us to marry." Jocelyn almost spit the last word.

What was it with the women nowadays? With half the men gone to war in the past decade, had the fairer sex decided in their absence that they didn't need husbands?

The sister who had the best chance of landing a husband, Carolyn, looked down at her hands.

"I beg to differ, madam," said Randleton. "You might not want a husband, but I would wager that at least one of your sisters might. Beyond that, I do not think this estate can support the three of you and three upstairs maids for very much longer. What will you do then?"

Rosalyn drew in a sharp breath. "We shall sell the lower pasture."

"Just who is buying all the pieces of the estate?" Major Sheridan asked.

"Lord Carlton," said Carolyn. "He has been quite fair with us."

"And what will you do when there are no more pieces you can parcel off?"

William resisted the urge to speak, hoping to learn more by silence.

Rosalyn stood and paced to a window, forcing the two sitting men to their feet. "I hardly think our financial affairs are any of your concern."

"Do you have any male relatives to look after you?" asked Randleton.

"No," answered Carolyn. "We do not."

"Then I suggest that you heed my advice," said Major Sheridan. "As your brother's superior officer, I am offering what assistance I can."

The room grew so quiet that William's growling stomach was unfortunately heard by all.

"I think it is time we took our leave. We have a dinner engagement." Randleton stood. "Truly, ladies, we want only the best for you."

The major bowed. "We shall return." He strode out of the room with Randleton fast on his heels, and William nearly ran to catch up.

They stood on the front steps, waiting for their horses to be brought to the drive.

"I say," said William. "I don't recall agreeing to escort them about town."

"We discussed it on the ride over. Doesn't look like you'll have to worry much about it, though." Major Sheridan rubbed the back of his neck. "They are obviously not on the hunt for husbands."

"Well, they ain't put on mobcaps, either," answered Bedford sarcastically. Couldn't trust a spinster who hadn't put on her mobcap and consigned herself to the shelves. They were prone to desperate acts in order to land a husband, and an escort was likely to be a prime target of these.

Just then the maid who had answered the door came bursting around the corner of the house. She scurried up the stairs, her feet moving quickly on each step, and a small tied bundle bouncing in her hands. She stopped on the step in front of William and spoke. "Please, sir." Her eyes contained desperation. "Take me with you."

Meg lay on the dimity counterpane, staring up at the tester overhead. The bedroom was the most luxurious she'd ever been in, yet Aunt Felicity had apologized for the meanness of it.

Meg had told her it was much nicer than what she'd had at school and that she was more than pleased with it. Besides, the room was situated very near the servants' stairs on the third floor, and Meg wanted to keep her escape routes open. She was entirely sure her ruse would be discovered at any minute.

A soft tap on the door made her swing her head in that direction. For a second she held her breath, sure that the authorities had connected her to the body found in the Thames.

"Diana, may I come in?"

Meg swung her feet to the floor and sat. "Of course, Aunt Felicity."

The door opened gently.

"Are you feeling unwell?" asked Felicity in a soft voice. Her unsolicited concern made Meg feel weepy. Nobody had ever really cared enough to inquire so gently after her health. But this was concern about Diana, she reminded herself.

"I'm feeling in prime twig."

"Good, then, I've sent for the mantua maker. She'll be by tomorrow for your fittings."

Felicity crossed the room with a graceful glide that made Meg envious. Perching on the edge of the bed, she said, "We should talk about the coming season."

"I am looking forward to it."

Felicity took Meg's hand in hers. "You do understand what a season is all about, don't you?"

"I shall be trying to get a husband." Which was fine by

Meg. She wanted to be respectably married. Besides that, the more distance she could put between Felicity, Charles, and herself, the better off she would be. Not that she didn't adore them, but she felt sure she would make some slip sooner or later. Even now she feared that the coarseness of her hands, which had known work, would give her away.

She had read and reread all of Felicity's letters to Diana, but what she didn't have were Diana's letters to her aunt. A husband would be even less familiar with her assumed background, and a slip even less likely to be found out—if this charade worked long enough to carry her that far.

Felicity had an odd look on her face. "If that is what you want."

"I want to be married and have a family. I want that very much."

Her aunt looked away at the flowered wallpaper. "Well, to that end, I have arranged for you to have a dowry of ten thousand pounds."

Ten thousand pounds! That was a veritable fortune. She would be rich. The thought was incredible.

Felicity had continued talking, and Meg hadn't heard a word. She tried desperately to school her features into an accepting expression. As if a girl heard every day that she would have more money than Midas.

When she could contain herself no longer, Meg said, "Oh, thank you, Aunt Felicity."

Felicity squeezed her hand. "Hmm. I am not so sure you'll be thanking me in a year or two."

Meg blinked.

With a man like Major Sheridan following her around, why wasn't Felicity keen on marriage? Admittedly, Major Sheridan seemed a little domineering, but that only served to make a man more interesting, in Meg's opinion.

And Meg knew far too much about soldiers for a girl raised in a Swiss finishing school, which was why she should not even consider army officers. But then, she'd always had a penchant for military men. If she could find one who would be posted far away from England, she'd run even less risk of discovery.

Tony stabbed a piece of burnt meat with his fork at the Boar's Head Inn. The three men had leased a private room to have dinner. He wished he could concentrate on the matter at hand. Instead, he kept thinking about Felicity and her son—or rather, *their* son. "Did we learn anything today?"

Randy talked around a bite of food. "We learned Bedford here shouldn't dally with the maids."

"There was no dalliance."

"The maid is neither here nor there." Tony dismissed the brief encounter with the servant. If he made it back to town at a decent hour, perhaps he could call on Felicity. He had the excuse of needing to find a place for the defecting maid. She, much to Bedford's relief, had only wanted to be taken to London so she might find better employment.

"Although, if she had not been paid in two years, probably all the servants are a bit disgruntled," said Randy.

"But why shoot Captain Lungren? She said he had promised to catch up their wages," Bedford said.

"I think you were right to avoid involving Lord Carlton. What do you make of his buying the pieces of the estate?"

"He could be trying to help. He could plan to assimilate the whole estate into his own." Tony shrugged.

"What if he hasn't been as fair as the sisters think, and Lungren discovered it?"

"We shall have to discover some evidence. Being greedy doesn't make a man a murderer."

Bedford put down his fork. He'd been stirring his meal around his plate without taking a bite for some time. "How could Lungren have considered this food edible?"

Tony looked down at his plate. Part of his roast beef was charred beyond crisp; another part was nearly raw. He glanced at Randy's plate, which contained a pork chop that Randy had been sawing on, to no avail. Bedford's meal wasn't any better. Admittedly, he and Randy were used to eating whatever they had to eat, but Bedford hadn't marched around the Peninsula with an empty belly, as they had.

"The ale is tolerable," said Randy.

"I suppose Lungren was trying to tell you the food was worse at his home." Tony rubbed his aching thigh.

"Perhaps there was no food at his home," said Randy.

"There is food there. None of those women are starving to death." Tony turned to Bedford. "We can find out what Lord Carlton is about, if you go to him and offer him first chance to buy the estate."

"I just want to be rid of the thing."

"We will all go, and you can tell him you plan to settle the money on the girls as dowries," said Randy. "And that you are concerned they won't be able to take care of themselves adequately. That you want to do the right thing by them."

Tony felt that he was missing something right under his nose. Of course, that could be because he had missed the fact that Felicity's son was also his at first. He'd spent years being angry with this Merriwether fellow, and now he realized he should be thanking the man for raising his son for the past six years—*almost* six years.

Bedford shuddered.

Tony removed the title and the quitclaim deed from his pocket and put them on the table by Bedford. "Do as you think best. I had hoped someone besides Lungren's sisters would show interest in the deed's whereabouts."

"Have we waited long enough to know?" protested Randy.

"It is Bedford's to do with as he pleases. No reason he can't deliver it on his own, now."

Bedford eyed the papers as if they might bite him. "Did you see the water spots on the ceiling? The damn place would cost a fortune to fix. No wonder Lungren kept gambling. He needed the blunt to keep his house from falling in about his ears."

He belatedly grabbed the papers and stuffed them into his coat pocket. "Very well, but I'm not going to Lord Carlton's alone."

Randy set down his knife. "You know, there is something cursed unlucky about that family. Three brothers and a father gone, all in the last couple of years, and—when did their mother die?"

Bedford had torn off the crust, of the doughy loaf of bread and was examining it carefully. "She's not dead."

Satisfied with the condition of his crust, he popped it in his mouth while Tony and Randy waited for enlightenment.

When Bedford realized he was being watched, his blue-green eyes opened wide. "She's mad. They packed her off to an asylum long ago."

"Could she be the murderer?" squeaked Randy. "Should we warn the ladies?"

"No, we need to play our cards even closer to our chest. But we shall keep an eye on them." Tony shoved his plate back and reached for a bottle of canary. They were supposed to be narrowing the field of suspects, not broadening it. "We will have to visit this asylum and see if there was any chance Mrs. Lungren was able to get out." He looked at Bedford. "Can you find out where she is?"

"I'll see if I can't gather some information on it," said Randy.

"What will you do?" Bedford asked Tony.

"I shall visit the tax assessor's office and try to determine when parts of the Lungren estate were sold off, and I shall make myself available to accompany either of you on your tasks."

"You won't forget the maid, will you?" asked Bedford earnestly.

"No, I shall attempt to find her a position tonight." Tony grew silent.

Randleton gave him an odd look. "You have been remarkably inattentive today. What is plaguing you?"

Tony took a long draught of canary and put it down to find

both men still staring at him. He shrugged. "What else? A woman."

Randy's expression flashed from surprised to suspicious in a heartbeat. "Not one of the Lungren sisters?"

Tony cocked his head at Randy, puzzled by his response. "No, not at all."

Randy leaned back in his chair, looking a bit relieved.

Bedford took the moment to pipe up. "Does it seem odd that none of his sisters is questioning Lungren's supposed suicide?"

Randy looked sharply at Bedford. "You didn't question it before you saw the letter."

"I certainly questioned *why* he would do such a thing. It seemed rather out of character for him."

"I should agree." Randy turned to Tony. "Just about as unexpected as for you to be distracted by a woman."

Tony shrugged and took another drink of canary. "It seems like the whole world has gone as queer as Dick's hatband."

At which point Randy turned a bright shade of scarlet.

EIGHT

Felicity decided the best thing to do in her situation was never to allow herself to be alone with Tony. So when he showed up on her doorstep at a late hour, she told her butler to tell Tony she had retired for the evening. She hadn't, but she really preferred to be left alone as she went through the correspondence relating to Layton's businesses.

Disasters had filled the week. A shaft had collapsed in the Cornwall coal mine, trapping six men for two days, and the overseer of the sugar plantation in Haiti was warning of revolt. The only spot of good news was from the textile mill in Cumberland. There had been a minor riot among the applicants to fill the latest openings. Only three bloodied noses and a broken hand, if that could be considered good news. And the manager there had thought they would lose workers when Felicity insisted on providing half a day of free schooling for the children instead of working them fourteen hours straight. On the contrary, families were clamoring for work at the Merriwether Mill.

She tapped her pen against her teeth, trying to think what to do about the plantation in Haiti. She hated that they owned slaves, and had been pondering a radical move, perhaps freeing them and offering wages. But being so far away, she couldn't really know if she would end up with no laborers at all, or if a move like that would worsen the situation for the other plantation owners and create more animosity and unrest.

She had at one time intended to get rid of the plantation

altogether, but selling it would leave her powerless to effect any change.

"You look deep in thought."

Felicity dropped her pen and nearly jumped out of her seat. Tony was leaning against the door frame, and her heart was pounding. This was not good. "Were you not informed that I had retired?"

"You haven't."

"I am quite busy, though." She should have known he wouldn't take no for an answer.

"Doing what?"

Felicity retrieved her pen from the floor. Thank goodness she hadn't dipped it in the inkwell yet. "Well, now, I am contemplating dismissing my butler."

"I doubt that you should find one that could block my entrance if I was of a mind to get in." Tony folded his arms across his chest. His expression was distant, closed.

"Exactly. You have little or no consideration for other people. I need to work."

"I see."

"Do you?" She stood up and then decided she was better served keeping the desk between them and sat back down.

"We need to talk, madam, and I have a favor to ask of you. When would it be convenient for me to call?"

She had every intention of sending him on his way with a flea in his ear, but what came out of her mouth was, "Sit."

He quirked an eyebrow at her terse command but followed it.

Just then her butler and two footmen, one still thrusting his arms into his jacket, appeared at the study door. "Sir, if you would be so good as to follow me, I shall show you out."

Tony leaned forward to rise, his pale blue gaze holding hers every inch he moved.

"Oh, never mind. Major Sheridan shall be leaving shortly of his own accord."

"Or of yours," he said with a nod that had the formality of a bow.

Her butler backed out of the room and shut the door.

Layton had once given her a piece of very good advice, and she recited it in her mind. *Begin as you mean to go on.* Simple advice, really, but not always easy to follow. Tony's request for a discussion would have to be considered. It was a discussion they absolutely needed to have.

But she would write the letter to her plantation manager first. Not that she had any brilliant advice, but he could find a holiday or special occasion and reward the workers with rum and roasted pig.

She had pigs on the brain, given that Tony was sitting just across the room, looking far too tempting. But pigs would never fly, she reminded herself.

"You do mean only to talk. Because I shan't tolerate anything more than conversation, Major Sheridan."

"Just talk," he said.

She didn't believe him. "Nothing like in the green drawing room." She couldn't have him kissing her. Her will was too weak. "Your word on it, sir."

He tilted his head as if trying to assess how serious she was. Felicity dipped her pen in the ink and held her hand poised above the paper. "Well?"

"My word on it."

"Good, then, we shall talk when I am done with this."

When she finished the letter, set down her pen, scattered sand over the surface, and laced her fingers together and placed her hands on the top of the desk, she said, "Now, what favor have you come to ask?"

"There is a maid who needs a position."

Felicity didn't know if she was disappointed that the favor was not more personal. She listened as Tony delivered a quick explanation of Molly's experience and qualifications to be at least an upstairs maid, if not a lady's maid.

Felicity was inclined to grant Tony's reasonable request, since her parents had announced at dinner that they would be going down to the country Tuesday next. And since her niece had arrived without a personal servant, she would need an attendant.

"Does she have references?"

"The Lungrens claim to be unable to do without her."

"Then why is she leaving them?"

"Since Captain Lungren's death, she has little hope of being paid."

Felicity blinked. It had been a long time since she had needed to worry about things like having enough income to pay the help, although she had been raised in a household where Peter was always being robbed to pay Paul. "I shall try her with Miss Fielding for four weeks. If all goes well, I shall then keep her on."

A slow smile curled up the corner of Tony's mouth and caused a sensual warmth to travel through her veins. Pigs, pigs, pigs, she reminded herself.

"When did you become so resolute?" he asked.

"Probably when I realized the consequences of doing otherwise." That was the ticket, recalling how difficult her life had become because of that one misspent, misguided, magical night.

He leaned forward, his gaze holding hers. "Were the consequences so very bad?"

Felicity shifted some of the letters on her desk. "Let us say, irrevocably altering." At best, marriage had been trying, no doubt for both her and her husband. Once Layton learned she'd come to him carrying another man's child, he'd been devastated. And in turn he'd tried to decimate her.

Then there was her beloved son Charles, and nothing would prompt her to give him up, even if she had to do everything over again in exactly the same way.

Tony remained silent until she shifted the letters back into their original position.

"I am grateful you decided to tell my mother we are engaged, but as we had not come to terms, it would not be fair of you to have any expectations."

"No expectations—I don't have the right." He stood and walked across the room and stood in front of the fireplace with his back to her. The flickering fire silhouetted him and glinted off the gold streaks in his hair, glowing around his head like a halo. He looked like an angel—a bold angel—but his words marked him as human. "Just wants and . . . needs."

Something raw and exposed in his words tugged at her. He was perilously close to undoing her defenses again. Years ago, he'd said a few words about his expectations of loneliness in the army, and she'd leaped to inviting him into her bedroom. She rubbed her hand across her forehead.

Tony was always so forceful, commanding, domineering, that she melted at a hint of his occasional vulnerability. Though she wasn't sure she heard him correctly when he turned around and spoke.

"What?" she whispered.

"I said that when your year of mourning concludes, we will announce our engagement."

William's claim that he was near death from starvation had been all that was needed for Randleton to invite him home for a second supper. William had never needed an excuse to take someone up on a free meal, although it was starting to seem that the cost might have been too dear.

Before they sat down to eat, Randleton requested that his batman attend them. Then he sent the scarred fellow off on a quest for information.

His hunger finally appeased, William had almost forgotten the errand the servant had been sent on. While he was tipping back Randleton's excellent port, the batman slipped into the room.

If he had thought the major's disdainful gaze frightening, Randleton's servant was not a man to cross. The scar slashing across his eyebrow and cheek could only have been made by a knife, but the grizzled, almost arrogant set to his chin, so out of place on a servant, would suggest the batman had won that fight and many others.

"I've found Mrs. Lungren, sir," the batman had said simply. "You could see her tonight."

Randleton had leaned forward. "Where?"

"Bedlam."

William dropped his glass and then scrambled to flee from the path of the dark, purplish-red liquid. He tossed a napkin in the direction of the spill, while the batman moved silently and effectively to right the glass and blot the wine from the table.

"Bedlam?" whispered William.

"Yes, sir." The batman didn't lift his eyes from the task of cleaning William's mess. "Fellow I spoke with said for a bull's eye he'd let you two gentlemen inside tonight."

William had been there once and never wanted to go back again. He'd been unpleasantly reminded of seeing animals in a menagerie, except in Bedlam these tortured creatures weren't animals. They were human, or something close to it.

Randleton pushed back from the table. "Shall we go, then?"

Apparently he hadn't heard the horror in William's voice. William looked between the batman and the nonchalant Randleton. Either Randleton didn't know what he was getting into, or he expected his servant to guard them well.

While the rough-looking fellow could probably protect his master, William had no doubt that if a choice had to made, he would be the one left to be torn apart by the mad inmates of the asylum. "Have you ever been there?"

"No."

"Perhaps we shouldn't."

Randleton looked at him and blinked. "Are you troubled by idea of visiting Mrs. Lungren?"

The last thing William wanted to admit was fear, especially not to Randleton, who would likely report it to Sheridan, and the two of them would have a good laugh about it. "Not Mrs. Lungren specifically, but . . . the people there are truly insane."

Randleton gave him an odd look. "I should rather hope so."

William swallowed hard. He wasn't going to get out of this with his pride intact. That was the trouble with soldiers—they didn't have the common sense to be frightened. He had encountered the same reckless attitude with Lungren, and where had that got him? "Very well, let us get on with it then."

As they were being led down a dark corridor in the new location of Bethlehem Royal Hospital, south of the Thames, William started to relax. Perhaps the oft-mentioned reforms had taken place. Certainly this new building hadn't developed the stench of the old, and in the dark he only caught the merest glimpse of sleeping inmates, who might or might not be chained.

An inhuman scream assaulted their ears. William clutched at Randleton's arm.

"Easy there, old fellow," said Randleton. "I'm sure Mrs. Lungren isn't the violent sort."

"Actually, guv, she attacked her daughter. That's why they brought 'er 'ere. But we ain't had a spot of trouble with 'er, though I recommends never turning yer back."

William felt only mildly vindicated but a great deal more goosish. He let go of Randleton's sleeve.

The keeper shoved a key into a lock and turned it. He walked in and set the lantern he'd been carrying on the small table in the center of the cell. "I be back for you in twenty minutes. Missus Lungren, yer visitors is 'ere."

The three of them walked into the room: Randleton, his batman, and William, bringing up the tail. The door clicked shut, and William heard the tumble of locks as the guard turned the key.

The space closed in, and William swallowed hard. The last thing he wanted was to be held over in here. A single cot stood against one wall, and a rickety wood chair held the room's occupant. She didn't exactly have her back to them, but the chair was sideways to the room, as if she spent a lot of time staring out the barred window, as she was doing now.

"Mrs. Lungren?" said Randleton softly.

"I suppose you've come to tell me another one of my sons is dead."

Randleton started. "We did not know if you knew, ma'am."

She swiveled in her chair to face them. Her face was lined, and a tuft of gray hair peeked out below her cap. With a birdlike hand she reached up and tucked it in.

William noticed that the mended elbow in her loose green gown had been patched with a bit of material not quite the right shade.

"I didn't, not really." She plucked at the threadbare fabric of her gown. "But it is the only time I receive calls anymore. I'd offer you gentlemen seats, but they only give me the one."

William mumbled a protest that he didn't mind standing.

"I suppose my Jonathon was poisoned too," she said.

He and Randleton exchanged glances.

"No, madam," said Randleton. "Jonathon was shot."

She looked puzzled a moment and then brightened. "Oh, that's right, Jonathon was in the army. Did he fall in battle? I was always worried he would turn out no better than he ought, but he was doing well in the army, wasn't he?"

"Yes," said Randleton. "I served with him."

Mrs. Lungren's face took on a distant look, and the silence stretched out. William could sense Randleton's reluctance to say anything that might upset the woman.

"How are my gardens? The girls kept planting vegetables and they were choking off the flowers. They planted peas next to my asters. Quite overtook the bed. They planted greens, and turnips, and castor beans. I can't imagine why we needed so many castor beans."

The gardens had looked in desperate need of tending when William had seen them last, and of course nothing was growing in February, but he said, "Why, they're lovely. The roses are quite beautiful."

Mrs. Lungren nodded as if satisfied. "How are the girls? Has Rosalyn married Lord Carlton yet?"

"Is she affianced to him, then?"

Mrs. Lungren looked confused. "Isn't she? He keeps asking her to marry him. I don't know why she refuses. Silly notions that girl has, both her and Jocelyn."

"Mrs. Lungren, do you know of any reason someone would want to kill your son?" Randleton asked gently.

She laughed, and there was a hysterical edge to it. "They tell me I can't say my sons were murdered. It is a delusion of madness."

"One of your sons was murdered, madam," said Randleton.

Her face crumpled, and she seemed to fold in on herself. Her narrow shoulders slumped, and her head fell forward. "No, it is quite comforting to be insane and know that these thoughts of murders are delusions. I should not be able to bear it if I knew all my sons and my husband had been murdered." She stood suddenly and curtsied. "I thank you, gentlemen, for your call. It has been quite lovely."

Mrs. Lungren reseated herself to look out the window, staring into the gaping darkness. The pause, as they waited for the guard, escalated into an awkward hush.

William stepped forward. "Mrs. Lungren, if your thoughts aren't delusions and someone did murder your sons and husband, whom do you suspect?"

She turned around, and for the first time, William saw the glassy stare of madness in her eyes. He backed away even before she answered.

"Tell them to send money for my keep, or they shall put me in a ward. Although I suppose that shan't be so bad." She cackled gleefully. "No worse than going home."

* * *

Felicity stared at Tony as if he had been suddenly transformed into a four-headed jackal.

When she spoke, each syllable was stressed with a slow cadence born of anger. "Ab-so-lute-ly not."

Tony winced. He'd never meant to allow her the opportunity to wound him again. Yet he might as well have slit open his chest and exposed his beating heart to her. He turned and kicked his Hessian boot against the grate. "It is the right thing to do, Felicity."

"It would have been the right thing to do once, but that time is long past."

He heard the rustle of her dress as she stood. Nothing could mimic the sound of expensive China silk. He never would have been able to afford to clothe her so well. Yet, the idea that she probably wore silk all the way down to her skin tormented him.

"I think you should leave now."

"We need to settle this." He turned around to see her hand on the door. His gut twisted. At times she seemed to hate him, and God forgive him, now he understood why. Just as he had wasted years feeling she had betrayed him.

"There is nothing more to settle. I don't intend to marry you, and if that is the price you thought you could extract for a pretend proposal, then I should have preferred you continued with your original demand for an affair."

He stepped toward her. "Not too late for that."

"In either case I should have said no." She pulled open the door and frowned as she stared out at the empty passageway.

He reached her side. "Felicity, just give me ten minutes. I will make no demands on you tonight."

She swiveled, and her skirts fluttered around his legs for an instant before they were still. It was as if she had touched him herself. The thought made him tremble.

"No, but you will tomorrow and the next day, and the next, until you get what you want."

He rubbed his fingers against his temples. "I want what is best for you and . . . for Charles." *And for me,* he didn't say.

Her dark eyes flashed as she wagged her finger in his face and stepped toward him angrily. "You have never given one thought to what is best for Charles. You've never asked after him, never thought about him, never—"

"How could I, when I didn't know he existed?"

She stopped advancing, but she was so close . . . so close he could simply wrap his arms around her and close the gap. He clenched his fists. She couldn't stand this near, so near he breathed in the scent of her, so near he could almost taste the silk of her skin, and expect him to pass on holding her.

Her mouth dropped open, and she stared at him.

He thrust his arms behind his back and clenched one hand around the wrist of the other. "Why didn't you tell me?"

She swayed. "I did tell you." Turning swiftly, she shut the open door. "I did."

Facing the shut door, she leaned her head against the wood.

Tony raked a hand through his hair. "In the letter where you told me you wanted to join me in Spain?"

"You told me to stay in England," she said in a small voice.

It made sense.

He couldn't resist the lure of touching her anymore. He caressed her shoulder. "Come away from the door, and let me explain."

"Don't," she said tersely. "How can you explain? Don't make a mockery of my situation. I did what I had to do."

"I'm sorry. I didn't know you were with child."

She spun away and leaned against the door. Her palms pressed back against the panels, as if she needed to feel something solid. "How could you mistake the first line of the letter: *I am with child, your child?*"

Her brown eyes glistened with unshed tears, and Tony felt his emotions throttling his throat.

He pulled her forward into his embrace and buried his face in her hair. She resisted at first, but he could feel her slowly going limp as he spoke in a low voice. "I bled all over the letter. Parts of it were obliterated. It came the day I was shot."

"Oh, Tony," she said with a skeptical sigh.

He pressed his lips against her nape. Desire threaded through him and bid for dominance over his intention to offer just comfort. Partly it was because he wanted comfort for himself; partly it was because he wanted the mistrust to disappear from her eyes. He wanted to heal.

"Would that I had not been such a fool. I should have realized why you were asking to come to Spain. But I did not want you to arrive and find me less than a whole man . . . or dead."

She wound her arms around his neck with a loose hold that drove him to distraction. He wanted her clutching him as if she wouldn't ever let him go.

He trailed kisses along her neck, seeking her surrender, her seduction, and *his* soul. His mouth found hers, and he tasted her, drowning in the swirling softness of her kiss . . . until she turned her head away.

"Felicity?" he whispered, his heart stopping in his chest. Didn't she understand he had never abandoned her?

She shoved his shoulders, and Tony stumbled away, his bad leg faltering. Shamed by his inadequacy, he reached for a chair back to lean against.

"All that changes nothing. I do not want to marry you."

The words burned through him like a criminal's brand. Sorrow overwhelmed him, yet he tried to make light of it. "An affair, then?"

If he tried to walk before the spasm in his leg calmed, it would give out on him.

"No. I will not be forced into marriage again." She stalked past him. "I won't take that chance."

"There are precautions I could take to ensure I do not get you with child. Measures I was too green to know about before." He frowned. "I should have protected you better."

He wasn't saying what he meant to say, but the words were jumbled in his head, and his leg was cramping ferociously.

"I can't trust a man who cannot keep his word for ten minutes." She crossed to the fireplace and turned her back to him.

"Then you should not extract an impossible promise." Wasn't all supposed to be fair in love and war? "I am more a soldier than a gentleman."

"Please leave."

Tony bent and massaged his thigh. Why wasn't he getting through to her? Years ago these lines would have worked. She was stronger now, tougher. He changed his tactics. "We should be a family now. You, me, and Charles."

"Charles and I are a family, and you are bound for India. I see no reason to deviate from that."

Tony felt as if his head were in a vise, and he couldn't think to get out the words he wanted to say. "I may never go to India; my leg is not improving. I can't continue in the army like this."

"So you thought you should marry me instead?"

"Yes." As he said the word, he knew it was wrong. "No." She pointed toward the door. "Go on, leave."

He hobbled away from the chair. "We aren't done yet."

"No, I suppose not," she said wearily.

He paused at the door. He'd gone about this all wrong; he could see that. He didn't know if he knew how to do it right.

What he knew was how to wage war. He knew how to direct a battle, how to command men, how to march them around and keep their spirits up while they waited for the mud to be just right to wage war. He knew how to kill.

He didn't know if he could remember how to be tender, how to protect a woman, how to love. Did he have it in him to be a father? Or was his son better off with him in India? Was Felicity better off without him?

NINE

Felicity didn't sleep well. She spent the night tossing and turning and thinking of what Tony had said . . . and hadn't said. She knew his abrupt volte-face had much to do with realizing Charles was his son and little to do with his feelings toward her.

The only thing that he clearly wanted from her was to be her lover. That was the part that kept her tossing and turning and punching her pillow and alternately kicking off her sheets and pulling them back over her again. His claim that there were methods he could use to prevent pregnancy had fired her curiosity—fired more than curiosity—and had her questioning her convictions.

So she was already in a foul mood when she awoke late and entered the breakfast room only to be greeted with her father's spleen.

"Felicity, your niece has burned this morning's issue of the *Post*." Her father's words contained an appropriate amount indignation as though Diana had tossed a Bible or racing scores on the fire.

Diana sat across the breakfast table, looking down at her plate, her shoulders hunched about her ears, which was not a very good posture, given her apparel. What had gotten into her?

"Then purchase another," said Felicity dismissively as she studied her niece's clothes.

"You know your father likes to read the *Morning Post* as he breaks his fast," said her mother, ignoring Diana.

Yes, but at home his copy was nearly a week old by the time it arrived. He had grown accustomed, unfortunately, to having a fresh newspaper. Felicity sent a footman out to buy a new copy and filled her plate from the sideboard.

She made a point of sitting down next to her niece. Although she hesitated to say anything about what Diana wore, Felicity knew she would have to broach the subject sooner or later. "Good morning, Diana."

"Good morning, ma'am," mumbled her niece. In a sprigged muslin gown that was much too tight through the chest, and without a fichu to properly cover her in the daytime, Diana looked blowsy. Felicity had to get her niece properly outfitted. Although it wasn't the gown itself that was inappropriate—just the fit and the lack of a neckerchief. However, that amount of exposure wouldn't have been given a second thought in a ballroom.

Lady Greyston took that moment to glance meaningfully at Diana's uncovered bosom and then lift her eyebrows as if to point out that someone with less breeding couldn't be expected to dress appropriately.

Her niece looked nervous, her winged eyebrows arched higher than normal, and her dark eyes wide. She twisted her bare hands together as she stood, making her decolletage more apparent.

"Really, Miss Fielding, you should have on gloves and something covering your chest during the daytime," said Lady Greyston. All right, so now that her mother had torn into the subject like a wild boar, Felicity wouldn't have to open the conversation, but she preferred to address the issue alone with her niece.

Felicity's father, who probably was feeling the lack of his morning's paper, narrowed his gaze and looked at Diana's nearly exposed breasts.

Diana put her hand against the spill of flesh. "Oh, I'm sorry."

Surprised that the expensive Swiss school hadn't taught Diana the basics of how a lady dressed, Felicity shook her head. But the only diversion she could think of was to return to Diana's original transgression. "Did you burn the *Morning Post*?"

Diana's lips trembled. "It was cold in the breakfast room."

Sir Edmund Greyston seemed to be trying to determine the veracity of that statement by examining Diana's bodily responses. Since it appeared her niece wasn't wearing the appropriate undergarments either, Felicity hoped the straining seams of the bodice wouldn't split and make obvious whether the chill of the room affected her niece unduly.

She probably had been cold because she was inadequately dressed. "Then it would be appropriate to fetch a shawl or wrapper, or ask a servant to stoke the fire. Please don't burn the newspaper anymore."

"Yes, Aunt."

"Had the fire gone out? Do I need to speak with the housekeeper?"

Diana shook her head.

Charles darted into the room and dashed to the sideboard and snatched a roll. Felicity made a grab for him as he headed back toward the door. She shook her head. Speaking of being inappropriately dressed, her son's long pants were every bit as egregious as Diana's immodest gown.

"Well, then I have hired a lady's maid for you. Her name is Molly." Felicity wished now that she had put more effort into making sure the maid would know the niceties of dress. But if she had acted in the capacity for three ladies, she couldn't have less knowledge than her niece. "She should be arriving this afternoon. The mantua maker will be here at one; please be ready for her."

"Yes, thank you, Aunt Felicity." Diana bobbed another of her awkward, inappropriate curtsies.

Lady Greyston harrumphed.

Presenting her niece to society might prove a more daunting task than Felicity had expected. She doubted that Diana would be the least bit ready for the dinner they were scheduled to hold in less than a week. Still, the girl's sweetness would win out in the end. Or at least Felicity hoped it would. Besides, the invitations had already gone out. Too late to call them back.

"Mama, let me go," pleaded Charles.

"Why are you in such a hurry?"

Charles broke free of her grasp then. "Got to walk the dog!"

Felicity's morning hadn't gone above a quarter hour, and it was already out of control. She narrowed her eyes and looked at her father. Had he bought Charles a dog—against her wishes? But her father maintained his fascinated stare at Diana's charms, and her mother turned and said, "What dog?"

Surely, her mother would know if Lord Greyston had bought Charles a dog. Then Felicity had a horrible suspicion that she knew what dog.

Bedford woke with a jolt. "Damn it, Lungren, leave me alone," he shouted.

Then he felt quite foolish. Just because he was having nightmares didn't mean his old gambling companion was causing them. Up until recently his main fear was that he would permanently reside in Queer Street—that, or worse, be cast in debtors' prison. Now he knew there was a murderer on the loose who might want the worthless deed he held. And he had grown suddenly fearful that someone might grow wise to his follies and toss him into Bedlam.

He tossed back the covers. He had business of his own to take care of before he joined Randleton today. He would have to visit a cent-per-center or two, and he needed a plan to get out of their clutches. A real plan this time—betting and gambling wasn't enough to keep him in the blunt. No help for it, but he must get back to the reason he came to London—to marry a woman with money.

After he dressed, he took out his notebook and studied the names he had listed, crossing off the first one. Mary Frances Chandler had eloped with an earl last season.

William really hadn't stood a chance with her. It had been clear from the beginning she was set on acquiring a title. Which was all well and good—she had seemed a bit shrill for William's taste, anyway.

He looked at the next name and grimaced, but he made himself note that the horse-faced Catherine Moulter was quite enamored of her bay named Apollo. The path to her hand would be through the stable. He would have to spend a goodly amount of his loan on decent horseflesh.

After reviewing the meager cast of candidates, the latest a rich widow he'd yet to meet, William tucked the notebook in his pocket and headed for the door. He opened it and found Randleton on the other side.

"Good, you are up and about." Randleton lowered the hand he'd undoubtedly had up to knock on the door. "Tony found your maid employment, and we must fetch her this afternoon."

"I . . ."

"Not to worry, I have a carriage we can transport her in. Thought you might want to take the opportunity to pay a call on Lord Carlton, while we're in the neighborhood and all that."

"Oh." William couldn't very well admit that he'd meant to spend the morning in search of a moneylender. "Who did Major Sheridan find to employ Molly?"

"A Mrs. Merriwether. Don't know her myself."

William did. Well, he didn't exactly *know* her, but her name was the last one he'd added to his notebook. Mrs. Merriwether, daughter of Sir Edmund Greyston, widow of the late, very wealthy Layton Merriwether of Moore, Merriwether and Turner Shipping, Merriwether Mill, and who knew how many other lucrative endeavors.

"Tony says he knew her before he got his colors. Do you suppose she's the woman he's been in a flap over?"

William certainly hoped not. How could he compete with Major Sheridan for a woman's interest? "Should we go by and inquire when we should deliver Molly?"

Randleton blinked. "I suppose we could. I understand her London house is not far from my family's home."

William had the address, at a rather impressive square in Mayfair. "What of Major Sheridan? Is he to accompany us, too?"

"Don't know. When I called at his lodgings, he'd just left to walk his dog. Thought we might head for Hyde Park, for I'm sure that is where he has gone."

The last thing William wanted to do was seek out Major Sheridan when he had that monstrosity he called a hound with him. "We should definitely go by Mrs. Merriwether's first."

So the two of them set out by way of Piccadilly. Just as they had started discussing their impressions of the night before, William saw a woman in a green dress with a patched elbow duck into one of the shops lining the busy thoroughfare. He stopped in his tracks and grabbed Randleton's arm. "Upon my honor, was that Mrs. Lungren?"

Randleton looked up the street and, of course, saw nothing. "Where?"

William took another step back. "In that apothecary shop."

"Hardly think it could be." Randleton took a step forward.

William would have preferred to go around another block. "No, you're right. It couldn't have been her."

"Come on, then," said Randleton.

William swallowed hard. How many women could own a loose green gown with a patch of the wrong shade on the elbow? Reluctantly William let loose of Randleton's arm and fell in step beside his new friend. He didn't dare look in the apothecary shop as they neared it. It cannot be her; it isn't her; he told himself.

"It is her!" Randleton drew to a halt in front of the shop window. "How the devil did she get out of Bedlam?"

"I suppose we should ask her," said William, although his voice took on an alarming adolescent squeak. Better yet, they could just run.

"Or find out just what exactly she is doing in an apothecary's shop?"

"Buying poison, most likely," said William weakly, and for once he was glad to have missed his breakfast, because quite likely he would have cast up his accounts right then and there.

Randleton yanked open the shop door, and William closed his eyes as the bell above the door jangled. He did not want to enter the shop with her in there. He debated staying outside, but he supposed it could have been worse. They could have run into the madwoman at Manton's gun shop.

Meg was ready to crumble as the footman brought in the replacement newspaper. Her knees knocked together beneath Diana's apparently inappropriate dress. Or perhaps it was only inappropriate on Meg. Of course Diana had been less endowed, and Meg had been forced to leave off her shift and stays to avoid bursting the seams.

She hadn't realized how many blunders she could make without knowing. Already she had dressed wrong, erred in thinking that a newspaper wouldn't be missed, and had Felicity's mother's jaw dropping when she'd used her spoon with her buttered eggs.

None of it would matter at all if anyone connected the lurid story of the body in the Thames to her and the real Diana. Sir Edmund Greyston glanced briefly at the front page and then opened the paper to another section.

Relief swarmed through her like a hive of bees with their pesky little buzzes. *See, you needn't think they'd notice a young lady's body in the Thames. They're above such stuff. Gentry don't throw themselves into rivers.*

Then the thoughts grew more pesky. *Just a matter of time before they figure out you're not the real Diana. You're an awful person for tricking them so. Even Felicity's father is not above looking his fill at what he should think of as an innocent girl's bosom. Oh, he can tell you were meant to be a whore.*

Meg bit her lip until she tasted blood.

"Diana, if you are done, you should go upstairs and find a fichu. I will send my dresser to you, since your maid won't be here until later." Felicity held her son tightly by his hand.

Meg stole a glance at the table and saw that her plate was gone. These servants fluttering around taking care of everything before she even thought on it unsettled Meg.

While Felicity moved toward the door, Charles tugged at his mother's hand and stuffed the roll he had snatched from the sideboard into his mouth.

After Meg realized that Sir Edmund and Lady Greyston weren't paying her any mind, she trailed along after Felicity and her son.

She tossed her head back. She would do this. She would just have to pay better attention to Aunt Felicity's dress, demeanor, and deportment.

Meg had thought she'd done a good job of erasing the sounds of the gutter from her speech, partly by imitating her father when she was young and partly by listening carefully to the officers and their wives when she was following the army. But speaking like a lady wasn't going to be enough.

However, as the three of them traipsed through the front hall, Felicity waved off a footman, marched to the front door, and threw it open.

Still holding Charles firmly by the hand, Felicity said, "What the devil were you thinking?"

Meg leaned sideways, trying to see around Felicity. Who was she talking to?

Charles tried to shake loose from his mother's grip. "Mama," he protested.

"Nothing more than that Charles and Phys get along famously and that Charles might enjoy a walk in the park with us. I asked your butler to inform Master Charles that he and his nanny could accompany me."

Meg could see Major Sheridan now that he had climbed the front stairs. She closed the distance and stood behind Charles. Major Sheridan only gave her a cursory glance. Instead, his pale blue eyes focused on Diana's small cousin.

"Did you ask your mother's permission?"

Charles turned his face into his mother's skirts.

Major Sheridan raked a hand through his hair.

Felicity put her fingers to the bridge of her nose.

"I fear that may be my fault. I assumed Master Charles would ask you." Major Sheridan shifted from one foot to the other and back again.

"She will only say no. She doesn't want me to have a dog," Charles said into his mother's skirts.

"Charles, we have a dozen dogs at home. I don't want one in London. That doesn't mean you cannot play with Major Sheridan's dog."

The major scowled.

Meg caught sight of the animal at the center of the controversy and stepped back, "Good Lord, that's a horse."

Major Sheridan gave her more than a cursory glance this time and blinked in surprise.

Meg resisted the urge to throw back her shoulders. She tried to slip behind Felicity. Besides, he clearly had his sights set on the lovely widow. He was even attempting to use her son. On the other hand, Meg might be able to help him out, or position herself to be scooped up as a replacement when he realized that Felicity wasn't going to give in.

Meg didn't know what Major Sheridan had done to deserve her aunt's anger, but it was so thick, Meg could have cut the air with her erroneously used breakfast spoon.

Charles risked peeking out from his mother's skirts.

"I would not broach a subject we haven't discussed first," the major said softly to Felicity.

She compressed her lips and gave a tiny shake of her head.

What was that all about? Meg wondered.

"You are more than welcome to come, too. You and your niece."

"I should like to go along," said Meg.

"No, you shouldn't. It is much too early for a young lady to be walking in the park, and you have an appointment with the dressmaker you must not miss."

Just then there was a shout from the street, and a pair of bucks trotted up to the door.

"There you are, Tony. Fancy meeting you here."

Meg looked the pair over. The taller one who had spoken had auburn hair and an open face full of freckles; the other . . . Meg didn't make it past the striking eyes, eyes the color of the Aegean sea on a clear day. The lovely eyes dropped to her sartorial *faux pas* and lingered there long enough that Meg felt a small surge of female triumph and blushed. Then he turned to Felicity and offered her a smooth-as-glass smile and a bow—and quite ignored Meg.

Major Sheridan performed the necessary introductions.

Randleton stepped back and signaled with a nod for the major to lean toward him.

Randleton cupped his hand and whispered, "You won't believe what we've learned about Lungren's mother."

Tony waved him off. Whatever they'd learned would have to wait until Charles wasn't with them.

Now that the boy, his son, was there, Tony hardly knew what he would say or do. And there was Randy and Bedford, Felicity's niece, and a bristling Felicity to think of as well.

Bedford nicely—a bit too nicely—thanked Felicity for offering Molly the position as maid.

Tony stared at Bedford. The little toady was fawning over Felicity. How dare he?

Felicity knelt down and faced Charles. "Now, you must hold Major Sheridan's hand when you cross the streets, because he was injured, and you want to make sure he doesn't fall."

Charles nodded solemnly. Tony bit back his protest, only

realizing at the last second that it was a ruse to get Charles to accept holding his hand while keeping the boy's pride intact. Tony's pride was apparently unworthy of consideration. Would she even have allowed Charles to accompany him if his friends weren't there?

Charles slipped his hand into Tony's.

As his fingers closed around the small palm, an unfamiliar emotion filled Tony. This was his child, his child with her. He met Felicity's soft brown eyes and whispered, "Thank you."

"Does it still hurt?" asked Charles.

"Sometimes," answered Tony.

Felicity stood and smiled prettily at Bedford and Randy. "I trust you shall have him back to me within the hour."

Tony looked at Felicity and realized she didn't trust him at all. Not with their son, not with their future, and certainly not with her affections.

TEN

"I say, we're not taking the boy with us, are we?" Bedford, no doubt wishing to be as far away from Phys as possible, had assumed the position outside of Charles, while Randleton flanked Tony on the leash side.

"Back off," growled Tony.

Bedford was so startled he stopped walking and then had to trot to catch up.

"I just meant we can't very well discuss . . . er . . ." Bedford swung his head around, scanning the potential audience. Then he dropped his voice to a whisper. ". . . murder, around a little limb."

Tony didn't know which exasperated him more, that Bedford had just referred to his perfectly behaved son as a limb of Satan or that Bedford was doing the pretty with Felicity.

"I think he means from Mrs. Merriwether," interjected Randy.

"Oh, I say, do you mean to marry her, then?" said Bedford.

"She has another four months of mourning. Don't pester her." Had Felicity been pestered by Bedford's attentions? Or just Tony's?

"My intentions are honorable, sir." Bedford drew himself up like a preening parrot. "If you intend to offer marriage, just say the word, and I'll give you a clear field."

"I did offer."

"Well, if she has spurned you than you shouldn't be so dog-in-the-mangerish."

"Grandmama says Major Sheridan is to marry my mama and that is as it ought to be."

Tony stopped and bent down to be on Charles's level. He couldn't let Charles think that everything was well and good between him and Felicity when it wasn't. So much for not broaching subjects he shouldn't talk about. "While I should like very much for that to happen, nothing is decided yet."

Charles looked puzzled a minute, and then guilty. "I 'spect I didn't hear right."

Tony tousled his son's tawny curls. "For now, this is just between your mama and me; do you take my meaning?"

Charles nodded solemnly. "Are we going to talk about murder now?"

Bedford had a dreadfully loose tongue, and Tony cast a disparaging look in his direction. "No, we shan't discuss murder."

"Well, you needn't think you can't talk in front of me, because I hear everything anyhow," Charles solemnly stated.

"So I gather," murmured Tony.

Physician took the opportunity to wander back. He wore a frown—if dogs could be said to frown—with his forehead crinkled in perplexity at these unusual delays to finding him a nice stretch of grass to water.

"Shall we make our way to the park, gentlemen?" Tony straightened. "Phys is growing impatient."

"He isn't the only one," muttered Bedford.

"Remind me, the next time I challenge you to a duel, to bring swords and cut out your tongue."

Bedford looked hurt, and Tony was instantly remorseful. Poor bounder just wasn't used to the forthright ways of soldiers.

Randleton, ever the peacemaker, stepped into the breach. "You know, the major is excessively polite to those he dislikes."

Bedford didn't look too reassured.

"Douse it, Randy."

Randleton just grinned. "See what I mean?"

"You fought a duel?" squeaked Charles finally, as if he had just worked up the courage to ask.

Good God, what was Felicity going to think of him now?

"You can't mean that!" Felicity stared at her parents, her worst fears suddenly realized.

Lady Greyston looked at her husband, and her lips pursed. "We can't leave you alone under these circumstances."

"I've been alone for eight months, and as ill as Layton was toward the end, I might as well have been alone for the last three years or more."

"That was in the country, where we weren't more than a few miles away."

"Launching that niece of yours is going to prove harder than you've allowed," said Sir Edmund Greyston.

"In spite of that expensive Swiss school, she doesn't have the first clue how to go on," said Lady Greyston. "You will need our help."

"As long as you act as if Diana is something the cat dragged in, I hardly think you will be of any help in presenting her to the ton." Felicity sat down hard on her couch. As it was, Felicity should be with Diana and the mantua maker now, to be sure that her inexperienced niece's dress choices were appropriate.

"Should have sent her to a nice Bath school, where they would have taught her good English manners," said Sir Edmund Greyston. "Those foreigners can't be trusted. Probably taught her to conjugate Latin verbs and do fearsome sums instead of embroidery and such."

"Papa, I didn't send her anywhere. Her father chose that school, and Layton decided to keep her there. By the time I had any say in the matter, the war was on and it seemed better to let her continue." Besides, the Swiss finishing school had been highly recommended.

Was it just Diana's lapses in judgment that had prompted her parents' decision to stay? Or was something else amiss?

"Shall I look into a place for you nearby? I'm sure there are several nice town houses available to let in Mayfair. Since you want to stay for the season."

"Oh, no, we wouldn't live somewhere else when you have plenty of room here," said Lady Greyston.

"Couldn't leave you unprotected anyhow." Her father cleared his throat. "After attending my club, I realized how much jeopardy you are in."

Felicity rubbed her forehead. "I'm not in any jeopardy."

Her father rocked back on his heels. "Afraid you are. They are placing bets on your outcome."

"My outcome?" Sounded like she was a race about to be run.

"The fortune hunters think you're the most promising filly to hit town in a score of years." Sir Edmund rocked forward on his toes. His color had grown high. "Tried to dissuade them from mentioning your name in the betting books, but I'm afraid I only changed the odds."

"Well, since I shall not marry a fortune hunter, I can't see that it matters."

"There are fortune hunters who will resort to terrible tactics," whispered Lady Greyston.

"Yes, there are." Sir Edmund shook his head. "All sorts of havey-cavey plots are hatching. I saw two bets in the book on whether or not you'll be carted off willy-nilly to Gretna Green."

"Even in Scotland a woman must consent to marriage."

"But you would already be well compromised; what choice should you have?" Her mother cupped a hand to her mouth as if sharing a scandalous secret, although who she might be excluding from the secret was hard to tell, since the room's two other occupants could hear her plainly. "Or one could hold Charles for ransom."

"With no man here to protect you, you are far too vulnerable."

All stuff and nonsense. Felicity rolled her eyes.

"Lord Brumly has been asking after you." Sir Edmund picked a piece of lint from his sleeve.

"I'm far too young to interest him."

"Then there's Lord Algany." Her mother's horrified expression said what she thought of him.

"I'm far too old for him. I don't think he's looking for a wife, anyway. Why does any of this matter when Major Sheridan will be watching out for me? We *are* to be married."

Her mother and father exchanged a look.

Felicity felt her stomach churning most uncomfortably. "What?"

"Apparently he doesn't think so."

"What do you mean?"

"He told Charles that nothing is decided yet."

After a sudden sickening moment, Felicity tried for nonchalance. Why would he be telling Charles anything after making it clear to her mother that Charles wasn't to be told—unless, of course, Charles had asked him. The little darling had undoubtedly been eavesdropping again. "He just means we haven't decided when we shall announce our engagement, or go through with . . . the . . . cere . . ." Felicity's voice trailed off.

Her parents were exchanging another look.

"It is quite a good thing you haven't announced your engagement yet," said Lady Greyston.

"Yes, we are quite sure that Major Sheridan is not the thing."

"I am a grown woman, capable of making my own decisions." Why, oh why, though, did her parents reduce her to the same quivering piece of reprimanded jelly as when she was seven, covered in dirt, wearing a torn pinafore, following a triumphant adventure of burrowing under a stone wall by the abandoned abbey and rescuing a lost ball?

"Talk of murder and mayhem: did you know he fought in a duel?"

"I know he has undoubtedly killed men. Frenchmen. That is what soldiers do." She shot to her feet. There was no way Tony would commit murder or fight duels or . . . do anything less than honorable . . . unless it concerned women . . . or just her.

"We shall just have to cast about for someone else for you to marry."

"I'm marrying Tony, and that is final!" Felicity felt as if she had been slammed against a wall. Had she just shouted to all the world that she was marrying, when she'd sworn she'd never marry? And marrying the last man on earth she'd ever consider—if she had the slightest inclination to enter the parson's pound ever again.

Her head hurt from the conflagration of thoughts blazing in her head.

She stalked across the room even though her heart pounded at the thought of brushing by her parents. But they parted and let her pass without incident. A feat she would have found quite remarkable had she reflected on it.

Instead, she headed straight for her desk, wrote a furious missive demanding that Tony escort her for a drive in the park at exactly five, then sent it out with a footman. She would know precisely what he had said to her son. Had her parents decided upon Tony's unsuitability from the prattling of a not-quite-six-year-old boy?

How else?

As it was, Tony was rather uncomfortably ensconced in Lord Carlton's drawing room. Uncomfortable because Lord Carlton found that Tony's suggestion that Mrs. Lungren was anything less than a complete lunatic who suffered from delusions and had even gone so far as to attack one of those poor, poor girls was, to put it mildly, preposterous.

Since Tony hadn't seen the woman himself, he could

only rely on Randy's sound judgment and Bedford's more skeptical agreement that she seemed, for the most part, lucid.

Carlton had less nicely accused Bedford of greed and malice in regard to his idea to sell the estate and give the money to the sisters as dowries.

"Why don't you just give the title over to me, and I'll see to it everything is handled nicely," said Lord Carlton.

Randy, who had up to this point escaped Lord Carlton's mettle, suggested in a mild sort of way, "We understand you've been acquiring pieces of the Lungren estate. If Bedford hands over the last piece, so you own the entire estate, could you tell me how that is helping the family?"

Lord Carlton sputtered. "Why, my buying a pasture and a farm here and there gives them money when they need it. Lord knows I've been responsible for putting food on the Lungren table for the last decade."

Tony rather thought Lord Carlton's righteous indignation was just a bit over the top. "It also makes the estate less able to support a family. Do you hope to convince Miss Lungren to marry you when she has no option left but dependence on you?"

"She should have accepted my offer long ago." Lord Carlton seemed taken aback that he'd admitted so much. "It would have made all this buying a plot here and livestock there unnecessary."

"So are we given to understand that Miss Lungren has accepted your offer?" asked Randy.

"She's considering it now."

Which sounded as if she was afraid she had no other choice. Tony studied Lord Carlton and wondered why the man would want to marry a woman past her last prayers, and a bit of a harridan to boot. But then, the middle-aged Lord Carlton with his fubsy figure wouldn't be a considered a prize, either.

"I say, if I am just to turn over the deed to the estate, I

might as well just give it to the Lungren sisters directly."
Bedford stood.

Lord Carlton looked like he was about to object, but instead cast a sly look in Randy and Tony's direction and said, "Well, sir, you must do as you think best."

Tony stood. It seemed as good a time as any to take their leave. For one thing, Tony wasn't sure they were best served by sharing their suspicions with Lord Carlton, who would denounce them as absurd. "Well, sir, I thank you for your time and for enlightening us about Mrs. Lungren's condition. I will admit we were all quite shocked by her accusations. I know that you have set my mind at ease, that she is not to be believed." *Unless, of course, it was about her delusion about Lord Carlton's myriad proposals to her eldest daughter.* "I do hope we have not trespassed on your hospitality with our concerns."

"No, no, of course not. I understand it is difficult to lose a friend, under such trying circumstances, too." Lord Carlton once again seemed his unflappable self, and too complacent to make a fuss about anything that didn't affect him directly.

The three of them found themselves on the front drive, when Randleton suggested they visit the sisters. Bedford groaned, and Tony wanted to be done with the murder investigation for the day—or at least have some time to mull over the developments.

Mrs. Lungren had been buying foxglove and laudanum, either of which, everyone knew, could kill when given in large doses. Lord Carlton had seemed almost frenzied when the suggestion of foul play in connection with Captain Lungren's brothers came into the conversation. No one had thought it wise to mention their convictions about the manner of Lungren's death.

"Tomorrow, or we shall be stuck dining at the Boar's Head," Bedford said.

"We really should strike while the iron is hot," Randy said.

"We are in the neighborhood." Tony looked at the angle of the sun, judging the amount of daylight left.

"I shall expire from hunger before this is solved," moaned Bedford. Then he straightened. "I am more confounded than ever, and I think better with a full stomach."

Randy's lips lifted in a half smile. He transferred his amused gaze to Tony, who was taking in Bedford's tasseled and spurred Hessians, cream pantaloons, and apple green morning coat.

Bedford scowled. "Very well, I know you two must think I'm a frippery fellow, but I cannot stomach the idea of eating at that awful inn."

It wasn't really that. Tony and Randy had discussed, after their years of service on the Continent, how many of the officers arrived as spoiled, pampered young society men, like Bedford. As they themselves had probably been. But it was hard to remember a time when creature comforts had seemed so important.

Then both men looked to Tony to decide. As much as he wanted to get back to the city, it didn't make sense to miss an opportunity to gather information. "We shall tell them we are just there for a short social call, as we were in the neighborhood."

"A quarter hour?" asked Bedford hopefully.

"Half hour," said Randy.

Of course it was neither. They had been at the Lungren estate nigh on an hour. William's stomach was rumbling, and he was freezing, having given his overcoat to a maid; and then was stuck sitting on a stone bench in the dead garden while Randleton and Sheridan were at least getting the benefit of the exertion of walking.

In addition to their extended stay, there had been an overlong pause on the ride over, to decide what they meant to discuss with the sisters and how to go about it.

The plan the three men agreed upon was based on the

best divide-and-conquer military strategy. Then they'd drawn straws—he and the major, that is; somehow Randleton had gotten out of it by holding the hastily picked blades of dry winter grass—as to who would be paired with the eldest sister, Rosalyn. That would be him, the inevitable loser of late in games of chance. Even when he won he lost.

Sheridan had suggested that he avoid giving over the deed to the estate, which sat well with William's plan to use the deed to help secure a loan from a moneylender. After that, he'd be glad to be rid of the thing.

However, as the eldest Miss Lungren finally grew indifferent to his banal chatter, William felt guiltier and guiltier by the minute. Rosalyn looked more careworn than the last time he'd seen her, with furrows between her eyebrows that wouldn't go away. She hadn't glared at any of them, which made him wonder if she was off her game. Even as he shared some of his best *on-dits* with her, stolen unashamedly from known wits of the day, the frown lines never completely went away and the corners of her lips only lifted in the narrowest of smiles.

"I say, I don't think I am cheering you in the least, and I assure you that, worthless fellow that I am, entertaining conversation is one of my few virtues."

With that she smiled just a bit more. "I appreciate your efforts, sir, but I am quite burdened with my situation."

"Is there anything I can do to help?"

She shook her head and looked down.

"It is our intention as friends of your brother to ease your burdens in whatever way we can."

"I know; Major Sheridan has already informed me that you three are willing to escort us about society. However, we can barely afford to eat, let alone dress appropriately."

William checked his cuffs to see that they weren't fraying. He quite understood how important clothing was to a successful season. "Unfortunately, I haven't the means to help you there, but we three could put our heads together and see what solution we might find, if I have your permission to speak on it."

Miss Lungren looked horrified.

"Truly, let us help you. While we cannot provide you with apparel—that wouldn't be thought proper—perhaps we can find some acceptable avenue."

She shook her head, looking almost as wild-eyed as her mother. "I should not have mentioned it."

"What are friends for?" William patted her hand and swallowed his bitter misgivings. Good Lord, he'd barely thought beyond seeing his own way through society. He'd never considered that he might need to assist someone else's entry, and he certainly didn't want to risk his own standing, but he had been terribly fond of Lungren—the rotter.

She jerked to her feet, forcing William to rise gracelessly, his bones stiff from the cold.

"I hate the idea of having to marry and be dependent on a man. It never was a good thing for Mama."

She strode forward, forcing William nearly to a trot to keep by her side. She pivoted, leaving him skidding on the loose gravel of the walk as he tried to turn about.

"Really, it is too late for me, but Carolyn might stand a chance."

"I'm sure Miss Jocelyn could manage a respectable match." William realized belatedly that he had all but agreed with her pronouncement that she was too old. Not a good thing to do, he reminded himself.

"She feels as strongly as I do about the terrible condition of women forced to be dependent on a husband." Pivot. "I'm not sure that she quite understands how desperate our situation is, since I can't find the deed to the estate."

Gravel clinked off his spur as he was once again left heading the wrong direction. The deuce with it. William stepped off the path and folded his arms across his chest. "I understand that you are not without prospects yourself,

Miss Lungren. It has come to my attention that a respectable man has cast the handkerchief in your direction
more than once."

She whirled to a sudden stop, making William's head
spin—probably due in part to the lack of food. Her face
paled, and her eyes took on nearly the bleakest look he'd
ever seen.

"Lord Carlton doesn't want a wife; he wants a . . ." She
looked around, marking the other two couples' out-of-hear-
ing but not out-of-sight distance. Then she studied the
ground; then, in something between a barely audible whisper and a hiss, she said, "He wants a slave to control."

"Rubbish!"

To which tears pooled in her dark eyes, and she swung
away and marched into the house. Her back ramrod-
straight, she slammed the door loud enough to jar the other
couples' attention.

The two other sisters broke away and followed the eldest into the house.

"Oh, I say," said William as Sheridan and Randleton approached, and William was at a complete loss whether he
believed the accusation or even should repeat it.

"What the devil did you say to her?"

William sputtered. Ten years it had been since his tutor
had beat his stutter right out of him, and it came back with
a vengeance as he tried to stammer some explanation, and
was sure he sounded like the merest ninny. Finally he managed, "I-m-m c-c-cold."

"You said you were cold, and Miss Lungren went running
in the house?" said Sheridan sternly.

It was easy to see how he'd kept his troops in line, because
William felt like whimpering. "Actually, I said 'r-r-rubbish,'
which wasn't precisely in argument with what she said, but
if it was true—hang it!" William needed to decide if he
wanted to slander Lord Carlton, and he couldn't think straight
with his knees knocking from the cold, and his spine and

navel rubbing together for want of food. "I say, we need to look a little closer at Lord Carlton's involvement in all this."

"This gets worse by the minute," said Randleton. "I don't know about you two, but I think, other than Miss Carolyn, Mrs. Lungren may be the sanest of them all."

Sheridan rubbed his face. "Then are we are agreed, all the men in this family have been murdered?"

ELEVEN

Five o'clock came and went, then six, then seven; Felicity heard the longcase clock in the entry hall chime eight times, then nine. Finally, her butler showed in Major Sheridan.

"I don't suppose you still want to go for a drive?"

Felicity put down her pen. She had long since given up on him and had moved to her study to get work done. "You have to stop these late-night visits. They're not proper."

She waved her butler away, anyway.

"Surely a pretend fiancé is allowed a little latitude." Tony limped into the room. His overcoat was draped over his arm, as if he or her butler was unsure of his welcome. "I came as soon as I got your note."

She rolled her eyes.

"It would appear I am not timely in response to your written missives." He sat down, draping his overcoat over his lap.

"Indeed." She softened a little at his self-deprecating remark.

"So why did you want to go for a drive?" He fastened his light blue gaze on her face. In the half-light from the lamp his eyes didn't look so devoid of feelings.

Felicity put her hand to her forehead. "To talk. My parents aren't leaving, after all. My father was in here earlier trying to 'assist' me." She doubted if Tony cared or even understood that merely the idea of her father meddling in

Layton's business affairs terrified her. "I understand you told Charles nothing was decided yet."

"And he told your parents?"

"I should imagine they grilled him thoroughly."

"I failed in my promise to avoid the subject."

"I imagine Charles raised the issue." She knew her son. Her anger had long since faded to the realization that Tony couldn't have known that Charles could be a very determined little imp, and he tended to hear far more than he should. Felicity wondered what other subjects he had questioned Tony about.

Tony gave her a tight smile. "I did not think I should lie to him, under the circumstances."

"No-o," Felicity drew out her response. It wouldn't bode well to begin a father-son relationship with dishonesty. It probably should have been better not to start the relationship at all.

"Nothing *is* decided yet."

"Apparently not," agreed Felicity. But they did need to reach some understanding.

She stood to move around the desk. He began a slow rise to his feet.

"No, stay." She held out her hand. The limitation caused by his wound made her want to reach out and comfort him. "I am only changing seats."

He watched her sink into the chair beside his. "So your parents believe your son is more informed than they when it comes to the truth of our engagement?"

Felicity rubbed her forehead. "Well, he is. And he does have an uncanny ability to ferret out the truth."

"Does he?" Tony leaned his elbow up against the arm of his chair, cradling the back of his head in his hand. He shut his eyes and opened them. "I could make good use of him, then."

She bristled.

The tiny shake of his head told her he had no intention of

using Charles in any such manner. "He hears a lot for a child, likely too much."

"Well, yes, there was some mention of a duel and murder."

"Murders, actually." Tony frowned, yet his pose remained relaxed. "Although I suppose this morning we hadn't yet concluded that there was more than one."

Felicity stared at Tony. "More than one?" she echoed weakly. What on earth? Was he somehow involved in a murder? Murders? "My parents are now convinced you are totally unsuitable. Perhaps they are right."

"Never think it. One of my captains was murdered the night of the ball. It would seem his brothers may have been murdered before him."

"Lord!" Felicity stared at him, waiting for more. "You are serious. Who? When? Who did it?"

"I should like to know who did it." Tony leaned toward her and put a hand on her arm. "Don't repeat this. It is not common knowledge."

She swallowed hard. "I was so irritated with you for forgetting my drink." The thought seemed petty and mean-spirited in light of the truth. He must have been called away because of the death.

"Yes, well, do you dislike lemonade now? I thought you liked it before."

"I do still like it—prefer it, actually."

She had forgotten that his hand rested on her arm, until he moved it and she remembered with a jolt of sparking pleasure. With a reluctance that made her arm feel like lead, she moved it away from his too-tempting touch.

"I was rather incensed that you married another man while we were engaged." He dropped his arm to lie on top of his coat. "So shall we just call it even and be done with it?"

He was inviting her to let bygones be bygones. While she didn't want to relive the past, she couldn't just ignore all that had happened. "No, I don't think we are at evens, Tony. I cannot believe that you did not know I was with child."

Felicity looked down at her hands, clenched in her lap. Heat burned her cheeks as she realized they were calmly discussing the consequences of the one night that had changed her life forever.

He watched her steadily a moment and finally said, "You have reason. I should have inquired after the possibility."

Tension drained from her shoulders, and she only then realized how tightly coiled her body was.

"So how is it that your father's offer of assistance is bothersome?"

"He doesn't know the first thing about business." She stood and paced across the small floor area. "He can't even run his estate well enough to pay his bills. I've tried to piece together why he cannot make ends meet, but there isn't any reason."

Tony watched her a while and then said, "I take it you're a wealthy woman."

"Charles is wealthy or will be. But obviously he is too young to manage his affairs for some time, so I . . . I suppose I'm wealthy enough in my own right. My father says they are placing bets on who will marry me."

"Bedford assures me his intentions are honorable, so you could marry him." Tony looked dreadfully serious. "But I suspect he is honorable in that it is the only way to get at your fortune. Of course, I am only after your person, so my intentions are less honorable, but no less sincere."

She knew he was trying to tempt a smile from her, but marriage was much too serious a burden to contemplate lightly. "I don't want to marry anyone. I just want some peace."

"Not planning on sharing your fortune?"

"Charles's. I shall not let anyone take over Charles's inheritance or mismanage it."

Felicity looked at the piles of ledgers and correspondence jumbled on her desk. There were so many figures she needed to transfer into the ledgers—prices paid for raw materials, manufactured goods, labor costs, equipment, and so on. Really, she was getting behind on her work.

Every time she headed for her study, her father would follow her and insist that he should help. Then she would hastily close all the books and shove them all in a cabinet, creating even longer subsequent delays. At home she had spent several hours each day with the stuff. She couldn't bear the idea of a husband coming in and taking that away from her. While much of the work was tedious, she enjoyed it and had worked very hard to keep the companies profitable.

"So do you wish to continue our arrangement?"

Felicity looked at him warily. "A pretend engagement only."

Tony reached under his coat. She watched in horrified fascination as his overcoat rippled with the hidden movement of his hand. "Perhaps your father will not insist on helping you with all this"—he waved the arm holding his coat, indicating the piles on her desk—"if he thinks I am taking it over."

Before he settled his overcoat back into his lap, she saw his long fingers massaging his injured thigh. She felt an odd, somewhat disappointed relief that he wasn't doing anything untoward. "I don't want you taking over. I *like* running the businesses. I've been doing it for quite some time."

"Since your husband's death?"

"No, before. Several years, now. He was ill. He couldn't . . ." She continued staring at his leg. While she tried to tell herself that she only wondered if she could ease Tony's pain by rubbing his leg, it wasn't really his pain she was thinking of easing. "He couldn't . . ."

She couldn't finish the thought. What kept coming to her mind was that there were a lot of things Layton couldn't do because of his illness, and that it had been a long, long time since she had done *that*. An even longer time since she had *enjoyed* doing that, and she had enjoyed it . . . once.

Tony tossed the overcoat into the chair she'd vacated, and caught her arm. He tugged her forward so quickly, she stumbled. He used her momentum to propel her into his lap.

With a deft motion as if she weighed no more than a fractious kitten, he shifted her to rest on his healthy leg.

"You can't continue standing, as it is making me rude to sit in your presence. And my injury is bothering me."

Felicity started to scramble off.

"Don't squirm, you're making me . . ."

It was quite obvious what she was making him, as he pulled her against him.

William woke with a jolt. He had been immersed in a dream in which he possessed a harem. Only it wasn't a pleasant male dream with beautiful, scantily clad concubines plying him with grapes and nectar. No, he had the three Lungren sisters as wives, and they were haranguing him for food. Not grapes, either.

It was an odd thump that had him rolling out of bed, half believing that his wives were so hungry and angry they were throwing things at him. As he hit the floor, he saw the flash of light and heard the crack from his bedroom doorway.

It took a moment for the gunshot to register. He shook off the fleeting thought that his wives had really given up on his ability to provide for them if they had decided to shoot him.

Good God, he was being shot at!

He lay on the floor in stunned disbelief for a moment before he heard the intruder—surely it wasn't his man, even though his wages were overdue—move. Then he heard his valet yell from the other room, "Sir, sir, are you all right, sir?"

William scrambled under his bed. Cowering in the dusty space, he heard the fleeing footfalls.

William didn't dare answer. In the dark, perhaps his assailant wouldn't know that the bullet had missed. His valet stumbled around, and he heard the concerned voice of his landlady from the stairs. William clenched his eyes shut, hoping no one would be hurt, and fearing the consequences to his valet and his landlady should they try to catch the shooter. He should climb out and assist them, but as the target in this absurd game of ducks and drakes, he would rather stay under the bed.

Slowly his room filled with light, and William's hiding place was exposed when the dust got the better of him and he sneezed.

His man latched onto an ankle and dragged him out from under the bed frame. Unable to resist, for sneezes had overtaken him, William ended up sprawled on the floor of his bedroom, the landlady standing over him with a lamp, and his man staring at the bed. His best nightshirt was covered in gray dust streaks. The landlady leaned closer, and William jerked his nightshirt down over his bare legs.

"Bring the light here," commanded his servant.

William scrambled to his feet, and though he kept casting a wary glance over his shoulders, he, too, looked at the hole shredded in the indentation in his pillow. His knees buckled as he realized that but for his nightmare and his falling out of bed, this bullet would have shattered his skull.

"Tony, I hardly think this is appropriate."

"Neither is a pretend engagement, but you do not seem to have any qualms about that." He'd be damned if he'd miss the opportunity when her eyes darkened like that, though. "And what do you think should be the best way to convince your parents your engagement is real?"

"We are not having an affair."

"We should. We must. I ought to tell your parents that I shall be here often, to be able to learn the business and—"

"You are not taking over the businesses!"

"Who better to look after Charles's best interests?"

"Me. You are not simply taking over. Not now, not ever." She glared at him.

Later, when she wasn't so ferociously caught up in protecting her son—their son—he would make her realize that he was quite capable of managing things. Damnation, war and troops had to be run much like a business. For now, he could concede the point and try to persuade her of the advantages of his at least being informed.

"No, I'm not, but I should give the appearance of doing so. Then, perhaps, your father shan't bother you. I wouldn't mind learning what goes on, so that when I depart for India, I shall have a good basis for becoming a nabob."

"You will never become a nabob."

Did she want him to stay in England? "What choice is there for a younger son but to build a fortune? Especially when an heiress won't have him."

Her cheeks were bright red, and Tony decided that if he could keep her distracted long enough, he could keep her on his lap too long for her to object.

"What heiress?"

"You."

She tried to slide off his lap.

"Mind the leg," he cautioned.

She froze. Her dark eyes fastened on his face, her brow puckered in concern. "I'm sorry. Is it bad?"

Perfect. He shifted her back to a comfortable position for him. "Only when you wriggle on my lap."

"Tony," she said on an exasperated note.

He had her tight against him now. "I'm trying not to be rude. Trying very hard."

"Your explanation defies logic."

"My dear Felicity, it will go so much better for us if you stop fighting me."

"You mean, it will go so much better for *you.*"

"If you do not want me to go to India, then you shall have to make an honest man of me."

"No. I will not."

"Is there anything we can agree upon?"

She leaned back away from him. "Doubtful."

He grinned and tugged her closer yet. "That you should kiss me?"

"Absolutely not."

He held her gaze and moved his mouth closer toward hers. She strained away from him but stopped when he didn't complete his approach. He simply lingered, her mouth a mere inch or so away from his. Her gaze dropped lower on his face; his mouth and her lips parted. Patience, he cautioned himself.

"Then don't," he whispered.

"I'm not," she answered, but she had shifted infinitesimally closer, and she waited like a woman sure of a man's next move.

It had to be hers. He could play these games, too. He wouldn't be accused of taking advantage of her, as if she hadn't participated in the kisses they'd shared thus far.

And he wasn't pleased with her contrariness. Had she been this prone to objecting to everything he said before?

Swinging her feet to the floor, he dumped her off his lap and struggled to his feet. The surprise on her face was almost worth the denial of his desire—almost. Except that the shock faltered into an uncertain, hurt expression, and she spun away, leaning her palms against her desk.

He held back a moment, but hurting her hadn't been his intention. Reaching out, he put his hands on her shoulders. He could feel the tenseness. "Felicity?"

"I think you should leave now."

"I should not if you are upset." He kneaded the tense knots between her shoulder blades. His mind tormented him with the idea that he should be doing this to her naked flesh. "Invite me to stay, Felicity." He leaned closer, and his voice dropped lower with each word, "Invite me to kiss you; invite me to hold you; invite me . . . in."

She turned around and studied him as if surprised by the desperation in his plea. He was surprised himself. It wasn't like him to beg. Not even for sexual favors.

He backed away. "Good God, I'm tired."

Tired, edgy, disillusioned—and empty. For a moment he'd believed she could fill the void in him. What he really wanted was to be the idealistic youth he'd been the last time she'd invited him into her bed, as if her invitation would restore his long-ago innocence. Would restore her faith in him.

He shook his head. She looked torn.

Neither of them was innocent anymore. She wouldn't invite him back to her bed, because she feared pregnancy. Yet she hadn't tried very hard to rise from his lap. She hadn't resisted his kisses—turned away once, but she hadn't really resisted. She hadn't extracted a vague promise that he wouldn't kiss her this time. And she certainly seemed to have no problem telling him no these days.

He wouldn't have pushed seven years ago, because he wouldn't have been sure she had the will to resist. But this was a different Felicity—stronger, and if not entirely self-assured, at least well on her way to it. And he wanted her more, not because he fancied himself in love as he had back then, but because she could meet him as an equal, as forcefully and as passionately as only a mature, experienced woman could.

"Ah, Felicity," he said, stepping forward and gathering her in his arms. He leaned down to kiss her, and she met him softly, her lips pliable but not open.

He wanted a better welcome than this. Disappointment warred with desire as he pressed her to open her mouth to his.

She complied, allowing him access, returning his kiss with an almost perfunctory acceptance. Where was the woman whose eyes had grown dark a moment ago? He continued the kiss, feeling a little desperate. He should withdraw, yet he couldn't bring himself to stop, to pull back. Had he misread her so badly?

Finally, she stretched up on her toes and slid her hands up his arms. Her fingers traced his muscles until she reached behind his head and pulled his head down. He deepened the kiss, pulling her tight against him, the soft mounds of her breasts pressed against his chest. He wanted to be closer. He wanted to remove all their clothes; but instead, he moaned into her mouth and slid his hands down to the curve of her hips. He cradled her hips against his hardness.

They stayed locked together like that for an eternity, until they both swayed and strained against each other. The kiss made them both breathe heavily. He wanted to rip off her clothes and make her his again, until the blood drained from his head and left him befuddled and urgent. Still he held back. He wanted more than this moment, more than one time, and he waited for an indication *she* wanted more— that this was more to her than compliance.

He waited, and she returned the kiss, returned the pressure against his groin, gave every indication of reception but none of a need as desperate as his. Why did it matter so much?

Because it did. Because that time years ago, she had reached for him in ways that left him shaking and awed. Because then she had wanted him . . . then.

Almost more than he wanted her, he wanted her to want him. He wanted her to need him, and it bothered him that she didn't.

He backed away from the kiss, feathering gentle nips on her lips as she strained up against him and gave a whimper of disapproval as if to indicate that she didn't want the kisses to end. Her unwillingness to let him pull away tore at him, gave him the encouragement to proceed. Her desire was slight compared to his, and it shamed him that it was enough. He wanted more, but this tiny sign of reluctance to let this end was enough for now.

He slid his hands to her derriére and lifted her up to rest on the edge of her desk. He barely managed to keep from grinding against her. Her hands slid down his back, down lower, until he pushed forward and she pulled him toward her woman's core, wrapping her legs and skirts around him. He thought he would die from this belated show of enthusiasm.

He delved in for a deeper kiss as he yanked his cravat

loose. She helped him slide his jacket down his arms as their lips remained locked together. His blood thundered in his ears, boiled in his bloodstream; his skin burned under his clothes.

This was what he wanted, needed, craved with a desperation that went deep into his soul. He slid his hand to her waist and up to the soft curve of her breast, and he brushed his thumb across the tantalizing peak of her nipple. Her whimper into his mouth made his blood thrum with triumphant pleasure. He caught the tight bud in his fingers and tugged. She squirmed against him, and heat rushed through him.

Eager, impatient for more, he pulled out pins, loosening the bodice of her gown. Tony tugged down her chemise, exposing a perfect, lily white breast. Lowering his head to take the rosy tip in his mouth, he reached down to find the hem of her gown. He bunched material in his hand as he suckled her tightened nipple. Finally, he could reach under her skirt. As he caressed the bare flesh of her leg, she trembled.

He rubbed his hand along the soft flesh of her thigh and then found the tapes to her pantaloons. While he untied the tapes, she strained against him, her back arched, giving him better access to her bare breast. He moved, kissing the upper slope of her breast, moving up the slender column of her neck until he reached the sensitive spot behind her ear. He savored her skin's salty sweetness, the brush of her silky hair against his cheek, and then he found her mouth for a soul-deep kiss.

He sought her woman's flesh, drawing his fingers through her warm, wet crevice. She shuddered and whimpered into his mouth. He pulled back and studied her flushed face. Gently he circled the little nubbin of her pleasure with his index finger. She gasped. Her face contorted with desire, and her breath came in heavy pants. Her hips circled as he continued his teasing torture of her.

"Absolutely not?" he whispered against her mouth. He feathered kisses along her swollen lips.

She blinked, her eyes dark and stormy with passion. "What?"

He tapped the tip of his finger against the tight little bud.

She shuddered and stared at him as if she couldn't comprehend his question. "Hold onto me," he commanded softly. With her arms around his neck, he pulled out the rest of the pins holding her bodice together and tugged her chemise down while keeping a steady, light rhythm with his other hand. He caressed her ivory breasts while she held on. He slowly and thoroughly brought her to completion.

"Oh, God," she whispered, her breath ragged against his neck. She clenched the material of his waistcoat in her hands.

"Let's go upstairs. Now." He splayed his hand across her bare skin on her back, half supporting her limp body while savoring the silky softness of her skin. He still pressed his hand against the pulsing center of her core. He was almost wild to tear off the remainder of her clothes and his. Yet he was far too aware of her initial resistance, and he waited for her full consent, his breath caught in his throat.

Instead, there was a knock on the door.

She jolted upright.

"Bloody hell," muttered Tony, yanking Felicity's skirts down and tugging up her chemise.

She slid off the edge of the desk, also attempting to right her disarrayed clothes. "W-what is it?"

Tony jerked across the room, holding the door shut.

"You have callers, ma'am," said her butler. "Actually, I think they are searching for Major Sheridan. I wouldn't have disturbed you, ma'am, but they say it is urgent. A Lieutenant Randleton and a Mr. William Bedford."

Tony glanced over his shoulder to see how Felicity was progressing with righting her clothes. Not well. She looked like a wounded doe struggling to regain its footing.

Tony opened the door a crack, making sure to keep his body between the room and the opening. "Put them in the green drawing room, if you please. We shall attend them in a moment."

Felicity squeaked something that Tony hoped passed for agreement, and he shut the door.

What in blazes were Randy and Bedford doing here? This time of night?

TWELVE

Felicity felt like a ninny as Tony helped her pin her gown back together. She couldn't believe what had just happened and that she'd let it go so far. What on earth had she been thinking? Or not thinking? How had he made her lose herself so completely?

"Go on up to bed, and I shall deal with Randy and Bedford."

"I hardly think that it is appropriate for you to receive callers without me in *my* house." She jabbed a pin in her bodice and stabbed herself. "Ouch! That would imply a great deal of familiarity."

"To appear looking like a well-satisfied woman would imply an even greater degree of familiarity." He took the pin out that she'd just put in, pulled her bodice tighter, and carefully reinserted it.

Her cheeks might as well be on fire, they burned so. "I think you are the one who looks well satisfied."

"Hardly, Felicity."

She couldn't bring herself to meet his eyes as she realized she had the only claim to satisfaction at the moment.

He picked his jacket up off the floor and thrust his arms into the sleeves. "I need a looking glass." He fingered his cravat. "Unless you care to do the honors."

"There's one in the front hall." She needed it first. She must look a fright. However, as she patted her hair, it seemed intact. How could that be, when she felt so undone?

She took a step toward the door and nearly tripped on her untied pantaloons. She *was* undone.

"You could just leave them off, and give me fair wicked thoughts."

She scowled at him and bent over to pull them into place. Turning her back to him, she hitched her skirts up enough to tie the tapes. "I didn't mean for this to happen."

His silence made her look in his direction.

He tossed her a look of ice-cold determination as he opened the door. "I did, but you need not have any pregnancy worries."

"Tony . . ." She was shocked and she wasn't. "I know that," she hissed. "But gracious, be careful what you say when the doors are open."

"Do your servants gossip?" he asked mildly.

She looked right and left in the corridor. "It's not the servants I'm worried about."

"Oh, Charles."

"And my parents, and Lord, I'm not sure what to make of my niece. Although I could hardly accuse her of being an eavesdropper, since that trait seems to manifest in my side of the family."

"I wouldn't want to cast your reputation to the wolves, but wouldn't it benefit me to see it tarnished?"

Felicity drew up sharply. "No, only Diana would be likely to be hurt by your machinations. I have a comfortable home and life that won't be affected overmuch by my reputation or lack thereof."

They entered the front hall. Felicity made her way to the looking glass. Tony's steps were more deliberate, slower. At times he seemed able to minimize his limp, but was it at the cost of speed? How could he lead infantrymen into battle without a confident stride?

She frowned at her reflection in the mirror. It wasn't that she looked different—well, not other than a certain starry-eyed quality, and her lips might be a little swollen. It was more that she looked at herself differently. Who was the woman staring back at her? Why would she jeopardize her hard-won autonomy to risk being trapped in a marriage with a man who would control her every move?

Tony pulled up behind her and began retying his neck cloth. A footman stared at them from his station beside the door.

"Would you please have cook prepare refreshments to be sent to the green drawing room? Perhaps some cold meat—whatever is ready—and a pot of tea."

The footman nodded and headed for the green baize door to go belowstairs, and they were once again alone, where no one could mark their ruffled appearance.

Tony waited until the man was out of earshot. "Feeding Bedford is a sure way to win his affections." His cravat tied, he leaned over and brushed a kiss on her temple. "I do think you should get on much better with me, though."

He ran a hand over her shoulder, then pivoted and headed for the staircase. She watched him, mesmerized both by his broad shoulders and his purposeful walk. What was she going to do now? Tony would think an affair was inevitable. Indeed, she thought an affair was inevitable. Therein lay the problem. Passion and prudence rarely went together.

The last thing she wanted to do was end up in a marriage where her husband ran roughshod over her, made all the decisions, and ignored her ideas because she was merely a woman, while he, the man, demanded complete obedience from a wife.

"What in blazes took you so long?" said Bedford the minute Tony entered the room. His turquoise eyes wild, Bedford paced back and forth and raked a hand through his tousled blond waves.

Tony hadn't ever seen Bedford so hastily dressed. Did his shoes match? Certainly his peach-and-green striped waistcoat clashed with his purple coat. He looked like the one who had been caught in flagrante delicto just minutes past.

Take A Trip Into A Timeless World of Passion and Adventure with Kensington Choice Historical Romances! —Absolutely FREE!

Enjoy the passion and adventure of another time with Kensington Choice Historical Romances. They are the finest novels of their kind, written by today's best-selling romance authors. Each Kensington Choice Historical Romance transports you to distant lands in a bygone age. Experience the adventure and share the delight as proud men and spirited women discover the wonder and passion of true love.

Get 4 FREE Books!

We created our convenient Home Subscription Service so you'll be sure to have the hottest new romances delivered each month right to your doorstep—usually before they are available in book stores. Just to show you how convenient the Zebra Home Subscription Service is, we would like to send you 4 FREE Kensington Choice Historical Romances. The books are worth up to $24.96, but you only pay $1.99 for shipping and handling. There's no obligation to buy additional books—ever!

Save Up To 30% With Home Delivery!

Accept your FREE books and each month we'll deliver 4 brand new titles as soon as they are published. They'll be yours to examine FREE for 10 days. Then if you decide to keep the books, you'll pay the preferred subscriber's price (up to 30% off the cover price!), plus shipping and handling. Remember, you are under no obligation to buy any of these books at any time! If you are not delighted with them, simply return them and owe nothing. But if you enjoy Kensington Choice Historical Romances as much as we think you will, pay the special preferred subscriber rate and save over $8.00 off the cover price!

We have **4 FREE BOOKS** for you as your introduction to
KENSINGTON CHOICE!
To get your FREE BOOKS, worth up to $24.96, mail the card below or call TOLL-FREE 1-800-770-1963.
Visit our website at www.kensingtonbooks.com.

Get 4 FREE *Kensington Choice Historical Romances!*

♡ **YES!** Please send me my 4 FREE KENSINGTON CHOICE HISTORICAL ROMANCES (without obligation to purchase other books). I only pay $1.99 for shipping and handling. Unless you hear from me after I receive my 4 FREE BOOKS, you may send me 4 new novels—as soon as they are published—to preview each month FREE for 10 days. If I am not satisfied, I may return them and owe nothing. Otherwise, I will pay the money-saving preferred subscriber's price (over $8.00 off the cover price), plus shipping and handling. I may return any shipment within 10 days and owe nothing, and I may cancel any time I wish. In any case the 4 FREE books will be mine to keep.

KN063A

Name _____

Address _____ Apt. _____

City _____ State _____ Zip _____

Telephone (___) _____

Signature _____

(If under 18, parent or guardian must sign)

Offer limited to one per household and not to current subscribers. Terms, offer and prices subject to change. Orders subject to acceptance by Kensington Choice Book Club.
Offer Valid in the U.S. only.

4 FREE

Kensington
Choice
Historical
Romances
(*worth up to
$24.96*)
*are waiting
for you to
claim them!*

*See details
inside...*

IIı.ı.ıllıı..ıllıl.ıl.ıl..ıl..ıllıl..lll..l

KENSINGTON CHOICE

Zebra Home Subscription Service, Inc.

P.O. Box 5214

Clifton NJ 07015-5214

"I don't believe it has been above five minutes," said Tony.

"Ten," countered the normally agreeable Randleton, who sat across the room on the chaise longue with the threatening crocodiles crawling up the legs. He rose quickly as Felicity entered the room.

Randleton's face was creased with concern, much the way it had been the night he informed Tony of Lungren's death.

Tony's heart leaped to his throat. "Who died?"

"Should we go elsewhere to—" Randleton started to say.

Bedford interrupted him, "Very nearly me."

When Tony's assessment of Bedford turned up nothing amiss, other than the odd choice of clothing, relief flooded through him. He limped over to a plush green velvet chair.

"Someone broke into my apartments and shot at me tonight. He would have killed me if I had not rolled to the floor just in the nick of time."

Tony's relief was short-lived as he realized that Bedford seemed to have the devil's own luck when it came to getting shot at. Were it anyone else, they might very well have another murder on their hands.

"Perhaps we should go to your lodgings, Tony, where we might be private," suggested Randy.

No doubt he was worried about involving Felicity, but Tony was reluctant to leave and surrender all the ground he had gained with her. If he returned to his lodgings, it would smack of retreat, just when victory was in sight.

"Mrs. Merriwether has ordered refreshments for us. We shall do as well to stay here." He glanced over at her. "I've told her that Captain Lungren was murdered."

Felicity stood near the closed door, looking dazed and thoughtful at the same time. However, she seemed of late not to remember that gentlemen could not sit as long as she stood. He limped back to her, gathered her hand in his, and led her over to the seats. He whispered, "My lap?"

She jerked free of him and sat on the couch. "Please be seated, gentlemen."

Bedford was clearly too agitated to sit, but he perched on the edge of a chair for a second before springing back up and pacing back and forth across the mint-and-emerald carpet. He barely spared a glance at Felicity before words began tumbling from his mouth. "I told you I didn't want to keep that damn title to Lungren's estate. Now I'm being shot at for it."

"If it is for the estate, then likely only Lord Carlton knows," said Tony.

Randy shook his head. "No, I saw his carriage coming up the lane as we were leaving the Lungrens' house. No doubt he informed them where the title resides."

"Have you summoned a runner?" asked Felicity.

"Well, that is the thing. We are not decided we should," said Bedford. "With everything that is going on, a runner is likely to think we're all Bedlamites."

Randy turned to Tony. "Do we still think it is easier to get answers if the killer thinks no one knows that there was a murder? Should we involve a runner, we'll have to reveal what we suspect."

"What *do* you suspect?" asked Felicity.

"That we shall all be murdered in our sleep," said Bedford, just as the door swung open.

Her footman carried a teatray into the room and set it on the table. His eyes darted from Bedford to Felicity, and then he scurried to the door, eager to leave any discussion in which murder figured.

"It has got rather convoluted," said Tony, which was half the reason he wanted her to know. She seemed to have a logical brain; perhaps she could puzzle out the culprit's identity. "I'll explain it all later."

"Wasn't there something in the *Post*? Didn't Captain Lungren die by his own hand?" she asked.

"He was shot in the head, but he couldn't have pulled the trigger himself," Randy said mildly, "although that is what people think."

"What was done with the gun used to shoot him?" Felicity asked.

"Should have been a deodand to the king. Did you see Lord Carlton confiscate it?" Randy looked thoughtful.

"I don't think so, unless he'd already had it removed to his carriage by the time we arrived." Tony thought he'd seen it on a side table. "But I believe I saw it in the library after he left."

"Just more havey-cavey business with Lord C. Or do you suppose he thought it should be too much trouble to turn it over to the crown?" said Bedford. "Although I don't think the shooter tonight was him, because the dastardly bastard—pardon me, madam—was able to get away quickly, and I didn't hear heavy footfalls."

"I wondered if it could have been the same gun." Felicity reached for the teapot and began pouring a cup.

"I suppose we could look at the size of the bullet hole in Bedford's bed. Or better yet, find the bullet," said Randy. "But we don't have the bullet from Lungren to compare."

Tony thought a moment. "The bullet went right through. It might still be embedded in the wall."

"Or the chair. Wouldn't have had much velocity left after piercing the brain box twice," said Randy. "Excuse me, I don't mean to speak of such things in the presence of a lady."

"Felicity is a trouper. Not the least bit missish," said Tony. Besides, it had been his experience that for all their pretense otherwise, women were much more resilient then men when it came to blood-and-guts. Already she was contributing worthwhile suggestions. "We'll have to see if we can find it."

"Don't tell me we shall have to go back there," wailed Bedford.

"Of course we shall. If nothing else, we are pledged to open up their prospects," said Randy.

Tony cocked his head sideways as he looked at his lieutenant. Randy had been resistant to the idea of escorting the women about town. Had he changed his mind? And why? "Was the shooter a woman?" asked Tony slowly.

Bedford slapped a hand to his forehead. "Do you suppose that mad Mrs. Lungren took that much exception to me?"

"Miss Carolyn believes her mother takes exception to being lied to. She attacked her sister because of a lie. So perhaps when you told her the roses were lovely . . ." Randy let his voice trail off.

"I should rather hate to think that Bedford was nearly killed because the roses aren't in bloom." Tony took the cup of tea that Felicity poured him. "I'm more inclined to believe that there is a link to the word getting out that Bedford has the title to the estate."

"But the estate is worthless," said Randleton.

"Mayhap not." Felicity poured another cup of tea.

"In any event, I am in a fine coil, and I am not going to sleep in my apartments until this is cleared up. So which of you gentlemen will put me up?"

"We should all stay somewhere unexpected. Somewhere there are enough servants to raise an alarm and put up a fight if there is a problem. Felicity, how many of us can you put up here?"

"What are you doing out here?" Meg asked the little boy who had his face pressed between the newel posts on the third floor landing. "Shouldn't you be abed?"

"Shouldn't you?" asked Charles.

"Likely so, but I am grown and therefore allowed a bit of . . ." Meg searched the suddenly meager-seeming store of words in her brain.

"Latitude?" supplied Charles.

Meg wasn't even sure she knew what the word meant. "Yes. Well, freedom." She hoped that was close to the meaning of the word Charles used. "Actually, I could not sleep, so I thought I might look for a book I could read."

She was doing a terrible job of carrying out this charade. She hadn't been able to sleep for worry about her mistakes today. She'd thought, even though she hadn't ever really taken to reading—although she did know how—that in the library she might find something to help her learn how to go on.

Charles turned to her solemnly. "Can't you read very well? I know I can't read all the books in Mama's library, but I can read some of them."

"I didn't mean it that way," snapped Meg. When Charles blinked his baby blue eyes at her, she felt ashamed of her peevishness. She knelt down on the floor beside her supposed cousin. Diana had been so eager to meet this little boy; Meg could at least be kind. "I meant something that might interest me, perhaps something on how to behave at balls and suchlike."

"Grandpapa says they didn't teach you a thing at that school."

Meg searched for a response. "Well, I was sick much of the time, so I often missed my lessons."

"Oh, like my papa—not my real papa, but the one who died. Are you going to die?"

What did he mean, his 'real papa'? Meg put an arm around the thin shoulders of the little boy. "We all will die someday, but I don't expect it will be soon in my case." Unless, of course, she was hanged for murder. Was impersonation of a dead woman a capital offense?

"You should tell Grandmama that you missed too many lessons, because she thinks you just have bad breeding."

Meg choked. Was it so obvious that her mother was a whore? No, she told herself. This was what Lady Greyston thought of *Diana*. In truth, Meg did have a better bloodline than Diana, at least on her paternal side.

"What you need is a Pocket Book," said Charles.

"What's that?"

"Mama looked at one at Hatchards, but she decided it didn't really tell her anything she didn't know. I guess they tell women how to live in London." Charles held out his hands a few inches apart to signify a smallish book. "You know, they're little like this. I could show you the one Mama looked at; then we could go get an ice at Gunters."

Meg grinned. The little devil was angling for a bribe. Well, she needed all the help she could get. She ruffled Charles's tawny curls. "I shall have to ask Aunt Felicity's permission to take you out, so we shall see. Now, I think I should take you back to bed. What do you say?"

"I don't want to go back to bed."

"Why not?"

"They are down there talking about murder, and if I don't listen, they'll never tell me."

Meg felt the floor drop out from under her. She clenched the newel posts with knuckles gone white. Had they learned about Diana? Were they even now discussing whether they should throw Meg in prison? Or worse? After a second she realized she was still on her knees beside Charles, who was eyeing her rather anxiously.

"You won't tell Mama that I told you that Mr. Merriwether isn't my father. I'm not supposed to tell anyone. I wasn't supposed to tell you."

"Who is your father?" Meg asked faintly.

Charles flattened his lips. "I 'spect it's Major Sheridan, but they won't tell me."

Meg supposed she might feel disappointment if it weren't for the fact that she wasn't likely to marry anyone if she was going to be swinging from a scaffold. She put her hand to her throat. At least she wasn't in France and likely to be separated from her head by a guillotine. With that cold comfort in mind, she urged Charles to his feet and shuffled him back to the nursery.

"If I knew, I would tell you," she said, and earned a beatific smile and Charles's compliance. She wasn't even sure if it was a lie.

Still, if they were discussing her possible involvement in Diana's death, Meg preferred to state that she hadn't killed the girl—just hadn't reported her death from illness—before their opinions were too deeply set to be changed. After settling Charles back into the third-floor nursery with his sleeping nanny, Meg leaned on the railing and gathered her courage. Once she felt brave enough, she would descend the stairs and confront her accusers.

Felicity sputtered. *How many of them could she put up?* Tony looked at her, his expression innocent. That rotter.

"I say, I should hardly need to move out of my brother's house." Randy stood and crossed the room for a plate of food. "They'll be up to town in the next few days, and we'll be filled to overflowing. It's just about the corner, anyway."

"If you have the room"—Tony looked around the green drawing room as if to mark the size of her house, which was on the large side for London—"then there can be no impropriety, as your parents are still in residence. Besides, we shan't want the news that we are staying here made known. That would defeat the whole purpose."

"I'm sure I don't mean to impose," said Bedford. He drew up in front of the food and filled a plate to overflowing with sliced beef and ham, bread, pickles, and two of the four scones and three dried apricots. "Whatever you decide shall be fine with me. Although it does seem a rather handy solution."

"A word with you, sir." Glaring at Tony, Felicity stood and marched toward the doors connecting with the rose drawing room.

Bedford took a hasty gulp of his food.

Tony followed her. Once she had shut the door, she turned. "Did it occur to you that you should consult with me before offering my home and hospitality to you and your friends?"

"No. I wanted to make it harder for you to refuse." Tony took a sip of his tea. "If you are going to stand, do you mind if I sit?"

If he was trying to remind her that he was a wounded veteran, it wouldn't wash. She waved impatiently at a chair.

What was she going to say to his suggestion, anyway? No,

she would look like the cruelest of the cruel. On the other hand, she had her son's and her niece's safety to think on. "What about Charles and Diana? What advantage is there to bringing the danger of a murderer's intended victims into my household? What about our safety?"

"The object would be to keep it secret that we're staying here."

"And you think that is feasible in London, during the season, when I'm launching my niece into society?"

"This won't go on forever. We will catch this killer. A few weeks, mayhap."

Felicity rubbed her forehead. "I don't like you deciding you want things your way and putting me in an untenable position."

Tony set down his teacup and saucer. He moved over beside her. "Felicity, there are some real advantages. It will give me a chance to get to know Charles without raising suspicions. I suppose he is about the age where fathers start teaching their sons to ride and shoot."

"Tony," Felicity began on an exasperated note. Why was it that he only thought as far as what *he* wanted?

He traced the line of her jaw with his fingers—his long, elegant, and far too talented fingers.

She shied away from him. "Don't do that. I can't think when you do that."

"Then I shall endeavor to do it more."

She stalked out of his range. One good thing about his limp: it meant she could quickly outdistance him. She had no doubt he would catch her if he had a mind to, but at least for a moment she could have a bit of space. "Tell me what are the advantages to me, if I were to have you and Mr. Bedford stay here."

Tony blinked his pale blue eyes, as if the thought had never occurred to him. It most likely hadn't. He was quick to answer, though; she had to grant him that. "Ready escorts for you and your niece to any event you wish to attend. Protection—I am a crack shot."

She tapped her foot. "I am sure the list of disadvantages is greater."

"Ah, well, you shall have me around to ensure you don't think too much."

"I like to think. I don't want to not think."

"That was a jest, Felicity." He was closing the distance between them. "I'd be here to deflect your father's interest in your affairs."

That could be an advantage. "You wouldn't expect to take it over? It should be just as bad for me if you decide *you* should run the businesses."

"No, I wouldn't want to take it over." His words were slow, as if he were thinking it out as he spoke. "If you want my help, I should be happy to assist."

"Let me be clear. Your help is not required."

He grinned mirthlessly. "I understand."

"I do not want that gigantic dog in the house. He can stay in the stables, if you must bring him."

"Phys is housebroken."

Felicity sighed. "I just had a battle with Charles about not having a dog. You cannot undermine my authority."

"Why can't he have a dog?"

"Tony!"

He caught her shoulders. "I'm just asking your reasoning, madam. If you don't want Phys in the house, I am sure he will eventually forgive you for it."

"Which he?"

"Phys, of course. He is a very good-natured beast." Tony rubbed his hands down her arms and tugged her closer. "I don't intend to undermine you, but please try to understand. Lots of boys have dogs."

"He has several at home. It's not really about dogs; it's that I'm trying to avoid spoiling him. He has so much money, and my father keeps telling him he can afford anything he wants. I hardly think it can be good for him to get everything he asks for, so I had resolved to say no to his next request." She shrugged. "It was for a dog."

"I see."

"Do you? Because I had been thinking of getting a small lap-dog before he asked. Of course, I can't now."

Tony rather looked like he was laughing at her.

"Only I live in deathly fear that my parents will go out and buy one for him. So you understand, don't you?"

"Felicity."

"What?"

"Thank you."

Somebody had tried to murder Mr. Bedford tonight, and she was chattering about raising Charles. "Oh, heavens, I'm sorry."

"Don't be, Bedford will be grateful for Phys's banishment." He steered her toward the door to the green drawing room. "Shall we see if they have eaten everything yet?"

"No, I'm chattering about nonsense, and people have been shot at."

"Raising Charles to be a decent man isn't nonsense."

Charles was only a little boy. She might want him mannerly, but manly was not in her plan. Oh, dear God, maybe her son did need a stepfather. Or Tony.

THIRTEEN

Meg's resolve faltered. Her palms were sweating. She didn't think she'd been this hen-hearted when she'd dragged Diana's body to the ship's railing. She clenched her fists and made herself race down the stairs.

She threw back the door and said, "I didn't kill her!"

The room was empty.

Her heart thundered in her chest. All that worry for naught. She almost laughed at herself. The rose drawing room was empty, and the green drawing room was never used. She'd never even been in a house with a drawing room before moving in with Felicity, and this one had two.

Meg backed out of the room and considered her next move. She might as well pursue her original plan and see if there was a book in the library that could help her go on. The longcase clock in the front hall chimed half past one, and she moved toward the stairs.

As she crossed in front of the green drawing room doors, they slid back. She leaped back and pressed against the wall. They *were* here! Something between a whimper and a squeal left her lips.

Four sets of eyes fastened on her: two pairs of brown, one of pale blue, and one set of brilliant, jewel-toned eyes that looked every bit as startled as she felt.

"Diana!" Felicity's expression changed from surprise to consternation.

"I told you I heard something," said Mr. Bedford.

Meg tried to catch her breath. Instead, tears welled up in her eyes. "Blimey, you gave me a fright."

They weren't calling her by her real name, or some dismissing non-name like "you, miss." They all looked shocked to see her, but Meg didn't sense any animosity or suspicion in their gazes. Likely, they hadn't realized the body pulled from the Thames was the real Diana. Likely, Charles had a lively imagination. Murder, indeed. Still, it was hard to will back the panic.

"What are you doing up and about?" Felicity stepped forward and took Meg's arm.

Meg fell back on her original plan. "I couldn't sleep, I thought I'd try the library for a book."

"You shouldn't be wandering about in your nightclothes," Felicity said in a low undertone as she pulled Meg toward the stairs.

Oh, no. She had undoubtedly committed another faux pas. "I'm sorry. I didn't know anyone was here."

Did her pretend aunt regularly entertain three gentlemen in the wee hours of the morning? Was that acceptable social behavior? Lord help her, Meg was trying to understand the rules, but there seemed to be more exceptions than not.

Felicity turned back around. "You will excuse us, won't you, gentlemen? If you could see yourselves out."

Meg realized that as Felicity steered her away from the curious gazes of the men, her aunt was trying to keep her body between Meg and the men's line of sight.

Meg glanced down at the lawn nightrail she was wearing, one of Diana's. Since the cut was loose, there was no tightness in the bodice. The material, however, was very fine. Thin. Oh, merciful God, the men could probably see straight through it.

At this point Meg decided she was better commenting on it than not. "Oh, heavens, I hope they didn't see me." Which seemed quite the most noddle-cocked thing she could have said. "Through my nightrail, that is."

"I doubt they had time enough to register the idea."

Not in Meg's experience. The first place most men looked was at a woman's chest. These gentlemen might be more discreet about it than ordinary blokes, but she didn't suppose they were all that different.

Now that she'd gotten her out of the men's line of sight, Felicity turned toward Meg. "You don't seem to have any sense of propriety, Diana. Where on earth did you learn to use a word like blimey?"

Meg studied her bare toes poking out under the nightgown. She took a hopeful stab in the dark. "My father used to say it."

She rubbed her foot across the carpet—so plush and rich, she didn't ever want to go back to the bare, splintering wood or jagged flagstone floors of the dozens of cheap cottages of her youth, each more squalid and dismal than the last. "Charles tells me I should get a Pocket Book to tell me how to go on."

"You probably need more than a Pocket Book," muttered Felicity. She pointed up the stairs and said in a firmer tone, "Go to bed, Diana. And a lady is never, ever outside of her bedroom in her nightrail. You must wear a dressing gown or change into day dress. I won't see you out of your room again like this, will I?"

"No, ma'am," said Meg. Too bad she wasn't really a lady. She would have known what to do. Instead, she just cried because she was quite sure that her masquerade was failing and she would never be able to fool a gentleman long enough to induce him to offer marriage. She would get the same kind of offer that she always got, a slip on the shoulder.

To which Felicity reached out and wrapped her arms around Meg, which made Meg feel worse, and she vowed to try harder to act like a lady and get herself married as fast as she could.

* * *

"I say, I wish she would have invited us to stay tonight," said William as they walked down the street.

"We're deuced lucky she invited us to stay at all," said Sheridan.

"She didn't, really," pointed out Randleton. "You forced her hand. I don't know what hold you have over Mrs. Merriwether—"

Sheridan snorted. "She has a hold over me, I'd say."

Randleton gave his major an odd look.

Sheridan stopped walking and leaned against a wrought iron railing. "Devil a bit, whose place are we closest to?"

"My brother's house," answered Randleton.

"You say the family isn't in residence yet. Can we go there? I need to sit."

"Your leg?" inquired William.

Sheridan turned in his direction. For a minute William thought he meant to darken his daylights, but Sheridan's fierce expression relented. "Hurts like the devil. I've been standing too long."

Randleton stared at his major. "Let us get a hackney."

Sheridan shook his head.

William held out his walking stick. Sheridan looked at it despairingly for a minute or two before asking, "Do you expect me to use that?"

William was rather fond of his ivory-handled cane. He was afraid he might need to pawn it. "Thought you might want a drink from the flask inside."

Sheridan took the cane and unscrewed the handle. He lifted it up while William winced.

"It's empty."

"Is it?" Bedford said as if he hadn't known. He looked hard at Randleton. "Must have forgotten to refill it."

"This way, then. I'm sure I can rummage up a bottle or two from the cellar." Randleton started up the street.

William fell in step beside him, leaving Major Sheridan to screw the lid back on the concealed flask and carry the cane or use it.

When the major was clearly choosing the latter course of action, he and Randleton slowed their steps so that the major might catch them.

"So tell me how it is the shooter managed to miss you," Sheridan asked when he rejoined their side.

If it had been anyone else, William probably would have tried to slant the story, but even in the dark, Sheridan's pale gaze had a way of cutting through William and making him fear for his soul. "I had a nightmare and must have heard a noise."

"And?"

"I fell out of bed. Then there was the shot. It all happened rather fast."

Fortunately, after exchanging a wry look, Randleton and Sheridan didn't comment on his cowardice. No doubt the last time either had fallen out of bed because of a bad dream, he had been in leading strings. William studied Sheridan and his heavy leaning on the walking stick and his stiff-legged gait. On second thought, he doubted Sheridan had ever fallen out of bed. A nightmare wouldn't dare intrude on his rest.

"Did you see anything?" Sheridan's face screwed up in a grimace.

"Just the flash from the gun and the hole in my pillow, right where I was lying."

"Got to figure this out"—Randleton reached inside his coat, pulled out a silver flask and handed it to the major—"before someone else ends up dead. Here, my good Irish whiskey."

William watched with envy as Sheridan drained the flask. After being shot at, he could have used some Irish comfort. "Rate we're going, the last one left standing will be the murderer."

Randleton took back the empty flask and upended it over the sidewalk. "Luck you have, that would be you."

William sputtered.

Sheridan playfully pushed his shoulder. "Odd thing is,

Miss Jocelyn just looked off to the distance when I asked her if she thought there might be something unnatural about all her brothers dying in such a short space of time. Seemed as if the idea was not new to her."

"Well, if her mother is the culprit, the idea wouldn't be new to her." When nothing more than a drop came out of the flask, Randleton frowned and screwed the lid back on.

"If her mother did them in, why is she allowed to go in and out at Bedlam?" William asked. Surely the woman would not be allowed to leave if there was the suspicion of murder.

"I gather a former inmate comes and claims to be her sister and they release Mrs. Lungren into her care," said Randleton. "I have had my batman following her."

Sheridan stopped walking. "Would he have followed her tonight?"

"Possibly, but I think she must be wise to him now." Randleton looked thoughtful. "I do not think it was the mother, though. I mean, a death from foxglove or laudanum would be quick and painless, would it not?"

"I should think so. An overdose of foxglove slows the heart until it stops, and too much laudanum simply puts one to sleep forever."

"Miss Carolyn said all the men died slowly, in agony. As soon as one died, the next got the symptoms." Randleton rubbed his back up against a lamppost, making William wince for the abuse to his jacket.

"Except for the captain." Sheridan resumed walking.

Randleton put his hands behind his back. "No, according to Miss Carolyn, for a brief time when he first came home, he showed signs of the family disease. Then he recovered."

"That would be when he stopped eating at home, then," said Sheridan. "Christ, what a dreadful coil."

"Lungren suspected poison in his brothers' deaths then." William scanned the empty street ahead. "That's why he tolerated the unspeakable food at the Boar's Head."

"Our killer has found a gun—that is much more to the

point." Sheridan leaned both his hands on William's cane, stopping in front of the Randleton town home.

Randleton fished a key out of his pocket. "Harder to explain away."

William glanced over his shoulder. "No one but us thinks that there is anything odd about Lungren's death, and what connection would people make to me?"

"That's another thing," Sheridan said. "There's no record of all these supposed sales of parts of the estate to Lord Carlton. I went to the assayer's office, and nothing has been recorded. In fact, just before Captain Lungren arrived home, the sisters paid taxes on the entire estate."

"He could be holding all the bills of sale until he has the entire thing, and then recording the sale." Randleton inserted the key in the knockerless door's lock.

"Why, though?" William asked.

Sheridan stepped over the threshold. "Mayhap it really is a worthless estate."

"I daresay the transactions wouldn't be legal if they took place during the true owners' illnesses. Not if the Lungren men weren't in their right minds. Weren't all these sales facilitated by the eldest Miss Lungren?" William followed the major into the quiet house.

"Without dates, I couldn't check the timing of the sales." Sheridan handed the cane back with a warning glare.

"There's something off about Miss Lungren's relationship to Lord Carlton." William wondered what she had meant by saying he wanted a slave to control. "She believes there is something less than honorable in his proposal to her."

"How is that?" Randleton shut and locked the front door.

William rocked back on his heels. "Just her reaction when I mentioned Lord Carlton's proposals."

"Miss Jocelyn is of the opinion that ladies shouldn't *have* to marry." Sheridan's disgust radiated in his voice.

"Seems to be a prevalent attitude nowadays, what with that Wollstonecraft woman spouting that sentiment," William said.

"All well and good if they believed in the free-love part of her philosophies too." Sheridan stumbled and crashed heavily against the wall. "Bloody hell."

"What the devil did you do to your leg?" asked Randleton, catching a vase that wobbled on a table near where Sheridan leaned against the wall.

"I told you, I stood too long."

William had started forward to assist the major but drew up short.

Randleton didn't seem the least bit threatened by Sheridan's menacing tone. He simply tossed Sheridan's free arm over his shoulder and pulled the man against him. "You must tell her you cannot do it standing."

"I didn't . . . we aren't . . . lovers. She doesn't want . . ." He put a hand to his head.

Since Sheridan's roar had reduced to a low moan, William stepped to his other side and pulled the major's other arm over his shoulders.

"You were once. You can't tell me that boy isn't yours," Randleton said. "He has your eyes."

What a trait to inherit: those pale, cold eyes. And with a sinking feeling, William realized Sheridan wasn't denying the child's parentage.

"Doesn' want me around." Sheridan was starting to slur his words. "Other than to pretend an 'gagement."

"That doesn't make sense," said William.

Sheridan turned and pierced him with his cold gaze, although his focus seemed a little unsteady. "Since when has what a woman wanted made sense?"

The two of them steered Sheridan toward the drawing room. Randleton braced Major Sheridan against him and reached out to open the door.

"She doesn't want me like she used . . . to."

Sheridan acted as if he was three sheets to the wind. Had he been drinking before they arrived? Surely a man his size couldn't be taken down by a mere flask of whiskey.

"'Course, only half the man I was." Sheridan swung his head toward Randleton. "Christ, tha' was strong drink."

"You didn't have to drink it all. Besides, it had laudanum in it."

William jerked. Then Sheridan's sudden dead weight required every ounce of his strength to hold. Why would Randleton have given the major whiskey tainted with laudanum? Why would he even *have* whiskey laced with laudanum?

Meg woke early to the sounds of furniture being moved in the room next to hers. Were the maids cleaning? She put her pillow over her head. Did they have to make so much noise?

It was no good. She was awake now, and the fear of what new story on Diana's body might show up in the paper urged her out of bed. Meg resisted the temptation to find out what was going on. She was in *en deshabille,* and *ladies* didn't go about in their nightwear. Instead, she yanked on the bellpull and waited for her new maid.

"What is all the noise?" Meg asked Molly.

"The mistress is moving in the bedroom next to yours. I gather we are expecting houseguests."

"Really? Do you know who?"

"Two gentlemen." Molly sniffed.

Meg supposed she was committing another error by talking to her maid as she helped her into her round gown. Or maybe the sniff was disapproval of Felicity's actions. Now, that was a novel thought.

"Is that a bad thing?"

"I'm sure I wouldn't know, miss," said Molly. "Even if I did think so, it wouldn't be my place to say."

Interesting. Meg moved toward the door.

"Miss, your gloves."

Meg would never remember she was to wear gloves everywhere. "Thank you, Molly."

She skipped down the three flights of stairs. Two gentlemen moving in? Surely it had to be something to do with last night's late-night visit by Major Sheridan, Mr. Bedford, and Lieutenant Randleton. Which two?

She reached for the breakfast room door, only to have a footman open the door before she reached the handle. Meg winced. Wait for the servants to do their job, she reminded herself. She entered the room, sedately preoccupied with which of the two men would be moving in and trying to decide if she was best served by pursuing only one of them.

Diana's likeness stared back at her from the paper. Meg gasped and took a step back.

Sir Edmund Greyston lowered the paper and stared at her. Felicity gave her a glance. Lady Greyston gave her a pursed-lipped shake of her head. Probably she had noticed Sir Edmund's pointed attention to Meg's properly—this time—covered chest.

Did Felicity recognize the picture of her niece? It was an uncanny resemblance.

"Now that we're all here, I have some news," Felicity said. "Sit down, Diana."

If Felicity knew, would she make her sit? Yes, because Meg wouldn't have a chance of running away if she was sitting. Still, what choice did she have but to pretend nothing was amiss? She moved toward a chair, her legs shaking.

Felicity pushed back her plate and then dismissed the footman, who removed it. She folded her hands on the table. Sir Edmund Greyston closed the paper and set it beside his plate, where Diana's likeness stared back at Meg, reminding her the world was closing in.

"I have invited Major Sheridan and his friend Mr. Bedford to move in with us here."

"You have done *what?*" Lady Greyston stood, her forgotten napkin falling to the floor. "What are you thinking?"

"I admit it is unconventional, and I never should have considered allowing them to stay here, were it not for the fact that you two are still here." Felicity smiled.

Lady Greyston gaped like a fish at a loss for water.

They hadn't figured out that Meg wasn't Diana?

"Why would you do such a thing?" asked Sir Edmund. "Just because you and Major Sheridan have an understanding doesn't mean he should be living here."

"We shan't want it known, and it has nothing to do with our arrangement." Felicity pushed back from the table. "I'm not at liberty to say why they are moving in, as of yet. But suffice it to say that when the truth is made known, I'm sure you will understand my decision."

Lady Greyston managed to get her mouth closed. "Have you thought of the repercussions to your niece? How will she secure a respectable offer if it is known she is residing with two unrelated bachelors in the house?"

"That is why it wouldn't be a good idea to bandy the information about."

Charles bounded into the room. He bounced over to his mother and hugged her. "Phys is here. Major Sheridan says he will live here."

"Only in the stable. Not in the house."

Charles leaned back from his mother with a startled expression. "You're putting Major Sheridan in the stables?"

Felicity rubbed her forehead. "No, Phys will stay in the stables."

"Oh, are they moving in because someone tried to kill Mr. Bedford?"

Felicity winced.

"My God, Bedford is the name of the chap your major fought a duel with," Sir Edmund contributed. "Slapped him with his glove in Watier's. Felicity, this will not do. You cannot have two men who are at each other's throats in the house."

"You can always leave if you don't like the way I run my household." Felicity moved toward the door with Charles's hand gripped in hers.

Lady Greyston dropped the pretense of being an ally of Diana's the minute Felicity left the room. Instead, she turned to Meg and, with bitterness in her voice, said, "What do you have to do with this?"

Meg almost would rather claim the connection to the missing girl's picture in the *Morning Post.* "Nothing."

Lady Greyston gave her a skeptical look.

Meg opened her eyes wide and pasted as much innocence as she could pretend on her face and said, "Will this damage my chances for a respectable marriage?"

Lady Greyston flattened her lips. "Not if I can help it. I see you are dressed demurely today. Very good choice, Miss Fielding. You look quite the lady."

To which Sir Edmund harrumphed and raised the newspaper again.

Of course, having Lady Greyston as an ally might be worse than having her as an enemy.

FOURTEEN

In the passageway outside the breakfast room, alone with her son, Felicity bent down to be on the same level with him. "Charles, were did you get the notion that someone tried to kill Mr. Bedford?"

"He said so, last night."

"How many times have I told you not to eavesdrop?"

"He was in the hall, Mama. Before you and Major Sheridan came out of the study. I wasn't trying to hear then, but I did. Major Sheridan had to tie his cravat, but doesn't he have a man to do that?"

Felicity felt her cheeks burn with mortification. "Nevertheless, you should not have listened. What were you doing out of bed at that hour, anyway?"

"I had to visit the garden," Charles whispered with his own affronted dignity.

"You were spying, Charles. You mustn't. Do you know what the government does to spies?"

Charles shook his head.

"In the army we just hang them. Don't usually bother with a trial," said Tony from behind her. "I've had to string up a few myself."

Instead of being deterred, her inquisitive son was enthralled. "Really? How many?"

Tony made a sound close to a choking noise.

Felicity couldn't tell if he was muffling a laugh or had got caught by surprise. She gave her wide-eyed son a swat on the rear. "Go get your breakfast."

"He's hanged spies, Mama," Charles said eagerly. "I want—"

"I don't want to know about it, and *you don't need* to know about it."

Charles stuffed his hands in his pockets and slunk into the breakfast room, his expression mulish.

"He's going to ask you about it. I don't want you making war into something glorious to him."

"Trust me, it wasn't glorious." Tony held out his hand to help her rise to her feet. "Are you ready for us?"

"Is Mr. Bedford here, too?"

Tony didn't let go of her hand. "He's outside. Randy is holding Phys for me. Bedford wouldn't take the leash. I thought I'd go ahead and see Phys settled in the stables after his morning walk. Then we are off to survey the damage at Bedford's place."

He stroked his thumb across the back of her hand and sent shivers down her spine.

"What do you expect to find there?"

"The bullet, and he'll need to pack his clothes, fetch his valet. If you are ready, we'll bring our things back with us." Tony looked over her head at the empty passageway; then he turned around and scanned behind him. Reaching out, he twisted the knob to her study and pulled her inside.

Felicity started to protest when her words were cut off by his kiss as the door clicked shut behind her.

"He is taking an eternity."

Randleton pulled out his watch. "It's only been six minutes."

"I should check on him, then."

"Only if you intend to remind him to lie down."

"He can't be doing *that,* this early in the morning." With his handkerchief William dusted off a stair and sank down onto it. Phys, of course, regarded that as an invitation to stick his big, wet nose in William's face.

"Perhaps we should go on to your place," suggested Randleton.

"Not with the monstrosity. My landlady would have a fit." William shoved the wolfhound's head away before the dog decided to lick his face.

"Oh, right." Randleton stared up the street.

William thought he might as well mention the events of last night. "I thought you were trying to kill him, giving him that laudanum."

Randleton jerked his gaze to William. "He never complains. Knew he must have been in a lot of pain."

"So you decided to overdose him."

"I thought he had a better tolerance for laudanum. The physicians poured it down his throat with a funnel at first. Must have weaned himself off it before coming home."

"Why do you carry around a flask with whiskey and laudanum?"

Randleton bent over—although he didn't actually have to bend down—and scratched Phys behind the ears.

William gave up on receiving an answer.

"You are not the only one who gets nightmares."

Felicity pushed him away.

His bad leg made Tony falter, and he had to let her go. Mindful of his thigh's overuse and cramping of the night before, he backed up to lean against her desk.

"You cannot continue dragging me around and kissing me everywhere."

Tony folded his arms across his chest. "I don't believe I've kissed you everywhere yet."

She gave him a scowl and moved to the far side of the smallish room. She picked up a cut-glass decanter from a tray on a sideboard.

"Early for that, don't you think?"

Her hand wrapped around the neck of the decanter, she set it back on the tray without removing the stopper. "I wonder why it is necessary for both you and Mr. Bedford to move in. Are you also in danger of being murdered? I mean, if he is in danger for owning the deed to the Lungren estate, then what danger are you in?"

"The danger that Bedford might usurp my position with you as your 'pretend' fiancé."

She grimaced, let loose of the decanter, and walked over to a window. "I hardly think that makes it necessary for you to move in with me."

"I will not let that bounder reside here unless I am here, too. I have no room to house him and Randy cannot in good conscience extend his brother's hospitality. And I very much doubt Bedford has the blunt to move into a hotel."

"It's only a pretense. I don't want to marry you." Felicity fingered the curtains and seemed entirely too pensive. Clearly, not only did she not want to marry him, she didn't want him here, didn't want him in her home. She might succumb to his seduction, but not willingly, not with enthusiasm, not the way she had before.

But they'd changed. He'd changed. He was much less of a man than he'd been when he left to serve in the military. What if she wanted Bedford to usurp his place? What if she thought she would be happier with the fashionable little toad? He reached down and rubbed his thigh.

She seemed to be noticing the motion of his hand.

He stopped.

"By all means, sit if you need to. Do not stand on ceremony with me."

Instead, he moved to the sideboard and poured himself a drink from the decanter she'd just held. A stiff drink might cure the dull ache in his head resulting from the deep sleep of the previous night. It also would give a reason to feel this burn under his breastbone.

He waited for her to tell him she'd reconsidered, that it wouldn't do for him to move in—waited with a patience born of spending months in hospital, knowing that any day the surgeons could determine that the infection had turned putrid, and no matter his protestation, the leg would have to come off.

"I suppose I should have voiced these concerns last night."

Tony didn't respond. What could he say? Last night he might have attempted to talk her out of her concerns, but now, if her mind was made up, there was little he could do. He told himself it was time to accept that whatever they had possessed before was gone. Gone like the strength in his leg, and to try to make it what it was before was pointless. The best he could do was salvage some goodwill, some friendship, so that he didn't lose his newfound son.

"I've put you on the second floor in my room."

Hope, that stubborn emotion—and more than hope, anticipation—resurged in his heart, and Tony nearly dropped his glass as he took a half-step toward her.

Felicity turned around to face him. "Mr. Bedford shall be in the adjoining room. I shall move up a flight and take the room between Diana's and the nursery."

His thoughts, hopes, and desires curled into dark-gray, wispy ashes.

Felicity's forehead crinkled, and she tilted her head sideways in inquiry.

"I will take it you would rather not share your room?" Tony raised the glass to his lips and swallowed a mouthful of brandy.

She ignored his sarcasm and said, "There will never be a reason for you or Mr. Bedford to be on the third floor. If you would convey that to him, I should appreciate it."

"Your servant." He bowed. "I should get back to them. We have much to do today."

Felicity looked perplexed as he reached for the doorknob. Well, she needn't worry. He understood all too well. He was only sorry it had taken him so long.

* * *

Felicity stared at the door after Tony closed it, wondering what had just happened. For a minute there had been a flicker of warmth, and then his expression turned frigid, unfathomable. She didn't know him anymore. He wasn't the young man who'd left her to fight in the war. She didn't know who he was anymore.

She shook her head and gathered her list of dinner party guests and the acceptances that had come in response to her invitations. Diana could help her with writing out place cards. She went to the breakfast room, where they could both use the table to write on.

Her niece was bent over the newspaper, chewing her thumb, and her forehead crinkled with concentration.

"Still in here, I see." Felicity closed the door. "Very good. I want you to help me with these place cards."

Diana jerked and hastily folded the newspaper backward and shoved it onto a chair at her side. Her furtiveness almost suggested guilt. Felicity looked at her niece. It wasn't as if she had caught her with a Minerva Press book, not that Felicity would have been bothered if Diana was reading one of the melodramatic romances. Did Diana believe she shouldn't be reading the newspaper?

"First, we shall see who has accepted to determine the order of precedence."

"Precedence?" Diana blinked her dark eyes at Felicity.

Lord, obviously the girl didn't know anything about ton parties. "Yes, everyone is seated by rank. We cannot slight anyone or give unintentional offense. Especially not this early in the season."

"Oh."

Felicity set the list of people she'd sent invitations to between them and divided the replies into two stacks. "Please go through these and cross out anyone who sent their regrets."

By the time Felicity was through her stack, Diana had only done about a fourth of hers. Felicity sighed, took another stack, and began all over again. At this rate Mr. Bedford and Tony would be moved in and—"Fiddlesticks!"

Diana looked at her.

Felicity rubbed her forehead. "I shall have to include Mr. Bedford, Lieutenant Randleton, and Major Sheridan."

"Is that a problem?"

"I shall have too many men."

"Oh." Diana stared at her, waiting until Felicity came up with a solution to this new dilemma.

Felicity supposed she was glad her niece had such great faith in her. She didn't know where she would find three women on such short notice. Especially three women who wouldn't expect their male family members to be invited also. She didn't have that much room available at the dining room table. She needed three widows or a widow with two daughters. "How many sisters did Captain Lungren have?"

Diana stared at her blankly a moment, then went back to her invitations with a shrug. "This woman says her husband is not yet in town, and asks if another gentleman might accompany her in his stead."

"Who?"

"A Mrs. Keeting. Oh!" Diana dropped the invitation and put her both her hands over her mouth.

Actually, Felicity had invited the woman's husband, George Keeting, since he was the one Felicity really knew from her first season. She reached over and plucked the response off the table. "The Earl of Wedmont," she read.

Diana's dark eyes were swimming in unshed tears. She pushed back from the table. "I'm sorry. I feel ill."

Really, this niece of hers could be awfully missish. "Do you know the earl?" asked Felicity. How would Diana know the earl?

Diana shook her head.

The previous Earl of Wedmont was a notorious rakehell. Perhaps Diana knew something of the father's reputation, even though he'd been dead for many years. "I assure you the present earl is nothing like his father."

"Oh," said Diana, which seemed to be her word of the day.

Perhaps Diana didn't want to deal with these social niceties. In which case, she would make an awkward hostess when she was on her own, or she would need a social secretary to take care of such matters. But Felicity's duty was to see her niece married, not worry about her social graces afterward. "I'll finish this. Why don't you go lie down for a bit, and have Molly fetch you a cold compress."

Diana nodded and fled the room as if the hounds of hell were after her. Felicity worked on the guest list for a while and then reached over and retrieved the newspaper. She refolded it correctly and looked at the illustrated likeness on the front page. Was this the story that Diana had been absorbed in when Felicity entered the room?

Curious, and with no great enthusiasm for the social niceties herself, Felicity read the article about the young girl's body that had been pulled from the river the day Diana arrived. What a shame no one knew who she was. Probably a soiled dove fallen on hard times. Felicity started to set the paper aside, but words from the accompanying article leaped off the page.

The writer declared otherwise.

The girl was an innocent, probably of good family. She'd been wearing an expensive lawn nightrail, no doubt like the one Diana had been wearing the other night, and had been most likely dead of natural causes before her body was tossed in the water. How odd. Why would anyone choose to dispose of an innocent young girl's body in such a manner?

"Got it!" exclaimed Bedford as he backed out from under his bed, holding a ball of lead between his thumb and index finger.

"Now we need to see if we can find the bullet Lungren took." Tony watched Bedford swipe dust from his sleeve with his arm.

Randy looked thoughtful as he placed the pierced pillow

back on the bed. "Been thinking. Perhaps Bedford here should register the estate in his name."

Bedford shook his head. "Not a good thought."

Tony looked at Randy. "Why?"

"Changes the whole picture, doesn't it?" Randy moved over to sit on the room's single chair. "If the estate is what the killer is after, then Bedford's legal and duly registered ownership would keep him out of danger."

"How so?" Bedford plunked down on the bed.

"Well, your untimely demise would mean that the estate transfers to your heirs, not back to the Lungrens."

"You think if he dies without registering the deed, the Lungren sisters could deny that he was the rightful owner. Would Rosalie be the heir if Lungren died intestate?" Tony shifted so that he was more sitting on the dressing table than not.

"I don't know, what about his mother?" Randy asked.

"Or Lord Carlton could eventually convince the sisters that they should turn over the deed to him," Tony added.

"This is a bad idea. The worst." Bedford folded his arms across his chest.

"Not so. It would thwart the killer. That is, if the estate is the motivation for murder," Randy argued.

"So would my just handing over the damn thing."

"How will we ever know who the killer is, if we can't induce them to take another shot at you?" asked Tony.

"Deuce take it, I wish you wouldn't discuss my being sent aloft with so little feeling. I should rather like to cock up my toes in a natural manner."

"Daresay you could name one or the other us in a will, so if we fail to catch the killer before he does you in, we shall be highly inspired to bring him down."

"Now, there is a comforting thought," said Tony.

Bedford gave him a nasty look, which was truly unwarranted because this was Randy's idea.

"There is, unfortunately, the matter of the quiteclaim deed Bedford signed. Shouldn't matter if he registers it or not if anyone gets their hands on that," Tony pointed out. "Let me see that bullet."

Bedford handed over the lead ball.

"Are we off to the Lungrens', then?" asked Randy.

"I, for one, should prefer to get settled at Mrs. Merriwether's first." Bedford sat on the edge of his bed.

Tony rolled the slightly flattened ball in his fingers. Bedford had pried it loose from the floorboard with a penknife. How could they know if this bullet was fired from the same gun that was used to kill Lungren?

The mold markings were still apparent on the ball's circumference. So it wasn't a bullet manufactured by dropping molten lead from a tower into a tub of water, but a poured bullet. As Tony studied it, he saw a slight indentation on one side. Was it just a random imperfection or one made exclusively by the mold that this one came from? "Where should we keep this? We don't want to lose it."

"I don't know what can be told by the bullet." Bedford handed him an empty snuffbox.

"For one thing"—Tony brushed out the stray bits of snuff left in the enameled box, and deposited the bullet inside—"that the bullet is molded and that there may be an imperfection in the mold." He turned it so that the indentation was up, and handed it to Randy.

Randy studied the bullet.

"Bedford is right. We should get settled into Mrs. Merri—Felicity's—before we do anything else." He tried, he really tried, to use her married name.

"But—" started Randy.

"Won't we need an excuse to visit the sisters again, beyond that we want to locate the bullet? I mean, unless we plan to tell them that we know their brother was murdered."

"You must be worried about what they will say now that they have learned you own the estate," said Randy.

Tony looked at his lieutenant. Randy seemed to be almost snappish. "What is it?"

"I plan to sell my commission."

Tony was surprised but not surprised. He supposed Randy had been afraid to tell him, his commanding officer for the past few years, but then now that Bonaparte was defeated once and for all, many of his officers were bound to resign or sell their commissions. Not everyone wanted an assignment in India or Canada. Tony wasn't sure that he did anymore. "Considering politics, are you?"

Randy blinked. "Perhaps. I have a small estate from an aunt. Enough land that I might eventually run for a seat in the House of Commons. I . . . I—my brother has suggested I do some secretarial work for him to get my feet wet."

Tony clapped him on the back. "You'll be good at politics. You already are."

Randy looked relieved.

"If I take the deed to the estate to Miss Lungren, I suppose that should be excuse enough." Bedford sounded about as enthusiastic as a duck in the desert.

"You're right, we need a better reason. Don't think he should turn it over yet. What do you think, Tony?"

"We need to regroup and ponder our strategy. I shall meet you two at Felicity's in an hour."

Of course, Sheridan wasn't there when William and Randleton showed up an hour and a half later with William's bags and boxes. It didn't seem to matter, as Felicity urged them into the atrocious green drawing room.

"How many sisters did Captain Lungren have?" she asked as soon as they had settled in the room.

"Three," answered Randleton.

"Perfect. Do you think you could persuade them to attend my dinner party the night after next? I wanted to launch my niece in society with a dinner. Since I assume the three of you will attend, I am in desperate need of three ladies to balance the table. You will attend, Lieutenant Randleton, won't you?"

"Of course. As for the Misses Lungren, I am sure—" started Randleton.

"They cannot attend without clothes," blurted out William.

Randleton stared at him as if he'd sprouted horns.

The door opened, and the butler ushered Major Sheridan into the room.

Mrs. Merriwether turned to him and said, "I was just inquiring after the possibility of the Lungren sisters attending my dinner party."

"That's a capital idea."

Randleton continued to stare at William.

Well, now that he'd started, he might as well finish. "You see, they are in some distress since their brother's passing, and their dresses are sadly threadbare." Now Sheridan's stare was added to Randleton's. "Miss Lungren told me as much."

Felicity rubbed her forehead. "It seemed such a convenient solution."

Sheridan turned to her. "What have you done with all your mourning clothes, ma'am?"

"Of course." Felicity snapped her fingers, her eyes never leaving Major Sheridan's. "I am just out of full mourning, with a clothespress full of blacks. I had no idea what I was going to do to get rid of them, since my dresser really doesn't want a heap of mourning wear. Could I impose upon you gentlemen to deliver them?"

"It appears we have an excuse to visit the Lungren sisters after all," said Tony.

"If you should just give me a few moments, I shall write out their invitations." Felicity pulled the bell rope. "And my maid will bundle up the clothes. You don't think it will insult them, will it?"

"Why should it?" asked Randleton. "You have no need of full mourning now."

"Might give offense if they don't fit," said Bedford.

Randleton cleared his throat. "Though Mrs. Merriwether is slender, the Lungren sisters are quite short. They'll probably have to raise the hems a bit."

Which was probably the most diplomatic way of saying that Mrs. Merriwether was larger than the Lungren sisters. Not that there was a thing wrong with her figure.

"Diana has some day dresses she's outgrown. I'll send those along, too. Besides, since the two of us are having new wardrobes done up, I'm sure we'll need the room in our presses."

William wondered if any of the day dresses that Felicity was expropriating from Diana's wardrobe resembled the one that her niece was nearly falling out of the other day. If so, he bit back disappointment. Although, if he could catch a glimpse of her in a delightfully transparent nightrail, he supposed he could stand the loss. No doubt anything that fit Miss Fielding now would be much too large through the bodice for the Misses Lungren.

And while he might enjoy seeing the charms of Miss Fielding, he really needed to concentrate on landing an heiress. Still . . . how much was Miss Fielding worth, anyway?

FIFTEEN

Meg couldn't believe she might be about to meet her half brother. The present Earl of Wedmont would have to be her brother. She didn't even know if she had other siblings. She hadn't even considered that she had family. Of course, she couldn't admit that he was her brother, and even if he knew about her, he would not be likely to claim her. Her hands shook as she pulled out Diana's dresses from her clothespress.

She hated to lose a one. They were better than anything Meg had ever owned, but they didn't fit right. Besides, Felicity had arranged for an entirely new wardrobe. The mantua maker was even now making them up for her. It was only because Meg had spent so much of her life scraping and scrimping and hoarding everything she owned that this propensity to discard perfectly good items seemed so very wasteful.

With the last of Diana's dresses draped over her arm, Meg made her way to the bottom of the stairs. On the second floor she encountered Mr. Bedford carrying in boxes. She peeked into his room and saw two trunks, several bandboxes, and a valise or two, not to mention several packing boxes.

"You have quite a lot of baggage." Diana hadn't had this much, and she had been moving permanently.

Mr. Bedford went red. "Yes, well, I expect I shan't be moving back to those rooms."

"Oh." Meg did her best to play an innocent. "I should

imagine it was frightening to be shot at. I don't think I would wish to return to such a place, either."

Mr. Bedford gave her a plaguey look, and Meg wondered if she'd overdone the wide-eyed innocence.

"Yes, well, that is not exactly why I shan't retu—I say, are those some of the dresses for the Lungren ladies?"

Meg extended her draped arm. "Are you to take them?"

"Well, yes, all of us. Your maid was to pack them but perhaps—"

Another false step. "I didn't think to call her. I haven't quite got used to having my own lady's maid." Meg looked at the stacks of boxes littering Mr. Bedford's room. She sauntered into the bedroom and laid the dresses across the bed. "We ought to just use one of your packing boxes if you've done with it."

Mr. Bedford turned a darker shade of red.

"If you tell me which one to unpack, I shall."

"Miss Fielding, I hardly think it appropriate that you barge into my bedroom. If I am not allowed even to set foot on the third floor, you should not be in here."

Meg couldn't resist. "You don't want me in your bedroom?" She batted her eyelashes. "No one could misconstrue events, since there are clothes all over your bed and the door is open."

Mr. Bedford stared at her, gape-mouthed.

All right, enough playing, Meg told herself firmly. This was obviously the wrong way to go about getting a husband. It had failed when she wasn't respectable, and didn't look like a ploy that was winning her the right kind of favors this time around. She backed out of the room. "I suppose you are right, though. I am so used to being in a school full of females that I quite forget about such things. I mean, it could hardly matter if one enters another's bedroom when there are only girls on the premises. We never worried about catching someone in a state of indecency, being all girls."

"There weren't any men about at all?" said Mr. Bedford in an unnaturally high voice.

Meg sighed forlornly and shook her head. "None at all." Which was entirely too mean of her. With a little wave she tripped down the stairs to the rose drawing room.

Dinner invitations and dresses in hand, the three men had made their way to the Lungren estate. When they arrived, the eldest Miss Lungren was gone to the village and Randy had settled right into a comfortable coze with the youngest, Miss Carolyn. Sheridan had done his best to be agreeable to Miss Jocelyn, leaving William the odd man out.

Which was fine with him. Well, other than that he'd have to make pretty with Miss Lungren when she returned. And judging by Miss Jocelyn's stunned reaction to his presence, the sisters knew he held the title to their estate. So any delay in meeting the inevitable vitriol filled him with relief.

He'd made an excuse to leave the drawing room and stole away to the library. His mission, since he was so conversant with the servants, was to locate the wing chair Lungren had been sitting in when shot to death. William didn't think it bore mentioning that the one servant he had known well was now employed at Mrs. Merriwether's.

William figured he might as well start with the library, where he knew Lungren had spent most of his time at home. The room was damp and dark. No fire burned in the fireplace, and the room had taken on the musty smell of a room no longer used. The stained chair sat in exactly the same place it always had.

William shuddered in distaste. They ought to have rid themselves of the macabre reminder. Since they hadn't, he supposed Sheridan and Randleton would expect him to retrieve the bullet. No doubt they would ride him mercilessly if he failed to make the attempt.

He promised himself that he might try and steal a kiss from Miss Fielding if he succeeded. A fellow needed all sorts of encouragement to do this sort of gruesome task, and Miss Fielding seemed a forward little baggage. Not at all like her reserved aunt. Although to think on it, Mrs. Merriwether couldn't be all that circumspect if she'd borne the major's child. William realized he was stalling.

He circled around to the back of the wing chair to examine it for a bullet hole. Finding none, he returned to the front, where, with a shudder of distaste, he prodded around in the padding. He tried not to mind the dried gore and reminded himself the blood had belonged to his friend.

It still was blood. And it made the back of his throat feel odd. All of his swallowing did nothing to rid him of the sensation.

After his tentative prodding produced nothing, he feared his extended absence would draw unwanted attention. So he put his fingers in the hole and ripped open the chair back.

The elusive bullet popped free and pinged on the floor, then promptly rolled under the other wing chair. William grimaced and bent down to kneel. Seeing that the ball would be easier to reach from the back side of the chair, he crawled on all fours toward the cold fireplace. He was just reaching under the chair, his face nearly to the floor, when the French door leading to the garden swung open.

Rosalyn fell through the door, and for the barest second William was on eye level with the wild-eyed, tear-streaked face of the eldest Miss Lungren. Her hair was falling down, and a bit of leaf was caught in it. With a sob she crawled through the door and hastily turned around and fastened the catch. As she stood, he could see the rip in her gown.

Her breath was coming in big, rough gulps, and she stared out the windowpanes for a long moment. She clenched her hands into fists, and just as William told himself he needed to make his presence known, she gave a howl of pure animal rage.

She swiveled, and much to his horror William felt himself cowering behind the chair, hoping she didn't see him.

Rosalyn moved to the desk and began yanking out drawers, one of them so hard the drawer and its contents fell to the floor. "Where the bloody hell is that damn gun?"

Another drawer came whizzing out. "Jocelyn!" Rosalyn spun around and put her hands on her hips, surveying the room. "Jocelyn, what have you done with the gun?"

William swallowed hard and decided he was best served staying hidden. He wanted nothing to do with Rosalyn and a gun, although at this moment he was rather glad she seemed to have misplaced it.

Rosalyn stamped her foot and yelled again, "Jocelyn!"

William tried to shrink farther into the space behind the chair, and feared she'd stumble upon him any second.

Felicity had just finished all the place cards and the seating arrangement when her butler entered the breakfast room and announced a visitor. He handed her a silver salver with a calling card, the edge turned down. Felicity picked it up and studied the name. Lord Algany. She hadn't thought he'd even noticed she was alive during her first season. Not that she had strong feelings one way or another about him.

As she remembered, he was an extremely attractive albeit mature bachelor, with a black reputation hovering over his head. As a debutante she had been warned to steer clear of him, because he was known to pluck the willing flower from the pick of the crop and fulfill her wildest fantasies. The ruined miss was usually scurried into a less than stellar marriage to someone else, and the whole thing kept as silent as could be among the gossiping ton.

Felicity suspected that far too many of the misses were all too willing to be seduced by such an attractive nobleman, sure that he would behave differently with them, that he would do the honorable thing: fall in love and offer marriage. He had never succumbed to that trap. Felicity supposed she might have had her head turned a bit if he had offered the slightest amount of attention. And she certainly couldn't sit in judgment of anyone, given her fiasco of a first season.

She inquired of her butler whether her parents and niece were installed in the rose drawing room. He replied that they were. So Felicity ordered a tea tray, and Lord Algany shown in, while she went upstairs to tidy up.

When she entered the rose drawing room a quarter hour later, Lord Algany stood and crossed the room. He took both her hands in his and with great sincerity, and a heartfelt look, said, "My dear Mrs. Merriwether, you must accept my condolences on your loss. I was so very sorry to hear about your husband's passing."

She nodded. "I appreciate your sympathy." She tried not to mind that it was eight months after the fact.

He held her hands and led her to the sofa as if she might break. "You must be bearing up quite well, because you look lovely."

He didn't wait for her to acknowledge his compliment as he turned and said, "Your parents have just introduced me to your niece. I understand she is to be presented this season."

"Yes, and you shall have to excuse us; Miss Fielding has a fitting she must see to." Lady Greyston stood with Diana's hand in hers. "I daresay you know how much preparation goes into preparing a gel for her first season." Lady Greyston practically yanked Diana to the doorway.

Felicity blinked at her mother. Was she holding Diana's hand? Good grief, her mother must think Algany the worst of the worst if she had leaped to Diana's defense. Of course, that didn't stop her mother from leaving her own daughter alone with the rake, except for her father, taking his mid-morning nap behind the newspaper on the far side of the room.

"Why, I shall feel greatly deprived to lose your company, Lady Greyston, and yours, Miss Fielding. I trust that I shall have ample opportunities during the season to enjoy your conversation." He bowed politely. "I shall simply have to console myself by reacquainting myself with Mrs. Merriwether."

After they left the room, he gave Felicity a smile and a small nod. "Hardly a dismal prospect, and a most agreeable way to spend a morning catching up with you."

She nodded in reply, wanting to say that he hadn't even noticed her during her first season. As he brought her up to date on all the gossip, Felicity paid little attention, wondering if the carefully arranged hair swooping across Lord Algany's brow was to hide wrinkles marking his age. Although he wasn't old, perhaps ten years older than she— younger than Layton had been—she wanted to tell him the style didn't suit him. It made him look as if he were trying to appear boyish.

He had switched to telling her of a lawn tennis match he'd had with a gentleman whose name escaped Felicity.

"You must come and join the spectators. I should enjoy that very much."

Felicity felt very much as if she were being invited to watch a gladiatorial combat in which Lord Algany was the star. To what purpose? she wondered.

"It is a shame that Major Sheridan shall likely never walk normally, isn't it? So many of our men were wounded or lost at Waterloo. Still, I suppose we should be grateful that he returned in one piece. You were once engaged to him, were you not?"

"A long time ago." How had they jumped to discussing Tony? She was simply going to have to pay more attention to the conversation, but since she was barely contributing, she supposed she was at the whim of Lord Algany's reflections.

"The company is a bit thin these days, what with so many of our own deserting us for Vienna and Brussels this year."

"Oh, but the season hasn't really started yet," said Felicity. She hoped the company would be so thin that Diana would have a hard time bringing a gentleman up to scratch.

She hadn't realized how impatient she would be with all the social niceties and chitchat in which she would have to participate. She checked the mantel clock, thinking of the business affairs that awaited her attention. She surely didn't want to be forced to do this again next year.

"I'm afraid word is out. Your dinner party is the opening event of this year."

"It is?" She had planned just a small soirée, with a light supper to follow. Something where Diana could get a little social experience without risk of drowning in a sea of ineptitude.

"Yes, well, do not act surprised. Your chef's culinary skills are renowned. Though I do realize you probably didn't know I was in town, I hope I am not too late to be included." He touched her hand and smiled.

His teeth seemed smallish in his mouth, and tilted inward, although really he had very nice teeth, very white and quite straight—and how on earth was she going to avoid inviting him?

She had forgotten that Layton had hired one of the chefs from Watier's, the exclusive gambling club. And that was hardly the point. "I shall be uneven," she heard herself say.

"Then allow me to suggest the perfect solution. Lady Penelope Fitzwilliam is newly arrived in town with her parents, the Duke and Duchess of Worcester. She is a beautiful young lady, certain to be on all the best guest lists this season, but I am sure that they should receive an invitation from you with the greatest pleasure."

No doubt Lady Penelope would be on all the best guest lists. Even if she were a cow, to be the daughter of a duke would ensure her welcome everywhere. How could Felicity not invite a duke and duchess? "Are you quite certain they would attend?"

"I assure you, 'pon my word as a gentleman, they would not miss it for the world."

Felicity's skepticism must have shown on her face. She

may be the daughter of a baronet, but her husband had been a vulgar commoner, a man who had made his fortune in business. And Diana didn't have any kind of right, beyond her tenuous connection to Felicity, to join the ranks of the upper ten thousand.

But to make her debut in society at an intimate—well, not so intimate now—dinner party with not only a duke and duchess but several other members of the ruling class in attendance was bound to add cachet to her niece's season. Felicity couldn't afford to refuse.

Felicity looked at Lord Algany and realized he'd played his trump card. She sincerely hoped he had one to play with the duchess. Likely he did, or he wouldn't have risked coming here.

"Do you have their direction? I'll write out an invitation just now."

Algany smiled his ferret smile, and Felicity wondered what scheme of his she had just fallen into. What did Lord Algany have to gain from her?

The hallway door snapped open, and the middle sister, Jocelyn, swung through it. "Stop your infernal screeching, Ros. We have guests."

"We do?" Rosalyn's voice wavered quite in counterpoint to her anger before. "I cannot see anyone now."

"Oh, dear God, what happened?" Jocelyn exclaimed.

William thought that he should like to know, too.

Rosalyn leaned against the escritoire. "He . . . he came after me . . . in the woods."

"That bastard."

William would surely like to be let in on who the bastard was, and Miss Jocelyn . . . He didn't know if he would have remarked it—was he not eavesdropping, as it were, and not able to see her expression?—but her tone was remarkably mild given her words.

"Did he . . . ?" Jocelyn let the sentence dangle.

"No, I got away. Why won't he leave me alone?" wailed Rosalyn.

William peeked around the edge of the chair. The middle sister was rubbing the elder one's back, but she didn't seem to be concentrating terribly hard on her comforting effort.

Rosalyn's shoulders shook. "He told me I shouldn't have any choice now. We don't have a place to live if Bedford owns the house. The estate won't support us, anyway."

"There's another solution; I'm sure of it."

Rosalyn spun around angrily. William tucked his head back behind the chair. "What solution? Mayhap he is right. I should marry him. He asks why I protest when we have been intimate."

If the way Rosalyn spit out the word "intimate" was any indication of her feelings toward the matter, it did not paint a pretty picture of it.

"That was years ago."

"I know. I would have thought that he would have found someone else, but he swears his devotion and . . ." Rosalyn began to pace across the floor. "Where is the gun? I should just shoot him and then myself."

"No, that won't do, love. We can't have two suicides in the family."

What an odd statement. As if social standing and good family name mattered to someone contemplating murder and suicide.

"If the world were without men, we should be so much better served." Rosalyn began coughing.

William hoped it was because she choked on the words.

"All he has ever done is try to make me dependent upon him, make *us* dependent upon him."

"Well, we shall take care of that, shan't we?"

"How?" wailed Rosalyn. "I see no course open to us but for me to marry him."

Jocelyn patted Rosalyn on the shoulder. "I shall take care of everything. Not much longer and you won't have to worry about a thing."

"How?" repeated Rosalyn.

"You shall see," said Jocelyn, and she headed for the door. "I'll tell our guests you're indisposed. Oh, by the bye, they have brought us invitations to a dinner party. Some widow friend of the major's."

"We can't go; we haven't anything to wear. Oh, no! Look, I have another rip in my gown."

"Seems they've thought of that. Wonder how they knew."

Rosalyn laughed without mirth. "All they had to do was look at us."

"It seems this widow is out of first mourning and thought we could make use of her weeds."

To which Rosalyn began another coughing paroxysm. Miss Jocelyn left the room without sparing her sister another word.

William couldn't in good conscience stay hidden while Miss Lungren was so afflicted. He plucked the fatal ball off the floor and tucked it in his watch pocket. "I say, Miss Lungren, allow me to fetch you some water."

She spun around and then doubled over again. "How . . . how . . . long have you been there?" The effort to suppress her coughs was making tears run down her face.

"Too long, I'm afraid. But never fear, your secrets are safe with me." He found his handkerchief and handed it to her.

She promptly wadded it in her fist.

He reached out to pluck the bit of dried leaf from her hair.

She ducked away so fast, he was almost surprised she didn't hit her head on the wall.

"You have some leaves in your hair. I was going to take them out."

She stared back at him, looking unnaturally pale; her dark eyes almost like holes in her white face. "You—you lied to me. You told me you didn't have the deed to our estate."

"I didn't at the time. Major Sheridan had it to return to you."

William tried again, and this time she held still. He showed her the brown bit of dried foliage he removed. She was as skittish as a doe.

She began coughing again. "You . . . you haven't . . . returned it."

"I had every intention of doing so, but things have become complicated. Let me assure you, Miss Lungren, I am not holding it to deny you anything that rightfully should be yours." He plucked his handkerchief from her hand and dabbed at the tracks of tears on her face. "Are you all right?"

The question was absurd. She appeared to be anything but all right.

She raised a shaking hand to her forehead. "Oh, no! You heard *everything,"* she whispered.

"About you and Lord Carlton, you mean?"

She clapped a hand over her mouth as if to keep herself from crying out. With his hands on her shoulders he guided her to sit in the other wing chair. He really didn't want to hear more, but like most men he couldn't stand to see a woman in distress without feeling a strong urge to set things right. He knelt down in front of the chair.

"Miss Lungren, it does not sound as if you actually enjoyed participating in these intimacies."

She closed her eyes, and with her hand still over her mouth, she sobbed.

"Could it be that he forced himself on you?"

She shook her head, and two small tears fell from her lashes. She dropped her hand just enough to whisper, "No, I'm afraid, I allowed . . . I allowed . . . things to go . . . too . . . far."

"But did you try to stop at some point? Did you protest the—forgive me for speaking so plainly—completion of the act?"

"He said—he said . . ." She gave a shuddering sob. "He said I had tempted him too far. That it was my fault he couldn't stop." She put her hand to her forehead as big, fat tears welled out beneath her shut eyelids.

"Miss Lungren, he raped you."

She shook her head.

"I believe so. Else it would not cause you so much distress now." William pulled her ever so gently toward him. "We men are not such beasts that we can't stop when a woman is frightened or in pain."

"But I encouraged him to kiss me and . . . and . . . oh, it hurt. I felt like he was ripping me in two."

"Hush . . . I assure you, Miss Lungren, Rosalyn, it was not your fault. Why, you are just a tiny thing; how could you have fended him off?"

For the longest time he held her while she sobbed, and he had to remind her to make use of his handkerchief. What kind of a beast was Lord Carlton, anyway? Likely a murderous beast. And as big a coward as William was, even he wanted to find the man and beat him black and blue.

After a while she leaned back, away from him. "I suppose it is you I have to thank for the clothes and the invitation."

"The major and Mrs. Merriwether can share credit."

Rosalyn wiped at her eyes. "I thank you for your faith in me," she said through a watery smile. "But I should not have allowed myself to be alone with him."

"Maybe so, but that does not excuse his behavior."

"Please, you said I could rely on you to keep your own counsel on this."

He couldn't tell? What could he do but keep his promise, even though it shielded a criminal? But then, Lord Carlton might very well be brought up on murder charges, and then the punishment for his dastardly ruining of Miss Lungren might be considered included. William swallowed hard. "Of course, you may rely on me to keep this matter silent."

"What are you doing in here, anyway?"

William had glanced at the twin wing chairs and then, too late, averted his eyes.

Miss Lungren studied the bloodstained chair. "What were you looking for? The bullet that killed my brother?"

"Well . . ." William couldn't think of anything to say. He could feel his face growing warm. "Well, you see . . ." He still hadn't conjured up a reasonable explanation.

Rosalyn pierced him with her penetrating stare. "I think you should keep the estate. I am starting to think that Jonathon didn't kill himself. I think that perhaps . . . perhaps he was murdered."

SIXTEEN

"What is the matter?" Meg asked Felicity, who was rubbing her forehead and going back over the dinner guest list, Meg had hoped it was finished, because she hadn't the slightest idea how to help with it. She reckoned there was more danger in admitting her ignorance. Better to appear lazy than attempt to assist her aunt with the work and make a muddle of it.

"If we add any more guests, I shall have to ask my parents to stay in their rooms."

"Oh, would they do that?"

"Not likely." Felicity glanced up. "But if I explained it was because a duke and duchess planned to attend my little supper . . ."

"A duke and duchess?" echoed Meg lamely. How did one greet a duke and duchess? Prostrating herself on the floor was the idea that sprang to mind, but no, that wouldn't be right. That was for sultans. There were a million ways to fail at this society stuff.

"Surprised me, too. But it seems they want to attend along with Algany. I presume my mother has warned you to steer clear of him."

Meg sat down hard. "Am I to cut him?"

"Oh, no, absolutely not. But you should never allow yourself to be alone with him—well, not with any gentleman, but especially not with him. You don't want to be forced into a marriage with a husband who has to be bought."

Why not? If a husband could be bought, Meg wouldn't mind—not in the least. "A husband can be bought?"

"It happens all the time," said Felicity. "You'll bring in a comfortable dowry. There are enough men who would take you on that consideration alone, but I don't know that they'd make worthwhile husbands."

"I see," said Meg. She didn't really, but Felicity couldn't know that just the prospect of a respectable marriage, bought or otherwise, was so much better than the life she'd been destined for. Meg wouldn't care if her husband was a bounder or a drunkard. Truly, there were worse things.

"I'm going to have to hire musicians," muttered Felicity.

"Why?"

"Well, now we are at forty-two, which is almost a dozen more than I anticipated. I think nearly everyone I originally invited accepted my invitation, which I did not expect. With so big a dinner party, we shall have to have dancing upstairs in the ballroom afterward. People will expect it."

Meg froze. She supposed the kind of high-spirited jigs she'd done around army campfires wasn't the kind of dancing that the ton did in their ballrooms. What did they do? Waltzes and stately quadrilles, she'd heard the officer's wives mention after the celebrations for victorious battles. She had no idea how to dance like a lady.

She could kick up her heels and toss her skirts about with abandon, but oh, Lord, how would she get out of dancing for a whole season? "I . . . I don't think I can dance."

Felicity stared at her, her eyebrows raised as if such a statement from a young miss making her debut was unheard of. "Why ever not?"

Meg fished about in her empty brain for an explanation, an escape from her words. "My shoulder is quite sore."

Felicity's dark eyes narrowed as she waited for more details.

Meg rubbed her shoulders. "I strained it on the ship." Her heart pounded. She *had* strained it . . . dumping Diana's body over the rail.

Felicity waited.

"You know, I 'spect I did it pulling my trunks around."

"You were pulling your trunks around? You shouldn't have been doing that. I should speak to the captain of that ship."

"No, oh, no!" Meg swallowed hard. "He probably would have sent a man if I asked for help, but he . . ." She searched desperately for a reason why a girl raised with all the privileges of wealth, as Diana had, wouldn't have, without a second thought, asked for help with her trunks. "He scared me."

Well, that much was the truth, anyway. Well, not exactly scared her, but worried her—*and rightfully so,* thought Meg, with the memory of her final night on the ship making her shudder.

Felicity patted her hand. "It may be better by then. Besides, you're not to dance the waltz until you're approved for Almack's, anyway. So you shan't need to raise your arm for any of the other dances, I shouldn't think."

"Yes, Aunt."

Oh, Lord, how was she going to pretend to dance when she hadn't the slightest idea how?

"Well, what were you doing?" Randy asked Bedford as they rode back to town.

Bedford had just given them his account of what had happened when he was missing from the Lungren drawing room. But his account seemed to have large gaps in it.

"I was crawling on the floor to get this." Bedford dug in his pocket and held out a chunk of lead.

Tony pulled up his horse and held out his hand. Bedford deposited the bullet in his hands. The once-round ball was mangled and deformed. Tony didn't know if it he could even compare it to the one fired at Bedford.

"So Miss Lungren didn't see you right away?" questioned Randy.

"I hid. She was screaming for the gun. I didn't think it was the best moment to pop up and announce myself."

Tony tried to suppress the grin that tugged at the corners of his lips, without much success. Poor Bedford seemed to get caught in the worst of situations, and his cowering became more a virtue than not—except that he had an honest streak that forced him to acknowledge his cowardice later.

"Then she could be the murderer." Randy turned his horse so that the three of them could circle tightly together, not that anyone could overhear their conversation on the road back to London.

"I hardly think she would admit that she thought her brother had been murdered if she was the murderess," objected Bedford.

"Then why was she calling for the gun?" asked Randy.

"Wouldn't she know where it was if she had fired it at Bedford last night?" Tony pocketed the bullet. The light was fading, and he hoped to examine it with the other bullet by its side. If nothing else, he could compare the weights of the two to determine if they were once of the identical size, a product of the same mold.

"Dash it all, I can't speak of it, but she was in quite a state when she came in—and I think we should focus our attentions on Lord Carlton. He is a lily-livered cad in more than one way."

"You can't speak of what?" asked Randy.

"If I could tell you, I would, but I pledged my silence on the subject."

"Why even mention it, if you can't discuss it?" Randy shook his head.

"Why, Miss Lungren was nearly in hysterics when she came in. I promised not to betray her confidence, but if you were to guess correctly . . ." Bedford screwed up his face as if in extreme concentration. "I would neither confirm nor deny your supposition."

"How should we know if we guessed correctly, then?" asked Randy, with an exasperated roll of his eyes.

Tony studied Bedford. He wasn't a complete corkbrain. "I should assume that if we guessed wrong, Will here could tell us we were wrong without breaking his promise. It's only if we guess right that he should have to seal his lips."

"Hardly in the spirit of honoring his word," objected Randy.

"Were we not dealing with someone who might also be a murderer, I should be completely closed about this. But I believe you should know, and I shouldn't have promised to keep my silence, but she was crying, you know. A fellow can't be expected to think straight when a woman is crying."

"So her distress concerns Lord Carlton?" asked Tony.

Bedford looked straight ahead.

"Something to do with his buying pieces of the estate?" prodded Tony.

"No," answered Bedford. "Though that is upsetting to her because she believes he's done it to make her totally dependent on him. But that is not the matter I am sworn to silence about."

"This is absurd," muttered Randy.

Tony ignored his lieutenant's spleen for the moment. "Did he attack her?"

Bedford pressed his lips together.

"Rape her?"

Bedford was having a hard time not nodding. Tony could tell that he wanted to wag his head up and down.

"Today?" squeaked Randy.

"No, not today," answered Bedford.

"Recently?" asked Tony.

"No, but I take it the threat of repeat is hung over her head often. And, well, she was running full tilt when she came in the house."

"Christ," muttered Randy, and pulled his horse ahead.

Tony trotted his horse up beside Randy's and grabbed his reins. "What is with you?"

Randy gave him a bleak look. "I could kiss a political

career good-bye if I marry a woman whose sister is a murderess."

"You suspect Rosalyn?" Bedford yelped.

Tony stared at Randy. "You've fallen for Miss Carolyn?"

"Don't look at me that way. It was all your fault for putting the idea in my head."

Bedford was still caught on the idea of Rosalyn as their main suspect. "I don't think she could have poisoned her brothers—she's too emotional for a method as painstaking as poison."

"I bought a book on poisons." Tony rubbed his forehead. "Do you really think our killer is one of the sisters?"

"I think it is Rosalyn," said Randy.

Bedford shook his head. "I'd believe it is the mother before I'd believe it is Miss Lungren."

Tony didn't know what he believed. "I don't know what to make of Miss Jocelyn. She avoids my questions and talks mostly of French fashions. She is the only one, however, who acted surprised to see Bedford. And who knows? Mayhap the bullet will tell us something."

After a satisfying dinner, his first at Mrs. Merriwether's house, William settled into his room. His man was in the powder room adjoining the bedroom, stacking up his boxes. William was putting his linens in the drawers when he heard a light tap at his door. Thinking it was probably Major Sheridan wanting to discuss the day's discoveries, William didn't think too much about the fact that he'd removed his coat and cravat and was in his stockings and shirtsleeves and breeches.

He pulled open the door and was dumbfounded by the sight of Miss Fielding and her little cousin.

"Mr. Bedford, could I ask a favor of you?" Miss Fielding began nervously.

His hopes of an assignation were dashed by the presence of Charles, who looked up at his cousin.

William recovered his composure somewhat. "Certainly, Miss Fielding. What can I do for you?"

Miss Fielding seemed to lose her nerve somewhat. "My aunt—that is, after the dinner party—my aunt thought she should have musicians in." Miss Fielding focused on his neck and then took a step back. "Oh, she thought . . ."

Charles piped up, "Cousin Diana wants to know if you would teach her to dance."

"I'm sorry, you are preparing to retire." Diana took another step backward. "I didn't mean to disturb you."

"You don't know how to dance?"

She shook her head, her dark eyes big in her blushing face. She really was a pretty thing. "I would have asked the major, but dancing cannot be easy for him with his injury."

"You didn't learn at finishing school?"

She shook her head in tiny movements, as if suddenly afraid to admit to anything.

William stepped out into the passage and pulled his door shut. That had to be more proper than standing in his bedroom, even if she had brought a chaperon. Not much of a chaperon, because what could a little boy do if he, William, attempted any impropriety?

Her tongue seemed to break free at that moment. "I don't know how to do any of the proper dances. Aunt Felicity tells me I can't waltz until I'm approved for Almack's, so I shouldn't have to learn that yet, but if you could show me how to do some of the steps, so I don't make a complete fool of myself . . . I should hate to embarrass Aunt Felicity. She is going to so much trouble for me, and I was afraid to tell her I don't know how to dance. I thought, I thought . . . if you wouldn't mind helping me . . ."

"She missed her lessons at school a lot on account of being sick a lot," said Charles.

"Yes, they thought dancing might be too strenuous for my weak constitution." She stared straight into his eyes.

If she had a weak constitution, he was a monkey's uncle. Still, he didn't really care what she had done to get out of her dancing lessons at school. Perhaps the dancing master had scheduled his terpsichorean tutoring first thing in the morning and she had preferred to feign illness rather than rise early.

"I thought Charles could count for us . . ." She searched his face with nervous eyes. ". . . since we don't have any music." Her eyes dropped to the carpet, and she backed up more. "Oh, never mind. Forget that I ever asked. I'm sorry."

"I should be happy to help."

"Really?" she asked, as if she didn't quite believe her good fortune.

"When and where do you propose we start?"

"Um, now. We could use the ballroom. I mean, we should use the ballroom, shouldn't we?"

"And it is where?"

"Upstairs."

On the third floor, where he had been warned not to set foot. He was torn.

"Aunt Felicity is in her study. She usually spends several hours in there."

Bedford had seen Sheridan take a book downstairs after dinner, so he supposed that there would be no interference on that front. "Very well, let me get my shoes."

Miss Fielding reached out and grabbed his arm. "Mayhap you shouldn't. We, um, we wouldn't want to be too noisy."

He supposed if he didn't need shoes—she was probably wearing slippers that would be noiseless—he didn't need a neck cloth, either. He didn't think it would be too outrageous if he requested a kiss from his student. Payment of sorts for lessons taught.

When Charles deserted them later in the midst of their giggles as he attempted to teach Diana the patterns of a country dance, he knew the kiss was inevitable, and he began to anticipate, with a bit more fervor than he should, the moment he would claim her lips.

* * *

Tony settled into the rose drawing room with his newly purchased book on poisons. Felicity had withdrawn to her study and her work; and her parents, as well as Bedford and Miss Fielding, had gone above stairs to retire, he presumed.

Pulling a footstool over, he placed his aching leg on it and opened his book.

Half an hour later his head was swirling with thoughts of arsenic, hemlock, henbane, and puffer fish. Tony hadn't quite realized there were so many poisons available, or that so many of the purges and emetics that physicians prescribed could actually kill someone over time.

He was going to have to try to figure out a poison based on what their suspects had available to them and the symptoms the deceased had suffered over the course of their illnesses.

Which suspects, though? Perhaps he should start in the neighborhood. All of the possible culprits had lived on or close to the Lungren estate at one time. Certainly all of them, including Mrs. Lungren, had at the time the first Lungren male fell ill. Poison, especially a course of poison specifically intended to kill each male family member in succession, had to be administered by someone close— someone with opportunity, access to poison, and a reason to kill.

What reason? And if it was Mrs. Lungren, was there even a reason that made sense to a sane person?

The door clicked open, and a little boy peeked around the edge. "What are you doing?" asked Charles.

"Reading and trying to puzzle something out."

"Really? I like puzzles." Charles crossed the room, his pale blue eyes bright and curious.

"Do you? I don't think this is a puzzle for a youngster, though."

"Is it about who tried to shoot Mr. Bedford?"

Tony patted his good leg. "Yes, that is part of it."

Charles scrambled onto his lap and settled into the crook of Tony's arm without hesitation. He looked at the book that

Tony held closed with his finger in the middle, holding his place. "P-o-i-s-o-n. What does that spell?"

"Poison."

"Does that got to do with Mr. Bedford being shot?" Charles was altogether too earnest.

"We suspect the person who tried to shoot Mr. Bedford might have poisoned some other men first."

"Capital!" said Charles, with far too much enthusiasm.

"Go get a storybook, and I shall read that to you."

Charles thrust out his lower lip. "You could just read to me from this." He tapped the book in Tony's hand.

"It's really very boring, and your mother would skin me alive if she knew I was discussing any of this with you."

"Yes, but mamas are that way. They always think they can keep all the bad things away by not telling us. But bad things are out there; we're bound to find out about it."

"She knows that you'll learn about it eventually. The trouble is, there is a lot of wickedness in the world, and mothers just want to protect their babies from it as long as they can."

"Papas are different."

"Not really."

"Mama reads to me from boring books. She explains about businesses and how to make money, and she makes me listen to the reports the managers send us." Charles's hopeful gaze focused on the book. "I don't like business much. When I get old, I just want her to keep taking care of them."

"Charles, you'll have to relieve your mother of the work when you're old enough to do it. You'll be a wealthy man, and you'll need to look after your assets."

"But she *likes* doing it. She's happy when she works on the businesses. She's happy when she makes a change—well, she's nervous about it at first but when it makes things better, she's very full of herself."

"Interesting." Felicity liked running the businesses? "But you know, Charles, you are very young, and you might find such work enjoyable when you grow up."

He shook his head. "I want to be a Robin Redbreast when I grow up, and solve mysteries. I'm very good at figuring things out, you know."

"So I've heard."

"Yes, well, I figured out that there is something odd about my cousin Diana. I don't know what it is yet, but I don't think she was at school the whole time she was in Switzerland. I think she ran away or something, except I can't figure out how she got the letters Mama sent her."

"Really?" said Tony, taken aback by the imaginings of the little boy. Although there was something not entirely innocent about Felicity's just-out-of-school niece.

"Sometimes you just have to ask the right questions. Sometimes the answer is right under your nose, and you just haven't thought of the question yet."

That was the trouble: Tony wasn't even sure he was asking the right questions about Lungren's murder.

"Diana lies a lot."

"How can you tell someone's telling a falsehood?"

Charles unconsciously plucked at Tony's sleeve and kicked a little foot back and forth. "Different ways. I can tell because a lot of times liars look you straight in the eyes. And sometimes they take too much time, because they think too hard of what to say."

"How do you know they aren't trying to remember something?"

Charles shrugged. "It's different. They blink more."

"How do you know these things, Charles?"

"I also figured out that you must be my real papa, because Mr. Merriwether wasn't, you know."

Tony wondered whether he could dissemble. Especially since the precocious child had just told him he could easily spot a liar. He decided not to, though it might mean risking Felicity's wrath. "I suspect so."

Charles expelled a big sigh, as if he'd been holding his breath. Tony pulled his son against him and kissed his forehead.

"How does one get a son? Because I know you weren't married to my mama, and she had to marry Mr. Merriwether."

Tony grinned. "That one I'm not answering until you're older."

"Very well . . ." Charles made it sound as though he had long pondered the question. "I shall just have to figure it out on my own."

Tony heard the longcase clock downstairs chiming eleven times. "You should be in bed."

Charles squirmed to the edge of Tony's lap, then paused. "You can tuck me in and read me a bedtime story."

"I can't. I'm not allowed on your floor."

"Oh." Charles looked thoughtful. "Can you tell me if making a baby involves kissing? Because I think Mr. Bedford was going to kiss Diana. And she said I shouldn't leave them alone, but it was boring just watching them dance."

Now what predicament had he gotten himself into? Tony might as well kill Bedford himself if he was going to compromise Felicity's niece before she had a chance to start her season.

SEVENTEEN

Meg knew Mr. Bedford was going to kiss her. She could see it in the way his sea-blue eyes fastened on her lips. She didn't care. More than not caring, she wanted him to. She hadn't thought, after the last time, with the captain on board the ship, that she would ever want that again, but she did.

However, she was supposed to be an innocent young miss, who'd never been kissed before, let alone done—well, everything there was to do. She tried to remember how she had responded when she'd been an innocent, and then she decided she'd never been innocent. She didn't want to pretend to be naive now. So when his lips found hers, she threaded her arms around his neck and arched up against him.

She could taste his surprise, but then it melted into eagerness as he slowly and patiently deepened the kiss, with such a coaxing sweetness and consideration for the maidenly sensibilities she should have had. All the while he held her tight, not crushingly so, but with the perfect blend of firmness and cradling.

That was before his hands began to stroke her back with a slow patience that made her melt. Her legs felt boneless as he tried to pull his hips back from hers, while he continued to kiss her again and again. She pushed harder against him, letting him support her. Enjoying, for once, a man trying to tempt her instead of expecting her to do all the work of seduction.

He began stroking the outer curve of her breast, slowly, oh, so exquisitely. She wanted to twist so his hand cupped her breast, but she trusted that if she waited he would get there, and the wait was perfect torment. She pulled his head down putting more pressure in her kisses. His thumb slid underneath, and a moan of impatience slipped from her lips.

He slid his hand down, away, and she could have died with frustration. Her nipples almost hurt. What was wrong?

Men liked her breasts. If they weren't too rough, she even liked it when they fondled and suckled, and—oh, dear God, he had started the same slow attention to her other breast, with his other hand.

Her breath was coming in little pants. His patience and concentration on her sensual arousal undid her completely. She couldn't remember ever wanting a man's touch so badly.

She could no longer return his kiss with any semblance of control. He pulled back, and his eyes, his beautiful eyes, watched her as he skimmed his hand over her breast, his palm dragging against the tightened tip, sparking liquid fire to race through her veins.

She shuddered and closed her eyes; her knees buckled with pleasure more intense than she could have imagined.

"Miss Fielding, I . . ."

Miss Fielding? Meg swung away, gasping, her knees weak, her heart all aflutter. What had she done? She wasn't supposed to behave like Meg Brown, the occasional prostitute. She was supposed to be a respectable young miss, who wouldn't consider letting a man hold her too tightly on a ballroom floor. "I should not have allowed you to do that."

Then she remembered Charles. Had she behaved like a slut in front of Diana's little cousin? Blimey, she had practically been rubbing against Mr. Bedford. She spun around, looking for the young imp. "Charles?"

"He left some time ago."

"I'm sorry, I shouldn't have encouraged you so." Meg paced across the wide-open floor. "I didn't . . . realize we were alone."

She folded her arms across her stomach. She had tossed poor Diana's body over a railing, denied her the opportunity to be buried by family, slept with that gross captain, all for the opportunity to marry into the gentry, and she was throwing it all away for an interested-in-bedding-her-but-not-wedding-her gentleman. "I didn't expect it to feel so good."

"Miss Fielding . . ." He sounded breathless.

The way she felt. She couldn't look at him. She knew that he wasn't the least bit interested in offering her marriage. He was much more interested in her aunt. She had seen the calculating way he looked at Felicity. Not that she minded particularly. She understood the desire to better one's situation through any possible means.

Meg had just wanted to enjoy one little quiet kiss. "I didn't mean to be alone with you. I know Aunt Felicity says I am rich enough to buy myself a husband, but I really didn't mean to . . . to . . . to,"

"Miss Fielding."

Meg was shaking with fury at herself and with frustrated passion.

"Oh, please promise you'll never say a word. I don't know what came over me." A sensual insanity, her mother's sluttish predispositions—likely the only legacy her mother had left her.

"Miss Fielding, I beg your forgiveness. It was all my fault."

No, it wasn't. She gave a huffy laugh. He had been gentle, tentative. He hadn't been likely to get carried away kissing an innocent miss. Without her encouragement, he would have indulged in a light dalliance and nothing more. But oh, she had encouraged him, enticed him, practically entreated him to take her right here on the ballroom floor.

"I should not have taken such liberties with your person."

She would never, ever allow herself to be alone with a man again, not until she was respectably married—assuming that could even happen now. "Please, go away."

"Shall I . . . shall I . . . shall I fetch your aunt to you?"

Oh, lud, it was worse than she thought. "I think it better she doesn't know. She might think you should have to marry me."

Meg watched Mr. Bedford turn white as a sheet. He backed toward the door. "Of course. Will you be all right? I'll . . . I'll send your maid to you."

Meg clapped a hand over her mouth.

He swiveled and practically ran toward the door, barely sliding to a stop in his stocking feet.

She doubled over in mirth the minute he left. Oh, poor Mr. Bedford was terrified he might have to marry her, and at the moment that struck her as hysterically funny.

Tony rapped on the connecting door between his and Bedford's rooms.

Bedford swung open the door, looking a bit wild-eyed.

"If you have compromised Felicity's niece, you shall have to marry her."

"I know."

Tony wasn't expecting Bedford's easy compliance. He looked over Bedford's shoulder, making sure that the girl wasn't stashed in his room. "Have you compromised her?"

"No, she came to her senses before things went that far."

Tony crossed his arms. "How far, exactly, did things go?"

"Well, not as far as things went between you and Mrs. Merriwether."

"Touché." All right, so it was a bit of the kettle calling the pot black. "However, I already had my suit accepted, and always was fully prepared to marry her. The war, and my removal to the Continent, became the problem."

Bedford ran his fingers into his hair and grabbed fistfuls

of it and pulled. "I might have to marry her anyway. I don't think I've ever wanted a woman so much."

Tony leaned against the doorjamb. "I thought you wanted to marry Felicity."

"I want to marry her fortune—although she'd have been a pleasant way to her money. But, I'm about to be thrown in debtor's prison—I have to marry a woman with some blunt. I can't even keep a horse."

"Felicity's niece is penniless?"

Bedford paced across the room and back. "My sources tell me that her father ran through his wife's share of the Merriwether fortune long ago."

Tony watched Bedford's stockinged feet with interest.

"It wasn't much compared to Mrs. Merriwether's current share. I mean, as I take it, Layton Merriwether had doubled his money twice over in the last couple of years."

While Felicity had been at the helm of her husband's enterprises.

"I can't marry a penniless chit. We'd have nothing to live on. I have no prospects, and my luck at gambling doesn't always hold steady. Lungren was teaching me some of his tricks, but that avenue is gone."

"Did he have tricks, then?"

"Oh, not like you're thinking. He didn't cheat; he just could persuade people to bet more than they ought—and I don't really like that. I always feel sorry for the poor sods who lose their money when they can't afford it, even though I need it as much or more than they do."

Bedford continued pacing. "I'm a younger son with no prospects. I can marry an heiress or become a vicar. Can you see me as a vicar?"

Tony was a younger son, too. So was Randy, for that matter. "There's always the military."

"Yes, I'm sure they can always use men who faint when they're fired upon."

"You didn't faint last time. In fact, you're getting rather handy at being fired upon."

"No, I just hid under my bed until my man pulled me out."

Poor Bedford, he probably was too honest to make a good Captain Sharp.

Bedford stopped in his tracks. "Oh!"

Tony pushed away from the doorjamb. "Oh, what?"

"She said something about being rich enough to buy a husband. Lord, I was in such a spin—you don't suppose Miss Fielding has money after all?"

"I don't know; Perhaps Felicity's husband bequeathed his niece a share of his fortune." Why wouldn't he have? Miss Fielding was his only flesh-and-blood relative at his death. That is, if he knew that Charles wasn't his son. "Even if he didn't, I should imagine Felicity was rather generous with her niece, if she is as rich as you say."

"She's rich, all right. Even Brumley is considering her as a possible bride."

"Brumley?"

"You have been away a long time, haven't you?"

"Six and a half years. Napoleon just wouldn't stay down."

"The Earl of Brumley has married five or six rich widows. Usually picks ones older than himself. Then he gambles away their money. Although, I have to say he never has stooped to marrying a Cit."

"What were you doing dancing with Miss Fielding, anyway?"

Bedford looked him straight in the eyes and spoke slowly.

"She was worried about the dinner party, and the evening's dancing and she wanted to . . . practice her steps. Make sure she was ready."

Tony shook his head. As he shut the door between their connecting rooms, he said, "You're a clumsy liar, Will."

Or maybe it was just that Charles had made it too clear how to pick out a falsehood. Trouble was, Tony wasn't sure if the lie originated with Bedford or Felicity's niece. Bedford did have a chivalrous streak deep in his soul.

* * *

Tony stretched out on the bed, fully clothed. He heard the longcase clock chime the midnight hour, and he wondered if he had missed Felicity's ascent to the floor above—or was the little businesswoman still downstairs building empires?

He finally picked up his poison book and made his way to her study. The light shining under the bottom of the door let him know she was still within, still working.

He opened the door. "Burning the midnight oil?"

She looked up at him and blinked, as if her thoughts were elsewhere. She lowered her head back to her papers. "I had a late start."

Tony nodded and moved into the room, taking a chair in front of her desk.

She looked up after a few minutes. "Is it that you need help with something?"

He shook his head.

"Could you leave, then? I have much work to do and little time."

"Would it trouble you if I just sat here and read?" He opened his book and looked down at it.

She put down her pen and smoothed her hands over her face. "Why do you want to read in here?"

"We need to talk about our son. I thought we might discuss things. No hurry, though; whenever you're done working."

"What about Charles?"

"Do you want to talk now? Or do you want to continue working?"

Felicity rolled her eyes. She also reached over and capped the ink bottle.

He guessed that meant now. "Did you tell him I'm his father?"

"No, but he knows Layton wasn't."

"Then he has guessed."

"Or overheard it."

"He was bound to find out sooner or later, he looks like me. Randy figured it out."

"Does everyone know?"

"Bedford knows. I don't think it has gone any further than that. I didn't tell them."

She stood with a rustle of her gray silk gown. "Didn't hint, didn't imply, didn't suggest." She waved her hand in the air.

"Other than my leaving you with child—though I would have arranged a marriage by proxy if I had known—what have I done to earn your low opinion?"

"Was that not enough?"

"Felicity, you know that I had not planned our one night together. And I shipped out the next day." She had invited him to her home, her bedroom. No man in his right mind would have refused, but he hadn't expected it, hadn't been able to refuse. Then there'd been the protracted war and nearly losing his leg three months after his departure.

"Well, then, it's more the things you haven't done, haven't thought about."

He shouldn't have started down this lane. Nothing could ever change the past. The important thing to consider was the future. "I want a relationship with my son."

She stood at the fireplace and fiddled with a pewter cup resting on the mantel.

"I want to teach him to ride, to shoot, to train hounds and pick out good horseflesh. I want to be his father."

"You *are* his father."

"I mean in practice. The easiest way would be for us to marry." He held up his hand as she swiveled around. "I've already missed nearly six years of his life."

"You were fighting a war. You couldn't have helped to raise him even if we had been married by proxy."

"But if you are going to deny me the opportunity to be around him for the rest of his growing years, then I should let him know immediately."

"I wouldn't deny you." She set the pewter cup back on the mantel with a bang. "I don't know how you will raise him from India, though. He's not going with you."

"Then I'm not going. I'll sell my commission, but I'll need employment. If you could use me to manage your estate, as a steward, that would be acceptable."

She turned back around and stared at him. "Have you given up on marriage?"

"You've made it abundantly clear that you will not marry me."

"I don't want to marry anyone."

"I suppose I could be your pretend fiancé in perpetuity, but employment as your steward would be a better arrangement. I'm not good for much. I was raised to be a gentleman, which means I can quote Plato and Socrates at whim, gamble at my leisure, and manage an estate. I'm a good officer, but most opportunities in the military are overseas."

She continued to stare at him.

"I might still consider India, and perhaps with your advice I could make myself rich there. You would allow me to correspond with you, wouldn't you?"

"My advice?"

"Yes, your advice. You're the one who has increased the Merriwether fortune fourfold in the last few years, are you not?"

"Layton taught me everything. The initial investments were his."

"Yet you have a shrewd head for business."

She looked stunned and moved to grasp the back of the chair next to his. "It was the only thing that ever earned me Layton's respect."

"Was that important to you—earning your husband's respect?" Had she actually loved this man she married?

She sank down in the chair beside his. "Not as much as I thought it would be."

Interesting. If Tony succeeded in earning her respect

again, would he find it not worth the effort? But then, he'd never figured someone else's opinion mattered as much as one's own. "It was more important to respect yourself."

She put her thumb against her lips and nodded.

"So what do you say?"

"I already have a steward who manages my estate."

"What other employment might there be in the neighborhood? Your father needs someone to straighten out his affairs. Perhaps you could convince him he needs to employ me."

"You wouldn't need such work. You could just stay with us. It's not as if you'd require money."

"Just self-respect." Felicity gave him a long, considering look as he went on. "I won't live off your money, even if you do have more than enough. I'll figure something out."

She looked at him, her dark eyes puzzled. "But if we were to wed, what would be the diff—never mind."

The difference would be simply that they were married— a permanent arrangement not subject to change at her whim. "What are you thinking?"

"All London would think that you were managing the businesses."

"I wouldn't take the credit. I don't think I fully realized until today that managing the business affairs was something you wanted and liked to do."

Her forehead furrowed. "I told you."

"Yes, well, I can be dense at times."

"Whether or not you are in charge, people will assume that is the case."

He reached out and put his hand on her knee. "Is that your main objection to marriage?"

She looked at him with a wounded and worried expression. "No," she said slowly.

"What is it, then? Is it something I can address?"

She popped up and paced to the darkened window. Pulling back the curtains, she stared out at the night. "I feel you've done a turnabout on me. I thought you wanted to have an affair."

"I wanted nothing more."

She turned around and watched him.

He glanced at the desk, thinking of what had happened the last time he was here, and the marked differences from the time when she had wanted to marry him. The comparison would haunt him forever. There was a world of difference between acceptance and eagerness. "So much has changed in six years. It seems you don't trust me any longer."

She looked down at the carpet and then back up at him. "I suppose if you were to come live with us at my home, an affair would be inevitable."

"I don't think so, Felicity. It wouldn't be the wisest course. It certainly wasn't the last time."

"What?"

He stood. "An affair with you would be smashing, a great do, but we should have the wedding first and the affair afterwards.

"By the bye, do you have any objection to Bedford as a suitor to your niece?"

"She should be introduced to society before she makes a decision."

"I gather his breeding is good enough, but he has no prospects."

Felicity winced. "I don't think she should fix her affections this early. Although she shan't be able to make a great match, I should want her to be comfortable." She looked a bit ill-at-ease. "I believe Mr. Bedford is an agreeable sort, and I like him, but if he has no prospects, then I should say no to his suit."

"I'll let him know." Tony bowed. "They may be fixing each other's affections prematurely."

"I shall speak with her, too."

"Now, see how well we work together." He tossed her a half smile and moved to the door.

Felicity stared at Tony's broad shoulders as he left the room. What had just happened? Beyond their casual agreement to look after Diana's best interests, he had withdrawn his demand for an affair.

Had she lost Tony's respect with the only thing that had earned her Layton's respect? Did he resent her business acumen? Much *had* changed in six years.

Never once in the conversation had the word *love* cropped up. When he heard her request for a pretend engagement, he'd been adamant. He had not wanted to marry her, only to begin an affair.

Now, since he had realized Charles was his son, he wanted marriage so he could be close to the boy. It had nothing to do with wanting to marry *her*. Now he didn't even want an affair?

She turned and stared out the window at the cold night. Leaning forward, she jumped when her overheated flesh encountered the cold panes of glass. He had brought her to heaven the other night, and now he didn't want to bother. She looked at the desk. Was it because he was left unsatisfied? Or did he truly no longer want her?

She stared up at the distant stars.

"No affair, Felicity," she spoke to the silent night. "It's what you wanted."

But did she want marriage?

She had married once for her son's sake. It had been the worst years of her life. Would it—could it—be different with Tony? Could such a man consider her feelings and thoughts and not try to control everything in their lives, in her life? Even in these more enlightened days, a man was king of the castle; the balance of power went, unchallenged, to him. How could she keep control of the business, let alone her person?

A man had a right to beat his wife as long as he used nothing broader than his thumb, and a woman had no recourse. No, Tony was right. She didn't trust him. She trusted no man. Because if you had asked her about

Layton's character when she married him, she never would have thought he would raise a hand to her, let alone a switch.

How could she expect happiness if he did not love her? Better never to give any man the right to control her. She would infinitely prefer an affair.

EIGHTEEN

Dressed in evening clothes, Tony, Bedford, and Randy drove in Randy's carriage to pick up the Lungren ladies for Felicity's dinner.

"Are we any closer to figuring out who the murderer is?" asked Bedford.

"Randy, what does your man say of Mrs. Lungren? Was she out of Bedlam on the night Will was shot at?"

Randy shook his head. "He's never seen her out at night. Her keeper swears that she is locked in after dark, so she can't wander off. In the days when she is out, she mostly just buys things, like tea and sugar and occasionally some laudanum and foxglove. Which her keeper says she uses herself."

"Perhaps it is time we crossed her off our list," said Tony.

"I think it is Rosalyn, the eldest sister," said Randy.

"No, I don't think it could be her. She is just not cool-headed enough," said Bedford.

"What about Lord Carlton?" Tony didn't know what to think. His head was spinning with the hastily acquired knowledge of different poisons and which ones could mimic the effects of a wasting disease.

"You said yourself that poison is a woman's weapon of choice," said Randy.

"Perhaps it is all the sisters together, then," suggested Bedford.

"Not a chance of it," swore Randy. "Miss Carolyn is most

distressed by all the happenings in the past few years. Nothing more would please her than to move far, far away from here. She cannot stand to watch any more of her siblings die."

Tony rubbed his head. "Who haven't we talked with that we should have?"

"We've talked to the physician who treated the men. He attributed the unexpected deaths to cancers, not poison. Some families are much afflicted with this dread disorder, he said. We've talked to the undertaker. We've talked to Mrs. Lungren. We've talked to the servants. Who else is there?"

"Mayhap we need to talk to them all again, if we had not asked the right questions before," offered Bedford.

"Every time we ask new questions, we suspect new people," muttered Randy. "Now Tony has added Miss Jocelyn to our list of possible candidates, as if one sister weren't enough."

"We can't rule her out," said Bedford.

"Mayhap we should all do our damnedest to enjoy the evening, for Felicity's sake."

"That's all well and good for you to say. You aren't the next intended victim," objected Bedford.

"We may very well be bringing the murderer into Mrs. Merriwether's house." Randy leaned back against the squabs of his carriage.

"Yes, but this is someone who behaves covertly. He/she doesn't want to be caught. A dinner party isn't a likely place for an attempt on someone's life," Tony reasoned.

"Except that it won't be expected, and that might make it a perfect opportunity." Bedford hit his fist against his leg. "Damnation! I wish we could figure out who did this."

"Then we shall make a pact to never leave you alone. Not even for a minute. One or the other of us shall remain by your side throughout the evening."

"Oh, I say, no need to go so far," objected Bedford. "I—"

"Don't need to be alone with Miss Fielding. Felicity says your suit would not be acceptable."

"Good grief, did I ask you to ask her?"

"No, but I was looking after Felicity's interests, not yours."

"A fine friend you are."

Tony clapped Bedford on the shoulder. "Sorry, chap. Her interests come before yours. Not that I am not on your side."

Bedford sulked.

"Think of her as the general, and yourself as a captain. We're all in the same army. And since you are dependent upon her hospitality, you should have a higher consideration for Felicity's wishes."

"You shouldn't call her by her given name if you don't mean to tell the world of your past relationship."

Tony felt the stab in the vicinity of his breastbone. "I can't stomach calling her by another man's name."

Bedford looked contrite.

"Shall we get back to the matter at hand—catching the murderess before she catches Bedford?" asked Randy.

"I want to know what was growing in that garden," said Tony. Mayhap if he knew what plants the sisters had replaced the flowers with, he could match it to something in his poison book.

The discussion continued for the length of the drive to the Lungren house, and they were no nearer solving the crime, or crimes, than before.

Felicity checked the name cards on the table and had to switch half a dozen that Diana had done. The girl didn't pay any attention to ranking. She wouldn't do well in society if she didn't get precedence right.

"I'm sorry. I did them wrong, didn't I?" asked Diana in a small voice.

"Never mind that. You should be upstairs getting ready."

"Yes, ma'am." Diana turned toward the door.

"Oh, and Diana . . ."

Diana stopped her back to Felicity. "Yes?"

"Don't encourage Mr. Bedford."

Diana turned and looked at her. "Why not?"

Felicity supposed it might be nerves, but her first inclination was to say, *because I told you so*. She managed to swallow back those pettish words and said, "You should see what other suitors you might have. Go slowly; you have a whole season before you to decide whom to marry."

"But I like Mr. Bedford." Diana twisted her hands in front of her. She wasn't wearing her gloves again.

"I've already passed the word on to him. Now, go get ready for your dinner party."

Diana shot her a dark glare that gave Felicity pause. "It's *your* dinner party."

For *Diana's* benefit. Felicity stared at the door that had closed behind her niece. She sank down onto one of the forty-four chairs squeezed around the vast dining room table meant to seat a mere forty. If it were up to Felicity, she never would have left home. She'd just retreat into her business work and never venture back into the confusing world of marriage and men and society.

She could always manage to be stronger, more resolute, when she did it in writing. And she had an awful feeling—premonition, really—that something was about to go dreadfully wrong this evening.

William grimaced as they arrived at the Lungren house at dusk. He was irritated that Mrs. Merriwether considered him no better than a fortune hunter and not good enough for her precious niece. That he was a fortune hunter in truth only made him angrier. And damn, he wished he had known Miss Fielding before he'd let Sheridan know that he needed to marry an heiress.

Since he wasn't likely to get to the bottom of the matter with Mrs. Merriwether, he'd just have to see if Miss Fielding knew what she was worth. Then there was always Gretna Green or special license.

They entered to find the household in an uproar. The men

were shown into the drawing room just as a bent-over Miss Lungren said, "I don't think I feel well enough to go."

"You have to," insisted Miss Jocelyn. She pulled on evening gloves and reached for a wrap that lay across a chair. "And look, the gentlemen are here to escort us."

"I can't. I really can't," whispered Rosalyn.

Miss Carolyn looked back and forth between her two older sisters. "Maybe she should stay home, Jocelyn. If she doesn't feel well—"

"Do you want to stay here with her?" Jocelyn walked toward the door. "If she stays home, one of us shall have to stay with her, and that means none of us might go, because neither of us can go alone with three gentlemen. It just wouldn't be proper. Come on, Rosalyn. You'll feel better for the fresh air."

Miss Lungren straightened, and William noticed she looked every one of her thirty-some years. Her skin was a pasty white with bright spots of color on each cheek. Frankly, he didn't want to ride in the carriage with her if she carried some contagion. Yet he crossed the room toward her, intending to help her to a chair.

"Papa was like this for months, and he still managed to get around to do his business," Miss Jocelyn said.

Tears sparkled in Miss Lungren's eyes when William reached her side. "I fear I have contracted the family disease, just like my brothers and father before me," she whispered.

The family disease was poison. A chill went down William's spine. He had to get her out of here.

He glanced across at Sheridan and Randleton and thought they were too far away to have heard what Rosalyn said.

"Then I must insist you come with us, Miss Lungren. The food prepared by Mrs. Merriwether's chef will cure anyone."

Sheridan gave him a sharp look, as if to remind him that he shouldn't know anything about the food at the

Merriwether house. Which hadn't been the point he'd been trying to make.

"I had the pleasure of dining on meals prepared by him when he cooked for Watier's." William kissed his fingers in a Gallic gesture of appreciation.

Miss Lungren looked at him as if he'd killed her last hope. Really, he must pull the others aside and let them know he thought she was being poisoned. But in the meantime he had to get her out of here. He put his arm around her shoulders and guided her to the door.

"Perhaps you would like to take a stroll in the garden and see if it helps restore feelings of health," suggested Sheridan as they moved past him. "A walk in fresh air can do remarkable things for the constitution."

Bedford wanted to growl at the major, but suddenly their eyes met and he realized Sheridan suspected the same thing that he did.

"Please, I should like that," said Miss Lungren. She was probably hoping that with the delay she could stay home. She really didn't look as if she wanted to go.

William leaned close and whispered, "Miss Lungren, if you are still feeling unwell when we get to Mrs. Merriwether's, she will find a place for you to lie down, but I must insist that you go. I fear for your safety if you stay here."

She gave him a wide-eyed stare and then a tiny nod of acquiescence. She probably thought he was concerned about Lord Carlton showing up on her doorstep.

They took a turn about the garden, and Randleton did his best to get the sisters to name the plants, while Sheridan seemed to be trying to commit each one to memory by staring at the withered foliage in the fading light, while he and William supported a sagging Miss Lungren as best they could.

"I think we should send for the physician," announced Miss Carolyn, looking at her sister.

"I already did," said Miss Lungren. She coughed a bit. "I received word back that he is attending Lord Carlton."

"Really?" said Miss Jocelyn.

The men all looked at each other, wondering why Lord Carlton needed the physician. When William could stand the question no longer, he said, "Do you know why?"

"They said he had an apoplexy," said Miss Lungren.

"Now, that should make you feel better, Miss Lungren." Of course it was an appalling thing for William to say, and Miss Lungren responded appropriately by fainting dead away.

William tried to catch her dead weight while Major Sheridan grabbed a wall to keep from tumbling down himself. Then William insisted they must with all due speed get Miss Lungren to London and a physician.

"Good show," said Sheridan as they headed for the carriage before the other two ladies could raise an objection.

"She's being poisoned, I daresay," whispered William as he and Randleton hoisted the inert frame of Miss Lungren into the vehicle.

"So I gathered," said Sheridan.

But Randleton shook his head, and the two of them took positions on the box while Sheridan climbed inside to ride with the ladies.

"She might be faking it, to throw us off the scent," said Randleton.

"I hardly think so." William was affronted.

"Look, no one would rather find that Lord Carlton is the culprit more than I, but even if this poisoning is real, after three murders our murderer would know what a fatal dose is. She might have even poisoned herself. Did you hear any of them name anything beyond turnips, peas, carrots, and rhubarb?"

"No. Maybe Lord Carlton didn't really call for the physician, either."

Then the coachman put an end to their speculations by
climbing up on the box with them.

William didn't know what to think, but something else was
niggling at him. How had Sheridan and Randleton known so
quickly about Captain Lungren's death?

Felicity checked the longcase clock. The men and the
Lungren sisters were taking longer than she had expected.
She had thought they would be among the first guests to arrive, but nearly all of the other thirty-four people had
arrived. She had received the duke and duchess and their
strikingly beautiful daughter and winced as Diana bobbed
one of her servantlike curtsies to them.

The next four people in line were chatting among themselves, and the dark-haired, dark-eyed Mr. Davies had to
prod a pretty blonde forward.

Two women stepped toward Felicity. The first woman,
with a mop of impish blond curls, came forward and held
out her hand.

"Sophie Davies," she said without a care that her hostess
might not know her by name. "That cad's wife." She pointed
at Keene Davies, future baron of Whitley. She smiled at her
husband with such warmth, and turned back to Felicity, her
smile filled with so much engaging charm, that Felicity
couldn't help but smile back.

The woman behind her gently tapped down Sophie's finger, her dark hair a sleek coil on her patrician head.

"And this is Amelia Keeting, a dear friend of ours."

"Thank you for letting me substitute Lord Wedmont. My
husband is still down in the country," said Amelia.

"Although you might not thank her later," Sophie added.

Felicity turned to introduce her niece, when Amelia
stepped back, her hand at her chest, and said, "Reggie."

Sophie looked Diana over and remarked, "Lud, she does
look like Regina, doesn't she? How nice to meet you, Miss
Fielding."

Amelia had recovered her composure, and with perfect politeness greeted Diana and moved on to Felicity's parents.

"A sister, do you think?"

Felicity whipped her head around to see Lord Wedmont and Keene Davies just as Keene said, "Shut up."

"He didn't mean you, Mrs. Merriwether. He means me. I have a tendency to speak before I think." Lord Wedmont bowed prettily over her hand. "Although I think you ought to address your wife so. I believe she just called you a cad."

Felicity exchanged greetings with the men and introduced them to her niece. As they moved away from the reception line, she strained to hear their whispered conversation.

"I hardly think the mother would fit into his pattern, would she?"

Lord Wedmont frowned. "Our dear papa's? No, not unless she was Haymarket ware. But she does look like Regina."

Felicity studied the two men, wondering why she had never noticed how very similar in appearance they were. They didn't have the same father; what were they talking about? And who was Regina?

Just then the door opened, and three women dressed in black entered, followed by Mr. Bedford, Lieutenant Randleton, and Tony. Lord Algany followed them in.

"Tony, you're back in town! When did that happen?" exclaimed Keene as he backed out of line and headed down the stairs to embrace Tony.

Wedmont followed him, and both men embraced Tony. She wondered if any of them would remark on their long-ago engagement. Mr. Bedford was leading two of the women up the stairs, with the third walking behind. They must be the Lungren sisters. He held on to one of them with a firm grip on her arm; another sister on the other side held her other arm.

Mr. Bedford presented her as Miss Lungren, and the one holding her other arm as Miss Carolyn Lungren. Felicity welcomed them and, concerned by the glassy look in Miss Lungren's eyes, and the furrows of pain in her face, leaned forward and asked if there was anything she could do for the sister.

Felicity was familiar with the woman's tragic history. She had lost three brothers and a father in the past few years.

"Thank you so much for everything you've done." Miss Lungren made a small gesture to indicate her black silk gown. "I'm feeling much better than I was earlier. I feared I might not be able to come, and I so did want to make your acquaintance."

"I am glad to have you, and so sorry about Captain Lungren."

The woman nodded and turned to be introduced to Diana.

Off to the side, Felicity could see Tony being introduced to Sophie and Amelia. He turned briefly and met her eyes. He gave her a small half smile, as if to apologize for their lateness and promise an explanation later.

Felicity realized with a gulp that it was far too easy to communicate with Tony. She turned back and greeted another Miss Lungren, Miss Jocelyn, and then Lord Algany, who lingered over her hand with his ferret smile and his odd, hanging-over-his-forehead hair.

Out of the corner of her eye she saw the smile on Sophie's face turn to a grimace as she watched Algany be introduced to Diana.

The Lungren sisters and Lieutenant Randleton and Mr. Bedford joined the cluster of her guests, and Sophie jerked her arm away with an "Ouch!" when Miss Jocelyn sidled up next to her.

Keene's arm went around his wife's waist almost without thought as he continued talking to Tony.

"Lud-cakes, what do you have in your reticule, an iron?" asked Sophie with no malice as she rubbed her elbow. "I don't believe we've met. I'm Sophie Davies." She extended her hand.

Miss Jocelyn was slow to respond to the buoyant greeting from Sophie. "I'm sorry. Did I bump you with my bag?"

"Oh, don't worry about it. Just caught my funny bone or something."

Lord Algany paused and looked around, his pleasant smile fading from his face as he saw Sophie. He almost took a step back into Diana but stopped himself in time.

Sophie took a determined step forward, and Lord Wedmont glanced at her and then moved to her side, as if the four of them had some unbroken code of protection that while her husband was occupied, Wedmont would step up.

"Hello, Lord Algany; what tricks are you up to this year?"

Algany put a hand to his forehead as if to smooth back his hair and for a moment lifted it up, exposing a black mark, and then, as if he had forgotten himself, he smoothed it back down. "No tricks, Mrs. Davies."

"That's lovely. Because I shall be watching," she said with a tap on his arm with her fan, and a smile that had nothing of the winsome sweetness of earlier.

Lord Algany moved toward the open door of the drawing room, quite neglecting to greet Felicity's parents.

"Well, I never . . ." started Lady Greyston.

Diana looked between Felicity and Lady Greyston.

"Let it be, mother. Please, let it be," whispered Felicity.

"Don't think you should invite that one to any more of your dos," said Sir Edmund Greyston.

"I didn't intend to invite him to this one," whispered Felicity. "He invited himself, along with the duke and duchess."

Wedmont bent close to Sophie's ear and said, "By God, I believe you tattooed him."

"I didn't. It was Indian ink—it should have worn off in a few weeks." She giggled, though, then clapped a hand over her mouth. "Oh, it is not funny."

Felicity wondered if she had a horrible contretemps on her hands. Obviously, there had been some sort of row between Sophie Davies and Lord Algany. And across the landing Miss Jocelyn was watching her with an odd expression. "Shall we move into the drawing room?" asked Felicity.

Tony began steering people in that direction, and Felicity raced down to the dining room to make sure that Lord Algany was seated far away from Sophie, her husband and friends, Lord Wedmont, and a wide-eyed Amelia Keeting.

NINETEEN

Meg watched as Mr. Bedford paid meticulous attention to one of the Lungren sisters. He led her into the rose drawing room and found her a seat. Had that kiss meant nothing to him, or was Felicity's rejection of his suit enough to get him to utterly disregard Meg?

She didn't understand why Felicity objected to Mr. Bedford as a suitor for her, and he must have approached her aunt for permission to court her, or whatever it was that these toffs did. Meg figured, a little desperately, that the sooner she was married, the sooner she could count herself in. She was desperately afraid one of her slips would lead to her discovery, and she was a bit unnerved by the two ladies who had looked at her as if she were familiar or at least reminded them of someone.

Then there was her half-brother, who had been eyeing her strangely, as if he was trying to puzzle her out. With the secrets and the pretense she was carrying out, she didn't want anyone paying her undue attention.

Felicity had brought over all the unmarried gentlemen to speak with her, and most of them, after a cursory glance at her bosom, brought their attentions back to her aunt.

Meg desperately wished the butler would announce dinner, so that she would no longer have to suffer through this incessant milling about with these full-of-themselves strangers.

"Diana, I'm sure Lord Algany would love to hear about Switzerland." Felicity turned to the gentleman she had brought over. "My niece has spent the last twelve years at school there."

"A beautiful place, isn't it?" responded Lord Algany. "I chanced to visit a few years back. Lodged at a handsome chalet near Lake Geneva. Where was your school, Miss Fielding?"

Meg searched her mind desperately and then remembered the direction on the letters Felicity had sent and realized she had no idea how to pronounce Lucerne and would probably botch it. She cleared her throat and whispered the name.

"And where is that, Miss Fielding?"

"Well, north of Geneva." Everything in Switzerland was north of Geneva to a degree, but that was exactly as far as Meg's geographical knowledge went. She hastened to fill in the silence with a change in subject. "There is nothing so lovely as the Alps, though, is there?"

Lord Algany gave her a sharp look and said, "Not quite as lovely as you and your aunt, but breathtaking all the same."

Meg, who had only seen the French side of the Alps, quite thought the loveliest thing she'd ever seen was the Aegean sea, with its blue-green waters reflecting the brilliant Mediterranean sky, but she supposed that the real Diana had never seen the Aegean sea. Blimey, she was going to be exposed.

Felicity murmured a thank-you for the overblown compliment.

Lord Algany leaned close to Felicity and wrapped his hand around her elbow. "I wonder if I might have a word with you in private, Mrs. Merriwether. Won't you excuse us, Miss Fielding? It won't take but a minute."

No, he could tell her aunt that she was an impostor in half that time.

She was doomed.

"I suppose we might step into the green drawing room for a moment," Felicity said.

"That would be wonderful, Mrs. Merriwether."

She moved to the curtained doorway that connected the rooms, and slid back one of the pocket doors. The last thing she wanted was to be alone with Lord Algany, but since he had managed to get the duke and duchess and their beautiful daughter, who was monopolizing all the eligible bachelors, to attend her dinner, then Felicity owed him that much.

Other than that Diana seemed more awkward and tongue-tied than usual, the party was starting out well. Since the men couldn't dance all at once with the lovely Lady Penelope, she supposed things would be all right. It probably would be much worse if the bachelors were forced to dance attendance on the uncharacteristically speechless Diana or the three Lungren sisters. At least this way, everyone seemed to be enjoying themselves.

Lord Algany and she entered the green drawing room, where Felicity had requested the servants to set up a table and chairs for the musicians to dine. She could smell the covered food across the room. But for the moment the room was empty. The musicians were upstairs tuning their instruments and would be led downstairs as soon as the formal dinner was under way.

Felicity turned around and asked, "What can I do for you, Lord Algany?"

He pulled the door shut behind him and moved toward her. "My dear Felicity—may I call you that?" He didn't wait for her answer. "Won't you have a seat?"

"I really can't be away from my guests for long," she said.

"You needn't worry. I'm sure your mother shall fulfill any hostessing duties in your absence. What I have to say is more important."

Felicity sat down on the chaise longue. There wasn't any point in telling Lord Algany that his advice not to worry would not make her stop. "All right."

He moved over in front of her and dropped down to one knee.

He wasn't going to . . . propose, was he? Panic fluttered

through Felicity's veins. If she had known this would happen . . . No, he wasn't the sort to propose, else he would not still be a bachelor at the advanced age of—what was he, perhaps thirty-five, thirty-six? She was likely to receive another offer for an affair.

There weren't words strong enough to express her disgust at that idea. Hell would have to freeze before she would even think of such a thing with Lord Algany.

"My dear Felicity . . ." He took her hands in his.

"I think you had best continue to call me Mrs. Merriwether."

He scowled at her interruption. "I remember you from your first season, and I have thought of you often in the intervening years."

She would have to suffer through this. It was the only thing a polite hostess could do under the circumstances. He was her guest. "Have you?"

"Oh, yes—well, to be honest . . ."

Something she suspected he rarely was.

". . . I was quite enamored of you then, but alas, you had already become engaged to Sheridan, and so I took it upon myself not to interfere. You were so young and seemed so in love with your dashing captain—he was a captain back then, was he not?"

"Yes."

Lord Algany dramatically placed his hand on his breast. "You see, I didn't want to dismay you with the violence of my affections when you were already fixed upon another man, but I swear to you, my heart has remained constant."

"It has?" said Felicity skeptically.

"I fear I am doing this badly. You see, I have never before—"

"Oh, excuse us."

Felicity looked up at Sophie Davies and Amelia Keeting. Never had she been more relieved to see anyone, but she feared they would exit, seeing Lord Algany on bended knee and all.

"Lud, we need to sit a moment," said Sophie, crossing the room and pulling out a chair. "When one is in the condition that Amelia and I are in, one can become overheated so easily."

Amelia snapped open her fan and began wagging it as if on queue. She tapped Sophie's arm, and Sophie waved her hand in front of her distinctly unflushed face.

"Lord Algany, whatever are you doing on your knee?" Sophie asked.

He swiftly stood and released Felicity's hand.

Amelia tugged at Sophie's arm. "Perhaps we should go."

"Nonsense," said Sophie. "If Lord Algany was doing the pretty and tossing his handkerchief in Mrs. Merriwether's direction, I'm sure he could have picked a more opportune time than during her dinner party." She shot him a look full of daggers. "Not that he ever has proposed before. What are you thinking, Amelia?"

"Can I get something for you?" asked Felicity. "Some water or lemonade?"

"We shall be fine in a trice. These feelings of weakness come and go, but you would know that. You have a son, don't you?"

"So I am to gather that congratulations are in order," said Lord Algany. "I shall offer my heartfelt best wishes to your husband, Keene, Mrs. Davies, and who should I offer congratulations to in your case, Mrs. Keeting?"

Amelia turned white, but Sophie didn't miss a step, "Why, her husband, George, of course. He's coming up soon, bringing Reggie with him. You should see how he dotes on his daughter. Now, I do think you should fetch our escorts since you have upset Amelia and your comments have become boorish."

"Haven't you done enough to interfere in my life?" he demanded of Sophie.

"Probably not yet," she answered. "I am curious, though, was it the blackness in your soul that made that mark permanent? It shouldn't have been, you know."

"Felicity, is there a problem?" asked Tony from the doorway.

Lord Algany backed into the table where the food was and spun around. A covered plate went flying, and Felicity stared as a pork roast sailed through the air.

A flying pig? Was this an omen she could not ignore?

Felicity stared at Tony. Her dinner party was going from disastrous to dreadful.

"Why, that was unhandsome of you, sir," said Tony with a steely menace that sent chills down Felicity's spine.

"An accident." Lord Algany looked dismayed.

Amelia rose from the chair where she was sitting. "Of course it was an accident. We all could see it was an accident. You just turned very quickly and . . ." How to explain it as a mischance must have escaped Amelia because she finished lamely, "An accident, I'm sure."

"Or an excess of emotion," said Sophie.

Amelia turned to her and said, "I told you we should leave. I daresay Lord Algany has every reason to hate you, Sophie."

"As do I," said Sophie.

"Lord Algany, I find I have an excessive desire to blow a cloud. Please accompany me. I find it most calming," said Tony.

"Mrs. Merriwether, I am so sorry. You can't imagine how sorry I am." Lord Algany looked sick at his tantrum. "I hope these were not dishes for us."

"No, just the musicians. I shall hold you accountable for their play if it is inferior."

Algany stared at her as if caught in a situation outside the bounds of his expectations, and he had no idea whether he should cry or shout, stand or fall, stay or go.

"Don't give it a thought, Lord Algany. I'm sure that this was an accident, and you can be sure my chef has prepared too much food. In fact, Tony, wouldn't Phys love this as a treat?"

"He would consider himself in hound heaven."

Sophie had already pulled the bell for a servant, and her butler came in. Felicity gestured to the mess of the roast on the floor. "Would you have someone clean this and take the roast to the stables for Major Sheridan's dog, if you please?"

"We shall be back in a few moments," said Tony.

"I shall have them hold dinner until you both rejoin us." She mouthed a thank-you to Tony and gave a short nod to the question in his eyes.

She knew she had all but said that Major Sheridan was living with her, and she hoped he understood that he had license to claim that fact or the pretend engagement with her. Anything to steer Algany away from the proposal he had been about to deliver.

"Lord, I'm sorry," said Sophie when the men left the room. "I'm afraid my emotions are running a little high. I didn't mean to spoil your dinner party."

"I don't think that most of the guests have any idea that anything happened," Felicity said. Else they probably would have all run into the green drawing room by now.

Amelia had a hand pressed against her throat. "Oh, my God, was he actually proposing? We thought . . . we thought . . ." She looked to Sophie for help.

Sophie looked flushed and upset, in truth now in need of the cooling-down she had claimed to need earlier.

Amelia swallowed down her reservations. "We thought he might be drugging you so he could . . ."

"Have his way with you," said Sophie finally.

"We should have left when we realized he was proposing," Amelia said.

"He must be after your money," said Sophie. She looked at Felicity. "Don't take that wrong. We thought, you know, he seduces beautiful women every year."

"Last year he was trying to ruin Sophie."

Felicity didn't know that she wasn't somewhat flattered. So the woman thought she was attractive enough to warrant the attentions of a known philanderer, but . . . "Well, I shouldn't have said yes if he had proposed." Something stopped her from saying she had no intention of marrying anyone.

"Oh, that is a relief," said Amelia.

"I know he has a title, but he stops at nothing. Last year when I kept telling him no, he resorted to trying to drug me." Sophie smiled one of her impish smiles. "You could do much better than that."

"Of course you could," agreed Amelia.

"Like the major," said Sophie as she sailed to the doorway. "We really should rejoin the company before Keene and Victor start tearing the house apart looking for us."

"We should all rejoin the company before anyone realizes anything is amiss," said Felicity, liking the two women but avoiding comment on Sophie's suggestion that Tony would be a better husband than Lord Algany.

She just had to get through the evening, and then she would have a chance to think whether a pork roast lofted through the air was the same thing as a pig flying, and whether that meant she was *supposed* to have an affair with Tony.

Which might not be so bad, but if he was insisting on marriage first, Felicity might need more than a sign from above to convince her.

In any case, she needed to concentrate on making sure the rest of the evening went off without a hitch.

Besides, what more could go wrong tonight?

"Miss Fielding, do you know where I might locate your aunt?" William asked Diana.

He was growing concerned about Miss Lungren's pallor. She insisted she was feeling much better, but he was worried nonetheless. He wanted to let Mrs. Merriwether know so she could take action if it became necessary. His allies—well, Major Sheridan was nowhere to be seen, and Lieutenant Randleton was knee-deep in conversation with Miss Carolyn. If he was right and it was one of the sisters, could it be her? He wanted someone else to keep an eye on Miss Lungren, in case she fainted again.

Diana turned around and shook her head, but her eyes were sparkling with unshed tears.

"Whatever is wrong?" he asked, pulling her elbow and guiding her to a corner of the drawing room, his concern suddenly all for her.

"Nothing."

"Not nothing. You may confide in me, Miss Fielding."

"It's just that I am doing so poorly, and this isn't what I thought it would be. I just wanted to get respectably married, but I keep doing the wrong thing, and I don't think I shall ever get a husband, and Aunt Felicity told me I must stay away from *you*."

"Miss Fielding, you are doing very well indeed."

"Am I? All the gentlemen are over there." She pointed to the cluster around the beautiful Lady Penelope.

Even William swallowed hard at the sight of such loveliness. But she was not for him. She would have the stingiest of dowries, her breeding and beauty being such that her father wouldn't need to waste any money on seeing her settled.

"Well, that is neither here nor there. They can't all have her."

"They all want her."

"I, as you must have noticed, am not joining the circle of her admirers."

"No, you're over there with that lady in black, and I am not to encourage you."

That was the second time she had mentioned that she wasn't supposed to be with him, and it rather seemed to be causing her distress. "You should take your time before fixing your affections. Your aunt is only looking to your best interests. She wants you to take your time and enjoy your season."

"Yes, but to be put on display and herded about makes me feel like I am a slave on the auction block. I just . . . You must think me the biggest ninny."

"I think you are just having a fit of nerves—quite understandable. You needn't worry about scooping up a husband at this event or any other."

"I cannot go through much more of this," Miss Fielding said on a low wail. "I shall go mad."

"Miss Fielding, your aunt only wants to protect you from a bounder like me who must marry a woman with a fortune."

"She thinks you are after my money?"

William didn't know if Felicity thought that. But he suspected she knew he was after *her* money. "Well, I am not after your money. I don't know that you have any, but she knows I do not have the means to support a wife."

"But I do have a fortune."

"A fortune?"

"Well, a lot. I'm sure I'm not as rich as Felicity, but it is enough to live on it for the rest of my life."

William studied her dark eyes, and they shone with sincerity. "I should be the basest cad if I offered for you under these circumstances. Your aunt will not approve."

"I don't care."

"Very well, Miss Fielding, would you do me the honor of—"

"Yes," she shrieked and would have thrown her arms around his neck but for his catching her elbows and saying, "Not here, not now," in a low voice. "We shall have to keep it secret because I am most vilely abusing your aunt's hospitality."

"When? Can we elope tonight?"

"No!" He had a murder to help solve. He couldn't run off for the two or three weeks it would take to get to Gretna Green and back. He forced himself to think. "We shall have to wait until you are twenty-one."

"But I am."

"Then I shall approach the archbishop for a special license, and then in a few days we shall find a minister to perform the service. You must keep it a secret until then."

She nodded, her eyes bright, as if shining with glorious emotion.

William wished his feelings were clearer. He liked Miss Fielding, very much. He wanted to bed her in the worst way. In fact, standing so close to her, he could feel the heat of her body, and he wondered if his head wasn't a little too muddled by her musky scent.

And she had circumvented his reservations by claiming she had a fortune, enough to live on the rest of her life, but he did wish he knew an actual figure. Then again, could he afford to be choosy when he had moneylenders looking for him and leaving angry letters and legal summonses at his former apartments?

"Sorry, old chum. I never smoke, but I thought we could take a short walk up the street and back," Tony said to Lord Algany.

"You don't mind if I blow a cloud, do you," asked Algany, pulling a case from his pocket. "It's cold as Hades out here."

"All the better to cool heads with."

"That woman . . . that woman . . ." Algany's hands shook as he rolled a cheroot.

Tony hoped he wasn't talking about Felicity, because then he would have to plant him a facer.

Lord Algany got his tobacco lit and drew a deep breath. "Just look what she did to me."

He lifted the hair off his forehead, and a black mark was there. It looked rather . . . permanent.

In any case, Felicity hadn't done that to him. "How did that happen?" asked Tony mildly, walking beside Algany.

"It . . . she . . . oh, never mind."

"Looks like a tattoo," said Tony.

"Well, I suspect it is. Hang it. She wrote on my forehead with ink, and I tried to wash it off. Washed until my forehead bled, and this is what it looks like now." Algany's voice shook with rage.

"I shan't ask how or why she came to write on your fore-head," said Tony. "But then, it never works to conceal one's scars."

Good God, was that what he himself had been doing? Was that why Felicity didn't trust him? Had he held onto the wounds and scars she had inflicted on him? And was he, worse yet, angry with her for letting her wounds show?

No, dash it all, she didn't want him. Perhaps she hadn't even wanted him years ago.

"Tony, there you are. We wondered where you dashed off to."

Tony turned around to see Wedmont and Davies approaching him.

"Drugged anyone tonight?" Wedmont asked Algany.

"Christ," muttered Algany as he ground out his half-smoked cheroot under his heel. "Time for me to return inside."

The three men watched Algany go back in the house.

"So your wife is the one who marked him for life?"

"She has her own way of confronting problems." Davies folded his arms behind his back. "We came out in case you needed assistance with Algany."

"I told you we didn't need to," said Wedmont. "Never known Algany to present a problem to another man. Let alone that Sheridan could handle more than either of us could, being a soldier and all."

"Officer. We probably ought to go back inside before we cause Felicity to postpone dinner." Tony, of course, couldn't walk as fast as Algany had, so he started his slow limp toward the house, and the other two fell in step beside him.

"You were engaged to her once, weren't you?" asked Wedmont.

"There, and I was hoping to curtail the awkward questions." Tony knew better. He'd been to Eton with these two and he'd never known Wedmont to keep his mouth shut.

"So why did she marry someone else?"

Davies reached out and thumped the back of Wedmont's

head. "Her boy is, what, almost six? You've been gone, what, six and half, not quite seven years, Tony?"

"Sir," Tony objected. Davies, he trusted, would keep his mouth shut, but Wedmont was a different story. Would everyone figure it out?

"Never fear, I'll shoot him again if he says anything."

"Again?" asked Tony weakly.

Wedmont shot Davies a dark look. "Yes, again; we fought a duel last year. Cursed pistols and all that."

"Well, I'm not entirely sure who won if the curse is true," muttered Davies.

"You did, you ninny. You are mad about Sophie."

"And where is Mary Frances? Why didn't you bring her to London? Although Sophie says her letters have been getting odd."

"You are mad about Sophie, and my wife is just plain mad."

Suddenly the two changed from squabbling boys to consoling men when Davies put his arm about Wedmont's shoulder. "I always thought there was something brittle about Sophie's friend."

Wedmont shrugged off the maudlin moment. "Are George and Amelia on the outs again?"

"Not that I know of . . ." Davies hesitated. "Bloody hell, she didn't!"

"Are these secrets for my consumption?" asked Tony, wondering if the other two men had forgotten his presence.

The two men exchanged a look, and Tony stepped back, realizing how similar they looked. How had he spent eight years in school with them and never realized?

"I suppose if you get us drunk enough, we'll tell all," said Wedmont. "Or at least I will. He won't last long before he'll have to go home to Sophie."

Davies shoved Wedmont away. "What have you been doing since you've been back in town, Sheridan?"

"Investigating a murder. Are you two . . . brothers?"

"Oh, he's good," said Wedmont.

"Never say so, but yes."

"And we are wondering if Miss Fielding is part of our big, happy family."

"I just can't see your father having an affair with a Cit's daughter," said Davies.

"No, I think he had pretty much moved onto cheap whores by the time Miss Fielding would have come into the world."

"Tell us about this murder," said Davies.

"Not if you're this loose-lipped."

"Only with each other," said Davies.

"And old school chums," said Wedmont. "We could always trust you, Sheridan."

"I'm glad someone feels that way," said Tony, opening the front door.

"You are living here, aren't you?" Davies said. "Sophie said so, but she's half-baked sometimes."

"Didn't hear it from me," said Tony, but he had erred in simply opening the door instead of knocking and waiting for a footman to do the honors.

TWENTY

"Oh, Mr. Bedford, you have made me the happiest of women." Meg clapped her hands together. The sound, of course, was muffled by the gloves she would have to wear all the way through dinner. Lord, how was she to manage eating with gloves on?

"Yes, well, look, we shall discuss it later, during the dancing after dinner. I will need to know your full name and all so I might put it on the special license."

He suddenly looked nervous.

Meg bit her lip and then plunged in. "Diana Margaret Brown Fielding." Surely the marriage could never be put aside if her real name was on the license.

"Brown Fielding?" echoed Mr. Bedford weakly.

Meg nodded, pasting on her most innocent face. *Oh, please, don't let him pull up now.* She very nearly had him. And frankly, she could have done much worse. He had quite the loveliest eyes.

She knew that ten thousand pounds was a lot of money. She hoped that Felicity wouldn't withdraw her dowry, because she was marrying a man Felicity objected to, but that mattered less than getting Mr. Bedford's ring on her finger, and the marriage right, tight, and legal. One bridge at a time.

Why would Felicity withdraw the offer, anyway? The only real danger was if she discovered that her niece was really dead and Meg Brown, illegitimate daughter of an earl, sometime prostitute and soon-to-be wife of a member of the ton, was posing as her niece.

"Miss Fielding, I want to beg a favor of you."

"Anything."

"See that woman over there, Miss Lungren?"

"The one you have been dancing attendance on all evening?" Meg pulled back. The last thing she wanted was to sound shrewish before the wedding. "I didn't mean that as it sounded."

Mr. Bedford—she should call him William now, which would mean he'd call her Diana, never mind, she'd change that after the wedding—looked a little nonplussed.

"Please, William . . ." She dipped her eyes and looked through her lashes in what she hoped was a cross between demure and flirtatious. "How can I help Miss Lungren?"

"She is ill, and I want you to keep an eye on her and re-move her from the company if she seems poorly."

"Should she be here? What if she carries some conta-gion?" Meg put her hand on his sleeve. "Not that I am worried for myself; I am never sick, but Felicity will be mortified if people fall ill after her dinner party."

It occurred to her, after she said that she never got sick, that she had just shot a giant hole in her pretense of being the sickly Diana. Blimey, she needed to get him to marry her fast. Then she should make sure they spent the first week of their marriage in bed, because nothing calmed a man better than that. Explaining away her skills between the sheets might be a little difficult, though.

She blinked rapidly, hardly listening as her future hus-band leaned close and whispered in her ear.

"There is no contagion. She's being poisoned."

"Poisoned!" blurted Meg.

William's wince would have more than expressed Meg's frustration with her own slip. She clapped a hand over her mouth, then lifted it to whisper, "I'm sorry. I just . . . poisoned?"

She looked over William's shoulder at the pale and pained woman. Only half the room was looking in their di-rection. The other half likely hadn't heard. Meg searched desperately for a cover for her outcry. "Robespierre did not use poison, did he? I mean, I thought he practically invented the guillotine."

It was enough; most of the faces turned away, bored with the talk of France and its criminals. Only the three Lungren sisters continued to stare in their direction.

Meg tried to rap William on the arm with her fan to imitate one of the society ladies, but the dratted thing came half open as she did it, and William stared at her as she tried to fold it back up.

"We'd better end this tête-à-tête, before someone summons your aunt."

Blimey, she'd broken the ivory spines of the dratted fan. Which only went to show that her female talents lay in a much more earthy realm. She yanked the cords free of her wrist as William turned away, and tossed the thing in the direction of the brass coal bucket.

Dinner went smoothly as course after course was served. Only the servants removing the dishes kept people from gorging on the food. Tony winked at Felicity. He could see how nervous she was from his vantage at mid-table. But then, this was likely the first ton party she'd ever arranged.

He knew she was worried about her niece and the row between Lord Algany and Sophie Davies. That was an interesting pairing: the outspoken Sophie and the reserved Keene. He turned his attention to Miss Lungren.

She stirred her food in a desultory way, but she had eaten some. It had perhaps been boorish of them to insist that she come with them. Then, of course, they would have to decide if it was safe for her to return home.

Felicity stood signaling the retreat of the ladies for tea, and the men were left to their port. Lord Algany left the table shortly after the ladies, in the midst of the gentlemen switching places and rearranging chairs. Tony wondered if he should follow him, and then decided he should do

Felicity more service by making sure the gentlemen didn't linger too long over their port, so the dancing might commence before midnight.

Not that Tony would be dancing, not with his leg.

Bedford took a chair to one side of him, and Randy grabbed the other.

"We can't let her go home and just be poisoned to death," said Bedford.

Randy rubbed his forehead. "Christ, what a coil. Don't know that we should allow any of them to go home."

"If I could just figure out what they grew in that garden besides vegetables," said Tony.

Bedford looked at him a minute, the churning thoughts in his brain box visible on his face. "Castor beans. My nurse used to make me take castor oil every day, until I started pouring it down the ashes chute." He shuddered. "Vile stuff. Didn't Mrs. Lungren say they replaced her asters with castor beans?"

"Peas, actually. But she did say they planted castor beans." Randy turned to Tony. "Are castor beans a poison?"

Tony looked down the table, keeping his voice low. "Yes, you can grind the beans into a poison that makes the blood congeal. I must look up to see if its effect is cumulative."

"That has to be it, then," said Randy. "What should we do now?"

"Bedford, you have the best luck with Miss Lungren. Find out what she's eaten lately, and who is preparing and serving her food. Randy, confirm with Miss Carolyn if they grew castor beans in the garden. I'm going to check my book, and then see if I can't learn from Miss Jocelyn who might have access to the kitchens or their meals."

"Then what do we do?" asked Bedford.

"Let's meet in the green drawing room just before it is time to take the ladies home, so we might discuss what we've learned and make a decision."

"Hope we will know something—anything. This situation grows more troublesome day by day," said Randy.

"We simply cannot allow another murder to take place," said Bedford.

"Especially not if it is yours," said Tony. "Let's clear the dining room, so Felicity can get the dancing under way."

After dinner everything seemed to be progressing smoothly. Felicity heaved a sigh of relief. Other than the incident with Lord Algany in the green drawing room, everything had gone as planned. The musicians were playing in the far corner of the ballroom. Lord Algany hadn't been seen since dinner, but Felicity supposed he might have just taken his leave. Tony was missing too, but no doubt he would show up sooner or later.

The only thing that made her evening odd was that during a waltz, she had received a marriage proposal from a gentleman she barely knew.

She hadn't realized there were so many fortune hunters in the world. Or that they would have so little finesse. Which quite made her wonder how many gentlemen were biding their time and seeking her interest before proposing. She grew skittish anytime a man approached her.

She knew most of them would only ask for a dance, but she would get busy with her servants or fixing a decoration or grabbing Diana and thrusting her in front of her. One poor gentleman had nearly run off when she said, "Oh, you have come to ask my niece to dance; how lovely."

He hadn't. She knew he hadn't. What was worse, he knew she knew he hadn't.

Tony finally entered the ballroom, and she sent him a desperate glance.

He limped across the floor toward her, and she wanted to run and meet him halfway.

"Would you like to dance, Felicity?"

"Oh, yes, please." To dance with Tony again would be lovely. She remembered how much she had enjoyed dancing with him her first season, and how handsome he had looked in his scarlet uniform.

Lord Wedmont stood in front of her, extending his elbow. "Mrs. Merriwether . . ."

For a confused second she looked at him, then at Tony, and realized Tony had summoned someone to dance with her rather than dance with her himself.

She placed her fingertips on Lord Wedmont's arm, and he led her onto the floor. "You need not worry, I shan't propose; I already have one rich wife. Shan't need another."

"Oh, did you see that?" she said, shocked into admitting that she had received a proposal.

"Amelia heard it. She was near you on the floor. Although I have to say, I wish I had waited a year."

Felicity blinked.

"I can pry Keene away from his wife to spare you a dance or two. I should imagine that between the lieutenant, Bedford, Keene, and me, we should be able to keep you well away from the fortune hunters and Algany. Although we might not allow you too much time in Bedford's company."

"I . . . he . . ."

"I know. As a former fortune hunter, he was ever underfoot last season."

Felicity decided she might as well let Lord Wedmont talk. "He was?"

"Now, what I want to know is, where did your niece spring from? Is she from your husband's side of the family?"

"Yes." Felicity turned to catch sight of Mr. Bedford, leading Diana into the figures.

"She has a different last name," prompted Wedmont.

"She is the daughter of Layton's sister. Layton was my husband."

"I see, and was she ever on the town, this sister of Layton's?"

Felicity focused her attention on Lord Wedmont's curious expression. "No, I don't believe she was brought out."

"Interesting."

The Merriwether empire hadn't been impressive enough to force their inclusion in society, especially not twenty years ago. Seven years ago Layton had barely been tolerated, and only on the fringe of the ton. He certainly wouldn't have been allowed in Almack's or invited to any of the royal fêtes.

He was better accepted after his death. She supposed that was because he wasn't around to make any missteps that might reveal his lack of breeding.

Felicity started. "Did you hear that?"

Wedmont frowned. "Was that a child yelling?"

Oh, dear God, what was Charles up to? Just that moment, a loud and shrill scream was heard from the front of the house. Not a child's scream, not a woman's scream, but . . . a man's? Falling, fading, as only the scream of a person falling a great distance could sound.

The cry was clear enough and shocking enough that the musicians at the back of the ballroom stopped playing.

Felicity ran to the street side of the ballroom, which ran the entire depth of the house. Unfortunately, all two score of her guests had the same idea.

She managed to see out. The screams and cries continued from a figure lying on the cobblestones in front of her house. Louder now that her guests had thrown open the windows. What on earth had happened?"

Her guests began to cry out.

"It's a man!"

"Did he fall?"

"Did he jump?"

"Oh, my!"

There on the street, between two of the empty waiting carriages, lay a figure. Felicity could see the coachmen begin to converge on the man, but not before she saw the odd angle of the twisted leg beneath him.

Felicity shouldered her way back through her guests. She hurried out to the stairs, and half her guests thumped down behind her. She shouted at her butler as she flew through the entry hall. "Send for the physician, quickly. Get a plank or a trestle to use as a stretcher. Bring a lamp. Get blankets and pillows and take them to the morning room."

Her servants, who had been standing about in a confused muddle, leaped into action; a footman yanked open the door.

Felicity ignored the cold February weather as she ran out to the street, where Lord Algany writhed and screamed in pain, and the angle of his left leg made Felicity want to lose her dinner. She swallowed hard and told herself there would be time for falling apart later. She knelt down beside him and held his arm while her servants and some of her male guests began restraining Lord Algany.

"Don't touch me! Don't touch my leg!" screamed Lord Algany.

"It must be straightened," said Lord Wedmont. "Allow me."

He grabbed Algany's ankle and pulled the leg to a more natural position. That it was badly broken was obvious.

Algany's scream was blood-curdling, but then he seemed spent and took in breaths in big, leaping gulps. Felicity knew it was small comfort, but she held his hand.

He practically cried as Lieutenant Randleton approached with a door removed from its hinges.

"Don't move me; please, don't move me," he begged, and tears ran down his face.

"I can't allow you to lie in the street," she said with a tight smile. Then she turned her attention to the guests blocking the doorway and spilling out onto the steps. "Everyone please return to the drawing room while we attend to Lord Algany. I will bring you news of his condition as soon as I know anything."

Most of them stayed where they stood.

She caught her butler's eye. "Has a physician been sent for?"

"I took the liberty of sending a manservant on horse and another on foot, ma'am."

He moved toward the doorway. "If you would please step inside, Your Grace," he said to the Duchess of Worcester. "Let the injured man through. Please, let's give him some room to breathe."

With not a small amount of herding skill, her butler quite efficiently moved her guests upstairs to the rose drawing room.

Felicity turned to the whimpering man now on the makeshift door stretcher. "Lord Algany, how did you come to fall? Were you pushed?"

Tony, with his injured leg, hadn't followed the mass exodus from the ballroom. Instead, he limped over to shut the windows that had been thrown wide open. Several of the candles on the chandelier in the center of the ballroom had blown out already in the stiff breeze. Only the weak gaslight from the wall sconces kept the darkness from the dimming room. Keene Davies's wife leaned out of one window while her friend Amelia held her skirt.

He'd heard Davies yell at her to stay put before he'd fled below.

"Is it Algany, can you tell?" Amelia asked anxiously.

"I think so," said Sophie. "Serves him right."

"You don't know that he did anything," protested Amelia.

"He must have been up to something, else he would not be lying in the street now. I wonder where he fell from." She leaned even farther out the window.

Amelia tugged the opposite direction on her skirts. "Sophie, if you fall again, Keene will skin me alive."

"I'm not going to fall."

Tony had reached their window to shut it when they both heard a tiny cry of "Help!"

"Gracious, there is a boy out on the roof!"

Tony's heart stopped beating. "Charles?"

"I'm here," came a thin, reedy voice. "Would you come and get me, please?"

Sophie whirled around fast and knocked into Tony, leaving him grasping the windowsill to remain standing.

"Sophie! No!" said Amelia. Sophie jerked away and left her sprawling on the floor, her hands empty of her friend's skirts. "Oh, stop her!"

But Tony didn't really hear her. His son was out on the roof. Instead, he ran—for the first time in months, ran—down the hall. He ignored the screaming pain in his thigh and ran down to the last room.

As if a part of him weren't really there, he could see himself watching Sophie as she ran ahead, her skirts hitched to her knees. The more demure Amelia scurried along behind him.

"Open window. Has to be an open window," Sophie panted as she ducked into the nursery, where a stiff breeze tossed the draperies this way and that.

Tony realized he should have looked for someone to assist them as they both raced across the room to the window that opened onto the roof.

"Charles," he breathed, seeing the small, huddled figure of his son on the roof slates.

"Could you come get me? I wasn't scared until the bad man fell."

"Stay there; we'll get you down," said Sophie.

"Please hurry," came the tiny voice of his son.

Tony felt a crushing despair knowing his bad leg made walking across the roof nearly impossible for him. Never had he felt more inadequate. "Would you fetch help, Mrs. Davies?"

She turned and stared at him. He wanted to sink into himself in mortification.

"I can't leave him alone, but with my leg I can't . . ."

She nodded quickly and turned.

"Papa, please come get me. That man keeps screaming, and I don't want to hear it anymore."

Lord Algany's screams kept drifting up from the street, and they were spine-chilling, even to a battle-hardened warrior like himself. All he could think was that Charles could fall and be in that much agony or worse. "Just stay put, Charles, and all will be well."

"I was just trying to get away from the bad man. He told me if I went with him he'd buy me a pony. I told him I already had a pony."

"Very good, Charles."

"Besides, I could buy myself another pony if I wanted."

"Quick thinking, son."

Charles leaned back. "Please come get me, Papa. I'm scared."

Tony's heart was breaking. Perhaps he could. That the boy was calling him "Papa" was killing him. But what would happen if he failed? If Charles had to witness another man, his own father, falling to certain injury, perhaps death, what would that do to him?

Tony's leg cramped viciously, no doubt in protest of the running he'd just done. He clenched his teeth against the pain.

He needed to keep talking to Charles, to help his son stay calm. "Why did the man offer you a pony?"

The window in the next room flew open. Relief flooded through Tony. Help was on the way at last.

"He said he had to marry Mama, and if I came with him that she would have to marry him, but I told him *you* were going to marry my mama. But he tried to take me anyway."

Tony watched in stunned disbelief as a pink-stockinged leg swung out over the windowsill in the next room, and then another leg and skirts.

"Hold still, Master Charles. I'm coming to get you."

Dread and dismay and the deepest feeling of inadequacy pounded down on Tony. "Mrs. Davies, what are you doing?"

She didn't even look at him as she eased down onto the roof and started inching toward Charles.

"You know, Papa, if he had promised me a dog, I might not have run away onto the roof."

She slipped, and Charles squealed in alarm and turned

his face down onto the roof tiles. Tony stood helpless, half the man he once was, watching while a woman—a thin slip of a girl, really—tried to rescue his son, and might very well plunge to her death.

"There you are."

William felt the unmistakable cold circle of a gun barrel in his back.

"I've been hoping to find you alone all evening," cooed the voice behind him.

William looked around the empty ballroom. Even the musicians were gone. He had watched Sheridan and those two women run out just seconds before, and they must have been the last of the party-goers to clear the room. He'd been looking for Miss Lungren, concerned she might have been overwhelmed by the mad rush of guests.

"I think it is time that you feel overpowered by your debts and decide to take your own life, don't you?"

"No, madam, I don't."

The gun barrel pushed into his back, right against his spine. William staggered a step forward. The last of the candles overhead flickered out, leaving them in a murky half-light.

"I do. Given the events of the night, I think a second leap from yonder window might make an interesting suicide, don't you?"

"No, I had rather you shot me."

"Move." Apparently she disagreed. She pushed with the gun.

"He's not dead. Can't you hear him screaming out there?"

"Yes, well, you shall have to leap headfirst. A bit messy, but it will do the trick."

"Look, we know that Jonathon didn't take his own life. You will not get away with this again."

"You know nothing. Now move. You are going to dive out that window."

"On second thought, I might rather prefer poison."

That seemed to surprise her.

Bedford swiveled and rammed his elbow backward, moving away from the gun shoved against his spine and toppling his assailant. "No, I really should prefer to be shot at."

Please just miss, he thought as he saw the black skirts fly up, and he ran toward the door. For a moment, the murderess was bested.

Outside in the street, they heard everything in quick succession: Charles's squeal of alarm, the scrabbling of someone on the roof, a shriek of rage through the open window of the ballroom, and then a shot.

Keene Davies dropped the corner of the makeshift stretcher and cried with almost as much anguish as Lord Algany displayed in his yowl of fresh pain: "Sophie!"

"Oh, my God!" Felicity stared up at the night sky, seeing the tiny figure of her son huddled on the roof, and two roof slates rained down and smashed into dust against the cobblestone street.

TWENTY-ONE

Meg wondered if it was her lot in life to take care of the sick. Miss Lungren looked dreadful and moved like a woman a hundred years old. She often had to pause and take deep, shuddery breaths as Meg led her away from the jam of people.

Meg had traipsed down the stairs with everyone else before she remembered that William had directed her to keep an eye on the woman. Then Meg had gone back up to find Miss Lungren squashed against the wall outside the ballroom while the guests rushed out the doors and down the stairs. Meg rather thought Miss Lungren might need to lie down and was leading her toward her own bedroom when Major Sheridan and two women came barreling down the hall.

Meg let them pass and then had just got Miss Lungren into her bedroom and convinced the woman to lie down when the shot rang out, quite loud, quite close, quite unmistakable.

"Oh, my Lord, no," wailed Miss Lungren. "We have to go back and find my sisters."

"I don't think so." Staying here until everything calmed down was just fine by her.

Miss Lungren coughed and sat up. Then, with more energy than she'd displayed all evening, she moved toward the door. "You don't understand. That shot was probably one of my sisters."

"Oh, I understand, all right. And you're being poisoned. Sorry, love, we're staying right here."

"What . . . what are you talking about?"

"William told me. Mr. Bedford," Meg clarified in case Miss Lungren didn't know, "told me you're being poisoned. And of course, with him being shot at and all, I 'spect he knows."

"What?"

Maybe the poison made her a bit of a slowtop. "You're being poisoned."

"Mr. Bedford was shot?"

"Well, shot at. Whoever it was missed. But he thought it was probably whoever killed your brother, the captain."

"What?"

"Are you always this slow?" asked Meg impatiently.

"No," wailed Miss Lungren. "No, no, no."

Her reply seemed overly vehement, despite the rudeness of Meg's question.

"We have to stop her."

"Your sister?" asked Meg uncertainly. She wasn't quite certain if Miss Lungren thought her sister was shot or if she was the shooter.

Miss Lungren threw her hands against her face hard enough to bruise. "I have to stop her. Oh, no, no, no."

"I'd rather not," said Meg, but she didn't suppose it would make any difference. For all her ill health, Miss Lungren seemed unexpectedly resolute—unstoppable even.

Mr. Davies and Lord Wedmont flew up the stairs ahead of Felicity. In fact, one of the gentlemen—Felicity wasn't sure which one; they looked so alike from the back— shoved the beautiful Lady Penelope out of the way as she stood on the landing at the top of the first flight of stairs near the drawing room entrance.

Felicity ran up the four flights to the third floor as fast as she could, but she was no match for the men.

"Sophie, what the bloody hell are you doing?" yelled Mr. Davies, which was how Felicity knew they were in her bedroom.

Her window stood wide open. Tony vied for room in the open window while Lord Wedmont tried to pull Mr. Davies back.

"I'm helping Master Charles back inside," came the faint but confident voice of Sophie.

"Don't move. I'm coming out to get you."

"Stay there, Keene. There are some loose tiles that probably caused Lord Algany to fall. Charles and I are light enough to not have a problem."

Felicity squeezed in between Mr. Davies and Tony. "Charles, are you all right?"

"I'm all right, Mama. I just got scared when the bad man fell."

"Yes, you are one brave lad, and we must slowly move toward the window. Bit by bit."

"Are we going to walk?"

"No, we are just going to scoot on our backsides," said the irrepressible Sophie.

"I shall kill her," muttered Mr. Davies. "I swear, I shall throttle her to death and then kill her again."

"I know," answered Lord Wedmont calmly.

"I can't watch," said Mr. Davies, but he continued to hang out the window. "Bloody hell, what is she thinking? She is with child."

"I want to be a godfather this time," said Lord Wedmont.

"If she makes it."

"And you don't kill her too badly."

All the while, Tony gripped Felicity's shoulder and said nothing.

"How could you let her go out there?" asked Mr. Davies, turning to look at Tony.

"I sent her for help."

There was a low quiet in Tony's voice that Felicity had never heard before. She turned and looked at the agony in his face, the terror that blanched his face. "Tony?"

He shook his head, his expression flat, emotionless.

"He'll be all right," she whispered.

His only response was to tighten his grip on her shoulder as they watched Sophie's painstakingly slow progress, inching over with her arm around Charles's waist. Felicity could hardly bear the wait, yet to will them to go faster was unthinkable. Finally, they made it to the window, and Lord Wedmont jerked Mr. Davies back.

Sophie lifted Charles across her body and handed him in to Felicity. She cuddled her son to her chest, his legs dangling down her sides. He was much too big to be held, but she wasn't letting loose of him, not for a long while. His arms wound tightly around her neck. She turned back around and saw Tony limp painfully toward the door.

Then Mr. Davies was pulling Sophie in the window, scolding her and rocking her in his arms.

Lord Wedmont looked over at Amelia. She motioned with her head to the door. Felicity hadn't even realized the other woman was there. Lord Wedmont tugged on Felicity's elbow, leading her out of the room. "He needs to kill her, you know."

Amelia pulled the door shut behind them.

Charles lifted his head up. "Is he really going to kill her?"

"It'll be a very small death, I'm sure."

To which Amelia flushed bright red.

"He won't kill her, but they need to be alone," said Felicity to Charles. She almost envied them their passion.

"If you mind terribly, I shall throw a bucket of water on them," offered Wedmont.

"No, oh, my God, what was that shot?" Felicity had quite forgotten, in her scare over Charles on the roof, that a gun had discharged. Perhaps that had been why Tony had left so quickly once Charles was safe in the house.

William knew he couldn't hide forever, but he cowered half behind the open ballroom door and next to a potted palm. He was afraid that if he tried to descend the stairs, he would be a sitting duck. He also would leave a trail of blood that would make it all too easy to be tracked.

He pressed his handkerchief against his sleeve. His best evening jacket, too. He lifted his hand away, and the red stain, the tattered material, made him light-headed. He couldn't even stomach looking at the wound in his arm. That was what physicians were for. He clamped his soggy handkerchief back over the wound.

He leaned back against the wall, hardly daring to breathe and wondering why it was taking so long for anyone to come and investigate. He might as well die here, for all anyone even noticed his absence. Not even his new fiancée, Miss Fielding, Diana, had come searching for him. Two men and Felicity had come running up the stairs, but they hadn't looked for him, or even in the ballroom, where the shot was fired.

His assailant, and damn, he wasn't sure which sister it was, had disappeared down the servants' stairs just before the crowd of party-goers stepped out of the rose drawing room on the floor below, following the shot. They milled about the passageway, and a few of them had looked up the staircase, but no one had ventured to the top to investigate.

Without knowing where the murderess was, he certainly wasn't going to step out into the open. It was with tremendous relief he heard an uneven gate. Must be Sheridan, and he leaned out of his hiding spot to come face to face with Miss Lungren.

It could have been loss of blood, but more likely he was a bloody coward, and with that new fright his world went dark. His last thought was that he was sliding down the wall and he couldn't stop falling.

"Oh, my God, he's been shot!" screamed Miss Lungren.

Tony hobbled forward and managed to kneel. The left sleeve of Bedford's jacket was soaked in blood. He pulled away the handkerchief and peeled back the ripped edges of the tear in Bedford's coat.

"Is he going to die?" asked a tearful Miss Fielding.

"Not today," said Tony, seeing that the bullet hadn't even

gone into his arm, although it left a nasty gouge along the top of it. "It is only a flesh wound."

Just in case, he checked Will's body to make sure the bullet hadn't skimmed over his arm and then entered elsewhere, but he could find no other holes. Even as he prodded at him, William's eyelids began fluttering.

"Tony, what is going on?" Felicity came down the passageway, carrying Charles, with Lord Wedmont and Mrs. Keeting trailing behind her. She drew up when she saw Bedford on the floor. "Oh, absolutely not."

She clapped a hand over Charles's eyes. "Is he dead?" she mouthed.

Bedford struggled to a sitting position.

"Not yet." Tony turned back to the injured man. "Who shot you, William?"

"One of the sisters. Couldn't see which one."

Miss Lungren put a hand to her forehead. "My sister brought the gun. Said we might need it in case we ran into robbers between home and London."

"Your sister brought a *gun* to a *dinner party?*" asked Amelia.

Rosalyn ignored Amelia's outrage at her sister's bad manners. "Mr. Bedford, did you say I was being poisoned?"

"We believe so," said Tony. "Which sis—?"

"Were my, were my . . ." Miss Lungren's dark eyes focused on his face.

"Your brothers and father poisoned? We suspect so."

"Oh, dear God!" She threw her hands over her face and began to shake like a dog emerging from a pond.

"Perhaps you should sit down," said Bedford.

But when she removed her hands, it was rage that showed on her face. "I shall kill her."

"There has been quite enough killing, Miss Lungren," said Tony.

She shot him a vicious look and ran down the stairs, calling for her sisters.

Tony lurched to his feet to follow her.

Just then Charles's nanny stumbled out of the servants' stairs and ran to Felicity, her gaze on the boy her mistress carried. "Oh, ma'am, I am so sorry. He told me I was wanted in the kitchen, and I thought with the party you might need me to help, and Charles was asleep. Is he all right?" She put her hand on Charles's back.

"He's fine and should be back in bed." She didn't set him down, though, or hand him over to his nanny. She looked agonized over the thought of putting her son back to bed after so near a miss with him, not to mention that a murderess still roamed the house.

Tony would gladly have volunteered to watch over him, but he said, "I must stop Miss Lungren and find her sisters before more damage is done."

Felicity stroked Charles's tawny curls. His hold had relaxed a little. "I have to go see to Lord Algany's welfare."

Lord Wedmont grabbed a chair from the empty ballroom and took it over to the servants' stairway door. He wedged it under the handle and walked back to them. "Other than the main stairs, is there any other way up here?"

Felicity shook her head. "Not without scaling a wall."

"Then I should happily stand guard here and not let anyone pass. I shouldn't think, other than Algany, anyone has an interest in your son, and I don't think Algany shall be tackling stairs anytime soon."

A scream wafted up the stairs, and all of them looked at each other.

"Was that Lord Algany?" asked Felicity, for the scream had seemed to come from a long way down.

"Oh, Lord, I hope so," whispered Amelia.

Tony grabbed the railing to begin his painful lurch down the stairs. He couldn't allow his leg to fail him now, when he'd brought a murderer into her house, into his child's home.

Bedford rose to his feet. "I'm going with you, Sheridan."

Felicity still had guests. She thrust Charles in Lord Wedmont's direction. "If anything happens to him, I shall not be responsible for my actions."

"Nor shall I," said Tony with a hard glare.

"You may have my liver if there is a hair out of place on his head. Once Keene is less occupied, he will assist me in guarding this brave chap."

"Tony, do you think this Miss Lungren has more ammunition?" asked Felicity as she followed him down the stairs.

He hoped not. Lord, he hoped not.

Felicity found Lord Algany propped on her breakfast table, alternately cursing and crying out, while a physician, with little regard for his misery, pulled on his leg.

"We're going to have to make a rig for him. Tie this leg up in the air," said the physician.

"Will he be all right?"

"It's a right bad break, though he will live. He'll be on his back a few weeks. Might have a limp forever, but I expect he'll walk again."

"Just shoot me; it is all I ask," whimpered Lord Algany.

"Could have been worse; could have landed on his crown and then you'd have had to call an undertaker instead," joked the physician. "I shall plaster his leg; then we'll just get him home."

"May I get you anything, Lord Algany?" Felicity leaned over him. "Perhaps brandy will—"

"Please, just put me out of my misery." He grabbed her arm.

"Don't tempt me." She leaned close and whispered, "You were, after all, trying to abduct my son."

"I . . . What? I swear, I was not. By all that is holy, I was only introducing myself to him. I don't know why he tried to run out on the roof."

"You don't?" Felicity didn't believe him for a moment.

"Then I tried to get him back inside. It is on account of

my attempt to *rescue* your son, from his foolhardy playing, that I have a broken leg."

With a sinking feeling, Felicity realized it would be her not-quite-six-year-old son's word against that of a peer. He'd effectively rid himself of any witnesses by sending Charles's nanny to help in the kitchens.

"I have an urge to send a servant for some black ink. What do you think, Lord Algany?"

"You bitch," he muttered.

"Worse yet, do you have any loans or such? No, don't answer, but if you do, be assured I shall own you before a fortnight is up. I'm a powerful woman, Lord Algany. You would have done better to admit the truth and throw yourself on the mercy of the court."

"Please, Mrs. Merriwether, you have nothing to gain by destroying me. I never meant to harm the child. Have I not suffered enough?"

"Likely not." *Let him stew on that a while.*

"Please get him out here as soon as you can," she said to the physician. "Then I need you to look at Mr. Bedford's arm."

"Very good, ma'am," said the physician as he gave Algany's leg another good yank.

Felicity took a deep breath and headed for the stairs. With any luck, the evil sister had been located.

"We can't find her," whispered William as soon as Felicity entered the pandemonium-filled rose drawing room. "The major and lieutenant are searching the house."

Lady Penelope was sobbing against her mother, the duchess's breast, several of the ladies were in various stages of the vapors, and the gentlemen were doing a good deal of harrumphing and pacing.

"We've told everyone that this was an accident." William lifted his arm.

Across the room, Lady Greyston threw up her hand and

fainted against the couch far too gracefully not to have practiced. That was when the guests realized that Felicity had entered the room.

Questions sailed at her head like a crowd of angry wasps. "Is Algany all right?" . . . "Is your son all right?" . . . "Whatever were they doing on the roof?"

"Good news; Lord Algany will be fine. He has a broken leg, but the physician assures me he will mend." He'd never know how much those words cost her. "My son is safe in his bed. And I must thank you all for coming, but under the circumstances, I think we might call it a night."

"Why was Lord Algany on the roof?"

"I'm afraid he claims he was rescuing my son, who had climbed out on the roof for no good reason." She delivered the words with a lofty air that, she hoped, conveyed her complete distrust of Lord Algany's explanations.

Felicity scanned the room. She saw two of the Lungren sisters and Diana, who seemed to be practically supporting the oldest. The other sister had her back to Felicity, and she couldn't tell if it was the middle sister or the youngest. She didn't see the black dress of the remaining sister, nor could she pick out the bright scarlet dress uniforms of Major Sheridan and Lieutenant Randleton. As she tried to count heads in the shifting cacophony of babbling, bawling, and blustering guests, she thought, but she wasn't sure, that everyone else was present.

She approached the duchess. "Lady Penelope looks quite distressed, Your Grace. Should I have your carriage brought round first so you might comfort her at home? I'm so sorry that things have turned out so dreadfully."

"He pushed me," sobbed Lady Penelope.

"Yes, my pet, never should have happened. Quite rude, but we can hardly hold Mrs. Merriwether accountable for the boorish behavior of her guests. Yes, Mrs. Merriwether, our carriage, please. We quite enjoyed the dinner."

Felicity summoned her butler and gave instructions for the carriages to be brought to the front door. That was when she heard a clatter in the green drawing room, as if someone had knocked over the stand of brass fire irons in there.

Across the room, the two Lungren sisters had heard the sound, and the oldest was marching across the room to the connecting door. Her sister—Felicity could see it was the youngest sister, Carolyn—followed behind, tugging on her older sister's arm, trying to hold her back but without much success.

"Mother, I need your help," said Felicity sharply.

Lady Greyston stirred from her fake swoon and jumped up from the couch.

Felicity grabbed her mother's arm and told her to get people out to their carriages as quickly as she could. She beckoned Diana over to help, too. They would do a bad job of it, but they would likely get it done.

Just then, Tony and Lieutenant Randleton burst into the room. Felicity pointed toward the green drawing room, and the two exchanged a look. The major headed back out in the hall, she presumed, to enter the room from the passageway, and Randleton cut through the room, beating Miss Lungren to the connecting door.

"Do something," Felicity hissed to Mr. Bedford as she watched half the guests turn toward the green drawing room.

He stood and, with a loud moan of pain, fell to the floor in a much less graceful fake swoon. Diana looked at Felicity and down at Mr. Bedford and, after a second's hesitation, let out a loud shriek and then ran to kneel by Mr. Bedford. "Oh, my stars." She clapped her hands to her chest. "He's dying."

Her niece was quite the little actress, thought Felicity as she watched Diana direct the men in the room to place Mr. Bedford on a couch and to go fetch the physician from downstairs, because surely a gunshot was a much more demanding wound than a broken leg. With a flirtatious flicker of her eyelashes, she made promises that had half the men falling all over themselves to assist her.

Felicity flew out the door and to the hallway entrance to the green drawing room. She entered just behind Tony as the group coming in from the rose drawing room slid back the pocket door.

In the center of the room stood the middle Lungren sister, her hands and arms full as she appeared to be trying to repack a pistol with the fireplace poker. Her large beaded reticule lay on the floor at her feet.

"Miss Jocelyn, what are you doing?" asked Tony.

She shrieked, whirled around, and dropped the pistol she held in her hand. A small pouch fell to the floor, spilling black powder on the mint-and-emerald carpet. As she spun, she must have hit her reticule, and a half-dozen round balls spun out, rolling across the carpet.

Felicity heard the swish of a sword unsheathing and looked to see Rosalyn pulling Lieutenant Randleton's sword free of his scabbard. He reached to grab it back, but the other sister, the youngest, wrapped her arms around his upper arms. Not that he couldn't have broken free, but he seemed caught off guard.

"I say, Miss Lungren, that is a real sword," said Tony. "Not a toy."

"Good," said Rosalyn as she pointed it outward and advanced on her sister, Jocelyn.

Jocelyn backed away.

After she let go of the lieutenant, the youngest Miss Lungren had the presence of mind to shut the door leading back into the rose drawing room. Felicity shut the door behind her.

"Are you poisoning me?" asked Rosalyn, advancing menacingly on her sister. Her foot caught in her sister's reticule, and she fell down to her knees, but she held the sword forward.

"What makes you think that?" Jocelyn fished behind her for a weapon to defend herself with as she backed away.

"Why were you planting castor beans?" asked Lieutenant Randleton.

Jocelyn took a frantic glance at the lieutenant and backed up until she encountered the chaise longue with the snapping crocodile legs and could retreat no farther. She looked more and more like a crazed animal with nowhere to go.

Felicity tried to step forward, but Tony barred her way with an arm, his other hand on the hilt of his sword.

From her knees, with the sword outstretched like some avenging angel or Joan of Arc emulator, Rosalyn cried out. "Why? Why would you kill all of us? Why Papa?"

"What are you talking about?"

Tony bent and picked up one of the bullets from the carpet. He rolled it between his fingers; the dark metal almost looked obscene against his white gloves. "Has the same imperfection as the shot fired the other night at Mr. Bedford's lodging."

He tossed it to Randleton, who caught it and examined it. "Same indentation, molded like the other. You may as well confess. We know you killed the captain as well as your other brothers."

"Mr. Bedford saw you before you shot him tonight." Tony took a step forward, closing in on the murderess.

"Or rather, as you shot him," said Randleton, also moving forward.

"I want to know why, why you would do such a thing," demanded Rosalyn. Tears were streaming down her face, but her eyes glittered with a focused rage. "Why me? Why poison me?"

The other Lungren sister, Carolyn, sobbed and clutched at Lieutenant Randleton's arm.

Jocelyn refused to answer, her gaze darting from one person to another as if looking for a way out.

"You will hang for them all, I'm sure," said Randleton.

There was no point in her refusing to admit her guilt, yet she remained silent.

Rosalyn inched forward on her knees, her other hand outstretched as if looking for some object to hold so she could rise without lowering the sword.

Finally Jocelyn's features twisted, and she looked at her sister. "You might as well put that down, Ros. You don't have the courage to run me through."

Rosalyn started to shudder. "I do! I will! You've nearly killed me. What is there to stop me?"

"Oh, not yet. You need more doses." Jocelyn swung around the chaise longue, putting it between herself and her sister.

"Just tell me why, and I'll spare you."

Jocelyn looked around with a gleam coming to her eye, as if she'd formulated a plan. "All right, I'll tell you why you. Because I shall own the estate after you're gone. Had to be done before you gave away more to that Lord Carlton."

Was she talking now to stall for time? Felicity tried to follow the line of her vision and saw the fireplace poker in the line of Jocelyn's sight. Felicity looked at Tony, who was slowly, without a whisper of sound, withdrawing his sword from his scabbard.

"But the estate is worthless," said Randleton.

Jocelyn laughed. "On, no, there is plenty of money in the house. Papa made a fortune smuggling French wines during the war."

"He did what?" said Rosalyn in a cross between a whisper and a cry of anguish.

Jocelyn took another look at the poker, and Felicity was sure she was going to lunge for it at any second.

"I couldn't let him do that, what with Jonathon over there fighting. Papa was likely to get him killed."

"But you killed Jonathon."

Jocelyn blinked, as if she couldn't quite reconcile the gaps in her logic, and then shrugged.

Felicity flew to Tony's side. "She's going to go for the poker," she whispered, with a cupped hand to his ear—or as near to it as she could reach.

"I know," he said. "Get back."

Felicity stepped back.

Rosalyn rose to her feet with renewed vigor and, with the sword held in front of her like an avenging angel, said in a sputter, "You let me go to that man and ask for help after what he did to me, and there was money all along?"

"Bad money. We couldn't spend it." Her eyes gleamed bizarrely, "Lots of money; he hid it in the walls."

Carolyn stepped forward, her face drained of color. "Why Jonathon?"

"Why Mr. Bedford?" asked Tony.

Rosalyn advanced with the sword outstretched. "Why Norman and Aaron? Why?"

"Norman thought I should marry; Aaron, too." She stared straight at her sister Rosalyn.

"So, Mama was right when she attacked you," whispered Carolyn. "And we thought *she* was insane."

"You think I would marry any man after I saw what Lord Carlton did to you? After I helped wash away the blood and . . ." She looked at the sword her sister held, her mouth twisted in a sneer that would do Lord Algany proud. "Do it, if you're going to. Kill me."

Rosalyn was still shaking, but she made no further advance. She simply held the sword out as if she no longer knew what to do with it.

Tony made a signal to Randleton, and they moved forward. Jocelyn, with the desperation of a cornered animal, leaped forward and grabbed the poker. Tony and Randleton were on both sides of her as she rose with the brass-handled poker in her hand. Randleton grabbed the poker before she could swing it.

She struggled with Randleton, no match for his superior strength. When she realized she wouldn't be able to wrest control of the fireplace tool from him, she shoved it toward him and spun around to flee. Tony started to lower his sword. He wouldn't need it to overpower an unarmed woman.

Jocelyn took two steps toward the door and Tony. Felicity stepped in front of the door, but Jocelyn, in a feint to maneuver around Tony, must have stepped on one of the bullets littering the carpet. Her feet went out from under her and crashed into Tony's bad leg.

Jocelyn went down.

Tony and the sword he was lowering fell. He tried to twist, to react, but it was too late. It all happened as both of them were falling, and in spite of his letting loose the weapon before either of them hit the floor, it was obvious it was far too late.

TWENTY-TWO

Tony was horrified as he realized he had impaled Miss Jocelyn. She lay on the floor, his sword extending from her abdomen, as he fell hard to his hands and knees. Pain ricocheted up and down his bad leg, and for a moment he couldn't move. He knelt on all fours, trapped beside his victim as she breathed in a surprised pant.

He'd loosened his grip on the sword as he fell, but to no avail. He'd felt it sink deep in the soft flesh of her midsection, and he knew the razor-sharp blade had run her completely through.

She stared at him, wide-eyed, the soul-deep fear of a wounded animal replacing the madness and insanity that was in her eyes a moment earlier.

He winced as he realized that the wound was mortal but the death would be agonizing and slow. Several days at best. He'd seen it dozens of times, whether it was a stab wound or a bullet wound to the gut. Twice he'd spent time in hospital watching young soldiers brought in with wounds like this one. Watching as their misery turned to agony, as the fevers came on and the stench grew. Sometimes there had been opium to dull their pain, most often not.

It was the leaking of their innards and the infection that came on that ultimately would bring on death, a young physician had explained to him as he begged him to help one of his men, who had taken a bayonet in the stomach. There was nothing they could do. Nothing to stop the inevitable gruesome death.

After six months in hospital, and six years of war he had watched a lot of men die—some mercifully fast, most not. He lurched to his feet. Gripping the sword with both hands, he heard the ladies gasp.

Jocelyn stared at him as he jerked the sword up through her body, making her death quick, certain, over. She twitched slightly and closed her eyes. Her breathing rattled to a stop, and then there was silence.

With a weary grief he pulled his sword free of the body and dropped it to the mint-and-emerald carpet. He'd known from the minute he'd entered the room that he didn't like the overgrown-jungle motif.

He turned to look at Felicity, and she stared at him as if he were some kind of monster, an evil woman-killer. He looked down at the body of Jocelyn. He should have felt some relief that his captain's murderer was dead. Justice was served.

He felt empty, as if the only thing he could do was kill.

He'd spent six years killing. He couldn't even rescue his son from a roof, but he could kill. No wonder Felicity wanted nothing to do with him. He had nothing but his skill at death.

One of the remaining Lungren sisters sobbed. Tony didn't know which one, didn't care which one. The only thing he cared about was the horrified look Felicity had turned in his direction. She didn't look at the body, didn't look at the others, didn't look anywhere but at him.

He could want her for the rest of time, and she would never forget this moment when she'd seen him revealed as the man he'd become, an efficient killer.

He knew then that it was over.

Felicity had managed to draw upon reserves she didn't know she had and regain her composure—well enough to see all her guests to their carriages. She thanked them for coming and apologized for the disruptions, knowing that most of them had no idea what had happened in the green drawing room. She even commiserated about how it was such horrible happenstance that Algany had broken his leg, and pushed them out the door when they started to question her about Mr. Bedford's "accident."

After a couple of hours she had seen the last of them in their carriages—well, the last of them except the Lungren sisters, who had decided to wait until everyone was gone before having the body of their sister removed. Lord Algany had been carted outside. In spite of his curses at the servants, they managed to load him in his carriage without banging his newly plastered leg. Though she had yet to see the Davieses emerge from her upstairs bedroom, the house was relatively empty of guests.

Her parents had gone to bed muttering about the disintegration of society, and Felicity no longer cared if they stayed to watch it fall or not. Her first ton party, and she'd had a guest break his leg, another shot, and another unmasked as a murderess and then stabbed to death. Quite a success.

If it were not for her obligation to find Diana a husband, she'd go back to the country tonight. She climbed the stairs, just wanting to check on Charles before she found Tony.

She could see a dim light under the door of the nursery as she approached. Charles had probably been unwilling to go to bed without a night-light. When she opened the door, the first thing she could see was that Charles was not in his bed. Her heart jolted.

It was quickly soothed by the sight of Tony in a chair, his eyes closed, his scarlet jacket unbuttoned, and Charles in his lap, leaning limply against Tony's chest. Her son was obviously sound asleep.

Tony's arm was curled around Charles, holding him securely. The sight brought tears to her eyes. Charles undoubtedly had missed having a father, and Tony—how could she have doubted that he wouldn't have made things right if he had known?—Tony looked like a father should.

Solid and fearless, a sure source of security and comfort when a little boy was scared. Especially when a mother was soft, weak and fearful, and in need of comfort herself.

"If you will lift him up, we might get him to bed without waking him."

Felicity met Tony's pale blue eyes. He seemed distant, unapproachable. She swallowed hard. She had no reason to fear him. He had never mistreated her, never done anything to make her fear him. It wasn't fair that Layton's sins should be visited on his head. "I am not sure we should move him. He looks quite comfortable there."

"It is time for me to leave, and I'm afraid I'll not be able to stand with any grace."

Felicity moved across the room. She didn't want him to leave. She wanted to tell him that she'd decided to have an affair with him, marry him if she must. Yet he seemed cool, remote. Did he no longer want her?

She lifted her sleeping son off Tony's lap and carried him to his bed.

Tony stood. "Is everyone gone now?"

Felicity tucked Charles under the covers. He didn't wake. "Lieutenant Randleton is helping the Lungrens get their sister's body home, and Mr. Bedford has been sent to bed by the physician. The Davieses, I believe, are still occupied in my room." She brushed Charles's tawny curls back. "He must be exhausted by all the excitement."

"You must be ready for bed," said Tony. He awkwardly leaned over and pressed a kiss on Charles's forehead.

Felicity found his gesture heartrending. He had missed years of this, and Charles had only ever had his mother's kisses before now. Perhaps through their son they could rebuild the love they had once had. Perhaps Tony could love her again. He had loved her once, and now he loved their son.

"I hoped to sleep in my own bed tonight."

Tony looked out the window. "Of course. Once I have helped Randleton see the Lungrens home, I'll return to my own apartments. No need for me to stay here, now that there isn't any danger. Bedford has let his place go, but he should be able to find another soon."

"Tony." She would have to spell it out for him. Her stomach knotted, and she feared he might still leave.

"I should not have brought her here into your home. I wasn't sure which sister was the killer, but I knew one of them was."

She put a hand on his arm, and he stared at her hand. "Tony, I haven't asked you to go."

He slowly raised his eyes from her hand and looked her in the eye. Confusion clouded his features. She stripped off her glove and raised her hand to cup his cheek. "You were not this dense years ago."

He put his hand over hers; the heat of it came through hers, burning a path to her heart. "But—"

She put her fingers over his lips. She didn't want to think about reasons they shouldn't make love. She didn't want to remember that he had loved her years ago but now just wanted to be her lover, at best. Undoubtedly the only reason he was still around this time was because of Charles. Nonetheless, she could pretend for tonight, at least, that he loved her. "Don't talk," she whispered.

"Are you sure?"

She smiled with the bittersweet memory and echo of that question from years before. Then she had been able to do no more than nod, her heart in her throat. This time she stared at him a long while and said slowly, "Absolutely."

His lips found hers, and there was no more talking except whispered compromises about getting from the nursery down a flight of stairs to her bedroom.

"I should carry you."

"You cannot," she whispered back, and her heart filled with tenderness and yearning. He cared enough to want her to feel romanced, seduced, wanted.

She put her bare hand in his, and he raised it to his lips and pressed a kiss on it. She led the way to the stairs and to her old room. Once in the bedroom, she felt shy and uncertain. Out of practice.

She stepped into the room and turned away from the bed. Tony rummaged in his things.

She felt awkward and wondered if he had expected her to remove her clothes and lie down on the bed. She hoped that the noises she heard behind her weren't of him stripping down. She wanted to ask him to go slowly for her but knew it was a stupid request, a stupid thought. He had not hurried with her the first time. She had no reason to think things might be different now, except that she knew tenderness could evaporate in a haze of lust. His concern for her wellbeing could disappear in a heartbeat.

Finally, Tony stepped inches behind her. She could feel the heat of his body, his breath on the nape of her neck a second before he pressed his lips there.

She shuddered, his gentle kiss burning through her.

He pulled back and then put his hands on her shoulders. "Quite a night this was."

His distance made her want to close the gap. Yet she was frightened that her memories of her one night with Tony were an illusion born of a desperate woman's dreams, that the harsh reality of her marriage with Layton was what relations between men and women were really like: progressing rapidly from sensual lovemaking to demanding use of her body without preliminaries.

But this was Tony, not Layton. Tony, whom she had once loved and trusted with every fiber of her being. She stepped back against his body . . . his strong, lean, hard body. "And it is not over yet."

He turned her around and looked for a long time into her eyes. "You are frightened of—"

She pressed her lips against his before he could finish the sentence. She *was* frightened, scared out of her mind, by everything.

His moan was half protest, half pleasure, and she strained up on her toes, touching the tip of her tongue to his lips, entreating him, begging him to continue, to help her forget her fears. His arms came around her, and he sought her mouth with his. His breath mingled with hers, his taste filling her mouth, and she nearly sobbed with relief.

She pressed up against the hard length of him, wanting to draw courage from him. "Don't talk; please don't talk; just make me feel the way you did the other night, please, Tony," she whispered.

He kissed her deeply and buried his hands in her hair, pulling out pins and dropping them to the floor. When he lifted her up, she wanted to protest the abuse to his leg, but didn't, as he carried her the four feet to the bed. He laid her down on the coverlet and sat to remove his shoes. His scarlet jacket, then his shirt, followed. He turned and bent over her, his lips pressing against her forehead before he moved back to the soul-deep kissing that had her panting, clutching at his firm, broad naked shoulders.

The feel of his skin, hot, smooth, made her want more. She pressed her palms against his chest, feeling the crisp, springy hair, the taut muscle under his skin. He pressed his hands over hers with encouragement, enthusiasm burning in his eyes.

With slow patience he peeled off her clothes, his hands reverently and gently caressing each bare inch of her skin. He watched her with such intensity in his unnaturally pale eyes; she wanted to close them, kiss his eyelids, and yet she held his gaze, and then suddenly she knew everything was all right.

She reached down to touch the hard, heavy length of him, and he groaned, pushing against her hand. She tugged at his breeches, trying to loosen them and move them out of the way. While she fumbled with his clothes, he made short work of what little she had left on. She succeeded in getting his breeches down and stopped when she saw the mangled, puckered, and white-laced scars on his thigh.

Tears sprang to her eyes, and she pressed her lips together. He kicked off the last of his clothes and pulled her up, his expression growing concerned as he wiped away a tear with his thumb.

Unwilling to lessen the moment, she pushed him back and threw a leg over him. He grasped her then, holding her tight against his body. They lay there together, skin against skin, heart beating against heart, for a long second, and then she squirmed against him, trying to find the right position. Then she had it, his hard male member against the core of her, and she pressed home.

"Oh, Christ, stop!" he moaned.

She froze. Was she hurting him? But his hips shoved upward and completed the penetration. She bit her lips at the feel of him inside her, stretching her, filling her, completing her. Then he shoved her hips away and broke the union of their bodies.

Fear once again crashed through her. Didn't he want her, even now, when his body was hard and ready? Didn't he want her at all? He shoved up on his elbows and twisted, reaching on the nightstand beside the bed. He fumbled, knocking something to the floor before he turned back around and placed a thin, transparent sheath over his erection.

His task done, he reached for her. He ran his hand down her side and pulled her hips toward his. "No babies," he whispered as he found her lips.

Her heart pounded harder, realizing that he hadn't forgotten his promise, and that he meant to protect her even when she hadn't asked or cared, even though an unintended pregnancy would force her down the path *he* wanted.

She held him tight to her as he completed them, as he brought their bodies back together and joined them in a timeless rhythm that stretched across to the moment they had created Charles. Her heart filled with tenderness for this thoughtful and giving man. Felicity realized she'd never stopped loving Tony.

Then she was caught in a place between heaven and

earth, floating, spinning out of control, yet here and now bound in the physical realm to the pulsing pleasure in her body. He was her mate, her other half, the twin of her soul, and somewhere in this haze of sensations she could feel the stars as she traveled with him through the throes of passion.

Tony stared out at the moonlight. He gripped the curtain in one hand and tilted his battered leg so he could rub it. He didn't know what had changed Felicity's mind about wanting to have an affair. Maybe it was the fascination women had for taming men they thought were out of control. No matter how he tried, he couldn't reconcile the past hour and their lovemaking with the expression on her face now. She had made it clear she didn't want to talk. Didn't want to sort out their differences. And God help him, he was too willing to take her on those terms, on any terms.

"What is this made of?" she asked from the bed.

He glanced over his shoulder and looked at her. He had thought she was asleep, she'd been so quiet and still in the aftermath, after their bodies had cooled and the breathing had returned to normal and he'd tucked her under the covers. Now she leaned up on an elbow, her dark hair tumbling around her lily white shoulders. The sheet barely concealed her rosy-tipped breasts, and he felt himself grow heavy at the thought. She was examining his supply of protection.

"Sheep intestine, I understand."

She wrinkled her nose and looked at him, something between disgust and amusement scrunching up her features. He turned back to the window. How would he be able to leave her this time? How could he not? It would be worse to watch her lack of respect and dismay at him turn to repugnance and disappointment.

"Shall we use another?" She waved one.

"Of course." He dropped the curtain, lingering for a moment, looking for an answer in the mystical light of the moon. He'd offered up his heart again, and she would carve it up and serve it in bite-size pieces eventually.

"The first time we were together . . ."

"Yes?"

"You stood like that in the moonlight and stared out the window. What were you thinking then?"

"Then? That it would be harder to leave in the morning, coming from your bed."

"Because you were tired?"

"No. Because I didn't want to go. I knew what pleasure I was forsaking." It wasn't as simple as all that. He'd been filled with emotion and didn't know what to do with it. There had been anger that he had to leave that morning. And sadness as well, and regret that he would only have that one night to sustain him for how many years, no one knew. He'd been almost afraid of the depth of his love for Felicity, and yet filled with joy.

"I thought you were beautiful standing in the moonlight. I looked at you for the longest time."

His hand stopped moving on his scarred thigh. "Not so beautiful now."

He heard the rustle of sheets, and she drew up behind him, pressing a kiss against his shoulder. "More. Is that something I can do for you?" Her hand slipped down over his. "Does massaging it help? I see you do it a lot."

He felt humbled by her willing acceptance of his scarred body. Her tender offer of massage awed him more than her willingness to become his lover, if that was possible. He wanted, craved, her love, yet he wasn't sure what she wanted to give.

He could feel the satin of her skin pressing against his back, the silky brush of her hair against his arm, the soft, womanly scent of her. He didn't know what he meant to say, but what came out was, "Felicity . . . you must not break my heart."

He felt her go tense. "But I am good at breaking hearts. No doubt I broke Layton's."

She turned away and moved back toward the rumpled bed. He stared out at the moonlight, sure he didn't want to hear about her marriage. He limped back to the bed and sat down. He reached out and stroked her hair. "Did you mean to?"

"No! Absolutely not." She looked at him, her dark eyes filled with unshed tears. "I meant to love him—I really did—but I could not, because you had my heart. But I thought I hated you, because you had ignored my being with child and told me to stay home. Layton hated me for not being able to love him."

She knelt on the bed beside him. She reached out with both hands and tentatively kneaded his sore thigh. "How much pressure?"

He put his hands over hers, stopping her. Then he gestured toward the bed. "So what does this night mean, Felicity?"

"It means I was ready to have an affair with you." She bit her lip and watched him with shadowed eyes.

"I have decided to go to India, after all."

She ducked her head and moved away. The silence stretched out in a long, endless dearth. Finally she spoke. "Would you marry me before you leave, this time?"

Her voice sounded tinny and hollow and barely controlled. And it wasn't what he expected to hear. "You are not with child."

"And I thought you prevented that for me." She swiped at her face, but since she was facing away, he didn't know for certain that she was crying until she sniffed.

"It is what you wanted, isn't it?" He reached for her shoulder, but she jerked away. "Why the change, Felicity?"

"Because I don't need Lord Algany or anyone like him trying to snatch my son so I might marry them."

She sounded angry. She moved off the end of the bed and grabbed the first article of clothing she stumbled across—which happened to be his shirt—and pulled it over her head. She stalked across the floor, her long legs eating up the carpet, his shirt hanging down only to the top of her thighs. "I had thought that perhaps we could try once more since you obviously care about Charles. I thought you wanted to be around to raise him, even were willing to marry me so you could be around him. I thought"—she gestured toward the bed—"that *that* meant something."

It meant everything; it meant too much. "Mayhap I am like Layton."

She swiveled and stared at him.

"I want everything or I want nothing."

She stepped closer to the bed. "You will have everything." She hesitated, pushing her palm against her forehead. "I have enough money to buy you anything you want."

"I don't want your money." He looked at his scarred thigh.

"What do you want, then?"

"Your affection, your regard, your respect."

"You have it."

"No, I don't. I saw how you looked at me in the green room when Miss Lungren was mortally wounded. I saw what you thought. I saw your horror and"—it hurt to say it—"your repulsion."

"I've never seen a death like that. Of course I felt ill."

"Killing is what I do."

"I know that." She stood at the foot of the bed, her arms, with the sleeves hanging over her hands, crossed in front of her.

"It is about the only thing I am good for. I could not even rescue my own son from a roof, because of this." He hit his leg. "I had to watch a woman do it."

"So what bothers you the most—that a woman had to do what you thought you should do, or that you couldn't go out on the roof yourself?"

"That I was not able."

"How ironic that a wound received in honor makes you feel less than honorable."

He looked at her. He hadn't thought of it in that light. She'd put one knee on the bed. She uncrossed her arms and put her hands on the bed, and began slowly moving toward him.

"I know that you ended it quickly for Miss Jocelyn. I suppose she would have taken a long time to die. I would not have thought that so terrible, since she poisoned three people to death. I just wasn't prepared to watch her slit open like a fish."

"And will the sight of what I did haunt you forever?"

Felicity crawled a bit closer. "I should imagine you have many more haunting scenes etched in your memory than I do."

So many echoes of screams, sights of dead and dying men, that he didn't know if he was human anymore. She would never know how broken he felt.

"Is my love enough?" she asked softly.

"What?"

"Enough of what you want?" Her eyes were bright with wary fear.

"You are frightened of me. I don't want you frightened of me." Had she said she loved him? No, she'd asked if her love would be enough. Of course she didn't love him. How could she when she was scared of him, frightened by his actions?

Her lower lip trembled, and she ducked away from him. "Not so much of you, but of submitting to your will, as the law and the church require. You cannot understand what it is like, being a woman, having no rights, no control." She plucked at the coverlet. "Yet I hoped maybe you could find it in your heart to love me again. I know that you want to be with Charles."

"I have never stopped loving you. But I have nothing to offer you. No fortune. No prospects . . ."

She laughed. Oh, what was wrong with her?

"Nothing, but the one thing I want. I have everything money can buy, but I want your love, and all the money in the world cannot buy me that. All I ever wanted was you . . . and, Charles, because he's part of you."

She wanted his love? He reached to hold her, and she turned into his arms and clutched him to her.

"Tony, if I had it all to do over, I wouldn't have written the letter telling you I was with child."

His heart plummeted to his stomach.

"I would have gone to Spain or wherever you were and found you."

His heart lifted, soared. He gestured to the opulent room. "You wouldn't have all this."

"Money means nothing when you are miserable. I never meant to break your heart; I never meant to break my own. I love you, and if you love me, what more do we need?"

What more indeed? "More children?" he suggested.

She stiffened. "Mayhap one or two."

He was in the mood to tease. "Sixteen."

There was a long silence before she muttered against his chest, "Three."

"Three it is. Including Charles."

She didn't look up. What reservations did she still have? "What, Felicity?"

"Shall it bother you terribly that I run all the Merriwether companies? I know, as my husband, I couldn't stop you from taking over, but—"

"You have a shrewd head for business, and I will not interfere. But you will have to let me do something, manage the estates or some such. I cannot be idle the rest of my life."

"You will never have time to be idle. Loving me and sixteen children will take all your strength."

He tilted her head back and kissed her. "I was gammoning you about the sixteen children."

"I know, but even three children are enough to drive you mad."

"I am willing to take that chance. Marry me, Felicity. I love you and I want you to be my wife—now."

"Absolutely not. I am still in half-mourning. We can wait four months to marry. But can we use one of those sheep things now?"

"Absolutely." He grinned, his heart filled with joy, but he would not let her hem and haw this time. No delays. "Not."

"Then I will marry you as soon as you can get a special license."

"Very well," he agreed, reaching for a condom. "I accept your surrender."

"I have not surrendered!" she said indignantly.

"Then you have settled on a compromise."

"Compromise? That was blackmail."

He breathed in a deep sigh. "We must post the banns. That will give us a month."

"Shall we discuss this when we aren't naked?"

"Naked? You are still wearing my shirt."

At that, she drew it over her head and tossed it on the floor.

"Capital idea!"

EPILOGUE

Nearly three months had passed, and Felicity was still being sought after as the hostess of the season. She rubbed the ring under her glove as she sat in the rose drawing room with her visitors, waiting for tea to be served.

She was Tony's wife. In the end it had been two impulsive proposals from social callers that made her track him down and demand he go get a special license.

"I must say, Miss Lungren, you are looking much healthier these days," Felicity said.

Rosalyn smiled. "Mayhap the poison just needed some time to wear off."

Miss Carolyn nodded. "We are hoping it has no lasting effects."

"And how are you enjoying your new home?"

The two sisters exchanged a glance. Rosalyn leaned forward. "I was quite shocked when Lord Carlton willed me his estate. I was not expecting that, but I find it much more comfortable than living where so much needless tragedy occurred."

"I never want to go back to our home," said Miss Carolyn.

"And you, Miss Carolyn, I hear you and Lieutenant Randleton have posted the banns."

"Yes, well, since all our scandals have been locked away in the closets, he believes I shan't be a detriment to his political career."

"I hope that was not stopping him from marrying you."

"Oh, not from wanting to marry me. He swore he would

marry me, even if he had to stay in the military to support a wife, but I knew he wanted a political career—and it wouldn't do to have a wife with a murderer in her family, not to mention smugglers. I never would have let him give up his dreams. But since it appears no one will ever know, I finally gave my consent . . ." Miss Carolyn smiled with a nervous look.

"We certainly will never tell," said Felicity.

"That is another reason we called. We hoped to find Mr. Bedford at home."

Mr. Bedford, whose arm had healed, had just last week clandestinely married her niece. They were temporarily living with Felicity, which seemed to make Diana a nervous wreck.

The tea tray was brought in, and Felicity sent the servant to inquire after Mr. Bedford.

"Who the devil *are* you?" William yelled at his wife.

"Felicity's niece, Diana Fielding."

"You are not. Then why did you ask me to call you Meg while we were making love? By the bye, no girl fresh out of finishing school knows what you know. And whatever made you think ten thousand pounds was a fortune?"

"*It is* a fortune." Her dark eyes flashed.

"'Tis not." William had been duped. Hook, line, and sinker, this woman had baited him, and he'd swallowed the whole line—probably the pole as well. "I owe over half that much, and we could only live a year or two on the rest."

"I could live forever on that kind of money."

"Like this?" he waved his arm around the room.

"Well, no. A bit more simply."

"We cannot take the dowry."

"What? Why not?" Diana—Meg, whatever her name was—said.

"Felicity *thinks* you're her niece—but that is plainly a lie."

There was a knock on the bedroom door. William opened

it with a heavy suspicion that he had made a fatal mistake. "What is it?"

"Mrs. Sheridan requests your attendance in the rose drawing room."

He nodded and straightened his cuffs.

His wife shot off the bed and shut the door. "Wait!"

God help him, he rather liked the tricks she knew. He flattened himself against the door, trying to avoid touching her, because then they would end up back on the rumpled bed.

"Why can't we take the money? Felicity doesn't need it."

"She provided for you, clothed you, launched you into polite society. You have taken gross advantage of a woman who is not even your aunt by marriage. Is that not enough?"

She dropped her eyes. "Do you want an annulment?"

William pressed his hands against his temples. "I want you to be who you said you were. I want the lies to stop. Right now, I don't even know who you are."

"I'm the illegitimate daughter of the Earl of Wedmont."

"Come down from that. He's barely older than you."

"His father. The current earl is my half-brother. Christ, look at him and me. You can tell by looking."

Perhaps she was. She did look a bit like Wedmont. All right, a *lot* like Wedmont. William crossed his arms. "And what happened to the real Miss Fielding?"

Tears dripped down her cheeks. "She died on the trip back from the Continent. I was nursing her aboard ship because she was ill."

"She just died?" William asked skeptically. Was he facing another Miss Jocelyn?

His wife flew across the room and pulled open a drawer. She pulled out several newspapers, then stuffed them in his hands. "This is her. I tossed her body overboard. I didn't kill her. I never thought about becoming her until she was dead. It says . . . it says in there she died naturally."

He looked down and saw that the paper was folded to an article about an unidentified body, of a young gentlewoman found in the Thames.

He put them on the dresser. "I shall read them later."
Right now he had to inform Felicity that her real niece was
dead and his wife was an impostor.

When he entered the drawing room, he found the two remaining Lungren sisters taking tea with Felicity. He sat
down woodenly and accepted a cup from Felicity.

"Mr. Bedford, we would like to return this to you."

He reached out and took the costly deed to the Lungren
estate. He looked up at Miss Rosalyn.

She smiled.

He should have tried to marry *her*. She was worth a fortune
herself now, what with the sacks of guineas they'd discovered
hidden in the walls, and her inheriting Lord Carlton's estate
when he did not survive his apoplexy attack.

"We think you should have it, since you did so much to
find out who the killer was," Miss Carolyn said.

"And were shot at," Miss Rosalyn added.

"Twice."

"It is not the losing proposition it once was, since all the
original land is restored to the property."

"And Lord Carlton kept no record of the land sales we
made to him." Carolyn added.

"So please, with our sincerest gratitude, keep the estate.
You won it fair and square from Jonathon. I think, under the
circumstances, he would have wanted you to have it."

"We just consider the payments Lord Carlton made to
Ros as restitution for his crime against her, instead of purchases of land."

"I know the house is in disrepair, but I think it could be
made habitable again."

William thought he might cry. "This is too much."

"Not really, Mr. Bedford. Neither of us ever wants to go
back there," said Miss Lungren.

"It is not a fond place for us. So please keep it."

The ladies took their leave, and William was left staring
dumbfounded at the deed to the Lungren estate. He looked
up to find Felicity watching him.

"You know, I think with that estate being so close to London, you could turn a handsome profit if you raised chickens. Fresh fowl are always in demand. Please feel free to use Diana's dowry for your nest egg, so to speak."

"My wife is not your niece," he blurted out.

"I know," said Felicity.

"You know?"

"You showed me the marriage certificate. It did not bear my niece's name. Or her signature."

"And you didn't say anything."

"I was not sure how much you knew, and I had introduced her to society as my niece." Felicity shrugged. "You might hold me accountable."

"And you were still prepared to give her the dowry?" William asked incredulously.

"I shan't miss it. And I thought we had agreed to keep our silence on all the scandals. My niece was always sickly; I suspect she died, and—Margaret, is it?—decided to take her place. Do you want me to denounce her? Tell the world that we were all duped?"

William shook his head.

Felicity stood and moved over to him, putting her hand on his shoulder. "I suspect she—whoever she is—rather loves you. And that is what really matters, is it not?"

"Absolutely," agreed Tony as he entered the room from what once was the green drawing room. "Come see what the workers have done, love. I, for one, am glad to see those crocodiles go."